The
STORYTELLER'S
SECRET

Center Point
Large Print

**This Large Print Book carries the
Seal of Approval of N.A.V.H.**

The STORYTELLER'S SECRET

A NOVEL

SEJAL BADANI

CENTER POINT LARGE PRINT
THORNDIKE, MAINE

This Center Point Large Print edition
is published in the year 2019 by arrangement with
Amazon Publishing, www.apub.com.

The text of this Large Print edition is unabridged.
In other aspects, this book may vary
from the original edition.
Printed in the United States of America
on permanent paper.
Set in 16-point Times New Roman type.

ISBN: 978-1-64358-285-6

Library of Congress Cataloging-in-Publication Data

The Library of Congress has cataloged this record
under Library of Congress Control Number: 2019942047

To Benee Knauer
I am forever grateful to you for your friendship,
guidance, and support,
and for always believing in this story. You are
truly one of a kind.
Thank you, my dearest friend.

The STORYTELLER'S SECRET

PROLOGUE

Summer 2000

Twenty percent of women miscarry. Of these, 80 percent lose the baby in the first twelve weeks of their pregnancy. If you are more than thirty years old, you have at least a 12 percent chance of miscarrying, the percentage points increasing with each advancing year.

I can recite these statistics and more by heart. I have researched them endlessly since we first started trying. That was over five years ago. Since then, I have spent countless hours in the library and on the Internet, hoping for a new study or drug that improves the odds of carrying to term and delivering a healthy baby. But the results are always the same—for every baby born, many others never reach gestation. For every woman who juggles a child in her arms, another yearns for the cry of a child to comfort. For every couple that successfully fills a home with a family, another will never become parents.

I stare at the sonogram picture gripped between my fingers. First I turn it sideways and then upside down. I've memorized the black-and-white squiggly lines that surround the only image I have of my child. I give color to the portrait where there is none and imagine that the fluid surrounding him or her is clear and warm, like a bath. I am convinced that the screeching of my daily commuter train's wheels against the tracks is altered to sound like a symphony, rocking my child to sleep. And the fear that permeates every cell of my body never breaches the uterus. Instead, my baby lives in a world of happiness and joy, assured of its future.

"Jaya." My office door opens just an inch—enough for the intern, Elizabeth, to pop her head in. "Patrick's on the phone." Seeming confused, she glances at my phone where two lights are blinking. "I tried you, but there was no answer."

"Sorry, I was working on a story," I say. She glances at my monitor that shows a blank screen, but she doesn't call me out. The truth is, I didn't hear the phone ring or her knock on the door. "I'll take the call." I wait for her to close the door behind her before I pick up the phone. "Patrick?"

"Hey, babe."

His voice is as familiar to me as my own. We've been together since college and married for eight years, so I know all of his tones and what each one means. The quick greeting tells me he's staring at his computer screen while holding the receiver between his ear and neck. It's late afternoon, so he's probably on his fifth cup of coffee. In law school, he tried to cut the habit and succeeded. However, by the time he became a first-year associate at the largest firm in New York, he had increased his daily intake to between six and eight cups.

"Did you want to pick up Chinese tonight?" In the background, I hear him typing and then the shuffle of papers. "Or we can do burgers and fries. Again," he teases.

It would be the fourth time this week, but since the pregnancy started fourteen weeks ago, burgers are the only thing I've craved. With the last pregnancy, it was Italian food, and during the one before that, I lost all appetite with the incessant nausea.

"Patrick." My fingers curl around the picture, gripping it tight. My other hand presses the receiver against my ear painfully. "I . . ." I pause, unsure how to say the words.

He stops typing and inhales deeply. "Jaya?" I hear the heartbreak in his voice, and with it my breath catches. Without my saying more, he knows. "Have you called the doctor?"

"Not yet," I whisper.

"When did the bleeding start?" His voice changes to the one he uses in the courtroom, while mine weakens until it's nearly muted. This is our dance—the one we learned by necessity, not choice. With each step, I falter and he gets stronger.

It's not who I ever thought I would be, but then I've learned life rarely works out as we hope.

11

Patrick is the exception to the rule. For him, everything has always gone according to plan. A born litigator, he comes alive in front of jaded judges and unconvinced juries. With his classic good looks, deep voice, and sharp intelligence, he has successfully won enough cases to be voted in as one of the youngest partners in the firm's history. It was what he expected, planned, when he graduated law school.

I, on the other hand, chose journalism. My love for the written word, matched with my obsession with facts and figures, made it the perfect career. My mother, disappointed, asked me, why not medicine instead?

"Two hours ago," I admit.

I wait for a response from him that will tell me who he is now—the lawyer, the man, or the grieving father.

"I'll meet you at the doctor's," he says, his tone clipped.

He is still the lawyer. In that mode, he will be able to lose himself in the medical details of the miscarriage and find acceptance in a way that I have failed to. I envy him his strength and yearn for my own, but it eludes me every time I reach for it.

"I'll see you there." I hang up before either of us can say anything else. Refusing to part with the picture, I tuck it into my pantsuit pocket for safekeeping.

I run my hand over my stomach and wait for a sign that tells me everything is fine. That there's no need to rush to the doctor or worry about what she'll say. I assure myself that inside my womb, my child rests safely, waiting to be born. I wait and wait. When there's no sign, no indication at all, I push my chair underneath the desk and turn off the computer. I hit the light switch, plunging the room into darkness, and walk out the door.

I fight to open my eyes from the anesthesia. I blink rapidly as Patrick and the obstetrician, talking quietly in the corner, come into focus. "She'll need bed rest for at least a week," the doctor says to Patrick. "No heavy lifting or strenuous activity."

"When can we try again?" I push past the weakness bearing down on me to find my voice. Both turn, shocked to see me awake. "How many months?"

They exchange a glance, telling me they've already discussed the matter. "Honey, let's concentrate on you right now." Patrick steps to my side and strokes my hair.

"Please, how long?" Like shards of glass, my words come out broken.

We waited six months between this pregnancy and the previous one. Patrick wanted to wait longer, but I was impatient and desperate for a child to love. Every pregnancy required months of IVF treatments, including injections, drugs, and detailed tracking of my ovulation schedule. Every miscarriage that followed became a failure to endure and a struggle to understand.

"During the D and C, your uterus was punctured." The doctor glances at her chart before meeting my gaze. "It's rare but happens."

Shock reverberates through my system. My gaze flies to Patrick, who stares at a spot on the wall. He grips my hand—the only sign I have of his pain. My hand lies lifeless in his.

"You were able to close the hole?" Grief lodges in my throat, choking off air.

"Yes." As if I were a science project, she tells me my future in clipped words devoid of emotion. "It was a small cut. You should heal fully with no complications."

"What does it mean?" I ask.

"That you must wait at least a year," she says with a finality I refuse to accept. "We'll check to make sure everything has healed, but on average, that's the amount of time we recommend."

"There has to be another way." Despair wraps around me like a noose and tightens until my body goes numb. After three miscarriages and a tidal wave of emotions, I search but fail to find a life raft. "Can I take medicine to speed up the healing?"

"Jaya." Patrick runs his hand through his hair.

After a deep sigh, he says, "Let's talk about this later, all right?"

Before I can answer, Patrick whispers a few words to the doctor. She nods, then walks out of the room. I twist the hospital bedsheet through my fingers while watching her leave. I give no other sign of my desolation.

"How are you feeling?" Once we are alone, Patrick lowers the bed's guardrail to sit next to me.

A searing pain rips through my abdomen and across my pelvis. After every miscarriage, we have been given a host of reasons as to why my body refuses to carry a child to term, but not one of them tells me how to solve the problem.

"It was supposed to be a simple D and C." I calculate the time it would take from the start of another round of IVF to an actual pregnancy. Desperation driving me, I decide on a course of action. "We need to see another doctor. Maybe we don't have to wait a full year."

"Honey." Patrick waits until I meet his gaze before saying, "Why don't we focus on your healing right now. We can worry about the rest later."

"I'll research some doctors and find the best one." I barely hear him as my mind whirs with ideas. Formulating a plan helps keep my focus off the reality of what has happened. "My dad should know someone."

"I don't want us to see another doctor," he says slowly.

"Why?" In the face of his silence, I sit up in the bed.

"Because I'm not sure this is what I want anymore."

JAYA

THREE MONTHS LATER

2000

ONE

I was five years old when I begged my mother for a dog. The breed or size didn't matter. I just wanted something of my own to love and to hold tight. Mom surprised me with a puppy waiting on a leash three days after I asked. It was perfect. I took the dog everywhere and slept with it every night. A few months later, the dog got out of the backyard and was lost. I sat on my bed and cried for hours while my mother watched me silently from the doorway of my room. I finally fell asleep, exhausted from my grief. Only the next morning did I discover she had come in during the night to pull the blanket over me and turn off the light. She never said a word to me about my loss.

I stare out at the water as it laps against the rocks. A horn blasts in the distance as a ship signals its navigation course down the Hudson River. I pull my jacket tighter around my frame. Weight I had put on with the baby has fallen off, robbing me of the layer of warmth I crave. The chill from the frigid air permeates the wool and leaves me shivering.

I slip my sunglasses off and raise my face toward the sun that peeks from behind the clouds.

Though it's only October, the temperature has fallen substantially, warning us that winter is coming soon. I don't mind the cold or snow. It offers an excuse to bundle my body under layers of clothes and hide from the world. I didn't always prefer my company to that of others, but then again, I never imagined my life would be what it is now.

I tuck my hands beneath my thighs and lean back against the bench. Seated and listening to honks from cars and blasts from ships' horns, I welcome the reprieve from the echoes of sadness that fill my head.

"I'm sorry I'm late."

I don't turn around. "It's fine," I say, though we both know I'm lying. Nothing is fine, and I wonder how anything can be again. "How was work?"

"Fine."

Is that what we are now—two people who parrot each other? Patrick takes the seat next to me on the bench. The wind blows his brown hair off his forehead. He's wrapped a scarf I bought for him two winters ago around his neck. Buying him things came naturally for me. I know his favorite shoe brand, the design of ties he prefers, and the cut of suits he likes. Between courtship and marriage, we have an insight into each other that can't be matched. But no amount of time together gave us a playbook on how to handle grief.

"Good." I return to staring out at the water,

wondering if the answers I've been searching for are within its depths. "That's good."

He covers my hand with his, and our fingers automatically intermingle. My eyes fly to his warily. It's been three months since the D&C. Since then, we've barely spoken.

"Do you remember the first day of junior year?" He doesn't wait for my answer. "You walked into class with your hair up in a bun and a pencil sticking out of it. You were wearing ripped jeans and a sweatshirt that read, 'If at first you don't succeed, skydiving isn't for you.'"

"I loved that ratty old thing." I threw it away when we moved in together right after college. A hole had started in the sleeve and made its way up to the shoulder. "You, on the other hand, were not a fan of skydiving."

"My mistake letting you choose our second date." His fingers tighten around mine. Unable to help myself, I squeeze back, welcoming the warmth from his touch. "If I had known . . ."

"Would you have said no?" Surprised, I meet his eyes and wait for the answer. Though I knew he was nervous that day, he suited up and hopped onto the plane without one objection.

"Would you have said yes to another date if I had?" he asks.

"I loved skydiving," I admit. The first time I went was on a dare in freshman year of college. For the straitlaced girl, it was a welcome departure from my daily existence. It became my drug, my natural high. "It would have been pretty tough if you had said no."

"Then I'm glad I didn't," he replies. I nod, understanding what he doesn't say—that he doesn't regret all the years we've had together. "You haven't been in a long time," he reminds me.

No, I haven't. Not since we started trying for a child. After the first miscarriage, he asked, then begged me to talk, but I told him there was nothing to say. I stayed focused on getting pregnant again—sure it would heal whatever wounds the first miscarriage had wrought. But each subsequent failure only served to drive us further apart.

"You should go again," he says gently. "You loved it so much."

"Sometimes loving something isn't enough, is it?" We both know I'm not talking about skydiving. He releases my fingers, and though I yearn to reach out and hold them tight, I let him go. "Have you found a place?"

Our separation has been accomplished in stages. After the D&C, he started sleeping in the guest room. On the weekends, he began joining his buddies for trips or visiting his family in Florida. I wondered aloud if we were separating. When he replied that he was searching for an apartment, another piece of me, already frayed, broke, but I said nothing.

"Yes." His answer is barely loud enough for me to hear. "Two blocks down from you. One bedroom. It's a sublease for six months while I look for something permanent."

A part of me yearns to believe he's staying close because of me, but the logical side of my brain tells me it's because it's convenient. Our current apartment is within walking distance to work and to all our favorite haunts. I wonder if I'll see him at our local restaurant or reading the paper on Sunday morning at the coffee shop where the bagels come out fresh from the oven and the owner knows just how we like them. Patrick prefers his lightly toasted but heavy on the cream cheese, whereas I take . . .

"Jaya?" From his tone, I know he's been repeating my name.

"Sorry." I rub my temple, hoping it helps bring me back. "Lost in my own thoughts for a minute." I turn away, refusing to let him see what I have kept hidden—that the blackouts are happening more and more. "What were you saying?"

"Have you told your parents?" He hesitates before saying, "About us."

"Yes." I rub the tension from my neck before facing him. "I called them last week." A ship passes slowly in front of us as I replay the conversation in my head. "Dad asked me how I was doing, while Mom stayed silent."

"Jaya," Patrick starts, but I cut him off with a wave of my hand.

"I'm going there for the weekend. I'll explain then."

"Do you need me to come with you?" His gaze bores into mine. "To help them understand."

Patrick is the son that my father never had. Though my mother was welcoming and seemed happy with our union, she maintained the distance she kept with everyone.

"It won't make a difference." Though he's trying to lessen my burden, we both know nothing will change my mother's detachment. "She'll still refuse to discuss it."

The lines around his mouth tighten, and I know he's holding back what he really wants to say. The space between us started when we began trying to get pregnant. He became withdrawn as I became impatient from the years of IVF treatments and fertility issues. Every discussion centered on the necessary steps to conceive. When we finally became pregnant the first time, it felt like the months of disconnection had never happened. Together we celebrated and daydreamed about the new addition to our family. When we miscarried twelve weeks later, I fell apart and he fell away. My grief became all-encompassing, leaving no room for our marriage or him. It started a cycle that took us through two more miscarriages.

He stands and wraps the scarf tighter around his neck, choking off any remaining oxygen between us. "I'll come by at the end of the weekend to get the rest of my stuff."

"I'll be home." Though he still has a key, I nod my head as if he were an uninvited guest.

"I'll see you then."

I yearn to ask him to stay, but the words fail me. My mouth dries up, and forming a sentence becomes impossible. Tears sting my eyes, but they don't fall. I watch him walk away until he is no longer in sight. Only then do I face forward and continue to stare at the flowing Hudson. When darkness falls and the lights of the city beckon, I start the long walk home.

TWO

When I was seven, I wanted to learn how to ride a bike. My mom bought me one with training wheels, but I took them off. My feet barely reached the pedals. Every day I got on the bike and every day I fell off. One fall was particularly hard and required ten stitches in my forehead. Afterward, Mom took the bike away and locked it in the garage. When I argued with her, she said I should either give up or wait until I was older to try again. I refused to listen to her and snuck the bike out. The next day, I broke my arm and busted my lip going down a hill. She immediately gave the bike away to a neighbor.

When I demanded to know why, she answered, "Sometimes, Jaya, it is best to leave things if they cause you harm."

I stand in front of the door of my childhood home in the sprawling suburbs right outside of the city. I finger my key, debating whether to slip it in or ring the doorbell. I finally pocket the piece of metal and push the doorbell twice.

"Sweetheart." Dad opens the door and immediately pulls me in for a tight hug.

"Hi, Dad." My words are lost in his clothes, and his laugh reverberates from his body into

26

mine. The smell of onions and garlic mixed with spices permeates the house.

"Mom's been cooking all day, hasn't she?"

"She just needs an excuse." He wraps an arm around my shoulder and steers me toward the kitchen. "She's made all of your favorites." He hesitates before asking, "How are you doing, honey?"

Grateful for his effort, I smile but hold back the truth. "I'm fine, Dad."

My father spent my childhood at work. Even when home, he ceded the responsibility of raising me and running the household to my mother. She set the course of our mother-daughter relationship and cemented it to what we are today—two strangers with blood as our bond.

Mom comes out of the kitchen, wearing a ridiculous apron that tells everyone the chef is always right. Like Dad, she pulls me in for a hug, but hers is quicker and her arms barely wrap around me.

"Just in time for dinner." Mom glances toward the foyer and then back at me. "Where are your bags? I thought you were staying for the weekend."

She's pulled her light-brown hair back with a clasp. Her dark-green eyes contrast with her light-olive skin. I grew up envying my mom's natural beauty. In our small community, she was openly admired for her looks. She always shrugged off the compliments and wore only the simplest of outfits and very little makeup.

I hold up my oversize purse. "Just one night. I threw some clothes in here." Eager to change the subject, I lift the cover off a pot on the stove and inhale. "It smells wonderful."

She's silent and then lowers her voice so I have to strain to hear. "You need to be with family right now. Especially after Patrick left . . ."

"Patrick didn't leave me." My voice is harsher than I meant it to be. "We decided together that we needed to separate."

I'm lying. It wasn't a decision. Instead, it was years of my crying and his stepping further and further away until he couldn't hear me.

"Because you can't have babies?" Mom asks, surprising me. She wrings her hands together.

My parents came from India as newlyweds. They had me, their only child, after Dad finished medical school and established his career. "You were such a blessing," my father used to tell me when I was growing up, whenever I asked why I had no brothers or sisters. "It wouldn't have been fair to other families if we had more than our share."

But I rarely felt like a blessing to my mother. If anything, I was a disappointment to her—I saw it in the way her lips pulled tight when I lost the fifth-grade spelling bee in the final round; in the way her face seemed to stiffen when I broke a tie at cheerleading tryouts and didn't make the squad; or in the faraway look to her eyes right now as she contemplates my failure to carry a child.

"Yes." Her face jerks up at my answer, but she remains silent. I swallow the lump in my throat, desperate for support but knowing better than to turn to her. "Because of the babies."

"Lena." My father pats my back while giving Mom a look. "Jaya just got here. Let's sit down for dinner and let her catch her breath."

He grabs plates and spoons and sets the table for three. Mom and I watch him, both of us statues frozen in place. He brings the dishes of food over and then pulls out two chairs. Mom takes her seat at the head of the table, and Dad and I sit on either side of her.

"How are you feeling?" asks Dad, always a doctor.

"Good," I lie. "My body is healing." Since I never confided in them before, I don't tell them the truth now—that moments of blackness still follow me everywhere and that the pain from the D&C is a daily reminder of my loss.

"Where will you live?" Mom leaves her plate of food untouched. She's clasped her hands in front of her, and her head is bowed as if in mourning.

"Patrick has found a place." I limit my words to facts without emotion. "A sublease for six months. One bedroom. In the same neighborhood."

"You'll stay in the apartment alone?" Her gaze flies to Dad and then back to me before she announces, "Jaya, you will move in with us."

My entire body stiffens at the idea of cramming myself back into the careful little box I lived in as a child under my mother's disapproving eye. "I'm fine, Mom," I say, dismissing her.

Given our history, I assume she will move on to other topics. I can't imagine she wants me here any more than I am eager to come back.

"You are not fine," she says, shocking me. "You can lie to yourself and us about the rest of it, but please admit that much. You are not fine."

The blackness starts to inch forward. "I don't want to talk about it," I say, desperate to shut the conversation down. "Not with you." With all the disappointments of the pregnancies, I am too tired to engage with her.

She stands up and neatly pushes her chair in. Without another word, she walks out of the kitchen and up the stairs to her room. In the ensuing silence, shame creeps over me.

"I'm sorry." My stomach growls from hunger, but I ignore the call. I take a deep breath to rein in the emotions that threaten to spill over. I look up and meet Dad's pained gaze. "I wasn't expecting her to discuss it."

"Your mother loves you."

I barely hold back my laugh. "Mom's idea of love was to take me to school and feed me food."

Even as I say it, guilt upbraids me. Though my mother was distant, every time she provided for me—my favorite foods meticulously prepared, my outfits carefully ironed, her face amid the crowd for every school event, watching anxiously—I convinced myself it was love. My mother was physically present for me in every tangible way that could matter. It is the intangible connection we have somehow always lacked.

"She can't ask for a seat at the table now."

"Your mother did the best she could," Dad says slowly.

"I know, Dad." Sensing it's safest to move past the discussion, I take out some Tupperware containers. "We can put the food in the fridge."

"Jaya." He waits until I face him before saying, "She's hurting right now." Anger stings me. I am hurting too, but my father always has taken my mother's side first. "She received some news from India," he explains. "Her mind isn't in the right place."

"India? What kind of news?"

Mom refused to talk about her childhood in India, and we never visited. Eager to learn, I would ask repeatedly as a child about their home country, but each time she would answer, "Focus on the future, Jaya, not the past." Dad's parents passed before I was born, and being an only child, he had little family left to return to. I vaguely remember the handful of times Mom's brothers visited from England and Australia.

"Dad?" I repeat when he glances worriedly toward the stairs.

He motions me into his cherry-paneled office that Mom spent hours decorating to perfection. The moldings are carved-oak motifs, and the dark-stained hardwood floor is covered with an Egyptian throw rug. An antique table lamp brightens the room.

Seeing her joy in decorating my father's office, I asked her to help me redecorate my room. At ten years old, I was desperate for a way to connect with her. Mom explored options and presented me with a dozen swaths of wall colors and magazine layouts of furniture. She left after telling me to make my decision. Taking her withdrawal as rejection, I discarded her selections and painted the room black with matching furniture. Though the Goth period lasted a full year, she never uttered a word in opposition.

From his desk drawer, Dad pulls out a crumpled letter. He reads it with fatigue and an unexpected wariness. No matter what was happening, he was always full of energy and life, whereas Mom was quiet and always seemed to watch her step. He offered lightness, a contrast to her heaviness. Yet never did he stray from her side.

"Your mother threw it away without telling me. I found it in the wastebasket." He hands me the letter with shaking hands. "Her brother reached out to her and asked her to come home. Her father, your grandfather—Deepak—is ill."

Dear Lena,
   I hope this letter finds you well, little sister. I am writing because our father is very ill. Ravi, a servant from our childhood, worries he may not have much longer on this earth. Ravi says there is something our father has for you. I would never ask you to return to a place that caused so much pain, but I would have failed in my duty as your brother if I did not inform you of our father's condition. Samir, Jay, and I said our goodbye to him decades ago when we left India. Whatever your decision, we support you and love you.

Your brother,
Paresh

   Without asking, I say with surety, "She isn't going."
   "No, she isn't." He leans back in his chair, the leather squeaking with his weight. "Nothing I say will change her mind." He rubs his eyes with his forefinger and thumb. "But I can tell she is troubled by her decision. I worry she will regret it for the rest of her life."

• • •

I lie in my childhood bed, watching the moon's rays bounce off the ceiling through the window. The clock lets out a small beep when the hour changes. Three a.m. Exhausted, I yearn for sleep, but it refuses me. I toss left and then right. I push up on my forearms and punch the pillow until it is flat, then try again. When that fails, I toss the pillow to the ground and sleep on the bare sheet.

I jerk upright on hearing a sound from downstairs. I listen to footsteps and then the refrigerator opening. Remembering my father's love of late-night snacks, I slip on my robe and make my way down the stairs. The sliver of light from beneath the kitchen door guides my final steps. I push open the swinging wood door to see Mom seated at the kitchen table, her head in her hands. She jolts up at my entrance, and we stare at each other.

"I thought it was Dad getting a bite," I murmur, automatically taking a step back.

"I wanted a glass of milk," Mom says, but there's no glass in sight. "Can I get you anything?" She stands without waiting for an answer and pulls out a saucepan and milk to heat up. While it's warming, she opens a carton of cookies and sets them on the table. "You've lost so much weight since the babies . . ." She pauses as if catching herself and falls silent.

"I'm fine." I stare at the space between us, unsure.

"I slept in this morning." She kneads her hands together and stares at the floor. "It always messes up my sleep schedule." Just before the milk overflows, she removes the pan from the stove, then pours the white liquid into two mugs and sets them on the table next to the cookies. When I continue to stand, she murmurs, "You should drink it while it's warm."

I take a seat, and only when I bite into a cookie does she sit down again. She is the perfect caregiver, attentive to all of my needs as if she were a well-trained servant. In the stillness, I can hear myself chew and then swallow a mouthful of milk. She watches me, her gaze focused on my every move. When the silence lingers, I finally say, "Dad told me about your father." I pause before adding, "I wish you had said something."

"It doesn't matter." Her face tightens, and her body seems to shrink into itself.

"He's your father." Shocked, I try to understand this woman I barely know. "Of course it matters."

"Let it go, Jaya."

She uses the same voice she did when I was a child—the one that allowed no room for discussion or argument. My spine tightens, and the hairs on the back of my neck stand up.

"He's dying, and you refuse to go home?" Her eyes narrow in warning, but I'm too tired to care. "Why?"

"Be careful speaking of things you do not know about," she says.

"Then tell me." As a child, I listened with envy when other kids spoke about visiting their grandparents. I begged to visit the grandfather and stepmother I knew nothing about. My requests and pleading were always met with a firm no and then silence. Now, having been denied my own family with children, I grasp at the only family I have. "Why didn't you ever talk about him? Why didn't we visit?"

"It's not your concern."

"Yes, it is." I can feel the darkness swirl around me. I blink to keep focus, but for a few seconds everything goes black. I close my eyes and breathe deeply. When I open them, she's staring at the table, her head downcast. I rub my hand over my face to get my bearings. "He's my family too," I remind her. "Why do you hate him?"

"You won't understand." She speaks quietly, her words slow and evenly spaced. "Please stop." She stands up to leave.

"You barely said two words to me when I was growing up." She slowly meets my gaze and flinches. "We never visited your brothers. And now you ignore your father?" I am driven by a need to hurt her, if only to distract myself from my own pain. "Who are you?" She recoils as if I've slapped her. Tears gather in her eyes, and guilt engulfs me. "Mom," I whisper, but she holds up her hand for silence.

"My stepmother made me promise never to return to India after my marriage." Her lower lip quivers. "And my father seconded her demand."

Shocked at the revelation, I ask, "What kind of father would do that?"

"The kind who knew it was the best thing." She lifts a frail hand and covers her face. She takes a deep breath before meeting my gaze.

"Mom?" I search my limited knowledge as to why her father would demand such a promise, but every explanation falls short. She starts to leave, when I stop her. "Please, tell me why."

For too long now I have been denied answers. I have been left in the dark as to why my body refuses to bear a child. I lost the man I love without reason. I never understood why the mother I needed kept her distance, as if she were afraid to come near.

Now I beg for a morsel of truth. The reporter in me yearns for the story behind why a father would ask such a thing. The daughter in me needs to understand why my mother agreed. But even as hope flares, it dies just as quickly. Today proves it is no different from every other day. I see her refusal before she shakes her head no.

"My promise was the price I had to pay for being born. That's all you need to know." With a tired voice she bids me good night.

THREE

I sit up on the sofa in my living room and rub the crick out of my neck caused from having fallen asleep on the armrest. The hours crawl into one another, and the nights turn into days. I have not spoken to Mom in the two days since our fight; nor do I expect to.

My foot hits an empty diet soda can as I wipe cheese residue off my shirt. I collect the garbage and toss it in the trash can. Hands empty, I start to head back to clean the rest, when my feet buckle beneath me. I grab the counter to keep my balance. In seconds, everything falls dark. Images of the children I couldn't give birth to fill my mind. The strength seeps out of me, and I slide against the wall until I'm seated on the floor.

These episodes have become fairly frequent. There's no explanation for the time lost with each occurrence when grief envelops me and I am blinded to the outside world. When I come out of it, time has stood still, but from the look on others' faces, I know it has paused only for me.

Scared of what has been happening to me, I recently made a doctor's appointment. After running every test imaginable, the physician declared me healthy. I laughed at his conclusion, wondering how you diagnosed heartbreak.

The last pregnancy held on the longest. We refused to learn the sex for fear of jinxing the pregnancy. But at the twelve-week mark, I couldn't help myself—I stopped off at a baby store after work and bought gender-neutral clothes and toys to fill the empty nursery. Over the next couple of weeks, I decorated the room until it was perfect.

I take deep breaths until the fog clears. I wrap my arms around my stomach and rest my chin on my knees. I stare at the nothingness in front of me and let my mind drift until I'm empty of thoughts. I'm a complete void with no thoughts or images of the babies or Patrick. No thoughts of the letter or the grandfather I have never met. Not even of my mother's silence in childhood.

"Jaya?" I jerk upright to find Patrick standing at the kitchen entrance. His brow furrowed with concern, he bends down until we're at eye level. Our apartment keys dangle off his finger. "Are you all right?"

"Yes, of course." I hate that he caught me in a vulnerable position. I jump up and brush past him into the living room. "I didn't realize you had arrived."

"I called out for you." He reaches out to grab my hand, but, hesitant to touch him, I move out of the way before we make contact. "You didn't hear anything, did you?"

I grip the back of the sofa with both hands and

silently beg for strength. I scan the apartment and see it through his eyes. There are rolled-up newspapers on the table and stacks of dirty dishes next to them. It's a far cry from the home of the woman who needed everything in its place for life to make sense.

"I tried to gather as many of your things as possible." I had spent hours dividing the memories of our life together. "If there's anything I forgot, feel free to take it." Eager to be alone, I say, "I'll go grab some coffee while you pack."

"I thought we could talk." In the home that we made together, he stands like an outsider. He waits until he has my attention before saying softly, "Stacey and I have been spending time together."

Stunned, I replay his words in my head, sure that I heard wrong. In the background, I catch the sound of the door across the hall open and close. Through the window, taxis honk as they maneuver for space. Every noise is magnified to drown out his words.

"Jaya?"

In a few strides, he's in front of me. On instinct, I retreat until my back hits the door. I stare at his features—as familiar to me as my own—and see a stranger. With every step away from each other, I never imagined him moving toward someone else. Especially not a friend I had known since college. Angry at my own naïveté and his betrayal, I look away before meeting his gaze.

I believe I see my pain mirrored in his eyes but then chide myself for my foolishness.

"I didn't want you to hear it from anyone else." In the face of my silence, he explains. "We were grabbing a drink after work, and there were some reporters from your paper there. They saw us together."

The blackness that has taken a permanent spot in the back of my brain starts to advance, threatening me with more lost time. I refuse to let him see me vulnerable, so I fight to hold it off.

"No wonder she wasn't returning my calls." I barely pull the words past the narrowing of my throat. My mind aches, while my body feels numb. "It's awkward to tell your friend that you're sleeping with her husband."

"It isn't like that." He flinches, then runs his hand through his hair, his telltale sign of worry. His words hold pain and regret, but I'm too angry to care. "We're just talking."

"Talking?" Confused, I ask, "What about?" When he's silent, I repeat my question. "What about?"

"About life. About our hopes." His words are precise, as if I were a member of the jury to be convinced.

I know from our years together that he's holding something back. Suddenly scared, I ask, "Do you talk about our . . ." I pause, stopping before I say the word *babies*.

"Yes." He reads my mind.

My breath catches, and my knees buckle in response. In all the time we were together, we never shared the subject with our friends; I assumed the topic too sacred to discuss with anyone else. "Do you love her?" Acid crawls up my stomach and settles into my mouth.

"No," he says quietly. "Of course not."

"Knowing Stacey, she'll expect to have her feelings reciprocated." I grip the doorknob behind me in hopes of staying steady. The safest thing is for me to leave, but my feet refuse to move. "Stacey is looking for marriage." I rack my brain for particulars. "White picket fence and two point five kids. She's mentioned enough times her clock is ticking." As if we were discussing our day, I inform him of the irony. "She'll probably be able to carry to term. Her issue has been finding the right partner."

His face falls, and for the first time since the miscarriages, I see his sorrow. I wonder if this is how most marriages end—with a calm discussion of the one who will replace you.

Though there's so much more I can tell him—Stacey's concerns about making partnership track, her neuroses, and the college sweetheart who dumped her when she left for a job in New York—I keep it to myself. He'll learn it all over time. That's what relationships are about, right? Seeing the good first and then slowly piecing in the bad until the full picture reveals itself.

"Why?" It is self-flagellation, but I need to know. "If you don't have feelings for her, then . . ."

He hesitates and I am sure he's not going to answer, when he says, "Because she listens. Because she talks." Anguish rips through me. I drop my head, but it is too late. He sees it and reaches out—"Jaya . . ."—but I step away.

When we met, a new world opened up to me. For the first time, I knew unconditional love and acceptance. In Patrick, I found a happiness I never believed existed. I was sure I had gotten my fairy tale, but he isn't a knight in shining armor, nor am I a princess. We are two people whose love has moved from the light into the shadows.

"You should be with someone who can make you happy." My heart breaks as I set him free. With all the love I have ever felt for him, I whisper, "You deserve that."

I struggle with the locks before finally wrenching open the door. I can hear him calling my name, but it doesn't matter. His call is no longer my beacon.

FOUR

"Please, you cannot go." Mom clasped her hands together as if in prayer.

The decision to travel to India came easily. For days after the conversation with Patrick, all I heard were his words: *She talks.* They echoed in my head everywhere I turned. Lost for too long, I became sure an escape was the solution. The miscarriages have stripped me of my sense of self. In my desperation for a child, everything else fell to the wayside—including me.

When I approached my boss to take an extended leave of absence, she offered me space on a friend's blog to write about my time away. Excited to continue writing, I gratefully accepted.

After cementing the plans, I went home to tell my parents. Tears welled in Mom's eyes as she begged me not to go. I wavered at her plea, but my own grief made it impossible to accede to her wishes.

"Please tell me what you are afraid of," I asked one final time.

"I am asking you not to go." She was resolute, refusing me as her confidante. "Let that be enough."

"I'm sorry." We both continued to keep our secrets. I didn't tell her that I no longer know who I am. Or that my roots have been stripped, leaving me adrift. In going to India, I am escaping my reality in the hopes of saving my sanity. "I have to go. For me." Her head dropped, and into the silence I whispered, "For you." She jerked her head up. I reached out and gripped her hand for barely a second before stepping away.

Seated on the plane, I smooth out the creases on the crumpled letter from my uncle. I read it one more time before slipping it back into my bag. I lay my hand over my barren stomach as I glance out the small oval window. The plane taxis on the runway of the airport in central India. I throw my light jacket over my jeans and top before grabbing my computer bag and backpack.

A weary couple next to me hushes their small children. Envy rips through me when the mother lifts the youngest into her arms and soothes his cries. I breathe into the V-neck of my shirt, blaming my sudden nausea on the smell of dirty diapers and curry that permeates the plane.

Finally, there is shuffling of feet. I follow passengers past the hovering flight attendants into the stifling heat inside the oversize terminal. Humidity fills my lungs, and my clothes mold to me like skin. Travelers bump me without apology as they rush toward baggage claim or connecting flights. Above me, large steel pipes crisscross the ceiling, and stray swallows fly freely.

A roar of voices fills the large, open space. One step farther into the terminal and I am met with beggars sleeping alongside grime-lined walls. Cigarette smoke mixed with the smell of sweat permeates the air. Haggard travelers hurry over the dirt-covered scuffed floor toward their destinations. Luggage porters in orange tops and white pants push carts filled with suitcases. Passenger names are repeated over the intercom as airport staff members help travelers find their gates.

I stop and take in my surroundings. Though I have seen pictures, nothing has prepared me for the reality of my parents' homeland and its contrast with mine. Unsure where to go, I search the signs hanging from the ceiling, when a group of children circles around me.

"Memsahib, you buy. You like." With thin fingers, they hold up their goods like prized possessions. Each child is bony with only threadbare clothes. Their faces plead while their words exalt the virtues of the cheap trinkets.

Living in New York, I'm used to beggars. As guilty as others, I give my standard response, shaking my head and walking away. But never have I been faced with children. The sight of them begging, some barely old enough to walk, turns my stomach. I glance around to gauge others' reactions, but no one seems surprised by their presence. The pain that has taken a permanent place in my heart folds into itself.

I find my voice and hold out a stack of bills. "Yes. Thank you."

Eyes wide, they take my offered money and scurry away. I follow them with my gaze as they move from one passenger to the next until they are lost in the throng.

I slip the plastic necklaces into my purse and follow the signs toward baggage claim. With every step away from the terminal gate and deeper into the heart of India, I search the faces around me. I recognize no one, and yet I know that, in this place I have never visited, I am a reflection of each one.

I wheel my bags through the exit door toward the sign that reads "Transportation." Overhead, the sky is hazy with built-up smog. The sun slips behind a cloud, but it barely offers a reprieve from the stifling heat. A large jet flies over the terminal as it climbs toward the sky. On first glance, the scene looks like one from any of the many large cities I've traveled to. Cars linger to pick up passengers. Officers in bright-orange vests whistle at them to keep traffic moving.

I spot a taxi stand and wait in line. A family bustles in front of me while a business traveler waits behind me. When it is my turn, the driver grabs my luggage and starts to load it into the small trunk space of the rickshaw. He's tall and young. A cigarette dangles from the edge of his long mustache.

When he asks me my destination, I repeat the name of the village I have memorized. My grandfather still lives in the same house my mother was raised in. It is my mother's birthplace, and yet I had never heard of it before now. When my father contacted my uncle Paresh about my trip, he helped to finalize the last few details.

As the driver pulls into the maze of traffic, I stare out the open window, refusing to miss a moment of this new world. Like a tourist, I watch excitedly as we pass through the modern construction and roadways of the airport before the asphalt turns to gravel and then simply to earth. The bustling activity from the airport spills into the neighboring streets as people rush about. I do a double take and then laugh with surprise as cows join the masses, demanding their space to saunter freely.

"There are no cows in your country?" The driver follows my gaze.

"Not roaming freely," I answer. "Is it common?" Though I know cows to be sacred, I have never imagined seeing them walking the streets unchecked.

"Yes. As do pigs, dogs, and any other animal that wishes to explore." He catches my gaze in his rearview mirror. "You are here for religion?" A gold cross hangs around his neck.

When I was growing up, we rarely attended religious events. I asked my mom once why, and in a rare moment of disclosure, she admitted she stopped believing in God when she was a child.

"No, not for religion," I answer.

"Then why the village? There are many towns in Madhya Pradesh," he says. "You will like better."

We maneuver through the center of the city onto a two-lane road bordered by sunburned fields. Sheep graze in the distance. Bone-thin women with saris tucked around their waists and knotted between their legs carry buckets of water atop their heads. Wailing infants dangle low on their hips, the sling their only cover from the midday sun. A small truck speeds ahead, pulling a cart filled with feed.

I take in my surroundings, mesmerized by scenes I had only ever before seen in movies. Everything I've grown up with stands in contrast to the abject poverty around me. "It's for my mother," I say quietly before telling the truth. "And for me." For the remainder of the trip, I stare out the open window, lost in my own thoughts.

Nearly forty-five minutes later, past miles of desolate fields barren of vegetation, we enter

49

a village filled with decrepit homes scattered among smaller houses. Like at the airport, throngs of people fill the streets. As the driver navigates the dirt lanes, villagers huddle together and watch our arrival. A young girl dressed in a tunic and pants waves shyly at me before running off.

We cross over a dirt street. The homes here are spread farther apart with ample land between. At the end of a long expanse, in front of a well-kept baked-cement home, the driver stops. The bungalow is white with small patches of peeling paint. A set of concrete steps leads to a porch where a hammock swings aimlessly in the dry air. Potted plants grace the sprawling manicured lawn. The next home sits nearly a quarter of an acre away. The soil-filled street contrasts with the modern dwelling.

The driver unloads my luggage. His eyes widen at my healthy tip, and he bows in gratitude. I watch him drive off until he's a speck in the distance. With a deep breath, I pick up my bags and slowly climb the steps to the home my mother called her own until she was wed at eighteen. I knock on the door, but there's no answer.

"Hello?" I call out softly and then louder. The bark of a dog in the distance shatters the silence. With no animal in sight, I wonder if I imagined the sound. I knock again, then step back, starting to doubt my decision to travel so far from everything familiar.

"*Yaha kaun heh?*" a hoarse voice calls from afar.

"Hello?" Now I'm sure I haven't imagined it. I rush down the steps and toward the voice.

"Amisha?" the voice demands.

Past the edge of the steps, I turn a corner and nearly collide with an aged man. He is hunched over slightly, the hair atop his head dark gray. A traditional long cotton shirt reaches his knees with matching loose pants beneath. His feet are encased in worn leather sandals. A large Labrador mix wags his tail by his side.

"Namaste." Though limited in my knowledge of Hindu customs, I know enough to clasp my hands together and bow slightly. Unsure of his ability to speak English, I point to the house and say slowly, "My mother, Lena, was raised here in this house." His eyes narrow, and he stares at me. "I've just arrived from America. We received a letter that my grandfather, Deepak, is ill."

His gasp silences me. He reaches out, but then his hand falls before making contact. Tears pool in his eyes and slide over his worn cheeks.

"You've come," he whispers in stilted English, overcome by emotion. His body shakes as his tears fall faster. "You have finally come."

Confused, I glance at the door and then back at him. "Are you my grandfather? Deepak?"

He shakes his head. "I am Ravi. A servant in your grandparents' home." He pauses and takes a deep breath. My gut starts to churn from the look on his face. "I am so sorry." On hearing his next words, I fall speechless. "You are too late. We scattered Deepak's ashes two days ago."

FIVE

" 'Mankind errs here.' " After letting us into my mother's childhood home, Ravi lights the oil lamps one by one. " 'By folly, darkening knowledge. But, for whom that darkness of the soul is chased by light, splendid and clear shines manifest the truth. As if a sun of wisdom sprang to shed its beams of dawn.' "

"That's beautiful. I've never heard it before." Though I yearn to ask him about my grandfather's death, I bide my time until he's ready.

"From the Gita. Some call it a book of poetry." He points to the lamps. "Used in time of celebration and mourning."

"My uncles—did they come?" I ask, though I know Paresh's letter said they wouldn't.

His face gives me the answer before he does. "No one."

"I'm sorry." The apology sounds hollow to my own ears. "My mother—she said she couldn't." Since he is a stranger, I don't confide in him what my mother told me.

"Your grandfather knew this, but he hoped nonetheless. I think it kept him alive until his body accepted what his mind couldn't."

As he continues to light the lamps, I walk around the small room, running my hand gingerly over the antique furniture. An intricately carved, dark marble chair sits in the corner of the room, alongside a gold-painted urn. The walls are painted a warm ivory color, and the floor is covered with an expensive rug. Ravi's dog follows him loyally as he finishes the last lamp.

"What's his name?" I ask.

"I call him Rokie. He seems to like it, so we are in agreement." He matches my smile, then motions me toward a large Rajasthan swing adorned with precious stones that sits in the middle of the room. "Please, sit."

"Thank you." I settle into the soft velvet cushions, tired after the long trip. "You speak English well."

"I grew up in a time when the British insisted we learn their language. It seemed a waste, but now"—he motions toward me—"I am grateful."

"How did he die?" I finally ask. I don't mourn a man I never knew, but given the long line of losses, it feels unfair to have another one. And now, with his death, I will never find the answer I came searching for.

"Peacefully." He rubs the top of Rokie's head, and the dog barks in approval before settling down.

"I'm sorry I wasn't in time."

"Maybe you still are."

I start to ask him what he means, when he grabs a larger cushion from a sofa and lays it

54

on the floor before settling atop it. Ashamed by his being on the floor while I'm on the settee, I quickly jump up. "No, please, you sit here."

"Your grandmother, Amisha, always said to me, 'Ravi, when you are next to the earth, you can hear her secrets.' Then she would laugh, climb onto the very seat you are on, and say, 'So please tell me what you find out.'" He signals for me to take my seat again as he settles comfortably into his own.

"You knew my grandmother?" She was a woman rarely mentioned. She died young, so her mention felt like a dark cloud that was always threatening. When my uncles spoke of her on their visits, it was in hushed tones and with few specifics. A veil would fall over my mother's face, and they would immediately change the subject. Soon enough she was never spoken of again. "I know she died many years ago."

"She did, though at times it feels like yesterday." Ravi fumbles for a pair of glasses from his shirt pocket and then cleans the lenses with his shirttail. "My grandson insists they are superior to the eyes that have served me for more than eighty years." He slips them on and blinks to get focus. "When suddenly I am able to see clearly, I fear he may be right."

"What was she like?" He had called for her earlier, as if she were still alive instead of a memory. "Amisha?"

"Her face was kind, and her heart was strong. When I heard you, I thought it was her voice carried by the wind." He closes his eyes. "I was sure she was standing behind me, but when you called again, I knew I was mistaken." He opens his eyes and winks at me. "I began to follow for fear you would lose your voice with the bellowing."

"I've only seen one picture of her," I admit.

I found the photo as a child. It was stored in a shoe box, buried beneath old receipts and clipped coupons. The image showed a woman seeking something in the distance, her eyes guarded against the glare of the flash. When I asked my mother about it, she took it without a word and returned to her room. I never saw the picture again.

"Your grandmother believed photographs hid the truth about a person, offering only an illusion instead." He pauses before adding, "I am sure she would have thought differently if she had known a picture was all that would be left to remember her by." Rokie growls at a passing bird outside the dust-laden window. We watch as he rushes out the open door. "How is your mother?"

There is desperation in his question that I don't understand. Unwilling to share too much with someone unfamiliar, I give him the answer that he seems to want. "Happy."

Joy flashes across Ravi's face. "Your grandmother would be pleased to know that."

"You were a friend of hers?" I ask, curious.

"I was a servant in the home, but your grandmother's heart was benevolent enough to call me a friend." His voice cracks like a man tormented. He averts his eyes, refusing to meet my stare. He swallows repeatedly and curls his fingers inward. The blood seems to drain from his face, leaving it haunted.

"Is everything all right?" He is hiding something, I am sure, but when I search his gaze, a mask falls over his face.

"Yes," he whispers. He gathers his emotions and finds his voice. "It was one of her many gifts, seeing past the circumstances of one's life and embracing the person." His body tightens as he lowers his head in shame. "I am a Dalit." He says it as if it were a sentence he is asking to be commuted.

"An untouchable?"

He nods. "We are often believed to be less than human in the Hindu caste system. Many times beaten or abused for minor reasons." I swallow my gasp, the journalist in me trained to listen without reaction. "Often conceived by accident, many of my people die before passing through childhood."

In history class via textbook pages and photos, I learned how the caste system defined generations of Hindus. Each person was slotted into a predetermined position of value based on his birth. The untouchables were on the lowest rung and were often considered worthless.

Furious at a system I didn't understand, I questioned first my teacher and then my father. He gave me the only answer he could—that history proved time and again it was difficult to change what people believed as truth. I argued in theory about the unfairness of it. Now, hearing Ravi's words, I am shamed by my naïveté and for not fully understanding the truth behind the practice.

"I'm sorry." The words sound inadequate even as I speak them.

"Do not be," he returns, surprising me. "It was because I was unwanted, dismissed as a burden on society, that I met your grandmother." His face softens at the mention of her. "For that I would live a hundred times as an untouchable." He sees the compassion in my eyes and smiles. "Your grandmother was a woman ahead of her time. Head of this house, she brought in my family members to work. She was a savior to us."

He speaks of her with reverence, with warmth that turns cold when he mentions my grandfather. I notice the contrast and wonder at the reason behind the difference. Before I can ask him to elaborate, he rises off the pillow and motions for me to follow.

"Come, I will show you her palace."

. . .

Ravi gives me a tour of the remainder of the house, proudly exclaiming that it was one of the first fitted for electricity—a luxury I have always taken for granted. The home is barely the equivalent of a large cottage in America. With every step, I try to imagine my mother playing in the halls, eating in the kitchen, and sleeping in the house. I wonder how she felt the night before her marriage, and if she mourned leaving her childhood home. I try to visualize and fail to understand how my mother would have felt when her father demanded she never return home after her wedding.

In the last room, Ravi presents the bed—a thin mattress atop metal springs—like a king's ransom. He hands me a set of rusted keys and promises to return in the morning. Though I booked a hotel in the neighboring town, I'm glad to be staying in my mother's childhood home to get a glimpse of the part of her she refuses to share.

As exhaustion creeps in, I lie in bed and stare through the protective mosquito net at the four bare walls, but thoughts of my mother keep me tossing and turning into the night. My gaze locked on the darkness, I wait for the mystery of her childhood to reveal itself. Minutes turn to hours, and I fall asleep with my questions unanswered.

At the first hint of sunrise, a rooster begins to crow. I slip one hand out from beneath the cover and search fruitlessly for an alarm clock before realizing the noise comes from a live animal. With a pained whimper, I cover my head with a thin pillow, but the rooster is relentless.

Ravi enters the room after a quick knock. "You do not care for the songs of our animals?" The rooster continues to crow in the background—insistent on waking even the dead. Ravi balances a tray with a cup and plate of food. "I could hear your protests from the living room." He toes the door open for Rokie. "I would ask if you are clothed, but since I am nearly blind, I believe it does not matter."

"I was too tired to change." I slip through the opening in the mosquito netting and reach for the tray. I inhale the fragrance wafting off the food. "You didn't have to bring me anything, but it smells wonderful. Thank you."

"You are her granddaughter," Ravi says as if no further explanation were necessary. "Chai and *ghatiya*—a proper breakfast." Yellow twists of fried flour lie next to a cup of foam-covered chai.

"I've never had it before." I cautiously take a sip. The rich concoction of fresh ginger and milk warms my mouth. "It's delicious." I nearly hum my approval.

"You may thank our goat for the milk." Ravi smiles when I raise an eyebrow in question. "In the field behind the house. She delivered it early this morning."

I glance curiously at the frothy mixture before taking another sip. "I look forward to the introductions."

"Your grandmother insisted it was the only way to start the morning." Ravi rests a hand on the old stone chair that matches the desk. "Finish your breakfast, and then I will show you where to shower. You don't want to frighten the goat when you make her acquaintance," he teases. "Later, we will talk."

I watch him leave before taking a small bite of food. The rooster finally stops crowing. In the stillness, I imagine telling Patrick about what I've seen so far. When we first met, I was quiet and reserved—a habit I learned from my mother. Patrick helped to bring me out, listening with interest when I spoke. He was the person I told everything to—good or bad—until there was nothing good left to tell. We were brutally tossed around in a cyclone of hope and hurt. To share my sorrow meant reliving the past with the one person who had already experienced it. I was too weak to carry his grief atop mine, so it seemed safer to stop sharing.

The memories of the past circle around me—a reminder of a time when my marriage was stronger than circumstance. I pass through the years like snippets of a film reel until I am moments away from the day he told me about Stacey. With the recollection, the pain comes flooding back.

I push away the plate of food and walk toward the window, where the sound of children starting a game wafts through the opening. After wiping the dust off the ledge, I push against the latch until it loosens. I slide it open and gaze at the children as they kick a barely inflated ball in a dirt field. Around them are fields with scattered vegetation and homes similar to this one. Their small voices become large with laughter.

I quickly shut the window and latch it closed. My back against the wall, I breathe deeply. For all of my surety about coming, I now wonder what I was thinking. I am all alone in a place that holds nothing for me and no one to care.

"This is the shower?" I ask, staring at the archaic bath.

Red clay bricks are stacked atop one another, forming makeshift walls. The branches of a broad-leafed tree provide camouflage as a roof. A small drain sits in the middle of the outdoor bath. From corner to corner, there's barely enough room for one person.

"Here are your three buckets of water." Ravi points to the two buckets on the far end of the wall. "They are for soaping but are very hot, so take caution." The third, he explains, is lukewarm for rinsing off. He hands me a small bar of soap. "It's sandalwood. Good for body and hair." Ravi starts to take his leave before pausing. "I nearly forgot. The geckos can be curious, so watch for them."

"Wait, what? Geckos?"

"Yes." He shields his eyes and scans the tree above the bath. "We have many here, and they seem to lose their fear when someone is bathing." He smiles at my astonishment. "Some have fallen on this old head, though they may think it is a nest. Enjoy."

I keep an eye out for wayward reptiles while I bathe quickly. I run the soap over my arms and then my stomach, tracing the faint stretch lines that formed with the last pregnancy. I never imagined one broken track could lead to an entire train falling off. Now I feel foolish for having believed otherwise.

Instead of washing my hair, I let warm water run through it to help relax the tension in my neck. Once finished, I dry myself with the thin towel. I slip on my flowered sundress and pull my wet hair up into a ponytail.

"There's a hotel in the next village that I booked before my trip." I swing idly on the hammock tied to the porch, while sipping the lemon sherbet Ravi made from fresh-squeezed lemons for me. The ice cubes start to melt in the heat.

Ravi uses a metal knife to carve the edge of a

small twig. He whittles the wood with the edge of a knife until the ends are shaved into fine bristles. Once finished, he hands me the stick. "To clean your teeth."

I turn the piece of wood over in my hand as I inspect it. It's as long and wide as a straw, and the bristles at the end look like the end of a broom. There is no way I am putting it in my mouth. "Thank you, but I have a toothbrush with me."

He refuses when I try to hand it back to him. "This is much better. You will see." When I continue to hold it out, he says, "I made it myself for you, and I am nearly blind."

Not wanting to hurt his feelings, I lay it down next to me. His lips curl into a small smile, and I know I've been played. "What's the best way to call a rickshaw?" I ask, hoping to get to the hotel by the afternoon.

"There is no need." He picks up another twig and starts the process again. "This is your home."

"I can't impose."

"This was *her* home, and now, for as long as you wish, this is your home." Ravi's choked voice falls low. He faces me and starts to speak, when something behind me catches his eye. I turn to see, but there's only the wall.

"Ravi?" I prompt when I see his mouth turn down. Sadness fills his eyes. "Is everything all right?"

"There are times when I am sure I see her," he

says quietly. "She's standing on the porch, teasing me for not having done the chores properly. Of course, many were her chores, but she was always busy writing. She had a unique light in her eyes when she told a story. She came alive." He raises his hands and demonstrates. "She would gesture wildly as she spun her tales. Made you listen even if you had no time." He shakes his head and seems to pull himself back to the present. "You came very far for the mutterings of an old man."

"She was a storyteller?" In an instant, I feel a connection to her I've never felt with my mother. I always wondered where my love of words came from.

"Yes." His fingers curl into a fist. "She was young, and death seemed powerless to touch her. She would write for hours and days. In her tales, she found happiness." He rubs his thumb over the palm of his other hand. He closes his eyes and shakes his head. "My apologies. In my old age, I seem to prefer the days of the past to those of the present."

"Do you have any of her writing?" I think about the letter that brought me here. "My uncle wrote that my grandfather had something for my mother. Was it the stories?" I hold my breath, waiting for him to say yes. To tell me he can give me something of the woman I will never know. When he shakes his head, I swallow my disappointment.

"They are all gone." He releases the knife he was using. It clatters to his feet and then onto the next step. Rokie barks at the sound. "She gave them all away. After that, she promised to never write again."

"Why?"

"They were her prized possessions and all she had left to give." He talks in riddles without explanation.

"Then do you know what my grandfather wanted to give my mother?"

"Yes." His face clouds over, and the warmth is replaced with detachment. "I do. But for me to tell you, first you must listen to a story."

"A story?"

"One your grandmother repeated to me in detail in the months before her death. It is the story of her, your grandfather, and your mother." He takes a deep breath, and his eyes fill with pain. "It is the story I have had to keep secret until now."

"Why now?" I ask, confused by his reaction.

"Because your grandfather has died." He hesitates, careful with his words. His bowed body leans back, making distance between him and his pronouncement.

"He made my mother promise never to return to India," I reveal, alert to his reaction. Ravi's eyes widen in shock and then lower with despair. "She said it was the price she had to pay for being born."

"I did not know." Ravi goes cold, and his lips flatten with fury. "Though it was best for her to never return to the place that hurt her, it was not his promise to exact."

"Hurt her how?" I ask quietly. The ache in his words is a warning to me. My instincts caution me to run, to refuse his offer, and let my mother's secrets stay safe. But the part of me that is broken, that yearns for something other than my relentless pain, demands the truth.

"The story will answer all of your questions," he says slowly. "But you must stay to hear it."

I remember what I left back home—pieces of a life that lay in ruin. "I will stay."

Relief covers his face. "Good. This was her home and your mother's. It is your birthright."

Ravi stands and motions for me to follow. We walk slowly past some mud houses mixed between bungalows similar to my grandmother's. The road shifts from dirt to asphalt. Large swaths of land are filled with vegetation, while others lie brown and unproductive. Burned leaves on trees lie still in the dry air. Fruit riddled with bird bites hangs off the lower branches. We pass a defunct windmill, and then the town becomes more modern with shops and open markets brimming with customers.

Ravi is quiet except for a few murmurs to Rokie, who follows loyally at his feet. I linger behind as my nervousness wars with anticipation about finally hearing my mother's story. In hopes of tempering both, I focus on the sights and sounds of this village where the villagers watch me warily, seeing me for the stranger that I am.

Ravi leads us toward an abandoned low-rise brownstone building that stands in the far distance. A smaller cottage, similar in design, sits to the side. With a key, he unlocks a gate and signals for me to follow. Once inside, he watches, waiting for my reaction.

Just inside the threshold, I stop and stare. "A garden?" Awed by the beauty, I stroll between the rows of diverse and fragrant flowers. I bend down and inhale the scent from a white flower with a yellow halo around a black center. "It's breathtaking."

"White alders, I believe," Ravi says. "Your grandmother was relentless in teaching me. After so many years, my mind is fearful of forgetting."

I point to a cluster of flowers next to the row of alders. "Red cassias in early bloom."

"You know your flowers," Ravi says as I inhale the powerful fragrance the pink blossoms exude.

"Mom liked to garden, and sometimes I helped her." They were some of the few times she allowed me in. We would work silently side by side, planting and trimming plants and bushes. "This is amazing." I gesture toward the array of plants and flowers, some still budding. The dusty village we walked through would give few allowances for such a garden to exist within its boundaries.

"It is your grandmother's from another time," Ravi says. "Come." He leads us to a bench beneath a beech tree. The leafy branches hover over us, providing shade from the relentless sun.

"Sit, and I shall tell you her story."

AMISHA

British Rule of India

1930s–1940s

SIX

Amisha giggled at the parade of cows with bells on their necks. Her mother had placed one on each cow, with vines of white karanda flowers woven into their tails. Ten cows were the agreed-upon dowry, and Amisha's parents had chosen the best ones for their daughter.

"The cows will dance to the music," Amisha sang into the star-filled night, her joy contagious. She swayed gracefully to the beat of the drums in front of the Shamiana gazebo. The marriage tent's double-layered roof glistened as the light of the moon reflected off the multicolored patchwork cotton sheet. The fire Amisha and Deepak rounded seven times within the voile curtain walls had since become a faint glow, with only a few embers still burning.

Amisha smiled broadly at her new husband as he watched her. Deepak, standing a few feet from her, returned her smile, only to grimace in shame when his mother, Chara, scolded him loudly. "It is not appropriate to look openly at your new bride."

The party continued into the night and fell over into the streets. The women were dressed in their elaborate wedding saris while the men sported fashionable *salwar kameezes*. The embroidered silk shirts fell to their knees with slim-fitting pants underneath. After eating their fill of the curried vegetables, they danced to songs sung by traveling gypsies.

When the stars began to give way to light, Amisha's brothers and parents gathered their things for the long journey home. When they took their leave, it would be a final farewell to Amisha whom until now they had called their own; though only fifteen, she was now considered a woman. Dread engulfed her at the thought of being left behind. Guests picked up their sleeping children off the ground and put them into the open cart. The men would lead the two oxen pulling the crate of wood on wheels while the women came up from the rear. Half the day would pass before they reached their homes, but this was their way. As tradition demanded, they had successfully passed on one of their daughters to another family.

"Mummy." When her mother held out her arms, Amisha ran into them. She hid her face in her mother's shoulders as sobs racked her small frame.

When Amisha's father laid his hand on her shoulder, she turned into his embrace. "This is your home now. Bring happiness to your husband," he said, his voice breaking, "and your new family." It could be months, years even, before she might see them again. Though they lived only two towns away, the trip would be considered burdensome and difficult to undertake.

Chara wrapped her arm around Amisha's shoulders as she continued to cry. Chara nodded to Amisha's parents, indicating it was time for them to go. Their daughter had been given to them in the common ritual of marriage, and she would now live with Deepak and his extended family in their home. From that day forward, Amisha would accept Chara as her mother, and her life would never again be her own.

"You are beautiful." Deepak closed the door to the bedroom behind him.

Through the thin door, Amisha heard Chara instructing the servant to lay down sheets and pillows for a makeshift bed. Deepak's two younger sisters and parents would sleep in the small open room adjacent to the living room. As the only son, Deepak had use of the bedroom. Amisha swallowed her nervousness and raised her jewelry-clad head to meet his gaze. They stood inches apart and assessed each other. Because their parents had decided their engagement, today was the first time they were meeting. He ran a finger over the pearl-and-diamond pendant that fell to the center of her forehead.

That morning, Amisha's mother and older

cousins had carefully placed the gold chain that graced the part in her hair. They had inserted gold hoops into her ears and looped two long necklaces around her neck. Amisha's aunt had slipped dozens of matching thin gold bangles over her hand and onto her wrists. "Treasure them," her aunt had said. "These are gifts from your family."

"Beautiful things help to make anyone look beautiful," Amisha now said with modesty.

"And a beautiful woman brings beauty to anything she wears," Deepak answered in kind.

Amisha considered him as he slid his fingers along the hem of her rose-colored sari. At nineteen, he was four years older, but he fidgeted nervously like a schoolboy. He was handsome, but more important, Amisha saw kindness in his eyes, and for that she was grateful.

Deepak handed her a velvet jewelry box off the table. She opened it slowly, revealing a *mangalsutra*—the traditional gold chain beaded with black onyx gemstones. The necklace was the time-honored gift from a husband to his new wife on their wedding night. It symbolized their bond for lifetimes.

"It is too much." Though it was simple in design, she recognized its worth immediately. The shiny gold was pure and the glistening stones of high quality. It was unlike any *mangalsutra* Amisha had ever seen on other village women.

She clasped the necklace in her small hand, making a silent promise never to remove it.

"I traveled to a store in the city for it." Deepak moved her hair aside to clasp it around her neck. "I wish I had something finer for someone so unique." With a shy glance he said, "I have never seen a woman dance for her husband at their wedding. You are different."

Amisha stumbled to explain. "I enjoy dancing. I meant no offense."

"Nor did I take any."

"There was once a bird who wanted to fly alone—away from the others." Amisha spoke quietly as Deepak began to remove each piece of her jewelry, leaving only the *mangalsutra* in place. A story was the best way she knew to share with her new husband her feelings—her fear and uncertainty, coupled with the pleasure she took at her parents' choice of husband for her.

"Why would he do such a thing?" Deepak stopped to meet her eyes.

"He worried if he followed the group, he would never find his own place." Her gaze drifting, she imagined the bird's course. "He flew alone for miles and days. When he reached his destination, he thought himself so brave and unique. But when he looked around, he realized that all the other birds had arrived at the same place days before." Deepak began to remove the rings that adorned her fingers. Amisha felt the first stirring of excitement as his fingers slid over hers. "In the end, he was no different. Nor am I."

"The bird was a fool," Deepak said, shocking her.

"The bird hoped to find his own place," she started, but Deepak cut her off.

"The bird's course was set from the start. He wasted time in trying to be different."

His admonishment cooled and then diminished her arousal. Amisha chided herself. Her mother's warning to keep her fictions to herself echoed in her head. In the silence, Deepak continued to undress her. He slowly unwound the sari until she was left only in her underskirts and blouse. He inhaled the scent of rose water and incense from the sari before laying it tenderly on the floor.

"Thank you." Amisha pushed the tale from her head to focus on his actions.

"For?" He raised his eyebrows in question.

"For treating it with care." She ignored the sting from his dismissal of her story and, instead, focused on trying to forge a bond. She pointed to the sari and admitted her trepidation. "The sari is all I have left from home."

"This is now your home," Deepak answered, his voice tense. He seemed to notice her surprise at his tone and stroked her cheek in apology. "I am glad to be married to you. I was hoping you would feel the same."

"I do." Taken aback by his admission, Amisha

softened her voice. "I hope you are as gentle with me as you were with my keepsakes." Though her mother and cousins had explained in detail what happened on a wedding night, she was still nervous. She had never been touched intimately by a man, and she worried about pleasing him.

"I'm scared." Deepak brought her body close and kissed the top of her head.

"You are the man." Amisha felt the vibrating tension in his body and saw his anxiety. Though it was her first time, she knew it was his also. Warmed by his nervousness, she said, "It is I who should be frightened."

"I don't want to hurt you." He rested his forehead against hers and ran his hand through her hair.

Amisha swallowed to dislodge her nervousness. A daughter's parents searched for the most suitable partner for her. They judged the boy from the parents' status in the community and word of mouth. Once the marriage was decided, they could only hope that the son had morals and would treat their daughter with care.

Amisha started to unbutton his shirt, when Deepak stepped back and finished it before removing his tunic. Still half-dressed, she held her hand out to him. Surprised, he lifted her into his arms and carried her the short distance to the bed.

"It is new," he said with pride. "Bought for our marriage."

He followed her down and rested on his elbows above her. Tentatively, he placed his lips on hers. Amisha opened them as her mother and aunts instructed her to do. He slowly raised her skirt and shut his eyes. Unsure, she watched him until finally shutting her eyes. When he entered, she turned away while accepting him as her new home.

After finishing, Deepak lay on his stomach and fell asleep. Amisha waited for his snores before slowly rising off the bed. She dressed quietly and then searched until she found a sheet of paper and pencil. In the far corner, she settled down and began to write.

Amisha sensed the moment Deepak awoke and watched her scribbling.

She glanced up and their eyes met. In them she saw confusion and then dismissal. Without a word to his new wife, Deepak fell back asleep under the glow of the fading moon. Amisha continued to write, finding solace in the only place she knew—the words that rose from within her.

Amisha slowly awoke to find Chara hovering over her. Her eyes flew to the empty space next to her in the bed. "It is time for chores," Chara announced. "Dress quickly and pull the sheets for washing."

"Yes, Mummy." Amisha stuffed the sheets into

the woven basket and balanced it on her head. On her way to the front porch, she passed Deepak and his father, who were eating breakfast seated cross-legged on the floor. Though he spared her a glance, Deepak stayed silent.

"There should be no bloodstains left on the sheets," Chara ordered. Her high-end sari hung off her heavy frame. With nimble fingers she redid her hair into a tightly held bun. Finished, she crossed her thick arms over her ample chest, her expensive jewelry clanking in the process. The large red bindi on her forehead adorned the entire space between her eyebrows. "These are sheets for the household's use, not just for you lying with my son."

"Of course, Mummy." Amisha injected a note of false subservience into her tone.

Chara's eyes narrowed in response. "You are lucky to be in this house, Daughter. Out of pity, we lowered our stature to allow you to marry my son."

Deepak's family owned the mill that fed the people of the village. Their house was built mostly of concrete rather than the mud and bricks used for the dwelling in which Amisha had been raised. On the night their engagement was decided, Amisha's mother had told her how fortunate she was, insisting she had been smiled upon by the gods.

"Your son is as kind as you, Mummy," Amisha

returned to Chara. Though it was rare to be friends with a mother-in-law, she had hoped for at least common decency between them. "I am fortunate that last night he too took such great pity on me. Twice."

Chara took a menacing step toward her. "You dare to speak to me in such a manner?"

Amisha bit her tongue, tasting copper as blood filled her mouth. "My apologies." She had been warned by her mother about speaking back. Amisha rushed down the steps and toward the river.

At the river, she scrubbed the sheet with a soapy rock. When the water ran clear, she gathered the sheet and headed toward home. She took the long route back, allowing herself time to enjoy her first walk through the village. She stopped to watch the children play while women gathered to talk. Other villagers returned from the market with baskets full of vegetables and new clothes.

From a distance, Amisha watched a group of British officers walk through the town square. From her father, she knew there was a Raj office in the neighboring village. In her own village, Amisha had witnessed officers beating Indians for minor infractions. As the officers came near, she lowered her head and waited for them to pass. Exhaling, she gathered her basket and ran toward home.

"You took your time, new daughter." Chara

stood on the top step of the porch, refusing Amisha entry. Heat from the sun enveloped Amisha as Chara detailed all of her new chores. "You will prepare the meals for the family, wash the laundry at the river, and keep the house clean." Chara glanced toward the house. "Deepak will be at the mill, working. Consider yourself fortunate if you see him on occasion."

"Yes, Mummy." In the hierarchy of her new home, Amisha knew she had no place of importance. She was subservient first to her elders and then to her husband. "Thank you."

Amisha walked past Chara toward the back porch, where she hung the sheet to dry. She started on cleaning next. That night she fell into bed, where she wrestled with sleep. Deepak followed her into the room a few hours later. Without a word to her, he fell asleep. To the sound of his snores, Amisha watched through the window as the night sky turned into day.

SEVEN

Amisha leaned against the wall of the front porch as she frantically scripted a discussion between a mongoose and a frog. Her broom lay unused at her feet. The frog argued that he would not be a delectable treat and was unworthy of the attention of such a fine animal as the mongoose. Amisha pushed loose tendrils of hair off her face as she began the mongoose's counterargument. Just then she spotted Chara and her friend in the distance, returning home from the temple. Amisha quickly hid the tablet and then splashed a handful of water on her face to look like sweat. She grabbed the broom and began to sweep.

"Amisha, we will have sherbet in the house." Chara fanned herself with a silk-top fan hand decorated with images of a sunset. "Hurry. We do not want our guest to faint from the heat." As Chara passed her, she tossed the delicate fan to Amisha to put away.

In the kitchen, Amisha poured two glasses of mango juice and threw some sweets onto a plate. In the living room, the two women were settled on the settee. Amisha served them and turned to leave. "I will finish cleaning the porch."

"The daughter-in-law of such a prestigious house does not have her own servant?" Chara's friend perused the sweets before choosing *halwa*—cooked carrots and sweetened milk topped with chopped nuts. She clucked her tongue in disgust at the water dripping off Amisha's forehead.

"Servant?" Amisha halted and stared at Chara. "What is Auntie talking about, Mummy?"

"I have not had time to find a suitable one." Focused on her drink, Chara ignored Amisha. "I am still forced to do many of the household chores while Amisha rests."

Chara's friend took a healthy swallow of her juice before speaking directly to Amisha. "You have been living here for over a month. It is past time for you to have a servant of your own." Since servants cost only a few cents per month, most homes employed three to four. Amisha's own family employed two in its home. With only one servant in her new home, Amisha had been running herself ragged.

She caught Chara's gaze and held it. "I'm sure you were going to tell me, weren't you?"

"Yes, of course." Backed into a corner, Chara was forced to agree. If she denied Amisha some help, she would be perceived as overtly cruel. If there was ever a fight between Chara and Amisha, the ladies of the community would be more sympathetic to Amisha and take her side. Neighbors often passed the time embroiled in one another's lives. "You may find one to your liking, or I can hire one." Clearly wishing for the discussion to be over, she concluded, "If you make the choice, then choose wisely. Your servant will know all your secrets."

Amisha swung the food-filled basket as she neared the mill. Delivering lunch to Deepak and her father-in-law at the grain-making factory was the highlight of her day. Besides washing clothes at the river, it was her only time away from the house.

With the edge of her sari she wiped the sweat off her forehead. The temperatures had reached record levels with no reprieve in sight. Inside the mill, she spotted the manager in his starched brown cotton top and pants talking to a young man. Amisha leaned against the wall to wait. She started to create another story in her head, when the manager began yelling.

"Ravi, how many times must I tell you?" The manager threatened the boy with a ruler. "Get out before I have you thrown out."

"Please, sir." Unflinching, the gaunt dark-skinned young man stood his ground. "I will sweep the floors at night. Wash the toilets. I will do anything, sir. I must earn a coin." Ravi fell to his knees and clasped his hands together.

"Earn a coin?" The manager spit in the boy's face. "An untouchable in the mill?" His laugh echoed off the walls, chilling Amisha. "You come from filth and are not worthy of earning a coin."

Amisha guessed the boy to be twelve, maybe thirteen, and yet his hungry, desperate eyes were of someone much older. His fear permeated the room. She wanted to turn away, but something about the way he stood his ground in the face of humiliation kept her attention.

"You are right, sir." Ravi nodded in agreement. "I can clean the toilets after the mill is closed so I do not offend anyone. I will work for little money, sir. Please."

"Get out now." The manager pushed Ravi so that he fell. Ravi scrambled off the floor and back into a kneeling position. "Allowing you to work here would be an insult to the food we make." Amisha searched the manager's face for sympathy but found none. "Leave before I beat you."

Amisha took a step toward them to catch the manager's attention. When he spotted her, his fury shifted immediately to respect. With a smile he took her offered basket. "I will deliver this to the sahib immediately."

"Thank you." Out of the corner of her eye, she saw Ravi's defeat as he walked out the door. "Who is that?" she asked.

"An untouchable," the manager spit out. "Doesn't understand the word *no*." He shook his head in disgust. "Every week, he comes begging for a job." He sniffed the tiffin. "It smells delicious. Deepak Sahib will be pleased." He left Amisha to deliver the goods.

Amisha rushed outside. She shielded her eyes from the sun's glare and searched for the man. She spotted his lone figure in the distance and ran toward him while yelling his name.

Ravi stopped and stared. When she finally reached him, he clasped his hands together and bowed in deference. "Yes, Shrimati?" he asked, using the respectful address for a married woman.

Amisha put both hands on her thighs and dropped her head to catch her breath. She took in deep breaths of the arid air as she struggled to get oxygen.

"Are you all right, Shrimati?" Taller than she was, he bent his knees and cocked his head to see her face. When she didn't answer right away, he glanced at the factory and back at her, seeming to gauge the distance. "It was not *that* far, Shrimati."

Amisha narrowed her eyes and glared at him. Seeing her reaction, he took a step back. "You try running in these clothes," she muttered. "It is like carrying a sheep around to get the warmth of a wool blanket." Gasping, she asked, "Why do you want to work at the mill?"

He seemed confused by her question but answered nonetheless. "I would work anywhere, Shrimati. The mill is only one of the many places I have been thrown out of."

Amisha remembered Chara's order to find

a servant she could trust. Because Ravi did not live in her village, he would not be part of the crowd whose loyalty would be to Chara first. She gnawed on her lip as her palms started to sweat and her heart fluttered. Even as the plan hatched, she feared she was inviting Chara's wrath.

"You would work anywhere?"

"Who are you?" Frustration laced his words.

He kept glancing around them. Amisha knew he was afraid of being beaten. She had seen it before when an untouchable spoke to a woman of a higher caste.

"I am the daughter-in-law of the mill's owner," Amisha replied quickly. She said it without pride since her position in society mattered little to her. At the widening of his eyes, she added, "Work for me." If she waited any longer, she feared talking herself out of it.

"It is cruel for you to joke." Ravi turned away, barely masking his disgust.

"I am not laughing, and neither should you be." The man's desire to be more than what was allowed struck a chord deep within her, and Amisha couldn't imagine a better comrade for herself. "Take the offer or don't. Just decide quickly so I know to look elsewhere."

"I am an untouchable." Ravi hit the dirt with his bare foot and glanced away in shame. "It is important for you to know."

"I am a woman." Her reality always a looming

shadow, she glanced at the sun. "We have now established our roles."

"You are the mill owner's daughter," Ravi argued. "My parents and siblings are also vagrants. Begging is our destiny." Furious, he paused before muttering, "No matter how hard I try to change it."

"Daughter-in-law," Amisha corrected. "Both of our circumstances dictate how we live." When his gaze met hers, she refused to look away. "My mother-in-law treats me no better than a servant."

"Is it acceptable for me to be a servant in your home?" Ravi seemed to accept that he couldn't win the war of semantics with her.

Unwilling to admit the truth, Amisha deflected. "I should tell you the story of a handsome singer."

"I would prefer you didn't," Ravi returned.

She ignored him. "This singer wanted to be part of a singing troupe famous for its melodies and striking appearance. When the troupe refused him, he protested the unfairness to the heavens." Her hands animated, Amisha wove the tale. "An old man offered the young man a flute for a loaf of bread. 'It will give you what you seek,' the old man said. Happily, the man made the trade, sure he would soon join the troupe. Before he left, the old man warned, 'If you reject the music, you will lose everything.'"

"Shrimati, as enjoyable as your story is, is there a point?" Ravi motioned around them. "There are many other fine establishments left for me to be kicked out of today."

Amisha raised an eyebrow in response but continued. "The young man played the flute in front of the troupe, but they were oblivious. Soon a song could be heard from over the hills. The voice was melodious and in perfect tune with the flute. Everyone stopped to listen. Out of the woods came a woman with the face of a troll and the body of a giant."

Ravi, intrigued, now listened intently.

"Her voice—that is where the heavens had smiled upon her. However, the young man believed he was better than her and refused her invitation for them to perform together. As he had been warned, he lost his ability to make music and fell into a deep depression."

"The fool," Ravi said.

"Desperate, he begged the woman for forgiveness. Together their popularity surpassed that of the troupe." Finished, she smiled confidently.

Ravi shrugged his shoulders and stared at her, confused. "The point of the story?"

"That we shouldn't judge each other," Amisha exclaimed, shocked that he didn't understand. "Let us make a pact. I will not judge you, and you mustn't judge me."

"Shrimati . . . ," Ravi began, but Amisha interrupted him.

"I need a servant." Anticipating his argument, she said, "I would be a fool to look for someone considered more appropriate when you are available and willing to work hard." She winked at him. "Plus, it would show the manager his place, yes?"

Amisha saw his desperation warring with his fear. He regarded her carefully before finally nodding in agreement. "You are a stranger but have offered me more than anyone ever has." He sank to his knees at her feet and clasped his hands together in gratitude. "Thank you, Shrimati. I promise to repay you in lifetimes for this gift."

Amisha jumped back and motioned for him to get up. "I will pay you, but I don't own you. We are near the same age, so you will work with me. Mummy said you will keep my secrets, but since I have none, I am more interested in your hearing my stories. Yes?"

Confused, he absently nodded. "Yes."

She sighed with relief. "Excellent. Also, do not fall to my feet again. There are plenty of important people around for that. I fear I am not one of them."

Amisha peeked around the wall separating the kitchen from the dining area. Chara spooned out lentil soup mixed with white rice to Deepak and his father. Amisha chewed on her nail as she silently ran through options on how to broach the subject.

"Amisha." Chara's booming voice carried over the clatter of the pots and pans as the servant continued to cook the food. "Bring the naan."

Amisha yearned to remain hidden. After hiring Ravi, she had fretted over her decision.

"Amisha, are you deaf?" Chara yelled.

"Coming, Mummy."

Another quick glance showed Chara serving Deepak and his father the cooked okra. It was their daily ritual—Chara served the food while Amisha brought warm naan as they were individually prepared over a small fire. Amisha grabbed the steel plate from the servant with a quick nod of thanks. She took a deep breath and sought courage.

"I have found a servant." Amisha kept her gaze glued to the wall as she entered. "He will start tomorrow."

"A servant?" Deepak stopped eating to glance at her.

They rarely spoke when he was home. Sometimes at night he turned to her silently in their hopes of making a child but then fell asleep right after. Early on, Amisha had hoped for more but soon accepted that their relationship was the norm for most marriages; to hope for more was foolish.

"Yes." Amisha met his gaze and found the

confidence she was seeking. "Mummy said I should have one."

"Who is he?" Chara barely paid her any attention as she continued to serve.

"His name is Ravi, and he was seeking work at the mill," Amisha said quickly. "There was nothing for him there, so I offered him a job."

"Ravi?" Chara glanced at her husband. "Do you know him?"

Deepak's father didn't answer his wife immediately. Instead, he considered Amisha, his eyes narrowing in appraisal. Feeling his gaze, Amisha shifted her eyes. As was common, they barely spoke to each other in the house. Deepak or Chara handled any dealing between them.

"An untouchable," he finally said.

Amisha heard Chara's gasp seconds before she saw the steel plate full of food coming at her head. On instinct, she ducked, and the plate hit the wall, scattering food everywhere. "You dare to bring an untouchable into my home?" Chara screamed.

"I thought he could work in the back," Amisha stammered. Desperate, she searched for a plausible explanation. "He won't enter the home."

"You're an idiot." Chara dismissed her with a wave of her hand. "I am ashamed to have you in my family. Your marriage to my son will end now."

Shocked, Amisha stumbled back. Her hand over her mouth, she barely held back her cry of misery. She tried and failed to find the words to undo the damage. Left with nothing, she could only stand there as her future crumbled around her.

"Amisha, why did you hire him?" Deepak asked, his gaze focused on Amisha.

Nervous, Amisha answered carefully, "His family is poor and in need of money. He had searched everywhere for employment. It seemed like nothing for us to help him."

"You knew of his status?" Deepak asked.

"He told me." Panicked, Amisha fidgeted with the hem of her top. "I thought it would not hurt for us to be humane." As a child, Amisha had refused to stone the untouchables as they went door-to-door, begging for food. It was a favorite pastime among many of the children, but it seemed too cruel. "Mahatma Gandhi says they are Harijans—children of God."

"When have you had time to read the words of Gandhi?" Chara demanded. "Is this why you are always behind on your chores?"

"Mummy." Deepak raised a hand for silence. A quick glance at his father gave him the support he needed. He paused in consideration before announcing his decision. "He will not handle the food."

"No," Amisha agreed quickly. She held her

breath for his judgment. Their wedding night was the last time Deepak had been outwardly affectionate. The few times Amisha tried to forge a bond since, he nodded off to sleep.

"He will only assist you in your duties and keep his distance from everyone," Deepak continued.

"Of course," Amisha stammered.

"Then this marriage will not end," Deepak decided. Amisha nearly buckled in relief. Focused on Chara, he said, "You told Amisha to find a servant, and she did. I am certain he will be treated no better than our other servant." His gaze locked on Amisha, he warned, "We will honor this decision, but in the future, be wiser in your choices."

"Yes." Amisha held back her tears of gratitude. Because of Deepak, she was safe. Willing to agree to anything, she said, "I will."

Furious, Chara stormed out of the house after yelling at the servant to have the place cleaned before she returned. From beneath her lowered eyelashes, Amisha watched her husband. For the first time in their marriage, she felt a stirring of genuine affection. As she returned to the kitchen, she sent a quiet prayer of thanks to the gods above for the man they chose for her.

EIGHT

Amisha fidgeted in the expensive ram's head chair Deepak had purchased a few months before for doing his paperwork in. The luxurious piece of furniture and its matching desk were crafted from bone. Detailed peacock feather designs were painted on every surface. With business booming, Deepak had presented them with pride to Amisha and Chara.

She scratched out the last two words and replaced them with synonyms. The final line of the verse had proven the most difficult. She had spent weeks attempting to transfer to paper what had sounded so eloquent in her head. The poem spoke of an intense rain and the splendor of the resulting flood. Finally satisfied with her creation, she laid the paper and pen down. It was always the same with a new story or poem. The words came to her at inopportune times and plagued her until they were expressed.

"Shrimati." After a quick knock, Ravi entered, his head bowed. "Your mother-in-law will soon arrive."

In the year since Ravi started working for them, Chara had hired another servant. The servants took advantage and ordered Ravi to do their bidding. He did so without complaint, clearly overjoyed to have honest employment. Chara initially refused to speak to Ravi and even now barely acknowledged his presence. She shunned Amisha for weeks after his hire and in retaliation increased her workload.

Amisha leaped off her chair, juggling her oversize belly in her palms. "Sorry, little one," she said to her first unborn child. "Ravi, I have not started dinner. She will have the hair off my head."

Ravi flinched at her sudden movement. "I know little of women's bodies, but I imagine the child did not wish to go for a run today."

Amisha smoothed her hands over her belly. When she began to vomit daily, she hoped she was with child. When she missed her period, Chara confirmed her suspicions. Besides an initial onslaught of fatigue, the pregnancy had been relatively easy. Amisha was surprised that the unexpected joy of carrying a child engendered an even greater desire to write. Stories swam in her head with not nearly enough time to write them.

"You worry too much, my friend." She gently patted her stomach. "This one is strong. It is Mummy's health I am concerned about. You've seen her tantrums when things are not done just right." She lifted an eyebrow and muttered, "At her age, it could lead to heart failure."

"It is finished," he said.

"What?" She stared at him, not understanding.

"We finished the cleaning earlier, so I began dinner," Ravi explained.

Ravi had begun taking on more of her duties. Early in her pregnancy, Amisha caught him starting the laundry before she could. Often, he stayed late to clean the house while she napped sitting up. Recently, he had secretly been helping out in the kitchen with the meals when Chara ate at a friend's house. Amisha, remembering her promise to Deepak, felt a twinge of anxiety. But Ravi's meals tasted better than hers. Even the other servants, who initially shunned him, welcomed his assistance.

"Another servant helped, and we were sure to burn every other naan, just as you do. This way she will not know." He said no more, but a grin played at his lips.

"The cauliflower and potato curry?" Amisha repeated the menu Chara had decided on.

"Finished, with too much salt and all the spices lacking, just as you . . ." Cut off by Amisha's hoot of laughter, he stood there, smiling.

"Thank you. Thank you," she said. "I could not tear myself away, and the time passed faster than it should have." Amisha wanted to give him a hug but knew better. Her mother often scolded her as a child for offering hugs to guests and relatives. After enough reprimands, she learned her lesson. She squeezed Ravi's bony shoulder instead. "You, my friend, have once again saved my life."

Amisha folded the paper in two. From beneath the bed, she pulled out a metal box and laid the paper atop a pile of other poems and stories. She closed the box with care and slid it back underneath where it was hidden from view.

"What is it about?" Ravi held open the door and followed her into the kitchen.

"The rain followed by an enchanting flood." She spoke softly so no one would overhear. Ravi was the only one who knew of her writing.

"Floods kill," Ravi said matter-of-factly.

"Yes, Ravi." She sighed deeply, a frequent habit around him. "But they also cleanse and clear the debris for new growth."

"Hmm." Ravi considered her words. "Is it done?"

"To my simple satisfaction, but it is best hidden." She nudged his shoulder with hers. "If anyone ever reads my ramblings, you will be embarrassed to have my company." Through the window they spied Chara climbing the steps. "Now, let's go serve the beast. I mean Mummy."

NINE

As Amisha readied to welcome another mourner, dressed in traditional white, the cry of her third son pierced the house. Having only given birth two weeks before, her body immediately responded with milk leaking from her swollen breasts. Deepak, oblivious to his son's cry, continued to speak to the guests.

Chara had died quietly in her sleep, and Amisha had genuinely grieved her passing. Over the years, an uneasy bond had formed between them. With every son Amisha birthed, Chara became kinder.

"You have proven your worth," Chara had said, delighted after the third son. Amisha, lying in bed, exhausted, had watched as her mother-in-law held the newborn. "Three grandsons are worth the price we paid when we allowed you into our home." Chara rocked him in her arms while the midwife laid a wet cloth on Amisha's head. "You have been blessed—a son will never leave you."

"A daughter would be just as precious," Amisha said weakly.

"Don't be foolish." Chara nuzzled the baby, cooing to him. "A daughter born to you is never truly yours."

Amisha had stood by Chara's side when her two daughters were married. Amisha had remembered her own wedding day and had laid her arm across Chara's shoulders in comfort and empathy. When Chara turned fully into Amisha's arms and sobbed, the two crossed an unspoken threshold and became one in sorrow.

Chara often said that a daughter's love was fleeting. A girl's time with her family was spent preparing for the day she would leave home to become a part of another's. A mother saw a daughter as a reflection of who she was—a stranger in every home she occupied. It was only when a son was raised and wedded that the mother could at last stake her place in the world. Because then she was able to look upon the bride entering the home as the stranger, and she, at last, was the familiar one.

Pulled from her memories, Amisha watched as the guests started the long walk to the cremation site. Amisha and her newborn were barred from the ceremony because the Brahmins taught that death could traumatize the infant and cause it to crave a return home to the heavens.

After the last caller departed, Amisha rushed to the back room, where her youngest had cried himself to sleep. Deepak joined her seconds later. Amisha took his hand and laid it over their newborn's head. Their two older sons stood solemnly next to them.

"A life is lost," Amisha said, hurting for her husband, "but a new one has just come. You will burn her body today, but never her soul. She will always remain with you and her daughters." She wrapped an arm around her two other boys. "Let your sons be your strength."

Deepak reached out and enfolded her in an embrace. Surprised, Amisha wrapped her arms around his waist. She savored the feel of his arms around her and relaxed into him. It was the first time Amisha could recall him hugging her. Though they had been married for years, he still felt like a stranger. Their communication was often limited to the happenings of the home. Their sons were the link in their fragile connection.

When Deepak stepped away seconds later, Amisha immediately released him. Silently, she watched as he gathered their older sons close. They joined Deepak's father, who had been waiting on the porch, and trailed the mourners toward the cremation site.

Amisha stood alone within the bare walls of the home and said a silent goodbye to the surrogate mother who had dictated years of her life. She bowed her head toward the statue of Vishnu, preserver of the universe, and gave thanks for her three sons and the meaning they gave her life. Her heart yearning for more, for the camaraderie of a kindred soul, she then silently wished for the birth of a daughter.

• • •

Deepak sat cross-legged on the floor in the middle of the two boys as they ate dinner. Amisha pulled on the string attached to Paresh's makeshift hammock to keep him asleep. Six months had passed since Chara's death. In that time, Deepak's father had joined his wife in the afterlife. Deepak was now solely responsible for his family's income, and Amisha had charge of the house.

Though they had recently wired the house for limited electricity, they still cooked their meals over a fire. "Ravi," Amisha said when he exited the kitchen with a stack of warm wheat bread on a plate, "you and the others eat while the food is still warm."

After Chara's death, Amisha had promoted Ravi to head servant. He now managed the others and dictated their individual duties. Bina was Ravi's cousin and their newest servant. Born with a cleft lip, she had little success with begging or marriage. When Ravi asked Amisha if he could hire her for some extra work, Amisha offered her a full-time job instead. Deepak had added additional space to the house, so there was more cleaning to do.

"I have decided to expand the business," Deepak announced between bites. "I have spoken to a farmer in Indore." At the mention of the town an hour away, Amisha raised her shocked glance to him. "It is a distance," Deepak said, seeing her reaction. "But he has been innovative in his ideas and is open to a partnership."

Deepak had always been reserved with everyone, including her. Amisha assumed it was because he was the only son and the eldest. His duty to take over his father's business was clear to him from birth. Any thoughts of college or opportunities outside the mill would have been dismissed. This was his home, his legacy, and Amisha knew he would honor it. So the light of excitement in his eyes caught her off guard.

"What about the Raj?" she asked. In Indore, the British had a larger presence. Deepak would need their approval before securing the business deal.

"It has been taken care of," Deepak answered quickly.

"It seems you already have everything decided." She thought about the trips back and forth to Indore. It would be lonely and barren along the way. Reports of robbers attacking carts late at night were rampant. If she did not want Deepak traveling late, he would have to spend the night in the city and return the following day. In his absence, Amisha would have to be both mother and father to their children. His decision would be her burden.

"It will better our family." Deepak glanced at the boys. "Their future will benefit." Finished with the discussion, Deepak finished his meal in silence while Amisha looked on.

TEN

"Ravi!" Amisha searched for him from the porch steps. She yelled again, louder and more insistent. "Ravi!"

"Every Ravi in this town and the next will be here momentarily." Ravi turned the corner with a basket of clothes in hand. "What are you going to tell them then?"

"That my Ravi did not answer when I called, so his apologies to each of you." She grabbed the basket and led him up the steps. "You won't believe my news."

"I can't believe it if you don't tell me." He retook the basket and began to sort the clothes.

"The British school?" The new construction outside the village boundaries had taken months to complete. Curious, Amisha had stopped by almost daily to watch the building go up. She had never seen another structure like it before. "Today I overheard a British teacher tell a father that all are welcome." Amisha helped Ravi lay out the clothes to dry. "They want to cultivate us. Here, in our small village, they will teach English writing."

Deepak had been traveling for months. In that time, Amisha began in earnest to read in the local papers about the war ravaging the world. She was

106

amazed that the same Raj occupying her country was fighting alongside America to protect the world from a man named Hitler. She read in detail about the heartaches and deprivations, and learned that the few victories for the Allies came at great cost.

At dinner parties, Amisha listened intently when the men discussed the large number of regiments and battalions of Indians fighting with British officers in charge. The men didn't agree about the decision to enter Indian soldiers into the war. While many of Deepak's friends supported the Raj unequivocally, others were enraged by the disregard for Indians' rights and opinions.

However, neither the war nor the increase in uprisings in the cities for India's freedom touched her family members' lives. Their rural village, part of a state that worked with the British in accordance with a subsidiary alliance called the Central India Agency, was run by a local government official named Vikram. Being one of the wealthiest individuals in the area, Vikram had a close relationship with the Raj.

"Sir Vikram has welcomed the school." Amisha assumed it was his way of looking good to the empire. "Maybe he hopes it will teach us about their ways."

"Who will attend?" Ravi asked. When Amisha pointed to herself, he didn't hide his surprise. "You?"

"They would not mind a grown woman wanting to learn, would they?" She saw Ravi's reaction and suddenly felt foolish for not having considered it. "Do you think I can do it?"

Wealthy families in the village often sent their daughters through primary school, and in the cities, some girls were able to attend university. Amisha, however, had been pulled out after elementary school to help in the house.

Desperate to learn, she'd stolen her brothers' textbooks and read by candlelight after everyone slept. From there she started writing her tales. She wrote at night and in between chores. It was when her brothers brought home books written in English that Amisha felt complete despair. No matter how hard she tried, she couldn't decipher the letters or make sense of the words.

"Because of you, I am an untouchable working in the home of a wealthy man, Shrimati. What are you not able to accomplish?" He stopped folding the clothes to ask, "But why English, Shrimati? You have never mentioned it before."

"The papers are starting to print in the language, and I cannot . . . I tried to teach myself, but I failed." Embarrassed, she reined in her disappointment and focused on the future. "Imagine my boys when they see their mother writing in English." Excited at the thought, she said, "I can help them with their studies." Silently she called out a plea to the gods, hoping they would heed her call. "One day they may even want to read the silly stories I will have written in English."

At times, Amisha's need to compose overwhelmed her. When one story was completed, she felt a sense of accomplishment. Rereading the words, she was amazed they came from her. When her tales had their ending, she was sure the closure was for her as well. But within days, new stories competed for her attention. Whether it was a man on a quest or a newborn's birth, the tale began. And when life permitted her the time, the journey found its end.

"Then do it," Ravi said.

Shocked, Amisha stared at him. "You don't want to tell me all the obstacles I will face? All the reasons I shouldn't do this?" Amisha teased. "I should check your head for fever."

"No illness, Shrimati," he assured her. "Tell the mighty Raj what you just told me. Only a heartless teacher could turn you away."

Amisha warmed the tiger oil before massaging it into Deepak's foot. The moon's light filtered through the window in the bedroom. The children had finally fallen asleep after a pillow fight with their father. They were excited to see him after his seven-day trip. After seeing the children to bed, Amisha joined Deepak in the bedroom.

"We will make good money for the year,"

Deepak said. "You can tell the Brahmins we will offer a meal meant for the gods at Diwali." When he moaned, she rubbed his sole harder.

During the New Year celebration, the wealthiest families in the village donated meals to the street beggars. Amisha and Deepak happily joined the other prosperous families in paying for hundreds of meals for the destitute. Beforehand, the priest would bless the food in an elaborate ceremony before requesting good karma in the upcoming years for the donors.

"Lakshmi has smiled upon you," Amisha said, speaking of the goddess of wealth and prosperity. "Your good fortune is a blessing for our family." Amisha swallowed her nervousness. A hundred times she had rehearsed her discussion with him regarding the school, but now, faced with the reality, she hesitated. With limited courage she said, "I need to speak to you about my writing."

Twice in their marriage Amisha had started to tell him about her writing. Hesitantly she had begun describing how important the words were to her, but he had interrupted her, telling her she was a fine woman and wonderful mother, and ended the discussion.

"It can wait." He pulled his feet off her lap and laid her flat on the bed. When she opened her mouth, he placed his gently atop hers. With deft fingers, he undid her blouse and bra, then pushed her petticoat above her waist.

"Please." Amisha knew her body was fertile. While other women in the village complained about how long it took them to get pregnant, for Amisha it had always come easy. "I don't want . . ." She struggled against her clawing anxiety as she tried to find the right words to convey her thoughts.

"What?" Deepak stopped in his ministrations to stare down at her.

Thoughts of school surrounded her. Though it seemed like only yesterday that she was asking for a daughter, now, with the opportunity of the school, she wanted to wait. She swallowed before saying, "My body is not ready for another child."

"They are keeping you busy, my boys?" Deepak grinned at her in the dark.

Without waiting for a response, he continued to caress her. When he entered her, Amisha turned her face away and started to pray—the only option left. She willed her body to shut down and begged her body to reject his seed. As his body moved within hers, she stared through the window and toward the sky. She silently appealed for the soul of a waiting child to be sent to another woman. *Find a mother who will welcome you,* she told the child.

When Deepak rocked against her, she closed her eyes. Images of the newly constructed school flashed before her and then faded. It was foolish of her to have believed it was possible. When she felt him tense, she accepted it was just a dream. Seconds before releasing, Deepak pulled out of her. He grabbed the bedsheet and sighed as his body reached fulfillment within the folds of the cotton.

"Why?" Amisha asked, shocked. She rolled out from beneath him and laid the dirty sheet in a corner before adjusting her clothes.

"You have given me three sons," he answered. "When you are ready for another child, speak to me. I'll see if I'm able." He folded his arms beneath the pillow and closed his eyes. Minutes later, he was sound asleep.

ELEVEN

The next morning, Amisha saw Deepak off to the train station before heading toward the school. She stood in front, listening as the Hindu men sang songs while putting the finishing touches on the school.

"Amisha." Sujata, a friend from the village, joined Amisha. Her hands were filled with bags of produce from the market.

Amisha gave her a warm hug. They had just spent the last weekend together, Amisha helping Sujata care for her ill father-in-law. "How is he doing?"

"Better," Sujata answered. "Thank you again for your help."

Amisha dismissed her gratitude with a wave. "It is good he is mending."

Sujata gave the school a cursory glance. "If the British teach us, they hope we will become British?"

Amisha grimaced. Hoping to avoid an argument, she said diplomatically, "Maybe it is their way of giving something back." From other villagers, Amisha had heard that the classes were filling up fast. "Children who attend here could go to university in England. Have an opportunity for more."

"My husband says the whites hope to convert us with one hand while beating us with the other." Sujata repeated the common sentiment from those who opposed the school. "You are not fooled?"

"No." Amisha herself had seen officers use their sticks to punish Indians for infractions. "I am not fooled."

Out of the corner of her eye, she spotted a British officer approach the school-ground workers. He said something that elicited a laugh, then stepped back to continue monitoring the final touches.

After Sujata said her goodbyes, Amisha stood alone, trying to summon the courage to enter the school and inquire about attending. The idea had seemed so perfect with Ravi. Now she wondered what she had been thinking. Even if there were classes for her, Deepak might not agree.

"If I didn't know better, I would think you were the supervisor of this job."

Amisha turned in shock to see the tall British officer now next to her. On instinct, she took two steps back and bowed her head in greeting. "Namaste."

"Namaste." His right arm was encased in a cast. Unable to clasp his hands together, he bowed slightly.

"You're hurt," Amisha said without thinking. "In the war?" Wincing, she lowered her eyes for speaking so directly. "I'm sorry. I shouldn't have . . ."

"It's fine." He waited for her to meet his eyes before holding up the cast. "I would love to say it was from fighting in the war, but unfortunately it was from falling out of a tree." He admitted ruefully, "My mates and I were having some fun with parachutes."

"There are not many trees in our village." Amisha kept her voice low so as not to attract attention.

Clearly pleased at her continuing to converse, he said conspiratorially, "It was outside of London." He added with a grimace, "My mates are still laughing about it."

Amisha glanced around the deserted street. Satisfied there was no one to witness their interaction, she answered his earlier question. "I'm not the supervisor."

He laughed aloud. "That's good, because I would be out of a job."

"This is your building?" Amisha silently wondered why he was spending time talking to an Indian woman. "You teach here?"

"Technically it's His Majesty's, but I am nothing if not a humble servant." He followed her lead and stole a quick glance around them. Amisha was warmed by his act of concern for her reputation. "I'm the head of school. I don't teach, but the teachers we have are very good. You have children?"

"Yes, three boys." Her gaze strayed again

toward the building. The school was built from brick with a stone base. The workers had climbed onto the roof and were setting down the last pieces of tile. "It isn't for them I'm asking."

"No?"

"I am . . ." Amisha hesitated to call herself a writer, and yet she had written from the time she learned her letters. "I write." She glanced at the sky and swallowed deeply. She remembered Deepak's reaction to her writing and downplayed her work. "Silly things. Not very important." She stole a glance at him, sure she would see mockery. When she found interest instead, Amisha was stunned. "But I write in Hindi and . . ."

"You want to learn English," he finished.

"Yes." Elated, she met his gaze fully. He was the first person to ever understand without her explaining. "I have tried but can't master the language." Suddenly self-conscious, Amisha brought the edge of her sari around her shoulders. That morning she had brushed her hair until it fell in waves to her shoulders. She had left her olive skin free of heavy makeup but slipped on small gold hoop earrings before heading out.

"Then I will be sure to reserve a place for you," he said. "In the English class."

"What?" Amisha couldn't believe it was that easy. There had to be forms and payment. "I'm a grown woman."

"The King and Queen are supportive of anyone who wants to learn."

It was the Raj's defense for their occupation—they were helping to save the poor and disenfranchised. However, in that moment, Amisha couldn't care about their reach or reason. All she could focus on was the chance she had.

"Thank you." Amisha exhaled, surprised she had been holding her breath. Then she started to laugh, full of happiness and unexpected joy. He seemed to fight his own grin as he raised an eyebrow at her. Undeterred and feeling stronger than she ever had before, Amisha said, "I don't even know your name."

"Stephen." He paused before adding, "I'm a lieutenant."

"Have you been in India long?" Though she knew it was past time to head home, she couldn't help herself. She didn't want the conversation to end.

He broke eye contact before answering, "Almost six months." Amisha started to empathize, to tell him she couldn't imagine being away from her children for that long, when he asked, "What's your name?"

"Amisha."

"That's it?" he prompted. "A surname?"

Unsure why she held back, she murmured, "Let us for now just be Amisha and Stephen." Like all women and children, Amisha's middle and last name were changed to her husband's.

He seemed to consider her answer before agreeing. "Amisha and Stephen it is. Do you live in the village?"

"Yes." In the midst of their conversation, she had, just for a moment, forgotten about her life and responsibilities. Her home was only moments away, but standing in front of the school and speaking about learning, she felt as if she'd been transported to another world. "My husband—his family," Amisha corrected before saying, "they own the mill in town."

His eyes widened with recognition. "Your family provides the grain for the village." Clearly impressed, he said, "Vikram has spoken highly of your business and husband."

"That was generous of him." His words served as a stark reminder of her place. She glanced toward the direction of her home. "I should go."

"Of course." Though they were already a few feet apart, he took another two steps back. "I'll see you in class on the first day?"

"Yes." She was unsure how, but nonetheless nodded her agreement. "In class."

With a curt nod, he walked away. When he reached the school grounds, she saw him turn once to glance at her, but her thoughts were on the school and what the future would hold.

TWELVE

"One tablet." Amisha negotiated with her middle son as she tried to take the paper he was holding. She had searched the supply drawer for other tablets but found it empty of any school materials. "It is good to share."

"Hmm." Jay bit his lower lip as his six-year-old mind weighed his options. "It is mine."

"I bought it from the market for you." Amisha reached again for the tablet of paper.

"Because you wish me to do well in school." He scooted away from her and hid it behind his back.

"In school they should teach you to honor your mother. Disobeying is not honoring." She wiggled her fingers dramatically and took two menacing steps toward him.

"They do teach honor, which is why I bring home the top grades that I do. For you." He ran behind the settee when she came closer and screamed with fake fear when she caught him and started tickling. "Four chocolates for my tablet," he said between his peals of laughter.

"Two," Amisha returned, amused and impressed at his bargaining. Amisha often included a cube of milk chocolate in their lunch sacks. Jay, who had a sweeter tooth than his brother, always begged for more. "Otherwise, your teeth will become chocolate." He agreed and handed her the tablet. She kissed his forehead and stood up. "Thank you, Beta."

"Why do you need it?" He started to adjust the buttons on his vest. He and Samir, who had left earlier to walk with friends, wore the same school uniform—brown shorts with a button-down shirt and a vest over it. "It's just a school tablet."

"Because . . ." Amisha wanted to raise her sons with the knowledge that women were equal to men. Yet it was rare for them to see older girls in school. "I need it for my work."

"What work, Mummy?" He stopped fidgeting with his clothes to stare at her.

"Jay." Amisha fell to her knees and took his small hand in her own. "Women and men are made the same way." She struggled with the words to help him understand. "You have two arms and two legs; I have the same." She shook her limbs, which made him laugh. "You have two eyes, a nose, and mouth. I have the same." She opened her mouth wide and made an exaggerated "Ahh" sound until he covered her mouth with his hand. "You have a heart; I have a heart." She kissed her fingers and laid them on his shirt over his breastbone. "You have a brain; I have a brain," she said, touching her forehead gently to his. "We are the same." She paused to see if he understood.

"So you can do anything? Same as Papa?" he asked, innocent.

"I think so." She smoothed the lines of confusion on his face. "I want to try to see if I can."

"Why can't you?"

"I don't know." She laid her chin atop his head and caressed his coarse black hair. His face was a miniature version of hers, though his eyes were Deepak's. Immediately a story came to her that could better explain. "There was once a little girl who wanted to play ball with the boys, but they wouldn't let her." She made sure she had his full attention before continuing. "So she went home and cut all her hair off."

"Why would she do that?"

"So she could pretend to be a boy." Jay stood up and grabbed a ball to bounce. "She then played and won the tournament for them."

"Did they find out?" He let the ball bounce away to stare at her.

"Yes," Amisha said. "And she was no longer allowed to play. The team struggled to win another tournament, and that's when they realized they should change the rules."

"But, Mummy, girls still can't play sports," Jay said, his young mind confused.

"No, they can't, but if they're not allowed to do things, we'll never find out what they can do." She tapped him on the nose to lighten the mood. "I am so lucky to have three smart sons." She set the strap of his satchel over his young shoulder. "Maybe one of you will help to change our world. What do you think?"

"I think I like you best as my mummy." He kissed her on both cheeks and then hugged her tight. Amisha held him until he wiggled to be released. With one hand on his satchel, he used the other to grab the tablet he had given her. "And you still don't get my tablet." He ran out the door, laughing.

Amisha watched him go, wondering if it was a sign that she couldn't attend, when the back door opened and Ravi entered.

"Your bag, Shrimati." Ravi held out a new satchel to her—one that was similar to the boys'. "You will be late if you don't leave soon."

"What?" Shocked, Amisha stared at the bag. Ravi had left early that morning, telling her he had to stop at the market. Amisha assumed it had been for vegetables. "A bag?"

"For school." He pulled it wide open and motioned for her to peer inside. "There are tablets and pencils. It cost me a rupee to have the carpenter sharpen them on short notice." He held up two erasers. "For all the mistakes you must make." He flipped the satchel and showed her the stitching. "It is not of the highest quality, but it carries the materials, so what more is needed?" When he finally looked up, he caught her swiping at her tears. "What is wrong? Is it the baby?"

"No. Paresh is fine." She fought to gather her composure before whispering, "Thank you."

"Did I do something wrong?" he asked, watching her carefully.

"I do not think that is possible," Amisha said, her heart full. "I'm fine," she assured him when he gave her a doubtful look. She felt silly and laughed to hide her reaction. "Everything is perfect."

"Then it is time to go," he said, motioning her toward the door.

"The children?" Her children and her home were all she knew. She remembered her conversation with Jay and wondered if she had the right to want more.

"They will be fine," he assured her. "I will collect them from school, and they will cause havoc as they do every day. Bina will have their evening meal ready." When she hesitated, he shrugged. "You're right. The children should not see their mother trying such things. It may scar them forever." He picked up a basket filled with dirty clothes and handed it to her. "Come, the river is waiting for us to wash all these clothes."

Lost in her own thoughts, Amisha said, "Ravi, I did not have the chance to speak to Deepak about this." He had not been home for weeks. "He may not like it."

"Then you should wait." He waved off her plans as if they were inconsequential. "What are a few more days, or is it weeks before he returns?"

His words had the desired effect. "I can do this?" Amisha stared at him, his answer meaning more to her than she realized.

"I think you must do this," Ravi said simply. "How will you feel if you don't?"

She handed the basket back and grabbed the satchel. "I am going. See me; I am going." She crossed the threshold of her home and ran with the sun's light guiding her way.

The satchel flapped against her fitted sari as Amisha ran toward the school. Puddles lined the street from the rain the night before. A group of piglets squealed in delight as they found food among the refuse thrown outside the doors of the village homes.

She waved to some local women but kept enough distance so she didn't get caught up in conversation. As she neared the school, she spotted Stephen waiting by the front door. She slowed down as their eyes met. He offered her a polite nod, but Amisha was sure she saw relief in his smile.

"I was worried you had decided not to attend." Stephen opened the door for her.

"My apologies." Concerned she had delayed

him, Amisha began to explain. "My son Jay was on his way to school, and I did not have a tablet for the work, and, well, he's a rascal and would not share, but my friend Ravi, he is so thoughtful, and from the market he . . ."

"You're not late," Stephen assured her. His gaze locked on hers, he asked, "Are you ready for class?"

"Yes." Amisha tried to sound convincing in the hope that he would be convinced as well.

"Perfect." Stephen motioned for Amisha to follow him. "I'll take you there."

"The sling has been removed," Amisha murmured as they walked alongside each other down the narrow hall. She kept enough distance so their arms didn't touch. "Your arm is healed?"

"Good as new." He pulled up his sleeve and flexed his elbow. The pale skin was crinkled and dry. "Still looks like one of the branches of the tree I got tangled up in." He laughed, pausing midstride to catch her gaze. "I'm happy you came. I wasn't sure you would."

Amisha hesitated in her answer. Denying the truth would have been lying, but admitting it felt like defeat. "I almost didn't." She scanned the assortment of colored drawings on the wall. They were similar to ones her boys did. "I feared my desires would infringe upon my responsibilities."

"And they won't?" He slipped a hand into the pocket of his khaki pants and rocked back on his heels. Focused on her, he pushed strands of his hair off his face and away from his eyes.

"I am privileged to have people around me who support this impulse." She thought of Ravi and then worried again about Deepak. She shook off her concern. "I couldn't be here otherwise."

"Then you are lucky. True kindness in people is a rarity, and when discovered, I believe it should be treasured."

"Yes." Amisha searched his face and found only sincerity. "I could not agree more."

"Then we have found the first thing we have in common."

He began to walk again, and Amisha followed. She noticed he took smaller steps—almost as though he understood her limited range of motion in the sari. They turned a hallway before stopping at the threshold of an open door. The smell of disinfectant and chalk wafted through the air.

"Here we are."

Amisha stared at the students inside. Though it was mostly young men, a few teenage girls were scattered throughout. She felt the same hesitation she had earlier. "They are children," she whispered.

"They are teenagers," Stephen replied. "I reviewed all of the class lists. This was the best fit."

"I am old in comparison." Though in her early twenties, Amisha carried the weight of her years.

She often vacillated between feeling like a child raising children and an aged woman who had never found her place. But the girls in ponytails were seated properly in their seats, innocent and hopeful.

"No," Stephen started to argue, but Amisha cut him off.

"I can't do this." Regret laced her every word. She glanced one last time into the classroom, and disappointment spiraled through her. All the children were dressed in Western uniforms, fully British if not for their skin color. She, in contrast, wore a sari and could practically have been their mother. "I am a woman seeking an education on a child's playground." The rules were not the same, and there was no way for her to win the game. She shook her head in frustration. "I don't know what I was thinking."

"You wanted to learn," Stephen answered.

Amisha barely heard him. She turned away from the room and the excitement she felt only moments ago. "I should go." Unsure where she was heading, she walked quickly down the corridor, searching for an exit sign.

Stephen followed her around the corner and toward another door in the back of the building. "Amisha, wait," he called out, fast on her heels.

She refused to heed his call. She opened the door to escape but came to a halt midflight at the sight that greeted her. An array of flowers bloomed among lush green bushes. Tall trees offered shade against the beating sun. Waterfalls flowed off meditation rocks while a small pond set in the middle reflected the sun's rays. Tables for lunch were placed strategically along the edge where high shrubs offered privacy. Lined walkways curved between the flowers and trees, immersing them in the garden's splendor.

"A garden?" The abundance of beauty caught her off guard. "It's a rainbow of colors." The flowers swayed in the light wind, reminding Amisha of hope and dreams, everything she couldn't have.

"Yes." He barely acknowledged the scene surrounding them, his attention focused on her instead.

"Amisha . . ."

"You are blessed to have so much beauty whenever you want," Amisha whispered. In their small village, growing a full garden was not a priority. She inhaled a deep breath of dry, dusty air. "I have never seen anything like it." She fell silent, her throat quivering with words she couldn't say.

"Don't leave," Stephen said. "We can work something out."

"This school is not meant for me," Amisha murmured, needing him to understand. She offered him a small smile. "I was foolish to think it was."

"It is for you." He took a small step toward her. "It is for anyone who wants to learn."

"Why are you so insistent?" Her voice rose above her own pain. "Why do you care?" With another breath she tried to reel in her emotions. Yet she couldn't quell her disappointment. Hope had driven her here. Now she had to face her foolishness.

"Because you want to learn, and that is a worthy aspiration." He grabbed a low-hanging branch and broke it in half. He lowered his voice. "It does not matter if you are younger or older."

"It does matter." She fought him, the only man she ever had. "I was unwise for accepting." She started to move past him, but he stopped her with his words.

"I saw you come to the school again and again." His hand tightened around the broken branch. "You reminded me of my brother."

Amisha's face shot up in shock. She had never noticed him and believed her visits went undetected. "Your brother," she asked, confused. "How?"

"You stood in front of this building, and you watched the walls go up," Stephen said. "Even from afar, I could see your hope." He stared into the distance before admitting, "He always wanted more also and believed others should be able to live their dreams. Drove me crazy talking about it." He laughed, seeming desperate to alleviate his memories.

"Wanted?" Amisha asked, picking up on the past tense.

"He died in the war." A mask fell over his face, shuttering his emotions. "I thought I could help you. For him."

"I'm sorry for your loss," Amisha said, feeling an odd connection to him. "I am grateful for your trying." She focused on the blooming flowers. "But I fear there are some things that cannot be." She quickly wiped away a lone tear that fell, hoping in vain he hadn't seen it.

THIRTEEN

Amisha walked home slowly, the satchel slapping against her thigh. She held back her tears, knowing that shedding them never solved the problem. She'd learned over time that life often offered disappointment without apology or explanation. Maybe, she considered, it was actually her fault. In wanting more, she had chanced failing. She entered the house to find Ravi holding a sobbing Jay. Shocked, she rushed toward them and scooped Jay onto her lap. That was when she spotted the angry welt on his palm.

"What happened?" she demanded.

"I told my teacher the story you told me," he said. Amisha wiped the tears off his face. "He said the story was inappropriate and whipped my hand with the ruler and then sent me home early." His tear-filled eyes met hers. "Why is it inappropriate, Mama?"

A terrible sense of guilt hit Amisha. "I don't know, Beta." She pulled him in tight. The tears she had been unable to shed for herself now fell freely for her child. She rocked him until he calmed down and began to nod off in her arms. "Do you want to sleep?"

"Can I have a chocolate first?" The injury forgotten, hope lit up his red-rimmed eyes.

"Yes." Unable to refuse him, Amisha said, "One chocolate and then a nap." Her heart breaking, she watched as Bina led him into the kitchen. Once he was out of hearing range, she said to Ravi, "It's my fault. I told him the story."

"No." Ravi's finger tightened around the bowl of turmeric paste he had used as balm for Jay's welt. "It was just a story."

"You are a fool if you think that." Defeat settled deep within her. Her gut tightened at what happened to her son. "We are both fools." Jay's laughter erupted from the kitchen, but it did little to ease her heartache.

"Why are you home, Shrimati?" Ravi eyed Amisha's satchel. "We were not expecting you for hours." On Amisha's silence, he asked again, "What happened?"

"Like I said, Ravi, we are both fools." Amisha threw the satchel into a drawer and, without another word, followed her son into the kitchen.

The first full moon of the month peeked out from behind the clouds. Legend taught that requests made on the day would be honored by the gods. After ensuring that Paresh was with Ravi and the two older boys were playing with friends, Amisha set out for the temple in the village. She had struggled to sleep every night since Jay's punishment. The image of the angry welt taunted her. Only when she finally realized what she had to do did she find some peace.

As she neared the temple, a small crowd was departing. The Brahmins had just finished the evening *puja* in preparation for the full moon. The air was thick with the smell of rose incense and coconut water. After slipping off her shoes, Amisha climbed the marble steps of the open-walled temple.

"Amisha." The priest, dressed in an orange lungi—a wraparound cloth—with a white shawl over his naked torso, paused in his ministrations to welcome her. "We have not seen you here for some time."

"No." She found it wiser not to give him the real reason for her absence—that she preferred praying in front of the makeshift shrine at home rather than at the temple. "I could come up with an excuse, but I worry you will find it lacking, so . . ." She bit back her smile when the priest failed to find any humor in her words.

"If you do not honor the gods, how will they honor your wishes?" His stern face made it clear that he wanted an explanation not laced with wit.

Instead of answering, Amisha handed him the steel plate filled with fruits and nuts she had gathered as an offering. She then reached for the bell that hung from the ceiling. Using the clapper, she struck the inside of the blended metal. She repeated it twice more, once for each of her three boys, then listened as the peals filled the room. The sound of the bell was said to last long enough to clear the mind and body of all other thoughts.

Amisha sank to her knees in front of the antique bronze statue of Lord Shiva. "Protect and cherish my sons." Her head lowered in deference, she said softly, "You have honored me with them, but never forget they are first your children and under your protection." She showered a handful of rose petals over the statue of the god of destruction and transformation.

She then moved in front of the matching bronze statue of the Goddess Parvati, Shiva's consort and the goddess of universal encrgy. As a child, Amisha would ask her mother to repeat Parvati's story.

"Parvati climbed to the summit of Mount Kailash, where Shiva sat in a state of perpetual meditation," her mother would begin. "She wanted to pay homage to his supreme being." Transfixed, Amisha would listen without interrupting, though she knew the story by heart. "Impressed with her conviction and ascetic nature, he asked her to be his wife, and together they watch over us."

"I have a request," she said to the statue. The goddess's refusal to let any obstacle stand in the way of her quest inspired Amisha. "I failed my family." Amisha glanced around the temple to check she was still alone. "My weakness hurt

134

them." With a deep breath she garnered her courage. "I tried to be more than I am allowed to be."

Her dashed hopes mixed with Jay's punishment circled around her. She had always welcomed the stories that were a constant part of her. Her failure was assuming no harm could come from them. Now she knew better.

"I beg you to rid me of this ailment." She pled to be like the others. "I should be more attentive to my duties." She lowered her voice. "Thank you for all you have blessed me with. I ask you to let it be enough. End my desire for more." She dropped her head, hiding from herself and from the need to be more than her life allowed.

FOURTEEN

Jay seemed to completely forget about the incident at school in the days after Amisha's visit to the temple. For Amisha, however, the memory served as a constant reminder of what couldn't be. She started to take a different route home from the village, bypassing the school, and accepted that the English education she longed for would never come to fruition.

"A story, Shrimati?" Seated on the floor, Bina kneaded the wheat flour for the samosas.

"It has been a while." Ravi glanced up from the potatoes he was peeling. Afterward, he would add in a bowl of peas and spices.

"They seem to have left me," Amisha lied. The truth was, the stories continued to plague her, though she tried her best to ignore them. She could only hope that her prayers would soon be answered. "Maybe it is best."

"Really?" Ravi's glance told her he didn't believe her. "The stories have disappeared like the sun in the sky?"

"The sun doesn't disappear, Ravi," Amisha started to explain. "We circle around it." She was about to go into the details she had learned from a book, when she saw his smirk. He knew the stories weren't gone. "Actually, yes," she said,

136

changing her mind. "They have disappeared like the sun. And you should repeat your theory to everyone you meet. They will be awed by your brilliance."

Before Ravi could respond, there was a knock on the front door. "Are you expecting company today?" Ravi asked, glancing toward the wall that separated the rest of the house from the kitchen. The older boys were at school and Deepak out of town. Otherwise, the house was quiet.

"No," Amisha answered just as there was a second knock. "It is probably a neighbor stopping in for some *lassi*." She quickly wiped her hands on a towel and then caressed Paresh's head as he played with some steel bowls before she headed to the living room.

At the door, Amisha quickly undid the lock and pulled it open. Standing on her porch, dressed in full British uniform, Stephen clasped his hands together and bowed slightly. "Namaste."

"Namaste," Amisha repeated, shocked. A quick glance behind him assured her there were no villagers around. A member of the Raj on her doorstep in the middle of the afternoon was fodder for gossip. "What are you doing here?" she asked, lowering her voice.

"May I come in?" Stephen glanced behind him, following her line of vision.

"Yes, of course. My apologies." She stepped back and ushered him in. "Please, sit," she said, motioning toward the new swing with a red coverlet in the middle of the living room. "Can I get you something? Chai? *Lassi*?"

"I'm fine." Stephen rocked back on his heels. Taller than Deepak, he filled the living room. He scanned the room, taking everything in quickly. "I'll only be a minute, actually. Is your husband home?"

"He's traveling." Suddenly nervous about his visit, Amisha tried to temper her anxiety. "Are you here because of the way I spoke to you at the school?" If he wanted a formal apology, she would gladly offer him one. There was no reason to involve Deepak. "I wasn't thinking straight. It was the excitement and then disappointment. My apologies for speaking out of turn." She wrung her hands together, unsure what word combination to use.

"Amisha, no," he said quickly, seeming almost embarrassed by her attempt. "There was no offense taken that day."

"Then why are you here?" The knot of tension slowly unraveled in her stomach but left an acid taste in its wake. His presence made her uneasy. In their village, Amisha had seen a number of British soldiers pass through as they toured the region, but Stephen was the only one who had ever entered her home.

"I want to make you an offer regarding the school," he said.

"Oh." Taken aback, Amisha fell silent. After their last meeting, she had assumed she would never see the soldier again. "You are thoughtful, but it is not going to work." She refused to raise her hopes only to face disappointment again. "I have accepted that."

"Listen to me," he said. "This wasn't easy to accomplish, so at least do me the courtesy of hearing what I have to say."

Shocked by his sense of familiarity and boldness, Amisha waited.

"A couple of days a week, teach a class to the group you were going to be in. Teach them writing, stories or poems." He paused while they stared at each other. "As payment for your services, I will tutor you in English." He said everything quickly, then fell silent.

Amisha froze with disbelief. "I am not a teacher," she said. It was the first thing that came to mind.

Seemingly calmer, he smiled at her. "Everyone is a student and a teacher." When he ran his hand through his hair, Amisha suddenly didn't see him as commanding but instead a young man struggling to appear older. "That is what I learned in university."

"You don't even know what I write." Amisha started to pace.

"Then I will sit in the class and learn with the others." His grin spread wider until it reached his eyes.

"Why?" She tried to make sense of his actions but came up empty. "There is no reason for you to offer this."

"Because," he replied immediately, as though he had rehearsed, "I do not give up, and I am hoping you don't either." A shadow crossed his face, but he quickly masked it, making Amisha wonder if he was thinking of his brother again. "You want to learn, and I want to help you."

"You will teach me?" Paresh began to whimper in the kitchen. Amisha started to go to him, when she heard Bina comfort him. "A member of the Raj?"

"Yes, I will."

His voice was urgent, and she wondered at the reason for it. "This matters to you?"

"I am here for only a limited time." He moved toward the window. Amisha wondered what he thought of their waste-filled streets and village bereft of any foliage. His shoulders hunched before he straightened and faced her again. "Helping you learn may be the only worthy thing I do in India."

"I may disappoint you," Amisha murmured. Years of conditioning compelled her to say, "Women are rumored to have very small brains." It was a common theory, and though Amisha refused to believe it, she wondered if he did. "We have little use for one."

"Then allow me to help you evolve," he said,

140

a teasing light coming into his eyes. "The Raj are here in fact to civilize and modernize." He considered her, seeming to understand her dilemma. "May I read something of yours?"

She glanced nervously at the bedroom where her stories were hidden. "They are all in Hindi."

"Then I will be able to test your skills as a teacher also," he teased.

She went quickly to the room and brought out a poem. After handing it to him, she paced behind him. Every so often, he pointed to a word and she read it aloud. When he was finished, he smiled at her. Her heart soared at the sight.

"This is wonderful," he said.

Amisha bit her lip to keep from shouting her joy. "I went to the temple." Hope rose within her, but she still fought against it. "I asked for the gods to take away my desire to write." She saw confusion cross his face and tried to explain so he would understand. "My son was punished harshly by his teacher for a story I told him. My thoughtlessness caused him pain."

"I'm sorry," Stephen said. Amisha saw he meant it, but his next words didn't allow her to keep making excuses. "But only you are to blame if you do not accept this offer to share your talent."

His words resonated deep within her. It was the first time she had been told she had talent. Amisha cringed at the irony. Her writing was her greatest contribution to a society that would not value it. Knowing that, she had kneeled before the goddess with the power to take away her gift and begged for her to do so. Yet the thought of writing again had her heart fluttering with excitement.

Perhaps her writing was not an affliction to be tolerated, but a gift to be cherished and protected. Her stories were her only passport to places she had never been. Without them, she would be forever trapped in this village.

"I was a fool," she acknowledged.

"Only if you say no," Stephen said, seeming to read her mind.

Amisha resumed her pacing, stopping a few times to stare at either the floor or the walls. She searched for any answer other than the obvious one. "Yes," she said at last, finding no other.

"Yes?" he repeated, as if needing the confirmation.

She nodded, promising without having consulted Deepak. "I will teach them, and you will teach me." Amisha smiled and then laughed, her happiness overflowing. "However, I warn you—if those innocent children's parents come after me with lit torches for my teachings, I will lead them directly to you and watch as you run," she teased.

"Then I'd better hope you teach them well," he said with obvious relief.

"I never expected to see you again," Amisha said after a pause.

"You should have," he said quietly. He glanced at his watch. "I will see you in class?"

"I will see you in class." She smiled broadly in spite of herself and followed him to the door. In just a few minutes, he had offered her more than any person ever had. "Thank you," she breathed, needing to say more but unsure of what.

He paused and searched her face. "You're welcome," he said gently before shutting the door behind him.

When Amisha leaned against it, she sensed him on the other side, not moving. There was only silence until she finally heard his footsteps walk away.

Ravi caught Amisha leaning against the door and raised an eyebrow in question. "Are you helping the door stay shut?"

"I am going to teach at the school." Amisha clasped her hands together in joy. "And Stephen, a British officer, will teach me English."

Smiling, Ravi turned back toward the kitchen. "So it seems the sun has reappeared after all."

FIFTEEN

Amisha slipped off her sandals and kneeled in front of the makeshift temple in the far corner of her home. Miniature metal statues of Lord Shiva and Parvati sat in the back of the shrine. Another of Ganesha, their son, sat between them.

She drew a long, deep breath as she lit the small piece of cotton wick surrounded by melted ghee. "Deepak returns home today." With the flame, Amisha ignited two incense sticks and placed them on a steel plate. She rotated the plate clockwise in the traditional show of respect. "Guide me, Parvati, and give me your courage. Give me your strength and give me honor. Today I will ask Deepak about teaching at the school."

In her own head, Amisha had replayed the scene with Stephen and his offer. Even as she repeated it to Ravi, it felt unreal. "I beg your forgiveness for asking you to rid me of my stories," she said now. "Give me your allowance to do as my heart demands without taking from my family who relies upon me."

Amisha glanced around the house—seeing all the signs of her children. The older boys' shoes were scattered by the front door. Jay's drawings covered the kitchen wall. Paresh's toys were strewn throughout the house. Her resolve wavering, Amisha asked, "Permit me to be a vessel for the tales that are in your keeping. Entrust them to me, and I promise never again to dishonor them."

Amisha glanced toward the window where village women walked with their children while keeping one another company. Servants carried laundry to the river to wash. Life as it was continued even as she begged to alter hers.

"Please guide Deepak to want this for me. I beg you for his understanding." She rang the small bell in her hand until the sound drowned out her fear.

"Business is going well." Deepak slipped his shoes off at the front entrance and settled onto the floor for dinner. He took a sip of buttermilk while he waited for Amisha to fill his plate. "My partner has a sharp mind," Deepak said, his excitement obvious.

"It was wise you chose him to work with."

Amisha was happy Deepak was able to expand his business even if it was at the cost of his not being home. In all honesty, she barely felt his absences. When in town, he often worked late at the mill. Afterward, he would walk through the village with the other men. At home, he spent his free time with the boys. The little time they did spend together was in the bedroom, but Amisha accepted that her marriage was no different from everyone else's.

She watched silently while Deepak finished his meal. She handed him a glass of warm water and a towel with which to wash his hands and a cup of fenugreek seeds as an after-dinner digestive treat. In the meantime, she stacked the dirty dishes after collecting the leftovers. Bina would feed them to the roaming cows in the morning.

"If you have some time, I wanted to speak with you."

"I have a few minutes before bed. Tell me what's on your mind."

Amisha glanced at the children, sound asleep. Paresh was content in his space, while Jay had wrapped himself over his older brother for warmth.

"The English school." Amisha sent a silent prayer to the heavens for help. "Near the market."

"Vikram spoke to me about it." Deepak had started to spend more time with Vikram. As their income and stature increased, Deepak was often invited over to smoke hand-rolled cigarettes and drink fresh lemonade. He leaned back on his forearms. The thin cotton shirt he wore pushed against his thin frame. "It is finished, I believe."

"It is." Amisha wrung her hands together. "I went by there, and they teach English writing." She paused, unsure how to continue. She tried to imagine his reaction but didn't know her husband well enough to guess.

"You want the boys to attend?" He didn't seem uneasy at the prospect, which gave Amisha hope.

"No," she said quickly. "They are happy at their school. They would miss their friends and the familiar faces." She chose not to mention the welt on Jay's hand. For that, Amisha accepted blame. "They wouldn't appreciate our changing their school." She heard Stephen's voice in her head. His words that day made her sure she could do this. Now she searched for strength to forge ahead. "Actually, I was thinking of myself."

"You want to attend school?" Deepak asked, surprised.

"The head of the school has offered me a job as a teacher." Amisha softened her voice, hoping he would agree without knowing the full details.

"Amisha, you working?" he demanded.

"Not for money." Amisha saw his bewilderment. Having never spoken to Deepak about her desires, she now struggled to find the words to explain herself. "In exchange, they will teach me to write in English."

"What use is that to you?" Already shaking his head no, he stood and swept the remaining crumbs off his shirt.

"It is something I want to learn." Left with nothing else, she begged. "I can help the boys with their studies in your absence." Desperate, she said, "They have begun staying after school for help."

Surprised at the news, Deepak nodded. "My apologies for not realizing. I will inquire about a tutor."

Believing the conversation over, he started to exit the kitchen, when Amisha called out, "I will do anything you ask of me. I just want to do this."

She stood against the wall, her hands clasped before her. She knew it didn't make sense to him. She, like every other woman, was expected to support first her father, then her husband, and finally her sons. Their failures and successes defined her place.

"You must always be different." Deepak stopped but still kept his back to her.

"What?" Amisha's hands began to shake. She dug her fingers into the folds of her sari to still the reaction.

"The day of our marriage, you danced even after the music had died," Deepak said. "You held your hand out to me as if it were you welcoming me into your home instead of the opposite."

"I was young," Amisha said, confused as to why he was bringing it up. To her, their wedding seemed lifetimes ago. "That night you seemed pleased."

But Amisha knew the boy she married was no longer the man who stood in front of her.

Time and tradition had molded them both into the people they were today—two individuals standing apart with their children as their link.

"Then bringing Ravi into our home," Deepak said as if she hadn't spoken. His small laugh left Amisha chilled. "I told you that first day he should never be allowed to touch our food. Yet we both know it is his cooking that we consume."

"He is no different from us," Amisha argued. "The untouchables are born the same as we are and return to God as we do." It was the first time they had ever discussed it. As unsure as Amisha felt, she nonetheless welcomed the back-and-forth. "It is not a crime that he wants to earn his way in life."

"No. Nor is it that you want to learn, correct?"

"Mahatma Gandhi speaks of women's intelligence," Amisha argued. "He said we are not weak; nor should we be seen as such." His speeches were in every paper and were well-known. "There are many reports of women joining him in the struggle against the British."

"You are repeating his words to justify attending a British school?" His clipped tone left no doubt of what he thought. Before she could respond, he said, "My mother warned me about you. 'A spirit trapped,' she said. She was sure you would break free no matter whom it hurt."

"Your mother did not know me." Misery consumed her with his every word. "It wasn't fair for her to say such things." Amisha realized she was in a no-win situation. No matter what she said, he turned her words against her. "You have been happy since pursuing your dream for the business. I was hoping to feel the same." Amisha started to leave the kitchen. "I meant no harm."

"What would happen with the children?"

Hopeful, Amisha froze with her back to him. "Bina and Ravi are here for Paresh. Samir and Jay are in school during the day. It is only a few hours a week."

"What will the townspeople say about my wife being in school?"

She turned and faced him. They both knew one piece of gossip could alienate them from the community. It wouldn't be just the loss of their social status; their livelihood would also suffer. Deepak was content with his life and expected her to be also. Their children were healthy and his business was prospering.

Amisha felt the grip of helplessness. It wasn't fair. Why were her hopes a threat to their life when he followed his own without consequences? Before she could speak, a sad resignation came over his face.

"Do it. Just be mindful of your duties."

Relief flooded through her even as she saw his disappointment that she asked for more than was allowed. "Thank you." She clasped her hands together and offered him a smile. Deepak started to leave without returning it. She swallowed before asking, "Why?"

"You have carried the burden of the house while I travel." He paused before saying, "I am grateful." He walked past the boys to the oil lamp flickering in the far corner. With a small blow, he extinguished the flame, casting the room into darkness. He went into the bedroom and shut the door behind him.

Amisha exited the kitchen silently. She gently moved Jay closer to his brother so she could lie next to Paresh's makeshift bed. Streaks of moonlight filtered through the glass, offering a reprieve from the darkness. To the rhythm of her sons' even breaths, Amisha imagined her future. Humbled and grateful, she fell into a deep sleep, happiness cloaking her through the night.

SIXTEEN

Amisha arrived early at the school and watched from her place against the wall as uniformed groups of students walked by. When a young boy glanced at her, she offered him an anxious smile. Teachers herded the children into their classrooms according to age.

She entered the school and searched until she found the door marked "Head Teacher" with the name "Miss Roberts" beneath. She knocked once and waited until a voice told her to enter. Inside, a stern woman sat behind a small brown desk. The woman stared blankly at her.

"I'm Amisha." Suddenly unsure, she asked, "Is Lieutenant Stephen available?"

"Three doors down the hall. He's with a parent." The woman came around the desk to stand in front of Amisha and crossed her arms. Though the teacher wore a Western long skirt and blouse, Amisha noticed a gold bangle popular with the village women on her right wrist. "So you've come to teach the children?"

"That is what the lieutenant asked me to do." Amisha had no idea what she had done to warrant the woman's anger.

"Do you have a teaching certificate?"

"No." Suddenly feeling exposed, Amisha held

her satchel tight against her stomach. "I don't."

"Then why are you teaching here?" She crossed one boot-clad foot over the other. "What could you possibly contribute? We are a prestigious primary school."

The only answer she had was that Stephen had asked her to. But then the woman already knew that. Her look of disdain, Amisha suspected, reflected the way many of the British viewed Indians.

Amisha pulled herself upright and gathered her limited strength, but she still felt small compared with the broad Englishwoman. "I will teach here because I have been asked." She thought of her stories and what they meant to her. "As for what I will teach, I am not sure," she admitted. She felt younger than her years in facing off with the woman. "Whatever is in their young hearts, I will tell them to write about. If their stories transplant them to faraway lands, I will encourage them to take the journey."

Amisha offered the unyielding woman a smile. "I will also advise that when they travel in their stories, they respect the people they meet and the values they hold. Their way of life is not for us to judge but our opportunity to learn." She ignored the widening of the teacher's eyes and ended with, "And to never forget that when you offer a hand of respect, you will in turn be welcomed."

Amisha stood behind her desk as the children shuffled into their seats. Each student wore a light-blue collared shirt. The girls matched it with a tan skirt while the boys wore shorts. Once seated, their backs straight, they removed paper and sharpened pencils from their satchels. Amisha did a quick head count—five girls and twelve boys.

Ready with white chalk in hand, Amisha welcomed them. "Good morning." There were murmured responses. On the chalkboard, Amisha scribbled her name in Hindi. The chalk squeaked against the board, reverberating in the silence. "I am Amisha."

"Madam?" A boy near the front pointed to her name. "Will this be a Hindi class?"

"No." Amisha realized her mistake and quickly wiped her name off with her hand, leaving white chalky residue on her palm. "We will speak in English but start out the first few written assignments in Hindi." Too ashamed to admit she didn't know how to write in English, she quickly changed the subject. "I am very excited to be teaching you." She scanned the class, guessing the children to be between thirteen and fifteen years old. "I have three children of my own," she announced.

"Do they go here?" a girl in the back asked, her voice timid.

"No. They are at another school." Amisha brought her chair closer to theirs. "I love my boys very much. I have learned something as their mother, though," she said conversationally. "When I try to teach them about life, they ignore me. 'Don't chase the baby pigs; you will fall in the mud,' I say, and yet they come home muddy. 'Don't eat too many sweets; the sugar will make you sick.' But when they are moaning in pain, do they say, 'Mama, why did I eat too many sweets?' "

The children's laughter helped to ease her anxiety. "I realized I wasn't teaching them the right way. So I sat my two oldest sons down and admitted something." The students leaned closer, as if waiting for a secret. " 'I had never been a parent before I had you,' I told them. 'I am learning to be your mama as you are to be my sons.' "

"You said that?" another female student asked.

Thrilled the children were responding to her, Amisha nodded. "I did. They were surprised. I think they believed I was born as a mama." She smiled at their laughter. "So I offered them a deal. They would help me to be a better mama, and I would help them to be good sons." Amisha stood and began to walk between the rows of desks. "I am offering each of you the same deal. I have never been a teacher before. If you will help me to become a good teacher, I will do my best to help you become better storytellers."

All those in the class murmured their agreement. Pleased, she said, "Excellent. Thank you." Ready to begin the lesson, she asked, "Where do stories come from?"

"From our minds," a student called out.

"From other stories we hear," said another.

"From our dreams." It was a girl's voice.

Amisha searched for the student who gave the dream answer. She spotted a young girl in the back. Her skin was a dark shade of brown, and her black hair was divided into two tight braids. "What is your name, Beti?"

"Neema."

"Neema, can you explain your answer?" With one look, Amisha silenced the boys who moaned.

Neema paused before answering. "We dream about what we don't know. We turn those dreams into stories."

"How can you write about what you don't know?" an older boy challenged her.

Before Amisha could say anything, Neema responded, "A dream may be the only window to the unknown." She fiddled with her paper. "Maybe to a different life."

Amisha nodded her approval. "Maybe without your own dreams, you are left to live other people's dreams?" In hopes of including the rest of the class in the discussion, she asked, "How many of you enjoy reading storybooks?" Hands shot up from all over the classroom, though

Amisha saw two boys grimace at the question. "Excellent. A better question—how many of you enjoy writing stories?" Half the students raised their hands.

"Good." Amisha had spent the previous night running through various lesson plans before deciding on a particular story. "A man is building his house. Though warned by his friends it isn't a safe design, he refuses to listen. There's an earthquake, and the house collapses. He and a bird that lived in a tree near the house become trapped."

Amisha searched the students' faces and was pleased to see their interest. "There is only one small hole through which to breathe. The man must decide who gets the oxygen." She paused to make sure she still had their attention. "Please write about what happens next."

"But what is the right answer?" a boy in the back called out.

"There is no correct answer," Neema answered before Amisha could. "It's about choices and how they're made."

"Very good." Amisha stopped at the girl's desk. Her face was scrubbed clean, and a small diamond pierced her nose. Two matching diamond studs adorned her ears. "Did you know your name means 'free'?" Amisha asked softly. At the girl's nod, Amisha said, "It's a beautiful name."

"Thank you, madam," Neema replied, her face downcast.

Amisha sensed her discomfort and changed the topic. "You raised your hand about writing stories?" The girl nodded. "How many stories have you written?"

"A few."

"I would love to read them." Before moving toward another desk, Amisha said, "Thank you for joining the class."

"It seems you did well today," Stephen said. He and Amisha walked together down the hallway. In silent agreement, they went out the back door and into the garden. Classes were still in session for another few hours, so they had the place to themselves. "The children were smiling when they exited your class."

"It may have been from relief that the class was finally over," Amisha teased. In actuality, she had been grateful for the students' obvious excitement and participation.

Once outside, Amisha noticed flowers that had been budding were now in full bloom. She fingered the petals of a white-and-gold one, admiring its beauty. Stephen reached out and broke it off, inhaling the scent before handing it to her. "Smell it."

Amisha held it to her nose but smelled nothing—no scent at all. Not wanting to seem stupid, she nodded politely. "It is lovely."

"Really?" He took the flower from her and

sniffed it again. "Because I couldn't smell anything." He laughed when she widened her eyes.

"You knew there was no smell?" At his childlike smile, she couldn't hold back hers. Happy, she asked, "May we start my lesson?"

"Now?" he asked, studying her.

"Having spent the morning watching the children learning, I find I am eager to begin my own lessons," she admitted.

"How about there?" Stephen led them to a bench near the far edge of the garden that was shielded by trees and a row of flower bushes.

"The scent of the flowers will lessen the sting of my ignorance," Amisha said, taking a seat.

She had barely slept last night. She had been anxious about teaching but at the same time excited to finally have the opportunity to learn. She had searched in vain for a reason why a man of Stephen's stature would take time to teach her. When the rooster crowed that morning at the first hint of light, Amisha was already awake.

"You shouldn't speak of yourself that way." Stephen sat far enough from her on the bench to be respectable.

"Then teach me well, and I will have no reason to."

On a small tablet of paper Stephen drew the capital letters of the alphabet as he sounded them out. Amisha listened carefully. Because she spoke the language, she was able to grasp the phonetics of the letters easily.

"Your turn."

She hesitantly took the tablet and pen and stared at his handwriting. She admired the certainty with which he wrote. He was a lieutenant in one of the most advanced military operations in the world, and he was here, wasting his time teaching her the alphabet.

"Why are you doing this?" she asked.

"Trying to distract yourself from your task will not work." He tapped on the pen, urging her to begin.

"There is a war going on." Nervous, Amisha began to draw the lines to form the letter *A*. Her eyes flitted back and forth between his letters and hers. She often watched Jay practice his letters. She mimicked her son's motions and drew a straight line and matched it with a parallel one. She realized her mistake and immediately crossed it out to begin again. This time she kept her pen on the top point to form the letter *A*.

"I wasn't aware," he said offhandedly, focused on her penmanship.

"Then it is good I told you." Amisha felt him watching her hand movements. She tried to be precise and accurate before quickly moving on to the others. "They may need you to fight for your king."

"He is not your king?" Stephen raised his eyes to meet hers.

Amisha considered her words, never having discussed the situation with a man. She feared sounding foolish. "I imagine he is a good person and means well. But India is not his to rule, and Indians are not puppets to be strung along."

"That's what you think we're doing? The British, I mean."

Amisha had heard Gandhi's speeches of peaceful resistance. Without answering his question, she asked instead, "Do you believe any country has the right to rule another?" As soon as the words left her mouth, she regretted them. Stephen was a British soldier who, in taking time to teach her, was showing her a kindness no one else ever had. "I spoke out of turn," she said, embarrassed. "Here I am, learning from a lieutenant, and I dare to speak in such a manner. Forgive me."

"Don't do that," he said, his voice urgent. "Please." Amisha started to speak, when he rose from his seat. She stared at him in puzzlement. "When we are together, learning, don't hold back your thoughts." Frustration laced his words. "If you do so, then how can we work together?"

She sensed how important this was to him and tried to explain. "It is not right to speak in such a manner. We must show respect."

"Shouldn't respect have to be earned?" he asked simply.

Unable to come up with an answer, Amisha stared at the flowers surrounding them. She wondered, for the first time in her life, why she had never asked herself the same question.

JAYA

SEVENTEEN

The sun has long since set, leaving a faint chill in the air. Ravi leans down to rub Rokie's chin, his spine cracking with the motion. The dog has waited patiently as day has yielded to afternoon and then to dusk. I have been sitting on the bench across from Ravi, mesmerized by the story.

When I came to India, I was hoping to meet my grandfather and learn something, anything, about my mother. Never did I expect to hear the story of a woman I had rarely heard about when I was growing up. Her story had always begun and ended with her death when my mother was young. Anything else was deemed irrelevant.

"I wish I had known her." Whereas Mom needed to follow every rule, do everything exactly right, Amisha pushed boundaries to find her place. If Mom had been raised by her mother, I wonder who she would have been then. "Does Mom know any of this?"

In the growing darkness beneath the beech tree's branches, Ravi wipes a lone tear from his cheek. "No," he whispers. "As I said before, I had promised your grandmother I would tell her story, but I was unable to until now." He coughs and struggles to catch his breath.

"Are you all right?" I ask.

"It was Amisha's tale to tell." He stares into the distance, his frail hands clasped together. "I wish more than ever she were here to remember the details this old mind has forgotten."

"What happens next?" I hate to push him to the point of exhaustion, but I am hungry for more.

"I am an old man, Beti." He massages his hands together. "Weariness has seeped deep into these muscles. If I do not give my mind its necessary rest, my body may rebel and break down completely." He raises his head and offers me a weak smile. "Then you will have to come and serve me my meals in bed for the completion of the story." He closes his eyes and leans back against the bench.

"I have never heard stories of my grandmother before," I say softly. Given my relationship with my mother, I never felt a connection to the distant land she came from. Though India was my ancestral soil, it held no memories for me, nor evoked longing. "My mom never spoke of her."

"Your mother knew only what others wished to tell her. That became her story."

"Did she know there was another story?" I try to make sense of the puzzle with the pieces he's giving me. He shakes his head no. "Did her brothers know?"

"You are the only one who has come." There is no malice in his words. "Amisha's sons left decades ago and never returned. Their father . . . ," he says with a pause, "waited for them for years." He glances at me. "In time, he accepted what we all must. That those who leave have a reason that is more powerful than the one to stay."

I think about the little I do know—that Mom was raised by a stepmother who couldn't have children of her own. She was wed at eighteen and left India immediately after. Facts recited to me by Dad when I begged for morsels of information.

Seeming to understand my desperation for more, Ravi pats my hand. "Be patient, Beti. Soon the story will reveal all of its secrets." He stands slowly and begins the trip home, navigating the worn trail skillfully.

When I was twelve years old, I asked my mother if we could host a mother-daughter Halloween party. She considered the question for so long that I worried she would say no. When she finally agreed, I was ecstatic. I grabbed a notebook and sat down next to her on the sofa to plan. She listened silently, never offering her own ideas, as I detailed the food, decorations, and music for our gathering.

"Costumes!" I cried, having forgotten the most critical detail. She drove us to a store where they had two witch costumes from *The Wizard of*

Oz. I fit into the smaller size—Glinda the Good Witch—while Mom took the one for the Wicked Witch. I loved her pointed hat and the extended chin that went with the outfit.

The day of the party, I woke up early to set everything up, only to come down the stairs to see Mom had already decorated. Streamers lined the walls, fake cobwebs and spiders crawled through the house, and mummies popped out of coffins at various corners of the living room. It was perfect. Excited, I gave her a grateful hug. Her body stiffened, and she quickly stepped back.

"Breakfast is ready," she said before heading to the kitchen.

That night we welcomed our guests as music blared from the speakers. Dad watched with amusement as the house filled with mothers and daughters dressed to the nines. Mom was laughing and embracing the party. There were rare instances throughout my childhood where her demeanor shifted and she was full of happiness. Thrilled this was one such occasion, I stayed close, wanting to be part of her joy. Twice she wrapped an arm around me and pulled me close for a hug.

"You both look adorable." A friend's mom admired our outfits. "Good Witch, Bad Witch, right?"

"Right," I said, happier than I could remember being in a long time. "I'm the Good Witch." Too caught up in the festivities, I didn't feel Mom's body stiffen or see her smile fall off. "Mom's the evil witch. She'll put an evil curse on everyone, but I'll save the day."

"Excuse me," Mom said quietly.

She removed her hand from my shoulder, and without another word to anyone, she went upstairs. I stared after her, hurt and confused. She came down ten minutes later, her costume replaced by jeans and a T-shirt. The rest of the party she was quiet and withdrawn, barely speaking. That night I cried myself to sleep and vowed never to engage with her again.

EIGHTEEN

I opened the window during the night to let some cool air in. It is early morning now, and a warm breeze wafts through, causing strands of my hair to tickle my face. The rooster once again crows at the first hint of light, and I hear the village come to life. On the bed, I lay my open palm over my stomach. I close my eyes and imagine the babies that I carried for such a short time. No matter how much I wanted them, they are gone forever.

Restless, I draw apart the netting and push out of the bed. Through the window, I see children start to play while groups of women begin their journey to the river for water and bathing. Atop their heads, they carry empty pots to fill with water for home.

Men in white tank tops stand on the balconies and brush their teeth using homemade brushes. They spit over the balcony and onto the street, then rinse and gargle with fresh-mint-leaf water. Fascinated, I stare at the ritual. Untouched on the desk sits the toothbrush Ravi fashioned for me.

"What happened to you here, Mom?" I ask aloud. "What made your father demand the promise he did?"

I try to imagine her as a child, desperate for

her mother's love. I think of my own childhood. No matter how distant my mother was, I always knew she was there. In the ups and downs of life, my parents and childhood home were my constant. What would have driven my mother away from hers?

"Good morning." Ravi enters after a quick knock, jolting me from my thoughts. "You are not ready." Disappointed, he asks, "You waste the day with sleep?"

"I don't think the sun has even fully risen." I nod toward the window, but he ignores me.

"But it has risen." Ravi sets the tray on the table with another piece of whittled wood next to the food. "I will return when you are ready."

"Wait." With the hope that his company will help to shake off the malaise from the morning, I say, "You brought me this wonderful breakfast, and so much of it. Please join me."

"No." He refuses without an explanation.

"You already ate?" I can't imagine he has unless he awoke when it was still dark.

"I will eat in my home." He heads toward the open door.

"You won't eat with me?" I pick up the tray and hand it back to him. "Then I won't eat."

"You will starve." He takes the tray and moves to exit.

Curious, I block his path. "You would let me go hungry rather than share a meal with me?"

"It is not appropriate for me to eat here, with you." He stares at the wall above my head.

"Then we'll eat in the living room." I take the tray and lead the way.

"I cannot eat with you in this home," he says softly.

"Why?" Confused, I try to understand. "Is there a reason you've brought me all of this food and then want to leave?" The scent from the aroma-filled cups swirls around us, making my mouth water. As if on cue, my stomach starts to grumble.

"In a palace such as this, it is expected that I eat in the back," he explains. "I am an untouchable."

"I know." I search my limited knowledge and combine it with what he told me to try to make sense of his actions. I set the tray down on the table in front of the swing. "You also told me that my grandmother invited you into this home and called you her friend. I assume you ate here with her?"

"She made an exception." He walks slowly toward the front door, where Rokie is playing on the porch.

"I ask you to make the same exception for me," I call out. He pauses, then turns back toward me. "I mean no disrespect to your customs, but I would argue it is dishonoring my grandmother to deny her granddaughter the same company that she enjoyed."

He stares at me, considering my words against the expectations that are steeped within him.

"Please." I motion toward the swing, waiting. A grin playing at his lips, he slowly walks toward it and takes a seat. I grab two plates from the kitchen and settle myself into the chair across from him. Together we uncover the various dishes on the tray.

"Smells delicious." He fills his plate, barely leaving any food for me. "You should try some." With his mouth full, he motions toward my plate. "Before there is nothing left."

Smiling, I take what remains, and we finish our meal in silence.

After our meal, I ask Ravi where I can make international phone calls and get Internet service. He recommends a café twenty minutes away. As the rickshaw wobbles over pebbles and debris, I picture Deepak as he traveled toward the same destination. Amisha's story told of barren and desolate roads, and only limited progress has been made in the decades since. The dirt path still stretches for miles alongside sunbaked fields with few fellow travelers in sight.

The driver pulls into a small town with modern shops lining the streets. The roads are made of asphalt, and lampposts mark the corners. The stores welcome customers with expertly clothed mannequins in Western and traditional outfits dressing the windows. The car maneuvers through businessmen and women mixed with students and mothers with children walking the streets. A Bollywood song blares from inside a store.

The driver stops in front of a café. "Our town equal to America, yes?" With obvious pride he points to the café. "You make calls from here. No problem."

Outside the café, tables are filled with young adults busy on their laptops. I laugh, amazed at the scene reminiscent of any café in New York. Inside, the young woman behind the counter asks me in flawless English for my order. Though there are only a few miles between the village and town, they are like two different worlds.

After ordering a chai with soy milk, I find an empty phone booth in the back. I take a deep breath before dialing the number by heart. Over the ocean, the phone rings before my mother picks up.

"Mom," I say, and then stop. Emotions that I have buried rise to the top, clogging my throat. I'm staying in her home, sleeping and eating in the house she grew up in, and yet, I realize, I am no closer to knowing her now than I did before. "How are you?" I am unsure of myself, and my words are stilted and formal.

"Jaya?" She sounds sad. "Is it you?" Over the miles, I hear her take a deep breath. "Are you OK?"

"Your father died," I say quietly. "Before I arrived."

There's deafening silence and then an intake of breath. "Then there's nothing keeping you there," she finally whispers. Her voice hardens, and if not for the pause in her words, I would have thought she truly did not care for the man. "You should come home."

"He died peacefully. They spread his ashes," I say, as if she hasn't spoken. "I've met the servant, Ravi. He's telling me the story about your mother."

"I never knew him," she says suddenly. Her voice anxious, she says, "There is no story."

"Mom . . ."

"Your life is here, Jaya. Your work, your home. Patrick . . ."

"No longer affects my life," I interrupt.

I don't tell her that I was collapsing from the weight of the miscarriages or that I never expected another woman to be the final rupture in our broken marriage. I keep to myself that hearing my grandmother's story, a reprieve from my own, has allowed me to breathe for the first time in months. I keep the truth from my mother because that is how we operate and I know nothing different.

"Our marriage is over." Before she can say anything else, I admit, "I can't come home. Not right now." I pause before begging, "Please, let it go."

In the silence, I imagine her retreating inward and disconnecting. She will square her shoulders and steel herself, as if preparing for disappointment. There is resignation and then detachment. I'm surprised when instead she says, "Your father is pacing the kitchen floor, waiting to talk to you. But I still have about an hour's worth of conversation left, so he'll just have to wait."

Taken aback, I stay silent. This is the side of my mother that I craved growing up. She would come to life and joke about things that would leave everyone in stitches of laughter. Her smile would linger for hours, but I refused to give in and steeled myself against her façade. I shut her out before she could me.

"Jaya." Her pain cuts through her words. I imagine her clutching the phone as she fights the tears. "I love you, Beti."

Still in shock, I maintain my silence. It's the first time I can remember her telling me she loves me. When the quiet continues, she hands the phone to my father without another word. He asks me a barrage of questions about the village and my plans. Throughout the conversation, my mom's declaration echoes in my head. I had longed for those words for years. Now, when she finally says them, I refuse to react.

After we hang up, I open my computer and draft a quick greeting to the editor of the blog I will be writing for. I run my fingers over the keyboard and consider what to write for my first post. I take a deep breath and then begin to type.

I traveled for twenty-four hours, leaving my home to visit my mother's. India is a place I have never been to before. If I'm honest, I never had the desire. They say home is where your heart is. Only when my heart was broken was I willing to undo the frayed tether and travel so far from everything I knew.

I'm in a small village where happiness is found playing with a ball in a dirt field or gathering together and sharing a meal. It is found in the daily rituals and in the stories hidden in passing clouds. It is realized in living life. I have never known what that looked like before. I lived my life as expected. I took all the steps necessary to create a perfect life. Every step up the ladder validated my place. I checked every box that society demanded. My power became dependent on the height of my achievements. But perfection may be an illusion and power a liability.

In India, I started hearing the story of a woman lost in her own time. She struggled to find herself while remaining loyal to the expectations of those around her. I have yet to learn whether she succeeded in either. Her story leaves me to wonder about the choices I make and why. Given the freedom to decide, have I ever made a decision, or have I blindly followed the steps laid out for me? When we reach, we always chance a fall.

I came to India because a grandfather I had never met lay dying. But my need to escape sprang from other reasons. I had three miscarriages. When I lost the babies, I lost myself. No matter where I turned or searched, I couldn't find the path to healing.

Before we started trying, I took for granted I would have children. They were the next step in my life that went according to plan. The first miscarriage I dismissed as an anomaly. Equating it with a midterm exam that I failed to study for, I assumed I would pass the final. When we tried again, I was sure I would rise to the responsibility to carry my child to term. I was sure the first nine months were the start of proving my worth as a mother. When it was clear the second pregnancy was on the verge of being lost, my soul cracked. I mourned the child I carried. I was constantly aware something was missing, just like a lost limb. Everywhere I turned, there was a child, reminding me of my own empty arms. The final miscarriage eviscerated the little I had left of myself.

I lost my marriage with my miscarriages. As a reporter, I write stories on children who fall ill and the strain it puts on a marriage. Fifty percent of all marriages end in divorce. For those with a special needs child or a child who is ill, that percentage is considerably higher. How about those of us who have never had a child? What is the chance our marriage can survive the tumultuous ups and downs of hope followed by disappointment and finally resignation? When it is too hard to stand, how do you help another? My marriage became another casualty of my fate. No matter how much I study the science of birth, dream of new beginnings, or pray for salvation, I remain empty. I can't help but wonder if it is the price I pay for having reached.

I reread the piece. Nowhere do I mention my mother or her silence. But it is from her I have learned to keep my secrets safe. Too conditioned to break the mold, I hit "Delete." I shut off my computer and stuff it into my bag. I lean my head back and close my eyes. The constant cloud of darkness hovers around me, trying to pull me in, but I fight against the loss of time. I toss the rest of the chai in the trash bin and flag a rickshaw to head back to my grandmother's home.

AMISHA

NINETEEN

"Sim-ple." Amisha sounded out each word. "Com-pli-cat-ed." Proud of herself, she stopped and stared at Stephen, who marked each word as she read it. In the silence, he glanced at her, curious.

"What?"

"How did I do?" She sighed in exasperation.

"You want me to compliment you after two words?" He pointed to the long list of words still waiting to be read. "You have about a hundred to go."

"But I already read two." Amisha pointed to the paper. "They were difficult, or complicated," she said, feeling smug.

"No, they weren't." He perused the list of words quickly and pointed to a word. "Read this one."

She narrowed her eyes in concentration. "Ex-as-per-at-ing," she stammered.

"Right—what you are." He handed her back the list with a sly smile. "Keep reading."

"No," she said. "*Exasperating*—it would seem to apply to more than just me." Amisha bit back a smile. "Is it common for the British not to give encouragement, or is that a personal trait?"

"You want encouragement?" Stephen leaned

back on his forearms. "I have another hundred words waiting in my office. You need to read seven words a minute to complete the task, and so far you are at one word every seven minutes. Speed up."

"It is a wonder you are not fighting in the front lines of the war." Amisha glanced at the next few words, assessing their difficulty. "I think they would benefit from your particular disposition." Not giving him a chance to respond, she began to read the words faster than before. As Stephen listened, his face lit up with pride. When she came to a difficult word, she sounded out the letters and matched them with her knowledge of the language until she got the right pronunciation.

More than a month had passed since they started working together. After class, they would begin their lesson. After repeatedly lingering past their allotted half hour, Stephen suggested they meet longer and make it three to four times a week. Thrilled, Amisha readily agreed.

"Done." Amisha beamed when she reached the end of the paper. Every time she finished a page, she felt a sense of accomplishment she had never experienced before.

"Good." Stephen took the sheet from her hand. "I'll go retrieve the next pages."

"When my students accomplish something, I am quick to offer them praise," Amisha hinted with a smile. Truthfully, she wanted to thank him. Without him, she wouldn't be reading at the level she was. She started to say the words, but he interrupted her.

"Your teenage students?" He shook his head at her. "I am pleased to know you are good to children. But then, of course, you relate to them so well—with like heart and mind, and love of compliments." Amisha saw the teasing light in his eyes. He was reeling her in, and she saw his delight when her mouth twisted in frustration.

"Please get the pages." They were playing with each other, Amisha realized. She had never done that with a man before. As a child, she had teased her brothers and their friends. But when she was still in pigtails, the sense of familiarity came to an end.

"I have homework for you also."

"Homework?" She rose to meet him eye to eye. Instinct, born from years of conditioning, told Amisha to lower hers. But she didn't and wondered why. "I don't have time for homework."

"No? Fine, then in a few years, you should be ready to translate your first story." His challenge was clear.

"A few years?" Insecurity seeped through the protective wall that surrounded her when she was in his company. Amisha stepped away from him and his words. A few years felt like another lifetime. Stories were already hammering at her, waiting to be told in her newfound language.

"Amisha." Stephen was in front of her in mere steps. He saw her reaction and said, "You're doing wonderfully." He was sincere, all teasing forgotten. "Better than I could have imagined. Before we know it, your stories will flow and you won't need me."

"You will be happy to be rid of me." Whenever Amisha thought about him helping her, she was still shocked. Ravi, thrilled for her, repeatedly advised her to accept her good fortune without question.

"Promise me one thing." He stared at the cloudless sky above their heads. "One story, written in English. As a parting gift."

No one had ever asked for one of her stories. Though she had tried to tell Deepak numerous times about her writing, each time he changed the subject to the children, the house, or his business. Soon enough she stopped trying.

"Why?"

"So I can remind myself what a great teacher I am."

His words broke the tension that vibrated between them. Amisha's laughter on his heels, Stephen retreated inside the building to fetch the additional materials for their session.

Amisha arrived early at school. Paresh had been sick the night before with a stomach virus. With Deepak out of town, Amisha welcomed Bina and Ravi's offer to stay the night. Ravi cared for the other boys while Bina washed the bile-soaked cloths in the back. When Amisha left this morning, all signs of the illness were gone. Paresh was happily playing while sucking on a *kulfi*. Torn about leaving him, she was relieved when he gave her a toothy grin as he waved goodbye.

At her desk in the classroom, Amisha began reading the stack of stories from the students. Her prompt had been simple: a fairy would grant the person two wishes—anything at all. It could be something small or life changing. But in return, the fairy would demand that the recipient give up one thing the person held dear.

Many of the children wished their family had more money. Others were willing to sacrifice clothes for toys and vegetables for chocolates. Those stories made Amisha fear they hadn't grasped the full purpose of the prompt. She had started to read another when Neema arrived.

"Good morning, madam," she said. Her hair was pulled back into a ponytail. Her clothes were wrinkle-free, likely pressed with a flat iron heated on a stove or over a fire.

"You're here early." Amisha held up the sheaf of papers. "I'm reading the wonderful stories from your class."

"You read mine?"

Amisha shuffled through the stack until she found Neema's near the bottom. "I will read it now."

"It is not very good," Neema said apologetically.

"That is hard for me to believe." Amisha hid her grin when Neema started pacing. The story began with a young fairy telling a girl she had two wishes. In seconds, the girl made her request—unlimited books and the time to read them. With a wave of her wand, the fairy granted her wish. When the girl pulled one book off the shelf, another magically appeared to take its place. The fairy then asked what the young girl would give in return. Without hesitation, she offered her planned marriage.

"Her marriage was a grand sacrifice." Amisha glanced at Neema.

"To the fairy it was." Neema spoke in barely a whisper. "The girl didn't want it." Neema pulled off her rubber band and let her long black hair cascade around her shoulders. It shone from the oil used to keep lice at bay. "But all girls should want marriage, right? So the fairy believed it to be a grand sacrifice."

"Don't you have some time before you need to talk about marriage?" Amisha still remembered her own father coming home to tell her she was engaged. While Amisha's mother and brothers celebrated, Amisha hid in the outhouse and cried for hours.

"I am fifteen. My marriage has been decided." Neema glanced at the clock and then at the door, avoiding Amisha's eyes.

Amisha, also married at fifteen, knew girls

were married at all ages. A poor family could barter its newborn away for a bag of rice. Fifteen, in some villages, was thought too old. Amisha wondered if the passage of time would change the ritual. But no one, not even the British, had been able to alter the practice thus far.

"Are you excited about your marriage?" Amisha asked.

"I am expected to be, aren't I?" Angry, she pursed her lips and narrowed her eyes. Amisha felt a burst of pride for her display of emotion. "Besides, it's just a story." At her desk, Neema started removing pencils and paper from her satchel. "I told you it wasn't any good."

"Neema, your story is wonderful." There was a time Amisha would have written a similar story. But from her marriage came her children, and no wish would make her sacrifice them. "You have done an excellent job with your words and imagery. I am very impressed."

Visibly moved by Amisha's words, Neema paused before hesitantly saying, "My fiancé wished for an educated wife. My father says I am very fortunate."

"Neema?" Amisha hesitated, knowing it wasn't her place. She was just her teacher, and Amisha knew, like everyone else, Neema had to live her life. "Do you wish you were the girl in the story?"

Neema remained quiet before finally answering, "Wouldn't that make me foolish?"

TWENTY

"Navaratri," Amisha repeated, hoping the second time would trigger something. "The holiday right before Diwali?"

"Saying it louder won't make me understand," Stephen said.

They were taking a break from studying to walk the boundary of the garden. It was a glorious day. The dust that normally swirled in the air had all but disappeared. Though clouds tempered the sun's heat, enough seeped through to warm Amisha's arms and the back of her neck.

"Dancing. Women adorned in their most expensive jewelry. On our ankles, we wear bracelets with little bells." Amisha raised her sari to show him the anklets she was wearing. "Twenty to thirty glass bangles on our wrists to match the color of our *chaniya choli*."

"So you jingle as you walk," he teased. He turned serious as her eyes narrowed in warning. "*Chaniya choli*?" he asked, encouraging her to continue.

"Our best attire." She gave him one more chastising look. "Short-sleeved blouses with matching silk skirts that fall to the knees with a thin matching wrap." Her parents had been able to afford only the simplest *chaniya choli*, so Amisha bought cheap glass beads and sewed them in to brighten the outfit. "The women stick bindis with small diamonds on their forehead." Amisha pointed to the area between her eyebrows.

"To show you are married."

"Yes." She recalled following Deepak around the fire seven times, and how he had then dipped his thumb into the vermilion paste and marked her forehead. The size of the red dot didn't matter, only that everyone knew she now belonged to him. "To show you are married," Amisha repeated quietly.

"You don't wear one," Stephen said, scanning her face.

"No." Amisha glanced at the ground. Soon after her marriage, she had worn a small one and then, after Samir's birth, stopped altogether. "I don't."

"Why?" Stephen asked.

Amisha hesitated, fearing she might sound silly. "Sometimes I forget." She glanced at Stephen to gauge his reaction. He smiled at her statement. Suddenly self-conscious, Amisha shrugged. "Young girls will wear bindis of any color, and widows don't wear one at all."

"Married women wear red, right?" Stephen asked. Amisha nodded in response. She knew that Stephen would have seen the bindis on the women in the village. "How did the tradition start?"

Amisha pointed to the area between her

eyebrows. "It's the third eye. When you see a bindi, it reminds you to see life's greater purpose, the supreme goal of self-realization. In the temples, it still means that. The third eye focuses on God, and the bindi signifies piety, reminding you to keep God at the center of your thoughts." She remembered Chara and her insistence that Amisha wear one. "I think the meaning got lost along the way."

"That happens more than you realize." When Amisha glanced at him in surprise, he said, "India wants the British out, but they forget why we came in the first place. It was to help."

Amisha fell silent, processing what he had just said. "Is that what you learned in school or what you believe?"

"Both," he said without hesitation. "What do you believe?"

It was similar to his previous question. Amisha thought of the repeated uprisings in the news—Indians fighting against the British. Given the increased instances, it seemed there was little time left for the British Raj to remain peacefully in India. Though they had established rule in 1858, India had fought hard beforehand during the Great Rebellion but failed to stave off the colonization. Now, under Gandhi's influence, Indians were again finding their voice and crying for independence.

However, England refused India's demand.

India was considered the jewel in the crown of the British Empire. India provided both material and economic gains. To lose the country would be a blow to England and its empire. The British continued to fight hard against it by increasing both their personnel and military presence. They had even imprisoned Mahatma Gandhi numerous times in hopes of silencing the revolt.

At dinner parties, Amisha listened intently when Deepak and the other men spoke about the situation in India. However, right now with Stephen, she didn't want to talk about the division between her people and his. Instead, she returned to the conversation about India's celebrations. "Navaratri," she said again. He had to have at least heard about the holiday. "The start of the Nine Nights of Lights?"

Seeming to understand her need to change the subject, he offered, "Assume I don't know and tell me."

"You want to know?" Amisha yearned to share the details with him about the festival. It was a time when family and friends danced into the night. A rare happiness flowed through the people. During Navaratri, Amisha gave thanks that she was born an Indian. "Sure?"

"I would be afraid to say no," he said, his face serious.

Stephen slowed down when they reached the farthest tree. He leaned against the trunk, throwing one khaki-clad leg over the other. He had rolled up his shirtsleeves, and Amisha saw the hair on his forearms glistening. She sank down on the grass, confident he would follow.

"It's the celebration of the New Year. *Diyas* light up every home." Small flames in clay lamps were continuously refilled with oil so they could burn for twenty-four hours. "For nine days we dance." Amisha's favorite was the first day, when people offered sweets and flowers to the gods and goddesses. "We begin with Navaratri and end with Diwali." Her voice rose with excitement. "Fireworks light up the sky. Mango leaves and flowers cover doors and windows." Amisha picked up a fully bloomed flower that had fallen. She inhaled its scent before passing it to Stephen. He took it and did the same. "We exchange gifts and sweets with our loved ones and then pray for spiritual growth and strength."

"Strength for what?" His face showed genuine interest.

Amisha considered all the reasons she prayed. Neema and her story of sacrifice came to mind. "To have the strength to accept all that life offers—good and bad."

Stephen glanced at the sky, and then his gaze fell back on Amisha. She saw him swallow deeply and wondered if he was thinking of his brother. He finally asked, "Whom do you pray to?"

It wasn't the question she was expecting. "Lord Ganesha and his parents." Ganesha was the remover of all obstacles. The fact that she was here, learning from Stephen, showed her that her reverence had paid off.

"The elephant god?" Stephen asked.

"Yes." Impressed that he knew, Amisha explained, "He's the son of Lord Shiva. Do you know the story?"

Stephen nodded, surprising Amisha. "His father cut off his head by accident, then replaced it with the head of the first animal he came across."

"As an apology, he granted his son the power to remove all of life's obstacles," Amisha finished.

"And with it to provide the path to enlightenment. Maybe I should convert."

Amisha's head shot up, but she saw the teasing look in his eyes. "Are you searching for enlightenment, Lieutenant?" She nudged him with her elbow but then immediately regretted her forwardness. Embarrassed, she folded her hands in her lap.

"Some would say I need to." His smile helped to ease her shame. Seeming restless, he stood and started to pace in the garden.

"The temple in the village would welcome you." She started to say it didn't discriminate, but then thinking of Ravi and Bina, she bit back her words.

"A member of the Raj in the temple?" Stephen

shook his head slightly. "I think this garden is where my enlightenment will begin and end."

Amisha didn't know how to respond, and both fell silent. Finally, she said, "The celebration also honors the goddesses." Amisha waited while Stephen retook his seat an acceptable distance from her beneath the shade of the tree. "The three most powerful goddesses—the goddess of power and strength, of wealth, and the goddess of knowledge and learning. Nine days of dancing, three days in honor of each of them." With a small stick, she drew letters of the English alphabet in the dirt. "Is there a celebration for goddesses in England?"

He leaned back on his forearms. "There are no goddesses to be found in the Bible, or elsewhere."

"No goddesses?" Amisha was shocked. "Then who are the gods with?"

"With? As in sleeping with?"

Heat rose over Amisha's neck and onto her cheeks. Stephen's eyes danced with amusement as he watched her.

"God doesn't sleep with anyone as far as we know," Stephen said. "And there is only one God. No multiples."

"Oh," Amisha said, silenced by the information.

"You seem surprised." He glanced at his watch. Classes wouldn't let out for another hour. "Were you taught about other religions in school?"

At the mention of school, Amisha shifted away

from his probing gaze. "I was pulled out after six years to assist with household duties."

"Six?" Stephen calculated the time. "You were eleven?"

"Yes," Amisha answered. She could imagine what he was thinking. She was an uneducated village girl, and he was a part of the powerful Raj. He had to be wondering why he was wasting his time with her. Suddenly she was self-conscious, and her previous exhilaration disappeared. She searched for an excuse so he could leave, sure he would want one. "You must have work to do. I have taken up too much of your time with my ramblings."

She was about to stand up, when Stephen's hand fluttered over hers. Only for a moment, making her wonder if she had imagined it. It wasn't long enough to catch anyone's attention. Not the attention of the gods to whom Amisha prayed nor the attention of any wandering eyes of the school staff. But long enough to remind her who he was—a man who cared enough to teach her.

"I'm sorry. That must have destroyed you," Stephen said quietly.

"It wasn't so bad." Amisha spoke past the lump of gratitude in her throat. "I stole my brothers' books in secret and read them." She paused, remembering that time. "Soon after, I began to write."

"A person with your abilities should have the world at her feet."

Overwhelmed by his words, Amisha stood abruptly to hide the emotions that threatened. She motioned for him to follow with a wave of her arm. "I'm going to teach you the Navaratri dance," she said.

"Oh no." He followed her but crossed his arms over his chest. "My nanny tried teaching me to dance." His stance left no room for argument. "I don't dance."

Amisha searched the ground for small branches. She handed two to him and then wandered around until she found two more. "Everyone dances." Dancing was a means of celebrating every major occasion—marriages, holidays, etc. For Amisha, it was the time when men and women came together without thought or concern of gender roles. Though she had never seen the British join in their festivities, she had started to view Stephen, in their garden, as his own person. "You teach me English, so I will teach you to dance."

"You want to learn English," Stephen griped. "I don't want to learn to dance."

Amisha ignored his complaints. She took the jagged point of his stick and positioned him. Taking her place across from him, she held up one stick in each hand and signaled for him to do the same. "Follow my lead." When he didn't immediately comply, she waved her sticks until, with a deep sigh, he followed suit.

"Satisfied?" he asked.

"Yes." Amisha bit back her laughter at the sight of him holding two branches of leaves. "Now, move one stick forward and hit mine, like this." Amisha demonstrated and then followed with her other stick. "Good," she said. "Notice my ability to complement?"

"Because I am able to hit your stick with mine? I'll be sure to return the favor when I teach you to play with pieces of wood," Stephen said dryly.

Amisha ignored him. "Now, we do this five times, and on the final hit, you turn in a full circle and move to the next person in the circle. See?" Amisha twirled around in her sari. Her hair flew around her as her sari loosened. Her foot caught in the hem, and she stumbled forward.

"Whoa!" He reached out just as she was about to fall. He caught her beneath her arms, his fingers resting against the side of her breasts as he steadied her. "Are you all right?"

"Yes," Amisha murmured. "Thank you." His warm breath graced her cheek. Embarrassed, she stepped out of his arms. The warmth his touch elicited warred against the expectations ingrained within her. "I'm sorry. I became overexcited."

"No apologies necessary," he assured her. He waited until she met his gaze to say, "Maybe it is important I learn the steps of your dance."

TWENTY-ONE

"Today we will write our first full story in English."
Amisha handed each student a booklet after writing
the assignment on the board in simple English.

Last night, Amisha had helped Jay for the first
time with his English homework. Afterward, he
climbed into her lap and thanked her. She had
swallowed the lump in her throat and hugged
him back before tickling him. When he ran off
laughing, she glanced at the makeshift temple
and nodded her thanks.

Now, using her limited artistic skills, she drew
a picture of the earth and colored the ocean blue
and the land green. "Who can tell me where we
come from?"

The assignment had come to Amisha after she
and Ravi had a discussion with the boys about
karma and the universe's determination of their
place. Jay had asked, in his innocence, what
crime Ravi had committed in his previous life
to be born an untouchable in this one. Amisha
started to scold, but Ravi had assured her it was
fine, and yet neither had the answer as to why
one was born into his station in life.

"God?" one student answered.

"Evolution. We came from apes," another
answered.

"And how do we live our life?" Amisha saw their confusion and tried to explain. "Once we are born, are we still controlled by the person or event that made us? Are we puppets?" The students shook their heads no. "Then how do we make our decisions?"

"Our hearts." Neema's answer was tentative, sounding more like a question. Amisha nodded her approval, offering encouragement.

"Our gut," a boy in the front added. "What feels right."

"Our soul?" Amisha asked the boy. At his nod, she said, "Excellent—all of you." Amisha made sure the class was focused before continuing. "The heart and soul work on emotions. They don't always stop to think about what is right or wrong, only what they want and need. So where do they get their direction?"

"From the brain." The answer came from the back of the room.

"Correct. Our minds guide us toward what is acceptable for us to create, protect, or destroy. And where does the brain get its intellect?" Amisha searched the room for an answer. At first the class was quiet, the children glancing at one another to see if anyone had the answer.

Finally, a student near the front answered, "From what we learn or have been taught. By knowledge?"

"Excellent. But even with our brains, heart, and

soul guiding us, can we do anything we want? Do we have the freedom to make our own choices?" When the class murmured no, she asked, "Why not?"

"Our parents," a student threw out, making everyone laugh.

"The Raj," a girl in the front whispered.

"Rules," Neema said.

Thrilled that the students were interested, Amisha said, "I want all of you to write about creating something you want, destroying something you don't need, and protecting what is vital. But you must explain how your heart, your soul, and your mind feel about each event."

Amisha was cleaning up the classroom when Stephen walked in. He glanced at the board. "The earth?"

"Their classwork." Amisha started to erase the picture.

"Wait." Stephen barely touched her hand as it held the eraser, but she immediately stepped back. He quickly read her notes. "The heart, the mind, and the soul?"

Unsure if he approved, Amisha said, "It seemed like a worthwhile topic."

He nodded his agreement, and Amisha felt a small sense of victory. "It is." He stuck his hands into his khaki pants. "I wish I had such assignments as a child. I would be a much wiser man." He leaned against the chalkboard and wondered aloud what he would create. "Maybe a really fast car?" He smiled when Amisha rolled her eyes.

"You are in a pleasant mood," she noted. "It must be the holidays. Christmas in your country, yes?"

"Yes." He waited while she gathered her things. In silent agreement, they headed toward the garden. Stephen held the door open for her and then followed her outside. He grabbed a heavy tree limb and pulled himself up with both arms. "My mother is coming to India."

"That's wonderful." Though he rarely spoke about his family, Amisha was sure he must be thrilled. When he gave her a look of unhappiness, she asked, "That's not wonderful?"

Shrugging, he grabbed another branch. "My mother is different."

"That's not nice." Amisha softened her words with a smile. She reached up and pulled a leaf off the branch he was hanging from. "She gave birth to you."

Stephen let go of the branch and landed on both feet. "Not by her choice, I believe." He took a seat on the bench and made room for her.

Amisha joined him. Over the last few months, she had become more comfortable sitting in close proximity to Stephen when no one else was around. Without realizing it, they had created their own rules inside the walls of the school. However, every time she was away from Stephen, Amisha worried about her behavior. She would think of Deepak and her marriage, and guilt would creep in. She would promise herself to step back and behave in accordance with society's standards. But then she and Stephen would spend time together; their interactions were natural and easy, and it was harder to pretend to be indifferent versus being herself with him.

"Your mother was not affectionate?" Amisha toed the stones beneath her foot with her sandal.

His short laugh was mirthless and empty. "My brother and I were more of an afterthought."

"What about your father?" Though she was fascinated, Amisha hesitated to pry. Her desire to learn more about him won out, so she asked, "Are you close?"

"That depends on your definition," Stephen answered. His gaze cut to the sky before meeting hers. "It's because of him I am here." He motioned around them. "Favors called in from university mates who now run the country."

"You're not happy here." Amisha knew that. He had told her as much when they met, but a part of her had hoped he was enjoying their sessions as much as she was.

"I'm not unhappy." He caught her gaze and held it before breaking away to glance over her head. His mind elsewhere, he murmured, "It's just that there's a war going on, and my mates are fighting in it."

"Why aren't you?"

He began to pace in front of her. His Adam's apple bobbed when he swallowed deep. "I told you my brother died?" He waited for her nod before continuing. "He died fighting. He was in the Royal Air Force. After that, I was assigned to India rather than the front lines. My father found the safest yet most respectable job he could for me."

Tears pricked the back of her eyelids. "Your brother was older?"

"Only by twenty months." He laughed at himself before admitting, "I always wanted to be him while hating him at the same time." Once he was lost in his memories, his shoulders relaxed and his face softened. "He used to play these crazy pranks on me. Every single time he got me."

"You loved him." It wasn't a question, but Stephen answered it nonetheless.

"I did. Still do," he corrected. He kicked a pebble and watched it bounce into a bush. "Guess it doesn't end with death." He took a deep breath before saying, "I don't know if I ever told him." Shaking his head, he said, "Now it's too late."

Amisha wanted to comfort him. To tell him that in time it would get better, but she had no idea whether it would. So instead, she listened and hurt for him silently. "Your father? Is he doing all right?"

"I don't know," Stephen said quietly. "Whenever I call home, he's not there for me to ask."

"But he must be a good person," Amisha said, sure of it.

"Why do you say that?" Stephen watched her carefully.

"Because you are such a good man," Amisha said. When his gaze held hers, she refused to look away. Whereas before she had felt uncomfortable and nervous, there was now an ease and familiarity.

"If he had a choice, I wouldn't be here." He lowered his voice before admitting, "My father thought living with the browns was the lesser of the two evils."

Amisha flinched at the derogatory term used so frequently by the British. Flustered, she asked, "Is that what you believe?" She hoped for his answer but feared it at the same time. If he admitted to her that he shared his father's views, then she wondered how they could continue their lessons.

"My brother traveled frequently before the war." Inside the building, the classes were letting out. The sound of children talking and walking through the halls spilled from the closed door into the garden. Stephen paused and listened until the halls were quiet again before continuing. "India was of course on his itinerary. When he returned, he told me it was different here, and that was frightening to a few. But the same blood runs in every human on the earth. You just have to see past the variations in skin and culture."

Relieved, Amisha nodded. "He sounds like a wise man."

"Then he punched me in the stomach as brothers do and told me I wasn't brave or man enough to ever leave home." Amisha saw his grief as he relived the memory. "Called me a mum's boy."

Amisha heard his pain and grieved for him. "Are you?"

He shuddered at the thought. "Bloody no. Mum and I aren't close." He assessed Amisha before saying, "She mostly keeps to herself. Exact opposite of you, I'm sure." It was the last thing Amisha expected to hear. He pushed his foot against her mound of pebbles. "I bet your children always know what is on your mind."

"Worry," Amisha said immediately. "I pray they don't kill themselves with their antics."

"Your boys know how much you love them," Stephen argued. "There is nothing you would not do for them."

"I would not be a good mother if they ever questioned my love and loyalty."

Amisha refused to sacrifice her time with them, so she waited to practice her words and check classwork until after they were in bed. That left many nights when she watched the sun rise as she finished her studies.

"Therein lies the difference between my mother and you," Stephen said. "You care what they know and think."

Unsure how to respond to the compliment, Amisha asked, "What will you do while she is here?"

He considered her question. "Taj Mahal, New Delhi, Bombay."

"A British tour, then?" Amisha teased.

"Where would you recommend instead?"

Amisha pulled a lone flower off a bush and offered it to Stephen. "Take her to Kashmir. Maybe Mount Abu."

"Mount Abu?"

"A treacherous winding road cut into the curves of a mountain." Amisha used her hands to demonstrate. "The road leads to a peak where a magnificent temple sits carved from marble." Her family had traveled there for a wedding. She still remembered her wonder at the sight. "Or the Dhal in Srinagar. It's a majestic lake surrounded by flowers that would make the one you are holding seem modest in comparison." She smiled, warmed by the memory.

"Go on," Stephen encouraged quietly.

"Kashmir is the grandest of all." Amisha had heard that the members of the Raj and their wives used Kashmir as their personal retreat and playground. "Heaven on earth, Lieutenant. Mountains surround open valleys. A painter's dream—lush green forests and a landscape that would make you weep." Amisha remembered her one visit there. Barely able to afford the trip, her family had slept on a friend's floor. Nearby, music spilled out of the doors of an opulent British hotel. "Even as the sun warms the petals of the flowers, snow caps the slopes in the distance," Amisha said. "But none of it compares to the people." She remembered those who lived there opening both their houseboats and hearts to guests.

Stephen listened quietly as she reminisced.

"It is breathtaking." Amisha would have loved to return, but the travel cost was extravagant and Deepak couldn't take the time away from business. "While there, my father said to me that beauty in such true form must be rare, for only then do humans appreciate it."

Amisha had been six when her father planned the trip for the family. Equal admirers of the splendor that surrounded them, she and her father had stood next to each other on the banks of the lake. Lost in the beauty of the region, they stared at the mountains that served as a backdrop to the fields of flowers.

"Take her there, Lieutenant, and show your mother the natural beauty that can compete with the magnificence of your castles in England." It was the first time Amisha had told anyone about the trip that meant so much to her, the only recollection she had of spending time with her father during her childhood. Like many men, he was busy with work and Amisha's brothers, leaving her to her mother.

Stephen, his hand moving of its own accord, reached out to grasp a strand of hair caught on her lower lip. He waited a breath of a second, his eyes meeting her before sliding it between his fingers and then tucking it behind her ear.

Amisha closed her eyes as his fingers brushed against her earlobe, lingering against her soft skin and the gold hoop of her earring. She nearly cried at the simple yet intimate act. Her pulse increased as guilt weighed on her for not turning her head. She convinced herself that to Stephen it meant nothing, and yet for her it was a violation of everything she had been taught as right and wrong. Regardless of the dictates, she couldn't move away.

"Your father is right," Stephen said softly. "It is so rare to see such beauty."

TWENTY-TWO

Amisha and Ravi were sweeping the front porch when a group of soldiers walked by. Though they were dressed in civilian clothes, the familiar small baton was strapped to each of their hips.

"Is something bothering you, Shrimati?" Ravi asked, continuing to sweep.

"Why do you ask?" Amisha returned absently as she stopped to watch the men.

"You seem unhappy," Ravi answered.

Amisha turned toward him with a raised eyebrow. "You are concerned with my happiness?"

Ravi shrugged and continued to sweep. "Usually not, but since you are increasing my workload, I find myself suddenly unhappy." Ravi had gathered a small pile of debris with his broom. Amisha, in her absentmindedness, had swept most of it all over the porch again. "Therefore, I will worry about yours if only to improve my own situation."

Amisha eyed the scattered debris and cringed. "Sorry." She leaned against her broom. "I was thinking of the lieutenant," she admitted.

"When does he return?" Ravi asked.

"Soon." Amisha didn't know the exact date. Though she imagined the teachers at school knew, she hesitated to ask them. On the surface, they had accepted her teaching at the school but made no overtures to welcome her.

"What makes the lieutenant different from them?" Ravi gestured toward the officers. They were watching a group of children play cricket. When one of the youngsters made a challenging hit, they joined the team in clapping and cheering.

"I don't know how to describe it." Amisha struggled to explain. "When we are in the garden, I can speak to him as I wish." He treated her as an equal. With him she felt safe to be herself and, in doing so, started to discover who she was. "I find myself happy," she said, not sure if she had known what that meant before.

Ravi listened without interrupting. When he saw the smile on her face, he returned it. "His absence must be difficult for you."

"You say that without judgment," she said carefully.

"You have been telling stories since before I met you." He paused before saying softly, "I know you have never been able to share them." *With Deepak* was what he didn't say. "I was judged for wanting more than I was allowed. Ridiculed and berated. You were the only one who understood and accepted. Who am I if I stand in judgment of you now?"

Amisha swallowed her lump of gratitude. "Thank you." She reined in her emotions and thought of a story to help better explain her feelings, both to herself and Ravi. "Shall I tell you about . . . the king and the prince?"

"Since you have doubled my duties, it would be an excellent time to entertain me." Ravi reached for Amisha's broom, and she happily handed it over. She settled into a chair and thought through the tale.

"A king ruled his land with an iron hand and strict rules as his ancestors had." She paused, waiting for the next part to come to her. "The king had only one son, the prince. When the prince inherited the throne, he remembered his father's advice to rule as he had."

Across the way, one of the officers joined the children's cricket game. The children's squeals of laughter interrupted the story. Amisha and Ravi both watched silently, neither voicing their thoughts.

"But the prince was blind and his tongue was deformed, so his speech was often garbled," Amisha started again. "He wondered how he could rule with his handicaps." She closed her eyes and imagined the prince and his heartache. The demand on him to be someone he wasn't. "He admitted his fears to his close friend. His friend said, 'Go to the people. When you can't see them, touch them. Instead of speaking your orders to them, listen and hear what your people have to say.'"

"A wise friend." Ravi set aside his broom to hear the rest of the story.

"So the prince did as he suggested. He hugged the children. When he did, he felt bones where flesh should be. When he held the women's faces, his hands came away wet from their tears. They were hungry and poor." Amisha choked up as the words flowed from her. "The fathers' words were filled with sorrow. They wanted better lives for their children. School and music. Sticks of color so the children could draw pictures. Poetry books to fall asleep with each night."

Riveted, Ravi asked, "What did the prince do?"

"He chose not to rule like the previous kings. Because of his friend, the prince ruled with his heart, and his handicaps became his strength." Amisha thought of her own place in life and the handicaps she carried with her. "And because of this, his people loved him." Unsettled, she glanced into the house and then back toward the game that was breaking up. Finally, she admitted, "The lieutenant makes me believe I have worth regardless of who or what I am." When she was with him, she believed herself to be intelligent and worthy. Because of the opportunity he gave her, she imagined anything was possible. "When he is gone, I wonder if that belief is an illusion."

Seeming to understand, Ravi nodded. "For you, I hope he returns soon."

The students fidgeted in their seats as they waited. Neema had volunteered to read her story first, but for the last five minutes she had stood in place, staring at the words. Her fingers gripped the thin paper so tight, Amisha wondered if it would tear.

"Beti," Amisha said gently. When Neema barely turned her head to glance at Amisha, she asked, "Would you like to start reading your story?"

"Yes, madam." Her voice shaking, Neema began to read aloud her story crafted for the assignment.

A young girl, recently married, walked alongside her husband to return home. He used a cane, while her young legs itched to dance. But there was no music, only the steady beat of the cane as she kept pace with him. One day and one night had passed since her marriage. When night fell, the girl sought out the shelter of the moon. She fell to her knees, her tears watering the ground that was his.

There was a flash of light, and she saw her life before and the one now, but when she searched for her future, the picture was empty. "Guide me to be who I want," she asked, but there was only silence. She searched for her own strength and became her own counsel. "I want to explore the world," she whispered. She looked to the stars and the sky and imagined a world other than hers. To a greater power she gave thanks for having created her. Then she laid her hand over her heart and asked it silently what it desired. "To be happy," the girl heard. She then laid her hand over her abdomen and whispered the same question. "To be free," she heard.

The girl raised her face to the moon, its rays the only light in the darkness. She set the pad of her fingers over her forehead and listened to the beat of her blood for the answer that lay dormant. There was another flash of light, and she nodded her head. She knew now what she needed to do to protect what was vital.

She bade goodbye to the house in which she had been sentenced to spend the rest of her life. With each step toward autonomy, her heart felt lighter and her soul more confident. At the edge of the cliff, she stared over the ledge. The embrace of the abyss called to her, and her final step took her to freedom.

"Neema." Amisha had waited for the class to empty out. Other students had read their stories aloud after Neema. Some took on world events such as hunger and the war, while others chose themes closer to their hearts. One boy wrote about evil versus good with warring monsters. But none elicited the shock and questions that Neema's did. "Your story was powerful."

"Thank you," she said quietly. Neema scooped up the pencils with the erasers chewed down and stuffed them into her bag.

"You're a very gifted writer." Amisha trod carefully and thought through her next words. "Do you enjoy school?"

The girl stared at the empty classroom around them. "My betrothed invites many of the British military into his home." Neema fidgeted with her diamond studs. Either she had not heard Amisha or was purposely ignoring her. "He wants me to be able to entertain them without sounding dull. An English education assures that."

"What do you want?" Amisha reached out for the girl's hand, but Neema jerked it away. Amisha was scared by the story—unsure whether it was a warning or a young girl's overactive imagination.

"It doesn't matter." Neema hunched her shoulders and curled her hands into fists. "How do you dream when your destiny has already been determined?" She grabbed her schoolbooks and opened the door.

"Neema," Amisha called out, trying to stop her, but it was pointless. Neema had already left.

JAYA

TWENTY-THREE

My father worked hard to build up his own thriving medical practice. Ever since I was young, it was assumed I would join him and then take over. My future as a doctor was firmly established before I fully understood what it entailed. As I grew up, I found I was less interested in medicine and more in words. When college came and it was time to decide my major, I revealed my choice of journalism to my parents. I braced myself for my father's disappointment but was surprised when he said he understood. Grateful, I started to leave the table, when my mother spoke up.

"Medicine has been decided," she said.

"No," I said, refusing to acquiesce. "I'm going to be a reporter."

"Jaya . . ."

"It's my life," I said before she could say more. "It's my right to do what makes me happy."

"Happiness cannot be assumed," she corrected. "You will be a doctor."

My father asked me to leave the room so he could speak to her alone. Close to thirty minutes later, they came out and told me they supported my decision. I thanked my father and left without a word to my mother. She never said another word about that day or my decision.

• • •

In the mornings, Ravi and I tour the village, and in the evening, he tells me the story while we eat. Tonight Ravi and I dine at a Punjabi restaurant. Unlike the spicy sautéed vegetable dishes that Ravi has been preparing for me, the Punjabi entrées are steeped in heavy cream and butter. I devour the rice pilaf mixed with vegetables.

"Everyone is so gracious and welcoming." I wave to a group of children who hover nearby.

"You have made their day." Ravi wipes his plate clean with his naan. "We are not used to foreigners."

"Foreigners, we have many," the restaurant owner says as he refills our glasses with mango *lassi*. Age lines cover his worn face and hands. He's paired his loose white cotton pants with a short-sleeved button-down shirt. His skin is nearly as dark as his hair. "It is rare to have a guest of Ravi Sahib."

"His particular charm doesn't attract hordes of people?" I give Ravi a teasing glance.

"He is too busy caring for the departed sahib's house and his other properties." The owner sets down a plate filled with dessert. "He hires people to tend to the garden and mill. The mill has been unused for years, but not even a spider dares to enter for fear for its life."

"You pay for the caretaking?" From our daily time together, I know he doesn't have an income source. "But there is no one left to pay you."

"Your family paid me a king's ransom when I worked for them," he says, as if that is reason enough. He finishes his sweet in two bites and then dips his napkin in the water glass to clean his hands. "It is my responsibility to care for what is theirs as they cared for me."

The owner bows his head in respect toward Ravi. To me, he says, "In their death, he is still your family's trusted servant. Your mother should be proud."

"You knew my mother?" Since my arrival, no one has mentioned her to me. It is as if she never existed.

His gaze collides with Ravi's, and a silent message seems to pass between the two. "Only by sight." He's evasive, clearly hiding something. "You look exactly like her." He nods to both of us before leaving.

"Why doesn't anyone know my mom?" I ask after the owner leaves. "She grew up here, and yet she's a stranger."

Instead of answering, he picks up a piece of *halwa* and hands it to me. Flies that have been wandering in and out of the open-walled restaurant land on our table in search of the sweet smell. I swat at them with my folded napkin but only succeed in bringing them closer.

"She kept to herself," he says. "She rarely went out when she was growing up."

"Not even to visit the garden?" I ask, wondering how she could have kept away.

"She did not know its significance." As so often happens when he is telling the story, his eyes are haunted and his words measured. "Your grandfather closed the school after your grandmother's death. Much of the garden died in the years in between." There's a flicker of sadness before he rubs his hand over his face. "Only after his second wife's death did he allow me back in."

"You brought it back to full bloom." His silence gives me my answer. He would have had to tend to every flower, every bush, with love. I wonder what my grandmother did to deserve such loyalty. "I did not know he owned the school. How did that come about?"

He shakes his head, and I know it will be the same answer—that the story will reveal its secrets soon enough. Since we have met, I have learned that pushing him will accomplish nothing.

"Were you this stubborn when my grandmother was alive?" When he smiles, I ask, "With my grandfather's death, who owns the school now?"

"Your mother." Shocked, I stare at him. "Your uncles relinquished their interest in the house and mill. Your grandfather left the school to your mother to do with what she wishes. He said it belonged to her."

"Does my mother know this?" She never mentioned it before my trip or during our call.

"I don't know." He shakes his head slowly, his fatigue apparent. "The property office says its letters remain unanswered." His shoulders slouch downward in defeat. "If the properties are not claimed within sixty days of Deepak's death, the government will sell them to the highest bidder." He swallows. "Your grandmother's memories—her legacy—will be lost forever."

I stand on the porch and stare into the darkened night. A full moon shines in the starlit sky, a view I'd rarely seen under Manhattan's city lights. After dinner, Ravi returned home, but I am too wound up to sleep.

I process Ravi's revelation as I walk among the unadorned walls. I run my hand over the various pieces of furniture, imagining the time when my grandparents and mother made this house their home. In the story, Amisha's love for her home and family is obvious. Why then would her children refuse what was hers?

I think of my own home, empty now. It was easier to walk away than I would have imagined. When we first moved in, Patrick and I spent hours decorating the expensive space that validated us and our careers. We arranged and rearranged every piece of art and furniture until it was perfectly placed. It seemed it could be the perfect home only if everything was absolutely right, and at the time, that was so important to us. Only when I yearned for the hands of a child to wreak havoc did I realize it is not the décor or the address that makes a home but the people occupying it.

I grab my computer and rest it on my lap. I skim my hands over the keyboard, feeling the calm that only the written word brings me. Too tired to censor what I say, I start to type.

I started my career as a reporter on the business beat. It suited my need for figures to support the facts. But after becoming jaded enough not to believe everything I heard, I was promoted to sports. I had never been a "fan," so imagine both my surprise and horror at hearing stats recited verbatim by men in locker rooms who believed I was equally invested in how fast a cut fastball was thrown this time versus the last twenty. After six months, I begged for a transfer to the technology section. My editor offered me literature instead. Books are a conundrum of sorts— though I value words above all else, stories were never a lure. But I opened my mind and came to appreciate that even in fiction there can be morsels of truth.

Imagine my fascination at learning that my grandmother—a woman who died before I was born—yearned to write tales. Hope was her life raft that one day they would be valued.

Hope is a four-letter word and one of the simplest in the English language; contrast that with floccinaucinihilipilification, one of the most complicated. Hope—for such a simple word its meaning is profound. The intellect in me dismisses its claim while the writer never understood the appeal of the intangible. Yet it was the only thing my grandmother and so many others like her held on to. My grandmother wished to write her stories in English, a language that was foreign to her. To me, the granddaughter who has had only the best of life, it seems like such a simple dream. I chose to write as my career. If I deem something important, I put the words on paper. They are safer to me than speaking words aloud. Never once when putting pen to paper have I feared the consequence of following my vocation. It never occurred to me to ask permission or wonder if I was allowed to be more than others wanted. In my life, I take my dreams for granted. No matter what they are, I assume they are possible.

It is sobering to learn of a woman one generation removed who lived a life I can't imagine or understand. I am mortified by my naïveté and ashamed to admit that my bubble became so dark that I saw only my shadow. In hindsight, I think we all protect ourselves from that which is too difficult to know. But that excuse is just that. My grandmother's pain seems incomprehensible while her strength inspires me. In comparison, I am weak. For all the beliefs I had of my own strength, it is humbling to know I am severely lacking. As a citizen of the world and as a woman, I can only strive to do better. What that means is still a mystery, but I'll take the first step of this journey in anticipation of where it leads. Along the way, I may learn a thing or two.

Maybe there's hope for me after all.

Finished, I start to hit "Send" but then again hesitate. The pain over the last few years became a secret well kept. When I needed Patrick, I didn't turn to him but instead kept my own counsel and let him keep his. It was easy to be together in the moments we were strong, but it felt impossible when I was weak.

Now, tired of hiding, I reread the blog entry and then hit "Send." Before I can question my decision, I shut off the computer and go to bed.

TWENTY-FOUR

I run a fine-tooth comb through my hair to check for lice. For the last few days, I haven't been able to stop scratching, and Ravi mentioned I may have been infected. I scrape the comb's teeth against my scalp and spot a small brown bug. I pick it out with a toothpick before repeating the procedure. Another one and then two more by the time I'm finally finished.

"Disgusting," I mutter.

"Something specific or just an observation?" Ravi asks, finding me on the back porch. When he spots the small comb, he nods in understanding. "Have our little friends welcomed you to India?"

"Calling them friends may be your first problem." Unamused, I point to my head. "Any advice on how to get rid of them?"

"I'll bring you a chamomile paste later. It suffocates them."

"Looking forward to it." I pull my hair back and quickly braid it. I showered early and threw on a long sundress. Ravi and I made plans yesterday to explore some of the other towns. When he told me he had been out of the village only a handful of times, I insisted we tour together. Inside the house, there's a knock on the main door. I glance at Ravi. "Are you expecting anyone?"

"I have no friends," Ravi says simply.

"Yes, that's why we're stopped repeatedly in town with people wanting to say hello." I roll my eyes before opening the door.

On the porch, a young girl, no older than eight, fidgets in place. Two braids fall over her shoulders, and her short dress with puffed sleeves reaches right above her scraped knees. Gold-colored sandals grace her feet with a flat ring adorning her toe. Plastic bangles line both of her tan arms.

"Hi." Surprised, I glance back at Ravi, who shrugs, telling me he doesn't know what this visit is about. "Can I help you?"

"Jaya Shrimati?"

"Yes, I'm Jaya. You are?" I ask her inside, but she gestures for me to follow her.

"There is a call for you, Shrimati. At my father's store." She jumps off the porch and lands on her feet. "Please, come quickly. The connection will be lost."

"I'll wait for you here," Ravi says when I glance at him.

Keeping pace with her rapid gait, I ask, "Who is it?"

"A man from another country. My father spoke to him."

It has to be my father. Worried, I move faster. "How did you know who I was?"

"It is well-known." Shy, she barely glances at me. "You are from the American States?"

"The United States?" Smiling at her enthu-siasm, I say, "Yes, I am."

"The store has never received a call from the American States." With a maturity that seems to surpass her age, she says, "The lines are not very good. Let us go."

Unable to keep up with her in my heels, I stop to slip them off. My feet slap against the dirt path. Before my trip, I would have challenged anyone who told me I would be running barefoot through villages in India. Now I can't imagine being anywhere else.

The dry air whips through my hair as we pass through the village until we're on the outskirts of the neighboring one. We approach a row of shops with tiled roofs and open fronts. A few people stare, but otherwise we're ignored.

"Here." The girl opens the door to a shop more modern than the others.

A blast of air-conditioning hits us in the face as we enter. Inside the store, surrounded by lush décor, are glass-covered cases filled with twenty-two-carat gold jewelry. Diamond studs and rings sit on top of the counter in revolving display holders with locks. A well-dressed man steps out from behind the counter on our arrival.

"Namaste. I am Sanjay, the owner of the store." Hands folded, he bows slightly. Unlike many of the other villagers, he wears suit pants and a dress shirt. The top few buttons are undone, revealing a lightweight gold chain with an Om pendant.

"Namaste." Smoke rises off burning incense inside a small makeshift temple. "Thank you for sending your daughter for me."

His face lights up at her mention. "The office is back here." He leads me through a back door into a small room. "The gentleman on the phone asked for you by name." He shuts the door to give me privacy.

The musty room is overcrowded with a small table and velvet-covered jewelry boxes stacked atop one another on the shelf next to an open container of pomegranate seeds. I lift the heavy receiver of the landline to my ear.

"Hello?" When there's no answer, I repeat, "Hello? Is anyone there?"

"Jaya?" Patrick's voice crackles over the static.

Emotions slam into me. I had fought thoughts of him every day since my arrival. Now I remember his warm breath against my neck as he held me at night. His excitement over new information that could influence a case he was working on, or his teasing laughter when I bought all the clothes for the baby. Suddenly, like running through a scene cut from a movie, I remember him finding me curled up on the bathroom floor after the first miscarriage. He picked me up and carried me to bed. There, we held each other as we cried. It was the first and last time we mourned our loss together.

"Patrick?" I grip the phone's wire. "Can you hear me?" There's static, and then the phone goes dead. Disappointed, I lay my head back against the chair as memories fight their way to the surface.

After the second miscarriage, I yearned to lean into Patrick—to pull him closer and hope his strength would seep into me—but I never took the first step. Patrick stood by me as he shouldered his own grief. He shed the tears I couldn't. He mourned when my grief refused me a reprieve. His path to healing was to return to daily life. Each step he took only left me farther behind. At the end, I was standing alone with no answers on how to fill the void.

But the past wasn't always filled with heartbreak. Before the miscarriages, our steps often matched each other's, and over the course of our courtship, we learned how to stand together.

When we first moved in together, Patrick and I had a huge fight over which show to watch one night. At the time, it felt all-encompassing, as though we were fighting about all aspects of our relationship, not just a TV show. I feared we were headed for failure if we couldn't find a compromise. In the moment, I failed to remember all the hours we had spent together before, cuddling in his apartment or mine and watching television together. The fight ended with Patrick wrestling me to the ground and kissing me until I calmed down. That night we spent hours making love.

Lost in the past, I wonder now if Patrick is calling me to say we can still work it out. That somehow, in the midst of our heartbreak, he has found us a path back to happiness. I pick up the phone to call him back. My gold wedding ring, the one I haven't taken off, glistens on my finger. As I dial, I fiddle with it, turning it around and around. So many times I had thought to take it off, but with all the heartaches of the last few months, I needed an anchor, even if it was only in my head.

The phone connects across the continents. I think about the last time we spoke and his admission about Stacey. I think of him holding her, kissing her. Bile rises in my throat. At his hello, I lay down the phone without saying a word. I close my eyes and wait for the pain to subside, and only then do I find my way home.

AMISHA

TWENTY-FIVE

Amisha was cleaning the desks. After each class, she made sure to tidy the room so the teachers wouldn't find cause to fault her. She'd started on the last desk when she heard someone behind her.

"Merry Christmas," Stephen said when she turned around. He closed the door before setting a large bag down on the ground.

"You're back." Amisha rushed toward him and stopped inches away.

"I am. Did you miss me?" he teased. He looked tired. His normally wrinkle-free clothes were disheveled and his tie was loose. There were circles beneath his eyes.

"Yes." Amisha didn't care if it was inappropriate. Her friend was back, and she refused to lie to him. "I did—so very much."

Amisha had missed him desperately. She passed the hours working with her students, but every time she approached the school grounds, her feet felt heavy and her mind lonely. She had missed their conversations and his company. During Stephen's absence, she had tried to talk to Deepak about some of the same topics she discussed with Stephen, but her husband had turned away, uninterested.

Now Stephen greeted her words with silence.

His eyes searched hers. Sure she had overstepped a boundary, Amisha, humiliated, took two steps back.

"I'm sorry," she stammered, her enthusiasm disappearing. She started to tell him she had spoken out of turn, when he interrupted her.

"I forced my mother to stay up into the late hours of the night talking about mundane topics." He closed the distance between them until she met his gaze. "It helped to pass the time until I returned."

Amisha swallowed and then struggled to take the next breath. She heard the words he didn't say. They were the same ones she feared but would never give voice to—that even though their time apart was brief, they had missed each other more than friends do.

He reached out until his hand was inches from her. He waited, giving her the chance to say no, but she couldn't. She was desperate to feel the connection with him, if only for a moment. When he saw the agreement in her eyes, mixed with guilt, he nodded in understanding. He grasped her hand in his only for a second before releasing it.

Amisha imagined Chara instructing her to walk away. Her mother-in-law would scream at her that in enjoying Stephen's company she was bringing shame upon herself and her family. For just a moment, Amisha considered her options.

Walking away was wisest, but for once she wanted to keep her own counsel. To determine what was wrong and right when it harmed no one else. Questions that she would never have imagined asking now began to gnaw at her, and yet ignoring them remained the only safe answer.

"Merry Christmas," Stephen said again, breaking the silence. He grabbed the bag by the door and held it out to her. "I brought you a gift."

"What?" Happy for the distraction, Amisha took the bag. "You didn't have to." The bag weighed heavy in her hands. "I don't celebrate Christmas." The last gift Amisha had been given was the jewelry from her dowry.

"Then I should take it back." He moved to reclaim it, but she stepped away.

Smiling, she held the bag close. "It's mine," she whispered. "Thank you." Amisha pulled out a package from inside the desk. "Merry Christmas." Hesitant, she held out the wrapped gift to him.

After telling him about Navaratri, she had asked him his favorite holiday. Without hesitation, he had told her about Christmas. When he mentioned presents, Amisha decided she would give him one. From the market, she had bought tissue paper and dyed it with saffron. With careful precision, she had wrapped her gift.

"This is for me?" Stephen's eyes widened at the package she was thrusting at him.

"No, for me. I enjoy giving myself gifts," Amisha murmured, feeling at ease with him.

"You got me a gift," he repeated, taking it.

She hadn't been sure how he would react, but his childlike joy was unexpected. "Yes," she said, delighted she had followed her instinct.

"It's tradition to shake a gift before you open it," Stephen said. Amisha laughed when he did and then, following his lead, shook the bag in a futile attempt to learn its contents. He laughed aloud. "You're shaking it now? You're going to break it if you're not careful."

"Now?" Amisha wasn't sure how it was done in his culture. She wondered if it was the same as hers—to open the gift and thank the giver profusely or wait until you were in private and then send a thank-you note.

"No, next Christmas," Stephen said. "When I'm off fighting in the war, you can send me a letter and tell me how you liked it."

His words echoed in her head. He was teasing, Amisha was certain. But her mind had already registered it. The last two weeks without him had been hard. She had missed him more than she thought imaginable. But the thought of never seeing him again left her reeling. Her next breath filled her lungs with dead air.

He must have seen the change on her face,

because the smile immediately disappeared off his. "I'm joking, Amisha," he said quietly. "I'm not going anywhere."

No matter how much he wants to, Amisha thought but didn't say aloud. Nonetheless, she fought to hide the range of emotions she knew were dancing across her face. When tears pooled in her eyes, his filled with pain. She scolded herself for her inappropriate reaction and quickly shuttered her emotions. Instead, she offered him a forced smile while struggling to find her footing.

"Of course." Feeling foolish, she murmured, "Please accept my apology. I just . . ." She stumbled over the words that tangled with her emotions. "The war is dangerous, and you are my friend," she said, hoping the explanation sounded reasonable.

"Open the gift," he said softly, offering her a reprieve.

She gently loosened the strings and pulled out her present. A small seedling was sprouting in a soil-filled pottery pot. "A tree?" Amisha stared at the gift in disbelief.

"From England," Stephen said gently. "It's a *Fagus sylvatica,* or European beech." He smiled at her. "It's native to England. Considered the queen of British trees."

"How did you get it here?" Her small hands easily wrapped around the base of the pot.

"I called in a favor." He fingered the thick leaves, lobed like the palm of a hand. "It was delivered while I was traveling. I wanted to surprise you." He paused, staring at the tree, and then at her. "I wanted to give you something from my home, for you to have here. It can live for over a thousand years."

"Long after you and I are gone." Amisha ran a finger over the leaf he had touched. She searched his face for the answer she already had. When he stayed silent, she said, "You have given me a wonderful gift, and I am indebted to you for bringing me such splendor."

"There is no debt, but if there were, you would have already repaid it with your gift to me." Stephen pulled on the string and tore at the paper until he revealed a small book. Amisha had written his name in perfect English letters on top with hers, smaller, on the bottom. He glanced at her, but she simply smiled and motioned for him to open the cover.

Inside, again in precise letters, was a short tale set in England. Transfixed, Stephen took a seat and read aloud the words that flowed from the pages.

A young man loses his brother. Inconsolable at the loss, the young man threatens the heavens with havoc unless he can see his brother one last time. When they do not respond, he begins to destroy things that the gods hold dear.

"Enough," the gods cry. "Why do you want to speak to him?"

"To tell him something that I didn't have the chance to," the young man says. He wants to tell his brother the things in his heart. The things he is sure the brother does not know.

"You will have five minutes," they say, agreeing. "But in return, we get your voice. Agreed?"

The young man quickly accepts the deal. When the lost brother comes forward and the young man starts to speak, the lost brother raises his hand for silence. "I already know," the lost brother says. "I know you loved me." He pauses, dropping his head as his emotions start to overwhelm him. "I always knew you respected me. Our memories will always be a part of you." When the young man stares at his lost brother in shock, the lost brother starts to explain. "In my heart," he says, "I've always known. We are brothers. Our hearts are the same."

By voicing what the young man was going to say, the lost brother ensured that his younger brother would keep his voice. They embrace, holding each other tight.

When the gods deem their time is up, the lost brother starts to tear up at the word goodbye. It is now the young man who raises his hand to stop him.

"Not goodbye," he says, shocking the lost brother, who was scared and alone. "Until we meet again."

And though he has lost his voice forever, the young man has given his brother the one thing he did not have: hope.

Amisha tried to finish cleaning but kept glancing at Stephen to gauge his reaction. When he finally turned the last page, he looked up, his eyes holding hers. "How did you do this?"

The story had come to Amisha the night after Stephen told her about his brother. When the holidays were approaching, Amisha decided to try her hand at the story. With it she wanted to tell him that his brother knew how much he loved him. It took her weeks to put the simple story together, but she persisted. She wrote it at night after Deepak was asleep. Though she knew she was doing nothing wrong, she felt guilty for spending time on a gift for another man.

"You like it?"

"More than you will ever know," Stephen said, the words seeming to choke him.

Amisha felt an unfamiliar lightness. Afraid she would say something and embarrass them both, she motioned toward the tree. "It is nothing compared to this." She cradled the pot. "I want to plant it. May I?"

"Here?" He seemed surprised. He ran his hand over his eyes, wiping away the moisture that had gathered. "I thought you would take it home."

"I can't." Her gaze locked with his. It was the first time she had acknowledged that their interactions had to be kept secret. She saw understanding in his eyes and looked away, afraid of what it meant. "It belongs in our garden," she said, injecting a false note of brightness into her voice.

He took the plant from her, and together they walked to the garden. She searched for the perfect place and found a spot near their regular bench. Amisha began digging at the earth with her hands. She was oblivious to the mud staining her cotton pants, her focus on providing his gift with the ideal place to grow its roots.

"Here, let me help you." Stephen found a small spade to spear the earth and then began digging. Once the hole was large enough, he rocked back on his heels and watched her. She gently removed the seedling from the pot and planted it in the spot. Stephen filled the hole and both patted down the dirt with their hands to secure the tree.

"Finished," Amisha said with satisfaction. "Now the tree has a home."

"Yes." Stephen stared down at the seedling that had only started to grow. "A place for you to come years from now and remember the time we spent here together."

"Amisha." Stephen stood in the doorway of her empty classroom. "Could you come to my office, please? Neema's father is here," he said quietly. "He wants to speak with us."

Neema had been absent for more than a week. Amisha had been concerned and even brought it up with Stephen, but he told her the school hadn't heard from the parents. Now, anxious to get more information, she quickly walked with Stephen to the office. He motioned her in first to the cramped space and then followed, shutting the door behind them.

"This is Amisha," Stephen said, introducing them. "She is Neema's teacher."

The Indian man clasped his hands together. "Namaste," he said. Speaking to Amisha, he said, "As I was telling the lieutenant, Neema was hurt in an accident."

"Is she all right?" Amisha demanded, worried for the young girl.

"I came to inform you that she will no longer be able to attend school." The father didn't answer Amisha's question but instead handed Stephen cash. "This should cover the remainder of my daughter's tuition for the year." He started to leave but then hesitated. "She spoke of your class often, Shrimati," he said to Amisha. "She enjoyed learning from you."

"I have some of her old work I would like to discuss with her," Amisha said as he started to leave again. She felt Stephen's gaze sharpen, but concern for the girl overrode his disapproval. "Could I stop by to give her my well wishes along with the work?"

"That is not necessary," the father said immediately. "I will pass on your good thoughts."

"Thank you for coming," Stephen interjected, standing next to Amisha. "Please let us know if there is anything we can do for Neema."

He walked the father out. When he returned, he found Amisha pacing his office. He started to speak, but Amisha interrupted him.

"I know you're angry, but I had to try."

"It is not our place." She started to protest, but he cut her off. "The school has to be very careful how it interacts with the students' families." He rubbed the back of his neck, clearly frustrated with the situation and the circumstances surrounding it. "The Raj can't force Indians to send their children to our schools. If the parents feel we're using their children's attendance to police their family's home life, then they will pull their children out."

"So that's it?" Though the explanation made sense, Amisha was scared.

"I'm sorry." His face clearly showed he meant it. "There's nothing we can do."

"That's not good enough," Amisha said, worried about the young girl.

"It has to be," Stephen replied. "I'm sorry. I know how much you cared for her."

JAYA

TWENTY-SIX

When I was sixteen years old, a neighbor down the street was diagnosed with cancer. It was a serious case with a poor prognosis, and he had an uphill battle ahead of him. The wife was a young mother with three children under the age of five. The neighborhood set up a food schedule, and though my parents barely knew the family, my mom signed up and took dinners every other week. After the first few months, the dinner offerings slowed down and people got back to their lives. Around that time, my mother came home with a slew of cookbooks featuring American cuisine. Every weeknight for the next few months, Mom tried a new recipe in lieu of her standard fare. Before serving dinner, she would deliver food for the family without leaving a note. She never talked about it at home or told anyone.

The man recovered, and the family threw a gathering at its home to celebrate. At the party, the wife made a toast to the individual who had provided dinner every night. She had no idea who it was and hoped the person would step forward. I glanced at my mother, who kept her face down and stared into her drink. The wife asked again, but there was only silence.

"If anyone knows who they are, please tell them how very grateful I am," the woman finally said.

At home later that night, Mom bid me good night and started for her room.

"I'm surprised you didn't say something," I said. "You could have gotten credit for all of your hard work."

At the time, it seemed to me she cared more about that family than she ever had for me. She learned to make meals they would like and took the steps to drop them off without being noticed. To the daughter who had spent her life desperate for any show of affection, it was an opportunity lost; the family would certainly have shown her appreciation, gratitude, and acknowledgment.

"It wasn't about me," she said quickly. She shook her head and wrung her hands together. "It was about them and what they needed. That's all."

She left for bed, but I stared after her, wondering at the glimpse of fear I saw in her face at the thought of their learning the truth.

I awoke this morning with thoughts of Patrick. When we dated, we rarely fought, but the few times we disagreed, we always talked it out. Never before would I have hung up on him. But those times are past. I hold up my hand and let the sun's ray glint off the gold ring. When he slipped it on my hand, we swore to love each other always. With my finger, I circle the band's diameter before slowly starting to slip it off. It stops at my knuckle and refuses to move. I tug at it, but it is stuck. Relieved, I push it back and jump out of bed.

Once dressed, I follow the throng of people to an outdoor market. The streets are lined with cart vendors and talkative customers. I walk by each cart, admiring and assessing everything from fresh produce to books. I stop to admire a row of scarves.

"I make it myself." The young woman behind the wooden cart on wheels holds out a silk scarf. The elegant base red is delicately mixed with intricate patterns of light green and finished with a hem of indigo blue. It's the perfect gift for Mom to wear on cold nights. A similar shawl would cost more than a hundred dollars in America. "Five rupees."

After buying three, I move to another cart where a young boy holds up soil-laden green and red peppers. "Fresh. See, no brown spots." His long fingernails are packed with the black dirt, making me wonder if he picked the vegetables that morning. "You buy? Very good."

"Yes, I buy."

Tonight, I decide, I'll return the favor of Ravi's meals. I pick through the rest of his cart and choose ripe tomatoes and onions. When I finish paying for my goods, the woman in the next cart holds up a toy rattle.

"For baby." The woman, who has to be nearing ninety, gives me a toothless grin. "I have good toys."

Her cart is filled with cheap plastic toys and clay blocks. Each block is brightly painted with letters from the Indian alphabet. "No. No baby." I move away just as she starts to try to convince me to buy.

Other vendors are equally solicitous, each one motioning me toward his merchandise. Unable to resist, I purchase a sari for Mom and a silk shirt for Dad along with various trinkets. There was a time when I never would have bought trinkets and teased any friends who did. I always insisted the cheap stuff was a waste of money. Now I think of Neema, my grandmother, and all the other people who were just trying to live their lives as best they could. If not for circumstance, I could be in their position.

Out of habit I start to ask for a shirt for Patrick before stopping myself. Angry at my near mistake, I start to chastise myself, when Rokie comes out of nowhere and jumps on me, nearly knocking me down.

"You either do not like my meals, or you're going to cook for me," Ravi says, a few steps behind the dog.

"I love your meals, but I am going to cook you

dinner." Jarred from my malaise, I hug Rokie as he lavishes me with licks. "I've been shopping." I hold up my full basket proudly.

"I see that, and I am nearly blind." He peruses the contents and then asks me what I paid. When I tell him, he lets out a hearty laugh. "You have funded our village for the next six months."

"They are presents for home."

He smiles at me. "You have the same stubborn look your grandmother had." He leans heavily on his cane. "It is good you paid so much—no price is too high for a gift from your heart." We pass the rest of the vendors as Ravi takes us on a roundabout path toward home. "Come, I shall show you where I live. You can cook for me there."

As we leave the market and head toward his neighborhood, the homes get smaller and more dilapidated. We turn into a narrow alley that is barely five feet wide. Wet mud and cow dung line the streets. Gutters carved into the side of the road are clogged with mango peels and roti. A pack of stray dogs scavenges through a pile of garbage in search of food. With every step, I process the level of poverty I have heard of but never seen. The children running through the streets barely have any clothes on. Their bodies are bone thin and their faces seem older than their age. Stress lines their faces. In my own childhood, I never worried about finding my next meal or having a safe roof over my head. What I took for granted would be a luxury for these children.

Ravi stops in front of a hovel in the middle of the slums. His home is attached to others in a long row. The roof is broken in places, and brown water drips off the corner and onto the street. "Home." He holds open the worn door with pride. "Welcome."

I flinch as I take in the dirt floor and grimy walls that make up two small rooms of his home. A third room—a kitchen—has a kerosene stove on the floor and a pot filled with dirty dishes.

"Ravi, this is . . ." I search for the appropriate words so as not to insult him but fail. "This is where you live?" My childhood home and my apartment in New York are mansions in comparison. I ache for him but cover my reaction so I don't offend him.

"And I welcome you in it," he says.

Ravi fills an old cup with water from a bucket and pours it into Rokie's bowl. We both watch Rokie lap it up before he saunters toward his blanket on the floor. He stretches before settling himself down for a nap.

"When did you get him?"

"Ten years ago," Ravi says. "I was walking into the village one day. He was walking the same way. We have been together ever since."

I smile at the simplicity of the bond. Both Ravi

and his dog are content in their humble home, and yet I struggle to understand it. I have always taken my material trappings for granted, but now, seeing Ravi's pride in the little that he has, I'm ashamed to admit I can't remember a time when I fully appreciated them. Disappointment for never having demanded better of myself washes over me.

"Why don't you live in my grandmother's house?" I finally ask.

A mouse scurries along the thin wall before disappearing into a small hole in the corner. Rokie wakes up to let out a ferocious bark at the mouse before settling back to sleep.

"It belongs to your family. Besides, my friends would miss me." He gestures to where the mouse ran into the hole. "They rely on me to provide them their food."

"Where is your family?" I remember he mentioned a grandson the day we met.

"My son and his wife live with my grandson and his family. They are not far from here." Ravi slips his sandals off and rubs the soles of his feet. "My son's wife is a daughter to me." He smiles to himself. "I am blessed that fate was so generous. She wants me to live with them so they can show their concern for me. And each time I tell her, 'Not yet, Daughter. Not yet.' "

"Why?" Confused, I ask, "They could take care of you."

"Yes, but then who would take care of Amisha's home and gardens?" he asks gently. He gestures toward his home. "I am happy here."

"Your wife?" The house lacks the touch of a woman. An oil lamp sits in the corner, and a torn afghan is spread over a mattress on the floor. Three pairs of outfits similar to the one Ravi is wearing are folded neatly and placed next to the bed.

It's hard to remember all the clothes I discarded over the years. Something being out of fashion, having a lost button, or simply seeming worn were just some of the excuses I used to update my wardrobe. In contrast, Ravi treats the little he has with care.

"I spread her ashes in the river years ago." He removes his glasses and rubs a hand over the sadness on his face. "We cremated a son before that; he died at three." He warms his hands over the oil lamp.

Though the sun is high and its rays powerful, I fight a chill of fear watching him. "Are you all right?"

"There is not enough skin on these bones, my son tells me." He blows on his warm hands. "I laugh, but when I feel cold in the heat of the day, I must admit he may be right."

"Have you seen a doctor?" I ask, worried. Even though we have known each other only a short while, it feels much longer. Maybe because of the story or the time we are spending together, I have come to care for him.

He smiles, telling me without words he appreciates my concern. "I made a promise to your grandmother. There is no disease that can take me until I have fulfilled it." He stares over my head, and his eyes glaze over. I wonder if he's imagining my grandmother again. "Then, when it is my time, even the best of health will not save me." He shakes his head and seems to come out of his malaise. "So I will enjoy your meal tonight and may even take seconds."

"I'm not a good cook," I say, touched by his declaration.

"Then I will savor it even more, for neither was your grandmother. This assures me you are truly her own."

I wash the vegetables in an old colander while Ravi lights the portable kerosene stove. Once they're washed, I slice the vegetables and toss them into the pan. Ravi follows them with pinches of various spices he adds to the mixture from unmarked containers.

"What are they?" I ask. The spices look the same as those I have seen my mother use over the years.

"Mustard seeds." He picks up a handful of small black seeds and then points to a red powder. "Chili pepper, and this"—he holds up a yellow powder—"is turmeric." He smashes a clove of garlic and ginger and stirs the pieces into the pot, followed by chopped onion. They start to sizzle with the rest of the food. Satisfied, he says, "It will be ready soon."

"I'm so glad you let me cook for you," I tease. The smell from the spices fills the room and makes my mouth water. I never thought before about things like a refrigerator or clean water. Now I wonder if I'll ever think of them in the same way.

"Your mother never taught you?"

As a child, I used to watch my mom cook. She seemed happiest when lost in creating meals. But whenever I asked to help, she shooed me away, told me to find something else to do. "No, she liked to cook alone." But her love of cooking had to come from somewhere. "My mother is an exceptional cook. Who taught her?"

He pauses, his hands going still on the pot he was readying to put away. "Her stepmother," he says quietly. "She insisted your mother learn."

"Out of tradition or . . . ," I ask, hoping he says yes.

Ravi shakes his head no. "She required Lena to make the family's three meals every day."

"She still does." There was never a meal not perfectly cooked or presented. I assumed it was her joy, but now disappointment sweeps over me. "Every day she cooks."

"Did your husband cook?" he asks when I don't say more.

"No." I appreciate his attempt to change the topic. "My husband, ex-husband," I correct, then stop. I shift in my seat, feeling a knot ravel in my stomach. It is the first time I have called him that. I take a deep breath and pinch the bridge of my nose as I try to remember his question. "We usually ate out," I finally answer.

"You are divorced?" Ravi asks gently, seeing my reaction.

"Soon to be." My head hurts as I think of the last few years. "We faced a lot of loss during our marriage." Darkness starts to swirl around me. It's been a few days since the last episode of losing time. With the reprieve, I had hoped it was over. "It proved stronger than us." I close my eyes, too weak to fight it.

"Jaya?" Ravi asks.

When I open my eyes, he's standing in front of me. From the concern on his face, I know I blacked out again. "I'm sorry," I whisper, hating the loss of control. It seems to happen every time I think of Patrick or the babies. "I lost myself for a minute there." When he continues to watch me with concern, I try to allay his worry. "I'm fine, I promise. I think sometimes my mind needs a break."

"Coming to India?" Ravi asks gently. "It has helped you to forget?"

"Maybe. The letter was the perfect excuse." I remember his earlier words about my uncles.

"At the time, getting away seemed smarter than staying."

"Sometimes it is the wisest answer." He gestures for me to take a seat across from him on the floor. "Let us eat your meal."

TWENTY-SEVEN

Feeling like a native, I walk past rows of mud-clustered walls with little space between them. Women are busy in their front yards, beating water out of washed clothes or bathing their screaming infants in buckets. Around us, birds sing in unison with the oxcarts that creak by. The men, mostly topless, whip the animals to move faster under the boiling sun. A stray dog barks at me but loses interest when a young boy tosses a lump of dripping mango peels in the dung-lined street. I watch all of it, amazed at the human mind and ability to make a home no matter the circumstances. These children, surviving with so little, are more resilient than I can ever hope to be.

The property and tax office is located one village over. The Indian flag waves atop a large pole. Half-naked children run through a sprinkler system in the front yard, though there is little grass to water.

Inside the office, three rotating table fans flutter the papers stacked on the desks. The office is cramped, with barely enough room to walk. A black-and-white picture of Mahatma Gandhi hangs on the wall. A uniformed man and woman are working with files. Another man, dressed in a similar brown top and shorts, asks me if I need assistance.

"I'm here about the house, mill, and school properties." I offer him my passport to verify my identity. "I'm the granddaughter of the deceased owner."

He pulls the file and sifts through it. "Your uncles relinquished their rights to the house and mill. Your mother is the sole owner," he says after verifying my identity.

He hands me the official paperwork that includes the letters from all three brothers. I read through their letters and the rest of the file. He pulls out one final letter and hands it to me.

"We received this a week ago. Your mother has no interest in the properties."

"What?" I take the letter and read through Mom's two sentences giving up all of her rights to the properties. She instructs the government to do with them whatever they wish.

"We will now sell the properties to the highest bidder," he explains when I look up. "It is good news. The mill can once again make grain. Local contractors will lease the school. Your grandfather always refused." The man hands me various offers from local businesses. I take them all with shaking hands. "You will receive a healthy return."

"Why didn't my grandfather sell the school?" I ask, hoping this man can give me answers.

"He said it was not his to sell." The man's

confusion matches mine. "It sat there, unattended for years, but every time he refused."

I envision my grandmother's garden and how she found herself within its splendor. The mill had provided both my mother and grandmother with sustenance while they lived in the village. My own history is intertwined with theirs, even though I am just now discovering it.

I run my thumb over the letters that burn in my lap. I still have no idea what happened to my mother or what would cause her three siblings to relinquish their rights, but every part of me senses that the school and house are as essential to the story as the people who spent time in them. Though unsure what I will do with the properties, I know there is only one decision I can make.

"We've changed our minds. We are not selling. I am here to claim the properties to keep them in the family."

"Ravi?" I knock on his door and wait. I had promised him I would come by after visiting the property office.

A boy, taller than me, opens the door. He's in the same uniform I've seen the village children wear to school—a white top over brown shorts with ankle-length socks. Wire-rimmed glasses cover his deep-set eyes.

"Namaste." I glance over his shoulder into the house. "Is Ravi home?"

"You are my great-grandfather's guest, from America?" At my nod, his young face lights up. "I am Amit, his great-grandson." His English is formal, with each word clearly enunciated. "My great-grandfather speaks of you often. It is a pleasure to meet you."

"You live a few villages over?" I ask, remembering Ravi mentioning it.

"Yes." He motions me into the house. "Can I offer you some water or cane sugar juice? I will go to the market now for it."

"No, please." I stop him with a hand on his, touched by his nervousness. "Water would be wonderful, thank you." He uses a ladle to fill a glass from the boiled pot. "You just returned from school?"

"Yes. I come as often as possible to check on Dada," he says, using the Indian word for *grandfather*.

He sits cross-legged on the floor while offering me a folded chair. I join him instead, folding my legs beneath me. Though his face shows his surprise, he says nothing.

"What grade are you in?" I ask while sipping the lukewarm water.

"Eighth." A blush spreads across his cheeks. "They moved me up a grade because of my test scores." He fiddles with the strings of the rug we're sitting on. "Do you like India?"

"Yes, very much."

Though my leaving for India was an excuse to run away, I have since learned about the women who came before me. Understanding each event, each detail that shaped their lives, is helping me to better understand mine.

I once interviewed a New Age guru who spoke about how unfinished business from ancestors can trickle down to generations twice, even three times, removed. Actions in the present can help to correct the mistakes made in the past. And even if there is no absolution to be had, an understanding may help keep the same mistake from being repeated.

"Your Ravi Dada has been kind to me," I say.

"He told me once that people will forget many things, but they will never forget a person who shows them kindness."

"He is a very smart man," I say, sure that Ravi had been talking about my grandmother. "Maybe you take after him?"

"I would be blessed if that was true." He uses the bottom of his shirt to clean Ravi's extra pair of glasses. "How many children do you have?"

Though the reminder stings, I take no offense at his innocent question. All over the village, women my age are mothering three to four children. One will be draped over her while others follow on foot. "I am not as blessed as your Ravi Dada to have a lovely child like you in my life."

"That is charitable of you to say." Amit stands after checking the time on the small watch on his wrist. "I must go. My sister . . ." He pauses, shuffling his feet. "She has trouble carrying her books."

I rinse out our glasses while Amit gathers his things. I watch him leave, making note to ask Ravi more about his great-grandchildren.

"I've decided to keep the properties." I hold the phone close to my ear.

"I don't want them, Jaya. They don't matter to me." I start to tell her how much they mean, when she says, "I don't want them to hold you there."

Suddenly I understand. She sent the letter relinquishing her rights to bring me home. Not wanting to argue with her, I change the subject. "Your mother wrote stories, constantly." Though I never gravitated toward fiction before, now I yearn to read Amisha's tales. "She was desperate to write in English. She taught at an English school in exchange for lessons from a member of the Raj."

"Was she . . ." Mom pauses, and I can hear her struggling with the information. I wait patiently as she finds her voice. "Happy?"

It's the same question Ravi asked about Mom. "I think so." In the story, her children were her greatest source of joy. In spite of the struggles of the time, she never lost sight of what was important. "She was strong. You would have been proud of her." Mom takes an audible breath, and then there's silence. I continue telling her about the mother she never knew. "She had a garden. It's beautiful. Filled with every flower you can imagine and a beech tree from England. She spent so much of her time in it while she was learning English."

"Why is he telling you this story?" she whispers. "Why tell you all these things?"

"I think it has to do with what your father wanted to give you." When she stays silent, I ask, "You still don't want to know?"

"No story is going to change what happened."

Something in the way she says it catches my attention. "What happened, Mom?" There's a hitch in her voice, a sound of sorrow that has no definition. "Mom?"

"Please come home." At the sound of her crying, I fight my own tears. "There are things I have never told you."

"Then tell me now," I beg. Around me, the café's noise fades until the noise in my own head drowns it out. "What are you hiding?"

"Some secrets, Jaya," she says quietly, "are meant to stay hidden."

Unbidden, I think of Patrick. Our marriage seemed an open book until we started trying to have a child. At the time, my own counsel felt sounder than Patrick's or advice from doctors. I was sure I knew the right steps, the best path toward our goal. I didn't hear him because I didn't want to.

When our marriage fell apart and he turned to Stacey, I was sure he was at fault. Now I think of how much I kept from him—my fears, my hurts, and the emptiness that crowded everything and everyone else out. It felt safest to keep it from him. How could I explain to him my desperate need to have a child and my sense of failure when I could barely understand them myself?

"No, Mom," I say, surprising myself, "they aren't. Your fears are telling you what you want to hear, but they're hurting you more than helping."

"Is that why you're in India, Jaya?" she asks softly. "Because you're facing your fears? Or are you running from them?"

I try to see past her words to the desperation to bring me home. "I'm running from them." Her intake of breath tells me I've surprised us both by my admission. I want to tell her that because of the story I'm feeling better. That every day doesn't feel like a burden to be carried. There are even moments, lost in the story, when I forget about the ache that has taken a permanent place in me. "I didn't know what else to do. When Patrick and I broke up, it felt like there was nothing left of me."

"He called here, to ask about you," she says softly.

The part of me that wants to hold on to belief is overridden by the facts and logic. Patrick has moved on with Stacey, and in time my heart and mind will have to accept it. The wedding ring I still cannot take off weighs heavy on my finger.

"He called here too." I don't tell her that it was probably tying up loose ends. That Stacey might be pushing him so they have the freedom to move forward. "We're both moving on," I lie. He was my first love, and it is hard to accept we'll never be together again.

"Then why do I hear hurt in your voice?" she asks.

"I don't have a choice, Mom." I pause, and the silence lingers.

"I've read your pieces." She changes the subject, surprising me. "They are very good." No matter how much Mom disapproved of my career choice, she never missed reading my articles. It was a conundrum I never understood.

"Why did you want me to be a doctor?" I have never asked before, but now, given what I'm learning about my grandmother, the question feels imperative.

"Because your father is a doctor," she says, the answer seemingly enough. "He's happy, successful. I wanted the same for you."

It's such a simple answer. If I see it from her

perspective, the first time I have tried to, then it is a mother wanting the best for her child. "I love what I do, Mom," I say softly. "It's what I'm meant to do."

"Then I am grateful."

"Mom?" I think about my next words, choosing them carefully. "No matter what the story tells me, please know that I love you. I always have."

I hear her tears before she slowly tells me that she loves me too. Seconds later, I hear the dial tone. As I set down my own receiver, I start to wonder if understanding her is the key to understanding myself. I sit for hours with those thoughts in my head. When the café starts to empty out and the barista announces closing time, I return to Ravi.

AMISHA

TWENTY-EIGHT

Amisha rose early the day of the Holi celebration. An ancient festival of color, it celebrated the arrival of spring. Around the country, fields were in bloom, and hope was alive for a productive harvest. The celebration brought out all castes and both genders as people celebrated with colors and merrymaking. Lord Krishna's followers honored him by imitating his playfulness. Legend had it that as a child, Krishna would mercilessly tease the *gopis*—the wives and daughters of cow herders.

Amisha brushed her hair until it shone, though she knew it would be saturated soon enough with colored paint. She glanced at the small clock that Deepak had brought from the city. It was an extravagance, but he insisted they should have it.

"It's getting late." Amisha checked her reflection one last time in the small mirror that hung on the wall, before rushing out of the room. They would first attend the public bonfire as a family and then join the community in the crowded streets to spray colored water and throw powder at one another. "Is everyone ready?"

The villagers would watch as children climbed atop the open roofs designed for sleeping and sprayed colored powder on people below. The vibrant shades fell through the sky like a rainbow melting in the air. Everyone laughed as it saturated their hair and clothes. For Holi, all worries and most prejudices were set aside as everyone decorated one another with equal strokes.

"Each of you looks perfect, as always." Amisha gave her two oldest boys a tight hug before straightening their clothes. The boys slipped on their sandals by the front door. Both wore identical long ivory shirts over matching fitted pants.

"My friends are already playing, Mama." Jay pointed to the group waiting outside. In the meantime, Samir slipped out the front door with a quick wave. "I don't want to look perfect." Jay, resisting her ministrations, began to twitch. "I want to play."

"Then play." As he started to pull away, Amisha gently wrapped her arms around him. "But I can't have a good Holi if I don't get one more hug from my best middle son." She brought his resistant body close, and when she tightened her arms around him, he relented and gave her a kiss on the shoulder. "Thank you." She stood in the open doorway and watched with delight as the two boys joined their friends.

Deepak exited the kitchen with a glass of buttermilk. Similar to Jay and Samir, he wore a long white tunic shirt over slim-fitting pants. "They are off?"

"Yes." He had arrived last night on the train. Jay and Paresh had thrown themselves at him, while Samir shook his hand solemnly. "They are happy to have their father home with them on Holi."

For Amisha, her husband's absences continued to have little effect on her day-to-day life. With Ravi's and Bina's help, she easily ran the household and cared for the children. When Deepak was home, he still spent most of the time at work or with the other men in the village. Their interactions remained limited in scope and rare.

"I will follow them to the town." Deepak set his glass down. "Vikram invited the lieutenant to celebrate the holiday with the villagers," he said, clearly as an afterthought. "He told me last night."

Though Stephen had already told Amisha about the invitation days earlier at the school, she hadn't mentioned it. Amisha had tried early on telling Deepak about her conversations with Stephen, but he had laughed them off, asking what a British officer and she could possibly have to talk about. Thereafter, she never spoke about their conversations in the garden or the hours they spent alone together.

She didn't share with Deepak how conversations with Stephen came easily, or that even when they weren't talking, she thought about what she would say. Nor could she tell Deepak she was excited for Stephen to see the Holi colors and learn their significance. She kept to herself how excited she was to see Stephen's eyes light up at the spectacle. She was confident he would enjoy the celebration as much as she did, and she yearned to be near him as he experienced it. To celebrate the festival with a man who had come to be her friend in a manner she had never imagined.

She wanted to show Stephen, at the end of the night, when there was no colored water left to be thrown and arms were weary, how everyone came together for a final meal. Brahmins laughed while Jains and other upper castes passed out meals. For just one night, people were not divided based on social hierarchy. For Amisha, that was the most delightful sight of all. For that reason only, she convinced herself, she was excited to have Stephen attend. But with every want came the reminder that her feelings were not allowed. In her desire to spend time with the officer, she was violating every rule of her society and culture.

Now she stood on the doorstep and watched her husband follow their sons into town. In caring for Stephen, she was betraying Deepak and the vows she had made in front of God and her family. With her head hanging, she waited until the last minute to join the festivities.

As the men talked, Amisha watched Stephen from her place among the women. Stephen patted a man on the back as he laughed at something he said. Even though he was standing among Deepak's group of friends, Amisha swore he kept a subtle distance. A distance she had never felt when they were together.

Deepak's friends were highly educated in comparison to many of the villagers. Some had businesses within the village, while others were entrepreneurs, active with their own ventures. Success was the common thread that connected them. Within their community and the surrounding ones, they controlled the direction of the village because they made more money than others. Sir Vikram, driven by his personal chauffeur, joined them.

"Lieutenant." Vikram shook Stephen's hand in welcome. "It is gracious of you to join in our celebration."

"I'm pleased to be here, Vikram," Stephen replied. "I would have regretted missing out on such a joyous occasion."

The men continued their discussion of business and the state of the local economy. Amisha, overhearing them, realized they avoided any topic of the unrest between the British and the natives. For that, she was grateful.

Noticing Amisha watching the men, her friend Sujata followed her gaze. When she spotted Stephen, Sujata took in a sharp breath and then quickly glanced toward Amisha. "A member of the Raj here?"

"Yes." Amisha tore her gaze away to focus on Sujata. "He is a lieutenant from the school." Though Amisha had never spoken about her time at the school, she knew in the small village it had become common knowledge. "He is here to celebrate Holi with us."

Sujata glared at Stephen. "He is not Indian. It is not his place to be here," she said, her scorn apparent. "The soldiers need to return to where they came from."

"England?" Amisha kept her voice light.

"The scourge of the earth."

"They are not all the same." Amisha hid her dismay at Stephen's being called such a thing. She bit back her true thoughts and said instead, "Some of them are benevolent."

"You spend time at the school, so now you like them? What—do you wish you were one of them?" Sujata raised her voice, catching the attention of the other women. "Our Amisha wishes she were British."

Amisha had to tread lightly. If she argued with them, they would continue to question her feelings. If she said nothing, they would rile her until she broke her silence. She glanced again at Stephen as he spoke to Deepak.

"I wish the soldiers gone as much as you do." The lie came easily to her, and she hoped it sounded convincing. She faced forward, turning her back on the men. "But they are not. Maybe if we learn from them, we will be strong enough to fight them?"

"Is that what you're doing, Amisha?" Another friend, Tara, joined the conversation. "Learning so you can free us from the Raj? Deepak bhai has been gone too much," Tara said, calling Deepak "brother" as was conventionally done. "Amisha is losing her mind with her free time." She wrapped an arm around Amisha's shoulders and pulled her in close for a quick hug.

These women were some of Amisha's oldest friends from the village. Many of them had been married around the same time, and they had become close over the years. But no matter how much they shared, none of them seemed to understand Amisha's desire to write.

Amisha laughed with them, relieved that the moment had passed. "I'm at the school so I don't have to spend my entire day with you ladies."

The women moved on to other topics while making their way toward the buffet tables. Every family brought entrées to share. The women began serving the food to the children. Holi often lasted two nights, but this first night was the height of the celebration.

Amisha glanced toward Stephen, and his eyes caught hers. His gaze ran over the red and blue paint that covered her sari before drifting toward the yellow that streaked her hair. He took a step toward her before seeming to remember where he was. Regret filled her throat. Instead, he raised his hand slightly and waved. Amisha readied to return his greeting, when she saw Deepak. She remembered her place, and regret overwhelmed her. Her face dropped, and she didn't return the greeting.

When one of the ladies asked for help, Amisha quickly turned away. She began to uncover the rest of the dishes, when she overheard Deepak say to Stephen, "My wife has been very happy in your school."

"We are happy to have her," Stephen murmured. Amisha heard the strain in his voice and knew he was worried about her reaction. "She is an asset."

"You are being charitable." Deepak's laugh was quick and easy, as if the two were old friends instead of new acquaintances. "It is hard to imagine my wife a teacher in a British school."

Dejected at Deepak's statement, Amisha strained to hear Stephen's response, but the clatter of dishes was too loud. Soon enough, the men joined them at the table for plates of food. Stephen stayed near the end, watching the interactions.

Amisha took her place behind the table and began to fill the plates. Suddenly ashamed, she kept her focus on serving everyone. Stephen knew her to be the woman who demanded he teach her more after they finished their lessons. She was the woman who taught him to dance and threatened to push him off the bench when he teased her. The woman Stephen knew was not limited by boundaries but instead soared free in the world she created as a storyteller.

After everyone was served and the women began eating, Stephen approached her. "Are you all right?" he asked softly. He kept a safe distance between them to avoid attention.

"Yes," she murmured.

Her glance strayed toward Deepak, and his gaze followed hers. Expressing understanding, his eyes were filled with apology.

"I'm sorry. I shouldn't have intruded on your family event," he said. "I should go."

"I'm happy you are here," she admitted quickly. She paused before saying, "It is just that I am not allowed to be."

Amisha imagined how he must see her now—subservient and anchored to the expectations of her world. Now, having seen her in her true light, he must be regretting the time wasted on teaching her. Her heart aching, she quickly filled a plate with a mix of nuts and raisins and a pudding of wheat, brown sugar, and butter.

"*Prasad*?" she asked quietly. When Stephen hesitated, Amisha pushed the plate toward him. "I made it, but it is still good."

As he reached for it, his fingers brushed against hers underneath the plate, entangling with them, just for a moment. Her eyes met his, confused and unsure.

"I'm grateful to have come today," he said quietly, out of earshot of everyone else. "Seeing you happy among your loved ones reminds me how lucky I am to have your friendship."

"As I am to have yours," Amisha breathed, grateful to him for giving their interactions a definition and boundaries. She sighed in relief and watched happily as he began to feast upon her *prasad*, clearing the plate of all the food.

TWENTY-NINE

Amisha was in her classroom when the door opened. She glanced up to see Neema standing in the doorway, her face covered by the edge of her sari. She wore a long-sleeved blouse, and the skirt beneath her sari reached the edge of her ankles.

"Neema." Amisha rushed toward her, stopping short of pulling the girl into an embrace. "It's been months, Beti." She squeezed Amisha's hand lightly. "How are you?"

Neema grimaced before pulling her hand out of Amisha's. "I'm fine." Her voice, though strong, lacked the conviction it had when she was in class. "My father told me you asked about me." She turned away, keeping her features hidden. "I begged him to allow me to come."

"Beti?" Amisha shut the classroom door quietly. "What happened?"

Neema shook her head no, and all of Amisha's motherly instincts kicked in. She tenderly pulled the edge of Neema's sari away and bit back her shock. The entire right side of Neema's face was wrinkled and deep brown from burns. She cupped a shaking hand over Neema's cheek.

"It doesn't matter." Neema moved away, forcing Amisha to release her. She wrapped her arms around her waist. Everything about her was broken and defeated.

"It does to me," Amisha said, her heart hurting for the child. "Please."

Tears began to flow down the young girl's cheeks. Amisha laid an arm around her shoulder, encouraging her. Slowly, between broken gasps, Neema said, "Before we pray, we light a fire, an *agni*." The edge of her sari floated over her shoulders, revealing the burns on her neck and upper shoulder. Amisha blinked back her tears and listened carefully. "The Agni is the deity that represents all other deities. It is the messenger of the gods. As the fire burns, it becomes our link with the supreme gods."

It was the reason *diyas* were lit before every prayer session and why the temples had dozens of *diyas* burning at any given time. It was also why bodies were cremated after death. The fire served as the gate for the soul to enter heaven.

"The fire was supposed to be my bridge. My escape from this world," Neema cried, tears rushing down her young face.

All the breath left Amisha's body. She struggled against her own tears as she brought the sobbing girl into her arms. "You set yourself on fire?" Amisha whispered.

"It was the only choice I could make."

Neema tore at the buttons on her sleeves, revealing both her forearms. Each one was burned far worse than her face. The skin had turned deep black, and the wrinkles reached beyond her elbow to her upper arm. Similar scarring covered her belly.

"Now I am less than I was before." Neema swiped at her tears. "He no longer wants me." She covered her face with her hands as she continued to sob. "My fiancé no longer believes me worthy."

Amisha held her as the sobs shook her young body. Minutes seemed like hours as the girl cried her heartbreak into Amisha's arms. All Amisha could do was hold her, their silence filling the emptiness. Drained of her tears, Neema stepped back and struggled to rebutton her blouse.

"Neema." Amisha ached for the young girl whose life was forever changed. "Beti . . ."

"When my body caught on fire, the pain was excruciating," Neema said, her voice filled with self-loathing. "My soul fought death. My brain demanded I scream for help. That's how they found me. Because I begged to be saved." She wrenched open the door and stared into the empty hallway. "Now, every day, my heart wonders why."

Amisha was quiet as she and Stephen walked in the empty garden. She was oblivious to the sun that beat down on them. Stephen had been standing in front of his office door when Neema exited the classroom. He had waited silently while Amisha saw the young girl into the rickshaw.

"Can we walk?" Amisha had asked softly once Neema had left. He immediately agreed and followed her outside.

"What happened?" Stephen asked now that they were alone.

"She set herself on fire." Her voice cracked, and the tears that she had been unable to cry in front of Neema now spilled down her cheeks. "She wanted to die."

"My god." Sadness tinged his words along with resignation.

"She cried out for help." Amisha picked up a small rock and threw it against the trunk of a tree. "So she's alive but broken." Angry, she took another rock and did the same thing. "She wanted to escape her fate. Death seemed the only way to make that happen." She folded her arms over her midsection. "The assignment—I told them to make a choice."

"Amisha, you didn't do this." Stephen reached out but closed his hand into a fist before letting it fall without having touched her. His tie hung loosely around his neck. "This was not your doing."

"Someone is responsible," Amisha argued. "Who takes blame for what happened to her?" When Stephen remained quiet, she added, "I could have done something to stop her." Her guilt and sadness weighed heavy. "I should have done something."

"How?" He laid a hand on her shoulder and squeezed. Amisha tensed and then relaxed into his touch. "There was nothing you or anyone could have done to save that girl." Frustrated, he admitted, "If you had stepped in, there would have been repercussions."

Amisha knew she was fortunate to be at the school. With the privilege came the knowledge that she had to tread carefully. Never could she cross a line with the students that would require Stephen's intervention. Yet right now it all felt like excuses, and she was ashamed for not having stepped up.

"Her story was a cry for help," Amisha admitted. "And I didn't heed the call."

"Neema's parents wouldn't have let you in," Stephen reminded her.

What Neema did wasn't unheard of. In their world, each person, in her own way, had to find her path and a way to navigate it. If it was an unpaved path, then the person chanced walking alone, abandoned by those who believed they knew better.

"I could have told her there was another way."

"Is there?" Stephen picked up the rock Amisha had thrown. "When I was a child, I spent hours fighting with a sword and shield. My father asked me who I was battling. 'Preparing for bad guys,' I told him. He said sometimes our fiercest battles are the ones we fight with ourselves."

"What did he mean?"

Pensive, Stephen thought before answering. "Everyone fights their wars. If my time here has taught me anything, it's that you don't always know who your enemy is. But if you're lucky, no matter who the adversary, you'll stand tall while fighting." Stephen handed the rock to her. "Neema was desperate. I think she fought the only way she knew how."

THIRTY

"Please tell me why." Ravi had never requested time off before. Now he was asking for a full week. "Are you ill?" Before he could answer, Amisha leaned over the laundry they were folding and touched his forehead with a finger. "You don't have a fever," she informed him.

"Maybe it is a good thing you were not allowed to attend university." He swatted her hand away. He handed a stack of towels to Bina to place in the cupboard. "If you had chosen to heal the sick, I fear they would not have survived one day in your care."

"You protest every time I touch you, so I dare not check your fever with my palm," Amisha returned.

"If the neighbors saw you laying your hand on an untouchable, I think I would meet with an unforeseen death as I slept," Ravi commented. "And if they knew you feed them meals and sweets from food cooked by an untouchable, you would meet the same fate."

Having rejoined them after putting away the towels, Bina said, "Because of you, Ravi, Shrimati is believed to be the best cook in the village."

"When I am on my deathbed, I will reveal my secret to our friends," Amisha promised.

"You'd better hope you have lost your hearing before your life. Their screams of fury will be loud," Ravi returned.

"Your attempt at changing the conversation has been noted, and may I say well done?" Amisha grinned at him. "Now, answer my question. Why the time off?"

"I need the rest," Ravi hedged. "This work has tired me out."

"Lying is not your best skill," Amisha decided, never having heard him tell an untruth before. "They say practice makes perfect. Keep trying, and I will tell you how you are doing."

"A week." Ravi sighed in frustration. "How can that be so difficult to accommodate?"

"This circle we keep going around in is making me dizzy." She brought out a stack of red peppers and scattered them on a plate to dry. Once dried, they would be crushed into flakes. "Please tell me so we can get off this track."

"He's getting married," Bina answered. "Ow," she cried when Ravi swatted her with a hand towel.

"Married?" Amisha's eyes widened with joy. "Really?"

"My parents have insisted," Ravi said hesitantly. "Because of you, we have been blessed with income. They want grandchildren."

He spent every waking moment in their home, doing any job that was necessary. For his dedication, Amisha paid him triple the amount he was due. With the money, Ravi had bought a home for himself, his parents, and his siblings. They had never had one before. Though it was small, he told Amisha it was their castle.

"This is wonderful news. Why didn't you tell me?" Amisha's mind whirred with gift ideas. A party in their honor and food for the Brahmins. They would need new furniture for their home. It was just a matter of maneuvering around him. "She must be beautiful." She nudged Bina. "Only the best for our handsome Ravi. Right, Bina?"

Amisha wanted to hug him to show her joy at the thought of his marriage. Yet she couldn't. Not when the wrath of any passerby could change their lives forever. Even alone, she never embraced him. So she settled for a smile and clasping her hands in thanks for his good news.

"I am lucky," Ravi said, looking overjoyed.

"It is she who is blessed. To have caught you is the best prize for a woman."

"I asked . . ." Ravi hesitated, suddenly reserved. "I asked for her to have your heart and generosity."

Amisha stopped what she was doing to stare at him. Her heart constricted. Chara's words from long ago echoed in her ear. *Find someone you can trust.* Fate gave her the gift of someone who had become her close friend and confidant.

"I am the privileged one," Amisha said, all

traces of playfulness gone. "Having you as my friend in this life assures me I did much good in my last one. Few are so blessed."

That afternoon, Amisha sat quietly while Sujata, Tara, and other women from the village discussed the recent happenings in the village. Amisha and Ravi had prepared *kachori* for the gathering. The round balls filled with yellow *moong daal*, black pepper, red chili powder, and ginger paste had taken all night to finish. Ravi accompanied it with a large bowl of *chevda*, a combination of fried lentils, peanuts, spices, and chickpea flour noodles.

They spent the afternoon discussing the best places to shop and the quality of the silk. "The city is the only place to shop," they agreed.

Tara took a sip of her coconut water. "Amisha, this food is excellent. You went out of your way."

"Thank you." Amisha didn't tell them that Ravi had helped. "It's my pleasure to have your company." Just as she started to say something else, there was a knock on the door. She excused herself and opened it to find Neema on her doorstep.

Shocked, Amisha ushered her in. It had been weeks since she had come to the school. "How are you, Beti?"

Neema kept her face hidden under the security of her sari. Spotting the other women, she said,

"I'm sorry. I didn't mean to interrupt. I can come another time."

"We should be leaving." Amisha's friends began to gather their things. "We need to start dinner for the children."

Neema moved to the side, away from their scrutiny, while they took their leave. Once the house was empty, she pulled out a cheaply made envelope from her bag. In perfect letters, Neema had written Amisha's name on the front. It was an engraved invitation to Neema's wedding that weekend.

"I came to give you this."

"You're getting married?" Amisha asked, shocked.

Neema wrung her hands together, the burned one intertwined with the smooth skin of the other. "I played with fire like a child," she whispered. "Now I must accept the consequences like an adult." She started to speak and then stopped, swallowing twice before explaining. "They have found me a groom three villages over. It is a small ceremony in two days, but I hope you can come."

"What does he do?" Amisha's palms began to sweat with fear. She knew the only type of man willing to take a disfigured bride would be one who could use her burns to invoke the sympathy of others. Though Amisha dreaded the answer, she waited.

"He begs," Neema said, confirming Amisha's fears. "For a small dowry, he has agreed to marry me and provide for me whatever he can."

"Come work for me." Amisha's mind raced with ideas. She refused to accept begging as Neema's only option. "You can have a job here."

"I can't." Neema blinked rapidly to keep her tears from spilling over. "The first day of class, you told us the story of the man and the bird." She stared at the floor. "There was only one small hole from which to breathe. We had to decide what happened next."

"I remember." Amisha's heart ached with sorrow. She knew Neema had the talent and potential to become an accomplished writer, and yet she would live her life as a beggar.

"I was sure the man needed to worry about his own life," Neema said. Most of the children had written a similar ending. "But now I understand he was at fault. He should have cradled the bird and offered him the fresh air."

"What about the man?" Amisha asked.

"His fate was decided the day he built the house. If the house hadn't collapsed with the earthquake, it would have fallen another time. But with his final action, he should have saved the innocent bird from the consequences of his own mistakes."

"Neema?" Amisha tried to understand the

story's connection to her offer for Neema to work for her.

"Your offer is generous, but I cannot accept it," Neema whispered. "My parents' status in the community would be diminished over time by my disfigurement if I work here and continue to live with them." Neema swiped at her tears. "I will be viewed as a bad omen. My brother is young, and his life is ahead of him. His future cannot suffer because of the choice I made." She offered Amisha a small smile. "It is a blessing that I will no longer be my parents' burden." She opened the door. "I hope you can come to the wedding."

Amisha rushed to school. When she arrived, Stephen was waiting for her at the entrance. Without a word he motioned her into his office. "Are you all right?" he asked.

"She's married," Amisha answered. She had come directly from the small wedding that Neema's parents had held. It was limited to immediate family and the *pujari* who presided over the ceremony. "I watched her walk seven times around the fire and leave with him after." Amisha wanted to throw something or hit someone. Instead, she paced the small space. "No one shed a tear. They simply watched her walk away," she cried.

"There's nothing that you could do," Stephen

said gently. He ran his hand over the back of his neck.

"What about the British?" Amisha faced him. It was the same argument they had before, but Amisha couldn't help herself. All she could see was Neema's pain and the fear for her future. "What can you do?"

"Amisha . . ."

"I know," she said, assuming his answer. "It's not your place." The small room started to close in around her, bereft of oxygen. She was angry and wanted to lash out. "My class is waiting."

"Maybe you should take the day off. You're hurting." Stephen stood between her and the door. Amisha saw his sympathy but couldn't react to it.

"I'm not the one destined to spend the rest of my life on the streets." Amisha moved past him and out the door. She felt him watching her.

In the classroom, all the students were already seated and waiting patiently. "My apologies for the delay." Amisha began to read aloud her planned assignment, but Neema kept crowding out all other thoughts. She shut her notebook and faced the class.

"Today, we are going to do something different," she said. Stephen slipped into the classroom from the rear door and stood against the back wall, the students not noticing him. Amisha ignored him and continued with the idea that had just occurred to her. "We are a colony of England that is ruled by a king and queen. Each of you is learning in a British school. But we are Indian, and we have many customs and behaviors that are different from theirs." Amisha stole a glance at Stephen, who watched her quietly.

"Your friend and my former student, Neema, was married this morning."

She reined in her emotions, knowing she walked a fine line. An inappropriate display of emotions would force Stephen to censure her, but at the same time these students were part of the future. They were the ones who could help bring about change. They could give an alternate ending to Neema's story. Offer another option to anyone who wanted something different— something other than what was decided for them.

"Was she happy?" a girl in the back asked.

Amisha shut her eyes at the question. Few, if any, students knew about Neema's accident. Her brother had kept the secret from his classmates, and Neema had been primarily confined to her house afterward.

"She accepted that marriage was her next step."

"What is the assignment?" Bored, a male in the front began to scribble on his paper.

Amisha thought about it. "We are going to write about how our country would change if a woman was our leader." In the back, Stephen straightened, his eyes intent on her. She ignored him as another student raised her hand. "Yes, Gita?"

"If the Queen was our leader?"

"No, not the Queen. Not the Raj. A woman born in India and raised with Indian social standards and belief systems. Each of you must imagine an Indian woman who defies those customs, who defies those norms, and leads our country."

"Like Gandhi?"

"Gandhi is fighting for our independence," Amisha said. "I am talking about the leader of an independent India. Tell me about this woman and how she would rule us."

"How is that a story?" One of the older boys was confused.

"Is it something you can imagine happening?" Amisha asked, her voice harsher than she meant it to be. Everyone stayed quiet. "That's why it's a story. Because it's fiction."

Stephen left the room as quietly as he had entered. Amisha continued with the class, making sure the students understood the assignment before giving them time to write.

Amisha read the students' stories after they left. She was proud that each one had tried his best to imagine a situation where a woman ruled India. Their stories, though sometimes comical, were sincere. She enclosed them in a large envelope and was sealing it when Stephen walked in.

"An Indian leader?" He thrust his hands into his pockets.

"I was surprised to see you in the classroom."

"I would imagine. If I knew you were going to encourage an uprising, I would have reconsidered my teaching offer."

"You fear a woman leader?" Amisha asked. She didn't realize she was holding her breath until his answer led her to exhale in relief.

"No." Stephen watched her carefully. "But I do have to worry about one of my teachers advocating an Indian leader to our students."

"I wasn't." Amisha paused, frustrated. "I wasn't taking a political stance. This is for Neema." She held up the envelope, her anger vibrating off her. "I wanted to send her something that would show her she shouldn't give up. That she can still hope."

"And you thought the children's stories would do that?" Stephen asked. Though his voice held no judgment, Amisha felt silly and small nonetheless.

"It was a ridiculous thought." She threw the envelope onto the desk.

"No, it wasn't." He took the envelope and wrote Neema's name on the front of it. "I'll have a courier take this to her new home."

"Thank you." His consideration surprised Amisha.

He bent so they were eye level. "Amisha, I'm

sorry about what happened to her. No matter what I said earlier, please know that."

"It wasn't fair." Amisha hung her head, her eyes filling with tears. "She deserved better." But Neema's story wasn't so different from others in their time and place. As much as Amisha wanted to nurture her, encourage her, Neema could have done little with her future.

"I know," Stephen said, watching her quietly.

THIRTY-ONE

A few days after Neema's wedding, Amisha still couldn't get the young girl out of her mind. She hurt every time she thought of her. She and Stephen spent hours in the garden talking about everything and nothing. It was as if he understood her need to lose herself in mundane topics to forget about the girl she couldn't help.

"Your brother?" Amisha asked as they walked. Ever since he had told Amisha about him, she yearned to ask him more. "Did you spend a lot of time with each other?"

Stephen didn't answer right away, and Amisha wondered if the topic was still too difficult. She started to tell him it was fine, when he said, "We were friends, and that was saying a lot for us." Stephen seemed to withdraw as he remembered home. "As children, we fought as all boys did. Forgiveness was offered with a tackle to the ground and punches to vulnerable body parts." As adults, he explained, they had become close and found they had more in common than just the blood coursing through their veins. "For that, I am grateful."

"You were not expecting to be?" Amisha asked.

"My parents didn't talk about their emotions,"

Stephen said. "I assumed my brother and I would follow suit."

"You're glad you didn't," Amisha said, sensing the affection he felt for the man he had lost. "Family is important." She remembered what he had told her about his father. "Your father made sure you were sent to India instead of the war. He must love you very much."

"A soldier in India." Stephen didn't bother to hide his anger. "My father wished for me to be yet another guardian of the King's pilfered treasure?"

"Is that what you think?" Amisha asked. It was the first time Stephen had admitted that India didn't belong to his home country. "That we deserve our freedom?"

"If I say yes, then I betray my people. If I say no, do I betray you?" he asked, silencing her.

"No," Amisha told him finally. "India's freedom doesn't guarantee everyone is free." Both seemed to understand she was talking about Neema.

"Is that what you want?" he asked. "Your freedom?"

"What would I do with it?" Amisha tried to make light of her words. "I'm speaking without thinking." Before he could say more or push her for a deeper answer, she changed the subject. "Do you regret your time here?"

"Not anymore." Stephen held her gaze while

he spoke. "But I miss my friends and sometimes my family"—he winked—"back at home." He paused. "You don't see your family very often, do you?" They had shared their histories in one of their many conversations.

"No," she answered. "After a woman marries, there's little reason for her to have contact." Amisha had learned to subvert the ache anytime she thought of them. They had been her entire existence until she was handed off in marriage and forgotten.

"Do they live far?" Stephen asked.

"By train it would not be far. But the distance doesn't matter. It's just not a priority."

With the children to take care of and Deepak out of town, it wasn't easy to make the trip. And though she yearned for the mother who bore her and then gave her away, she knew her mother had never really known her. Her dreams, her desires, became a secret kept well hidden.

"This is the woman's choice?" Stephen asked.

"No, by tradition," Amisha said. She wondered at the surprised look on his face. "Is it not that way in your country?"

"No," he answered. Amisha remembered his telling her that both of his grandparents lived near his childhood home. "Why separate a woman from her family after marriage?"

As a young girl, Amisha had watched her friends handed off to unknown families in marriage. Only years, if not months, older than Amisha, they would weep and beg not to be given away. Plead to be allowed to remain with their family and siblings and continue living in the only world they knew.

"So that the woman can begin to have children. Preferably boys." The dowry demand increased with age. A young daughter-in-law could begin producing sons immediately. Large, extended families crowded into small homes. Sons and their new families lived with their parents and unwed siblings.

"They help to support the father," Stephen said. After living in India for this amount of time, he was familiar with the customs. "Provide for the family."

"The marriage and bearing sons is all that matters." The threat of divorce or being banished always hung over a bride if she didn't fulfill her customary duties. "The wife's natural family serves no purpose. It's a waste of her time and productivity." Amisha tried to hide her dismay at the practice, but when she saw the sympathy on Stephen's face, she knew he saw through her.

"I'm sorry," Stephen said. He moved toward her before stopping.

"That's the way it is." Amisha valued her culture and its traditions that demanded unconditional love of children and family, and yet there were imperfections that she couldn't ignore. "There has to be a reason for it, right?" she asked, but didn't wait for an answer. "All traditions have to originate from somewhere. Maybe there was a need for the behavior at the time."

"That's very philosophical," Stephen teased, but Amisha saw the admiration in his eyes. "It makes sense. Women are the only ones who can give birth, leaving men free to provide for the family."

"What about when those roles are no longer necessary?" Amisha asked. Unable to ever have such a conversation with Deepak, she relished every moment of it. "What if tradition is just an excuse to keep things as they always have been?"

"You're talking about Ravi and Bina?" Stephen asked, seeming to read her mind. She had spoken often about her frustration with the limits imposed on them. "The temple still won't allow them in?"

"Among other things." Amisha knew many of the untouchables feared for their lives. They didn't dare to anger villagers for fear of the repercussions. "Sometimes it feels like an excuse to be unkind. When everyone is doing it, maybe it feels acceptable?"

"There are few consequences if society accepts the behavior," Stephen agreed.

"It would take a great person to stand against the norm." Amisha once again thought of Gandhi and his constant words of freedom. "Your king and queen seem to have found all the excuses they need to control India. Maybe they are no different from the rest of us."

"And I am their loyal foot soldier," he said, shocking her. "Using my role to keep the Indians in their place?" he seemed to ask himself. When she started to respond, he asked, "What would you do differently? If you were me?"

She imagined him saying no to coming to India, and her heart broke at the thought. "Nothing. It is easy to speak words, but one man," she said, pausing slightly, "or woman, cannot change an entire people's thinking." She struggled to make clear her thoughts. "I didn't mean for you not to be here." She took a deep breath and stole a glance at him, hoping he understood what she really meant to say. But his silence willed her to continue. "I would keep things exactly as they are so you could remain here." She fell silent after her admission, once again afraid she had said something out of line or crossed an unspoken boundary.

"Sacrifice India's freedom for tutoring lessons?" Stephen tried to lighten the air between them. "Your people may disown you."

"My people are fighting a battle no one should ever have to—the freedom to be themselves." Amisha knew that answer was too simple. Before Stephen could call her on it, she continued. "But with all the anger and hatred, it is impossible to see the good that came with the bad."

"Then why fight?" Stephen asked. He motioned toward the garden and the school. "We are offering the best of what we have. Better roads, schools. India had none of this before."

Amisha knew he wasn't arguing with her but instead valuing her opinion. It made her heart soar. "At what cost?" She thought of the struggles she read about—the oppression and dejection felt by even the strongest Indians. "We can't define ourselves as long as someone else gives us our definition."

"Is that what we're doing?" Stephen asked. He went silent as he thought. "Are we forcing Indians to become who we need you to be?" Before Amisha could disagree or agree, he asked, "Will freedom give you the right to be who you want to be? Will Ravi begin to be treated as an equal rather than an untouchable?"

"No," Amisha answered honestly. As much as she wanted to believe that independence for India meant independence for everyone, she knew it might not be. "But it's a start, right?" Above them, a flock of birds flew in formation, filling the sky with their calls. "When you are pushed down, it seems you have two choices. To lie down, or stand up and ask why."

"Like you?" Stephen asked. At her confusion, he explained, "When you talked about attending school, you said it was because you wanted more." He tilted his head to the side and considered her. "Do you always stand up for what you want?"

Amisha stared at him, amazed he had remembered her words from the conversation she had forgotten. "I think it's foolish not to stand, though it's not always the wisest choice. Especially if the consequence may hurt those you love. Neema stood up the best way she knew how, and the cost is one she never would have imagined."

"It is not this way everywhere," he said softly. "You have choices."

"No?" Amisha knew in the cities that there were more rights for women and untouchables. But in her small village, that world seemed far away. "Where? England?"

"England still has far to go, but a woman is considered equal to a man in daily life." He clasped his hands together and stretched them over his head. "Not to say there are not men who would prefer this way of life. A woman at the beck and call of a man can be a dream come true," he teased.

"Your dream?" Amisha challenged.

"I've never thought about it. Marriage seems a distant future, but when it comes time, I imagine I would want an equal." Stephen's gaze on her was unwavering. "Someone who is both my friend and a confidante."

"That sounds wonderful," Amisha admitted. Afraid to delve deeper, she nonetheless asked, "She would be English?" As soon as the words were out, she wanted to take them back, but it was too late.

The question hung between them. "Yes, I think so," Stephen stammered, clearly embarrassed. "An Englishman marrying an Indian?"

"No, that wouldn't work, would it?" It was unheard of. The members of the Raj were here to civilize, not socialize with the Indians. "Your parents wouldn't approve."

"No." Stephen sounded torn. He ran his hand through his hair, avoiding her gaze. "What would you want? If you could have chosen?"

"I—I don't know." Amisha turned away, unable to imagine romance, or a man who valued her beyond her ability to provide children and keep a home.

"You don't know?"

They were treading on uneven ground with an invisible boundary between them. Both were defined by their culture. Amisha had no choice but to bow to the conventions of her society. The few rules that she defied, she did so hoping there would be no cost.

"I would want someone who believed in me," Amisha finally answered.

"That's it?" he asked, amazed.

"That would be more than I could ever hope

for. It is what I would want for my daughter if I ever have one."

"A daughter, hmm?" Stephen smiled.

"But as things are," Amisha said, hesitating, "I don't know if here would be the right place for her."

Stephen seemed shocked. "You would not want her in India?"

"If India became a place where she could choose her path, then yes, I would want her here. It would be her home. We . . ." She paused, thinking of Deepak. "We would be her family." Amisha considered her world as it was now. The choices that didn't exist. "But I would want her to have more than I have."

"More?" Stephen asked, encouraging her to continue.

"A place where she can be anything," Amisha said. "Where her dreams could transport her anywhere and her only limits would be the ones she imposes on herself." She thought about it. "Do you know of such a place?"

"In England . . ." Stephen paused as they both remembered his earlier statement.

"She would be a brown," Amisha said, using the word many of the British used. He flinched but didn't correct her.

"Maybe America?" Stephen shrugged when Amisha glanced at him questioningly. "I've never been. But my brother . . ." He paused. "He made me promise to visit one day."

314

"When you do, you'll have to tell me how it is," Amisha said. Neither commented that once he left India, there was little chance of his returning. "Whether it is a place where my daughter would be happy."

"I promise."

JAYA

THIRTY-TWO

Ravi gathers flowers and fruits for the temple and arranges them carefully on the tray. He asked me yesterday if I wanted to go to the temple that my grandmother attended. It was common practice before the Holi celebration. Eager to see where she prayed, I immediately said yes.

"You believe in God?" Though I am not religious, the little faith I had was shaken after the multiple miscarriages. It was hard for me to accept that a kind god could be so cruel. After hearing Ravi's stories, it's even more difficult.

"I came into this world not believing. How could I?" he asks quietly. "My people are judged and sentenced by individuals for infractions that break no laws." He lowers his head, and I can see him struggling against the pain. "The past could be forgotten if not for present-day reminders." Lost in thought, he pauses before saying, "But the compassion of humans forced me to believe that there must be something or someone more powerful to have placed such perfection on this earth."

"You're talking about my grandmother."

"I am talking about her heart," he corrects. "As a human, she was imperfect, as all humans are. But her heart always fought to do right by others, even when she was not doing right by herself. Therein lies her perfection."

"She was lucky to have a friend who thought so highly of her," I say, touched by his words.

"Because of her, I live a life I could never have imagined. It is I who am lucky," he says before falling silent.

I start to ask him more, when he glances past me. His eyes glaze over, similar to the times he mentioned seeing Amisha, and his expression fills with guilt and apology. He shakes his head and comes out of his daze. In seconds, he has shuttered his emotions until his face is blank. He resumes walking with Rokie at his heels.

"When I was a student, I witnessed an exhumation of a generations-old body," I start, breaking the silence. "In this cemetery, the whites were buried separately from the blacks." Ravi listens carefully as we walk. "All the headstones spoke of how loved the person was and of his roles in life—parent, child, grandparent. Not one mentioned the color of the person."

"It did not matter in death," Ravi says.

"No. All that was left of the person was bones. The same as everyone else." I wondered if they knew that at the end, we are all the same, just a body with only our actions and others' memories to define who we are. "Whatever separates us in life has no relevance in death."

"Your grandmother once wrote a poem about

the only thing we take from life to death being the people whose lives we have touched. Everything else is a façade." He pauses midstride to glance at me. "I think your grandmother would have been very proud to know you." There is joy mixed with regret in his words that I don't understand.

"Thank you," I say, grateful. I take the tray from Ravi's hands so he can walk with his cane. "My mom doesn't remember you. How can that be?"

Ravi falls quiet. "I was not there for your mother's upbringing," he says, stumbling in his explanation. "Shortly after Amisha's death, other servants took my place in the home." His expression tightens momentarily, and the pace of his stride quickens. Without facing me, Ravi changes the subject. "Your childhood—what was it like?"

I hold back from pushing for more. "My dad was busy with work." Which meant it was usually just Mom and me. As a child, I attributed her distance to not caring, but now, given the story, I'm questioning my assumptions. "I had a good life." In comparison with the children I see on the streets, I was blessed. "I was always taken care of."

"You said Lena is happy?" Ravi asks slowly.

Still curious about the reason for the question, I try my best to be honest. "She isn't unhappy." His face tightens as he listens carefully. "My dad loves her very much." I pause. "She and I aren't very close."

"Why?" he asks quietly.

"I don't know," I admit. "She wasn't ever cruel, just distant."

"I'm sorry," he breathes.

"Don't be." I smile to lighten the mood. "If this trip has shown me anything, it is that I am lucky to have the life I do. I'm not sure I knew that before now."

He nods, seeming to accept my words. "You are good at reporting?" Ravi asks, making me laugh.

"Sometimes," I answer as honestly as I can. "It's important to me that I try my best." My work had fulfilled me and given me meaning. It was only after the miscarriages that I wondered about my place in the world. "But I needed some time off. Coming here allowed me that."

"The loss you mentioned," Ravi says.

"I had three miscarriages." I quickly wipe the tears away as they start to fall. Though the darkness of the days after still lingers, it doesn't hold the same bite it did before. "I wanted to give birth. I wanted to be a mother." During that time, it was all I had wanted. The process had overwhelmed every aspect of our lives. "Not being able to broke my heart."

"And your husband?"

"Patrick? He found a way to heal." After the first miscarriage, Patrick immediately went back to work, while I struggled at my job. I initially envied his ability to get past the loss but then began to resent his ability to lose himself in his career and everyday life. It never occurred to me to wonder how he felt about losing me to my grief. "I couldn't find the strength to. With their loss, I lost myself. And no matter how hard I tried, I couldn't find my way back."

Now, every time I see a child, I remember how much Patrick wanted a family. It was as much as I did, but I couldn't see his pain past mine. In hindsight, I try to imagine another path or steps to have prevented our fate. I was always so sure of our marriage and our life. Now I think of a life without him, and it feels empty.

"We're separated," I tell him quietly. "When I go back, I assume we'll start divorce proceedings."

"We are here," Ravi says, his words barely audible. He slows down and points ahead of us.

The exquisite structure is breathtaking. Ten pillars rounded from aged marble connect to a pyramid roof carved with elaborate designs of artistic beauty. The pillars are evenly spaced, with no walls to obstruct the smell of rich jasmine incense wafting through the air. Multiple tiers of small pavilions lead to a domed shrine from which hundreds of small bells hang. The temple sits high above the ground, with forty steps leading up to its frameless doorway.

"It is . . ." At a loss for words, I stare at the structure. The temple feels ancient. I imagine I can hear whispers of prayers from years past in the currents of air that pass by us. Ghosts of husbands and wives, and young love and old loss, linger in the air. "When was it built?"

"Many hundreds of years ago." Ravi stares at it as if seeing it for the first time.

"How often do you come here?" I wonder why he hasn't brought me before.

"There was a time I was not allowed," he answers honestly. "The first time I came was before your grandmother died. Then I stood at a distance, mocking its false supremacy. Afterward, I came to scream my fury and sorrow. By the time we were allowed, I wanted nothing to do with the religious sanctuary that failed to save my friend."

"You asked God to save her?"

"I begged," he corrects. "But my prayers went unanswered. I was sure then that God did not care about our wants or pain."

"Why did they allow untouchables?" I ask.

"We were ashamed by the world's reaction to our caste system. It forced us to make laws that held us equal, not lesser." He glances at the temple and then back at me. "But laws are slow to change what is in people's hearts." A family walks down the steps, each individual wearing shoes. "Come, let us say hello."

I follow Ravi's example and remove my shoes

at the foot of the steps. Dozens of other pairs lie about in disarray. "Why?" I ask, gesturing toward all the shoes.

"It is believed that meditative energy flows from the feet upward," he says. "Only with bare feet can you feel God within you." As we start to climb the marble steps, he adds, "And only with bare feet can you tell who has bathed and who has not, yes?"

Throngs of people travel up and down the steps. Women hold tight to their youngsters while older boys and girls run freely. Ravi leads me to a row of statues of deities placed against a wall. A small brass bell hangs from the ceiling with a matching brass-colored cord. "Ring the bell, my child. My arms are too old to reach the sky."

I take the fist-size ringer hanging from the cord and hit it against the side of the bell. The piercing echo rings in my ears. Ravi picks fruits and flowers from his silver plate and lays them at the base of the statue of Lord Shiva. The Brahmin *pujari*, an old man wrapped in an orange sari, accepts Ravi's offer of goods to the temple with a curt nod. As required of all *pujaris*, the man has abdicated all earthly pleasures for a higher calling.

The bell tolls through the temple and reverberates throughout the village. In perfect rhythm, the priest begins the verses to a song. Ravi sits where he stood and gestures for me to do the same. I fold my dress around my legs as I take a seat. The women and men join in song with the priest, together singing about love and praying that the future bodes well for them and their loved ones. Calmed by the lyrics, I close my eyes and lose myself in the music.

"*Prasad*." Ravi hands me a full plate of the food that the rest of the congregation is feasting on. "You must eat it."

I remember the part of the story when Amisha offers it to Stephen after Holi and scoop up the offering. The concoction melts on my tongue. I quickly empty my plate.

"Do they do the same thing for every *puja*?"

Ravi points to some burning candles. "They are lit first and then the incense." The *pujari* leads the group in songs of praise and gratitude.

"There are millions of divine manifestations." Ravi directs me toward some of the gold-covered statues set throughout the temple. "Everyone chooses which deity to pray to according to their religious practices. It is said that each god has a purpose, a power," he says, searching for the word.

"Similar to Greek mythology," I say.

"I do not know," Ravi admits without apology. "I did not attend school."

In a far corner sits a bronze-sculpted figure. She's balanced on one foot as if in a dance pose, while her multiple arms reach outward. "Who is she?" Her white crystal eyes are mesmerizing.

"You chose well," Ravi says. "Her name is Durga." He glances at me. "For Hindus, she is believed to be the universal source of all power, energy, and creativity." He stands next to me and admires the icon.

"She's breathtaking." I steal a flower from an assortment and lay it at the base of her feet.

"Yes," Ravi says, watching me. "She was also your grandmother's favorite." When I stay silent, he says, "Your grandmother was a very strong woman. I believe you, as her granddaughter, will find the same strength lies within you." He smiles at me. "Now, let us go celebrate Holi as your grandmother did."

After the *puja*, we join the throng of people headed toward the village square. The night before, Ravi had mentioned the Holi celebration to me. He thought I would enjoy the colors and vibrancy of the annual celebration that was eagerly anticipated by both children and adults. Any passerby in the vicinity was an open target. Laughter could be heard on the streets for hours after the sun set. Then, as they had done for years, every villager, regardless of caste, would gather together and share a meal.

Ravi and I had created two baskets of color-filled balloons to throw at passersby. As we approach, the crowd divides itself into round circles facing one another. The women are dressed in white skirts and blouses while the men are wearing white pants with long cotton shirts. Most are already streaked with color. They each hold two sticks and hit each other's in synchronization before moving to the next person in line. As the tempo of the music increases, they go faster until sweat pours down their faces.

"Dandiya Raas." Ravi watches me. "The dance your grandmother was teaching the lieutenant."

Those in the crowd laugh as they start to miss their steps and people fall out of line. Additional villagers arrive and start to throw paint balls. Soon the dance breaks up, and it is an all-out war as everyone throws color at one another.

"Will they dance again?" I ask, hoping.

"Tonight, after eating. You will join them?" he asks.

"Yes." I think of my grandmother and her attempt at teaching Stephen the steps. I imagine him learning in the confines of the garden as they used branches for sticks. If she were still alive, would I have learned from her? Would my mother have embraced her culture versus rejecting it? "I would love to."

Ravi nods, seeming pleased by my answer. I start to say something else, when I spot Amit in the distance. He walks toward us, holding tight to a young girl's hand. A braid falls down each side of her head and over her ears. Her hair is rich black and her skin the color of dark wood. Metal braces encase both her legs, leading upward to a full metal cast around her small body and ending with an enclosure around her neck.

"Who is that?" I ask. Ravi stays silent. "Ravi?"

"My great-granddaughter, Misha."

"Misha as in *Amisha*?" I ask slowly.

He smiles. "Yes. She was the first girl born to my family. It is her fortune to be named after your grandmother." I swallow my profound gratitude at his act of honoring my grandmother. "She is eight years old." Ravi returns Amit's wave when he spots us. "For years, my daughter-in-law was unable to have children. After many fasts and full moons, we were blessed with Amit. We didn't dare ask for another, for how can perfection be repeated?" Emotion clogs his voice. "Then Misha came to us, and we were proven wrong."

When they reach us, Ravi pulls them both in for a hug. Ravi introduces his great-granddaughter, who stares at me. "Meet my beautiful great-granddaughter, Misha."

I bend down until I'm eye level with her and hold out my hand. She glances at Amit, who nods his approval. When she slips her small hand into mine, I say, "It's a pleasure to meet you, Misha. You are as beautiful as your great-grandfather said."

Her face lights up at my compliment. "Thank

you." She points to my full basket of paint balls. "You will play with us?" Her own basket has only a handful of balloons.

"No, honey." I glance at her basket. "Your great-grandfather and I made these for you and your brother." When I hold them out to her, she stares at the basket, confused. Gently I push it toward her. "Please, take them."

I fight back tears. Misha is tinier than any eight-year-old I've seen. Since my arrival, I've met plenty of children during my walks to the village. Some were beggars to whom I gave money but never asked them their stories. Because there was nothing I could do to change their circumstances, it was safer not to know. However, this is Ravi's flesh and blood. The child is Ravi's future generation, and he is my friend. He's treated me as if we've known each other for ages when in reality we are only recent acquaintances.

"Remember to share with your brother," I say.

"Thank you." Amit glances at his sister. "You have made her Holi."

"You have given away your arsenal." Ravi and I watch as Amit and Misha join the other children and begin to play. "How will you play the game?"

"Why have I not met her before, Ravi?" I ask, ignoring his teasing. I face him, this man who is spending hours of his time sharing the story of my family while keeping his own shrouded in secrecy. I am embarrassed for my self-centeredness, for not having asked more about his life and focused only on mine. "Tell me about your family," I beg. "Please."

He hesitates. "My son is a hard worker and has a good wife. My grandson works as an assistant to a tailor. Like his father, he works hard and is a good man who cares deeply for his family." Ravi stops repeatedly to say hello to other villagers. "My great-grandchildren play with their hearts light and their minds free." He pauses. "I am grateful they are able to do so."

"Why didn't you tell me about Misha?"

"You have sat with me each day, listening to the story of a woman you never knew. Crying and laughing with your grandmother as she struggled to find her place." The squeal of a child breaks into our conversation. The children start to throw the balloons at one another, coloring each other in the various shades of the rainbow. "I didn't want Misha's story to overshadow your family's."

"Why would you think it would?"

He smiles, but his expression is filled with sadness. "Because you are Amisha's granddaughter."

I watch Misha run as fast as she can to keep up with her brother. The metal braces cause her to stumble. Amit, seeing his sister's distress, stops and comes to her side, helping her in her struggle to stand.

"What happened?" I ask.

"Polio," he says, his gaze following mine. "We are told she is lucky to walk. There are others for whom the disease is disabling." When I glance at him, he says, "They are destined to spend the rest of their lives in a chair, if it can be afforded."

"Is there anything I can do?"

"Your asking is enough. Thank you," he says. We both fall silent as the children continue to throw balloons at one another. Soon the adults join in, and colored powder falls from the sky. "I'm sorry you did not get to play."

I don't respond. My children, if they had been born, would have lived privileged lives. Diseases such as polio would never have crossed their paths. Their worries would have been about school and friends, the prom, and where to travel for spring break. It both shames and gives me pause that I have lived my life on the sidelines, never knowing or caring that others live in such misfortune.

"Are there untouchables in America, Jaya?" Amit asks, swinging on the hammock on the porch. He had called me Shrimati until I insisted on Jaya.

After the Holi celebration, Amit and Misha spent the night at the house with Ravi and me. Misha begged her parents, who agreed after I insisted it was fine. In the morning, Misha and Ravi disappear to get ready while Amit and

I wait. We watch the flow of people passing in front of the house. There is a general feeling of happiness in the air after the celebration that went late into the evening.

I don't respond immediately, cautious about his feelings. "No, there are no untouchables."

"Everyone is treated the same?" Envy colors his features.

"I wish they were." I think of America and its own issues of inequality. A history riddled with treating others as less. "There are people who are treated differently, unfairly compared to others."

He seems surprised by the information, making me wonder what his image of America is. "How do they decide who is second-class in America?"

I shudder at the question. He asks it with an assumption that a second class has to exist. That everyone doesn't have the right to be treated the same. "The law says everyone is equal, but sometimes people can be made to feel like they're second-class."

"Who?"

"Groups who are different may get singled out," I answer. "People are sometimes afraid of what they don't know. It can be because of the color of your skin or who you love. Maybe how much money you make. Different reasons."

"Have you ever been singled out?"

I think of the rights and privileges I take for

granted. A life filled with opportunities that my grandmother never had. That Ravi doesn't have. "No, I'm very lucky. I've always been treated like everyone else."

"You are lucky." Amit swings his legs, and the hammock sways back and forth. The motion causes his hair to flutter in the light wind.

"Are you . . ." I am reluctant to ask the question for fear of the answer. Though I don't want to believe that Ravi's great-grandson has faced prejudice, I know I am being foolish. "Have you ever been treated differently?"

"I am an untouchable," Amit says, as if that's answer enough. "My family treats Misha and me the same. But outside . . ." He trails off.

"Does it bother you?"

He glances at me for a fraction of a second before his eyes shift away. Tension vibrates off his body, and his face tightens. I wonder if it's from years of conditioning that he's learned to repress his emotions.

"Ravi Dada worked for a family that was prestigious," Amit says, his eyes pensive. "Because of them, we are treated with more respect. My sister and I attend the best school. Ravi Dada tells us we are lucky." He holds his head high and says the words with grace. As a twelve-year-old, he has a resilience that I envy. "But I know not everyone is as fortunate as we are, so I am grateful for what we do have. It is enough." He smiles at me, but a mask falls over his face, keeping his thoughts hidden.

"Ready?" Ravi asks, joining us on the porch. "It is time to water and prune the flowers in the garden."

Amit trails behind as Misha chatters the whole way, entertaining us with questions and stories about her day. Once at the school, Amit and Ravi start in the classrooms, while Misha and I choose the garden.

Misha holds the watering can and walks alongside me as I trim the roses. Her breaths become labored as she struggles to keep up. I slow down, taking smaller steps to keep up with hers. When she continues to breathe hard, I ask her if we can take a break. Without waiting for her response, I take a seat on the bench.

Misha hops up next to me and swings her legs back and forth, her braces banging against the bench. She points to a rosebush. "Ravi Dada always cuts the thorns off before giving them to us."

"That's a good idea." I let her steer the topics and sit back, enjoying the conversation.

"They need them; otherwise they would be too perfect." She pushes off the bench using both hands. Once she gets her balance, she walks toward a rosebush. She bends as far as she can and cuts a flower while avoiding the thorns. She inhales the scent before handing it to me. "Ravi

Dada says that if something is too perfect, God can't let it go."

"That sounds right."

Her words bring to mind images of the children I couldn't bear. Like a mother full of pride, I imagine them in all of their perfection. No matter who they were, I would have loved them unconditionally, like Amisha did her children and Ravi his great-grandchildren.

"Like me." Misha smells another rose, wrinkling her nose when the petals tickle her skin. She pulls the petals off one by one and showers them over the ground. "Ravi Dada said that's why I have the braces."

My breath catches at her unequivocal acceptance of Ravi's explanation. I remember my own baby pictures where a large black dot figured prominently on my temple. Mom explained to me once that the black mark was the best way to protect a child against God's eyes. If he realized he had let perfection go, as all babies are, then he might call the child back to heaven. The spot served as an imperfection.

"I think your Ravi Dada is exactly right." I blink back the tears that threaten.

"Me too." Full of energy, she starts to walk around the garden. Her metal braces clang against each other. I grab the waterpot and refill it. Together we trim and water the rest of the garden.

• • •

Last night I learned how to Dandiya Raas. It is the traditional dance performed during Hindu celebrations. Holding two sticks, you gather into two large circles and face one another. After five specific steps, you move to the next person and repeat the same steps with your new partner. For hours you go round and round, moving your body in motion to the music. It is beautiful both in its simplicity and ability to gather a large group together. Children, men, and women lose themselves for the hours they are synchronized in movement.

I haven't danced in years. The last time was at my wedding, when I didn't want the music to stop. Before then, I used to dance at clubs and parties, and even have impromptu jam sessions in my living room. As I got older, my thoughts intruded until I couldn't hear the lyrics through the music, and the rhythm was lost.

During my visit to India, I've spent time with a man who has become a dear friend. Today I met his great-granddaughter. Because they were born as untouchables, their hand was dealt before they learned how to play the game. They are considered undeserving and worthless to their society.

But even under the worst of circumstances, my friend holds his head high and teaches his great-grandchildren to value those things others take for granted.

History shows us we need labels to help define our place. For hundreds of years, people have categorized others as less so they could feel like more. Color, gender, class, religion, physical handicaps, sexual orientation, and pedigree are just a few ways in which one group is divided from another. For every person who stands superior, another must be inferior. But what does it say of us as a human race when we push others down for our own needs? Does it accomplish the intended goal or simply give rise to a pattern of behavior that can never be broken?

What if we all stood equal in one another's eyes and felt pride at our reflection? I speak of utopia and chance being ridiculed, but sitting in a village thousands of miles from everything, I will roll the dice. For one day only, maybe we could put aside our differences and come together in our sameness. For one day, we could see that past all the variations, we are all the same with similar hopes, dreams, fears, strengths, and weaknesses. For one day, we could stand together, not apart, and treat others as we would hope to be treated.

History teaches us that day will never come. Our differences give us purpose—both good and bad. Some see it as an opportunity to strive for what they aren't, while others take it to belittle those who frighten us. In the vein of my earlier appreciation for dancing, I would imagine a world where music defines us. The fall and rise of the tempo would dictate our moves, and our hearts and minds would sway to the beat. Each person would have a place on the stage, and every voice would be heard. The melodies would bridge our differences while celebrating our similarities. And at the end, we would be better for having danced together.

With age come wisdom and the knowledge that we can't dance through our lives. But I hope I can find a way where my labels of daughter, reporter, wife, and now soon to be divorcée don't define me. Instead, every new person will represent the chance to grow, and I will feel no shame in taking the first step. With humility may I reap my own power, and at the end of the journey, I hope I learn when to stand small so others can feel tall.

AMISHA

THIRTY-THREE

Deepak made room on the settee for Stephen to take a seat next to him. "It was kind of you to accept an invitation to eat in our home." He clasped Stephen's shoulder. Amisha had been shocked when her husband told her he had invited Stephen after running into him at Vikram's house. Deepak relayed that the lieutenant had accepted graciously, but she wondered how comfortable he was now.

She spent the morning cleaning the house with the servants for Raksha Bandhan—a celebration to honor the relationship between a brother and his sister. Janna, dressed in a georgette sari with gold bangles, spoke quietly to the children about their schooling while fanning herself. The younger of Deepak's sisters, Janna was never close with Amisha. But she was married to a man one village over, so they saw each other a few times a year.

"She must be trying to keep the maggots away with her fanning," Ravi whispered to Amisha while they reheated the food. Since Deepak had insisted neither Ravi nor Bina be allowed to serve the guests, they would stay in the back and help with the food preparation. "They are attracted to dung, in any form."

Amisha laughed while shushing him. "Do not let her hear you."

He stopped, but a smile lingered. Ravi had never liked Janna. After his hire, he often warned Amisha that her sister-in-law was manipulative and vindictive. Now, with a dexterity and efficiency that Amisha envied, Ravi scooped the vegetables into one bowl and the soup into another. He added squirts of lemon and ginger water over the dishes to aid in digestion. "Dinner is ready," Amisha called out from inside the kitchen. Deepak motioned for Stephen to walk ahead of them, and they took a seat together on the hard floor. Amisha carefully balanced three bowls. She glanced at Stephen when she entered the eating area. Deepak, busy discussing prospects for the production of a new crop with his brother-in-law, barely noticed her. As she stepped toward them, her foot caught on the hem of her sari. She jerked, nearly tripping under the weight of the meal. Stephen immediately braced one arm behind him to get up to help. Amisha gave him a frantic but quick shake of her head, insisting he stay seated. If he dared to help her, it would be seen as an insult to Deepak. Stephen, understanding, stayed seated, but his gaze remained locked on hers.

Amisha filled Deepak's plate first and then Stephen's with the curried vegetables. She handed a stack of naan to her brother-in-law, who then passed them to the other two men. Once the food was served, she gave them each a damp cloth to wipe their hands with after the meal. "We do not have utensils," Amisha said to Stephen. "I'm sorry."

"Amisha, you are worried for no reason. Our friend will eat like an Indian." Deepak pinched a piece of the flatbread between his fingers and scooped up some *sakh*, a cooked-vegetable dish. Stephen easily followed his example and began to eat. "You could not find food like this in your country. I am right, yes?" Deepak asked after his first bite.

"You are right, Deepak. It would be impossible to find an Amisha with such superb cooking talents in my country." By twisting Deepak's words, he thanked Amisha for the meal the only way he could. As he lowered his face to sip the soup, he raised his eyes to catch hers. He tore his gaze from her when Janna entered the eating area.

"Is this the first time you are sampling our Amisha's cooking, Lieutenant? I am surprised," Janna said, cattiness lacing her words. She rested against the door frame, continuing to fan herself. "Amisha spends a lot of her time at the school, doesn't she?"

Amisha cringed inwardly. She stole a quick glance at Deepak to see his reaction, but he continued to eat. "Janna," she said, her voice stern, "I am learning and teaching at the school. Not cooking."

"Yes, we are fortunate to have Amisha." Stephen stopped eating to look directly at Janna. Uncomfortable, she glanced away. "Though it is a shame she is the only one willing to take time to help the children learn. You are welcome to come and assist anytime."

"Gossiping, Lieutenant," Janna's husband chimed in. Unaware of the red fury that spread across his wife's cheeks, he continued. "Janna is too busy with it to teach. Deepak, it is good Amisha is occupied. You are not tortured by hearing the scandals of the villagers each and every day."

After dinner, everyone gathered in the living room. Amisha lit the *diyas* and recited a prayer in front of Lord Ganesha's statue as the group stood quietly, hands clasped in prayer.

"Lord Ganesha's father created him in childhood," Janna's husband said to Stephen. From his place on the other side of Amisha, he pointed to the statues inside the makeshift temple. Amisha motioned for Deepak and Janna to come closer.

"I heard that somewhere," Stephen said, smiling at Amisha.

Deepak started a prayer that wished his younger sister a lifetime of happiness and prosperity. The prayer ended with his promising to protect her if ever the occasion arose. Janna recited her own prayer in which she promised to love her brother forever.

"May the gods bestow upon you all the happiness you deserve, bhai," Janna said. She dipped her thumb into a bowl of red vermilion powder and then stamped it onto Deepak's forehead.

Janna took the offered *rakhi*, a sacred golden-red string, from Amisha and tied it around Deepak's wrist. Once it was secure, Deepak gifted Janna a stack of rupees as a thank-you, completing the ceremony.

"Lieutenant, what do you think of our traditions? Would the Raj approve?" Deepak asked while Amisha served fresh chai to the group. Deepak took a deep swallow of his drink as he waited for Stephen's answer. Outside the window, the children could be heard playing with a family of stray chicks.

Stephen had stood against the back wall while the proceedings took place. With a nod of thanks to Amisha, he took a cup of the hot liquid. "I think your people are lucky to have the opportunity to show openly how much you care for your siblings," he answered diplomatically. "It is unusual for us to have siblings feel such sincere affection for one another, so maybe the tradition would die a fast death regardless,"

Stephen joked, rewarded with laughter from the group.

"Do you have a sister, Lieutenant?" Janna joined the conversation.

"No, I am not as fortunate as Deepak," Stephen replied. He stole a glance at Amisha, who stifled her laughter behind a cough. "I do not have a sister."

"That is a shame." Janna turned toward Amisha. "The lieutenant has been so gracious to you, allowing someone of our low status to learn in his distinguished school. It is only right you show him some gratitude in return."

"Sister?" Deepak asked. "What are you saying?"

Amisha saw Deepak suppress a sigh. She knew he was never fond of her antics when she still lived with them. As the youngest, Janna had been allowed more freedom than the others and had always walked the fine line between good behavior and causing mischief. The night before her older sister's marriage, Janna complained her outfit was not fancy enough. When her complaints went unheeded, she spilled red henna all over it, forcing her parents to buy a new one.

"Lieutenant," Janna pressed on, ignoring Deepak, "it is common practice in Hinduism that when a man shows extreme generosity to a woman, she is to call him a brother. There is no better time to solidify your relationship than on the day of Raksha Bandhan."

"Sister," Amisha spoke up. Her nerves fraught, she kept her voice steady. "It is not appropriate for you to impose our beliefs on the lieutenant. He is a guest in our home and is here to appreciate, not partake." She kept her gaze focused on Janna while trying to calm her rapid heartbeat.

"I'm sure the lieutenant would be honored," Janna returned. "Right, Brother?" she asked, speaking directly to Deepak.

Deepak ignored his sister while considering Stephen. "You have been very kind in allowing my wife to learn at the school." He set his finished cup of chai on the table for the servants to pick up later. "Lieutenant, it would be an honor to have you as a brother of our humble home."

Amisha watched helplessly as Stephen surveyed the room. Unsure, she waited for him to speak, afraid of his answer.

"It would be an honor," Stephen said, "to accept this gift."

Shocked, Amisha stared at him before remembering she had an audience. She felt Stephen's gaze on her, assessing her reaction. "I don't know if we have another *rakhi*," she murmured. "I only bought one of the blessed strings from the temple."

"We can use red string." Janna went to the cupboard where Chara had always kept sewing supplies, and found a small piece of thread. She held it up like a prize. "It is thin but should do."

Amisha took the string, her fingers recoiling at the touch. Her steps slow, she didn't even realize she had stopped a few feet from Stephen until Deepak said her name. When she glanced up at him, he was watching her curiously. "Amisha," he said again, encouraging her.

"Of course." Her final steps toward Stephen felt as though she were walking on hot coals. Amisha would have preferred the steam of the black rocks to this. "Your hand?" she whispered when she reached him.

Stephen held her gaze as he unbuttoned his cuff and rolled up the sleeve, baring his wrist. Amisha saw the concern in his eyes, but he couldn't comfort her. Not now, in front of everyone. With shaking hands, Amisha brought the two sides of the string around his wrist. She shifted some of the hair so as not to catch it in the knot. Amisha heard his intake of breath, and her hands began to sweat in response. As she began to tie the thin edges together, she used her fingernail to strike at the string on the opposite side of his wrist in the hope of tearing it in two.

Stephen grimaced when Amisha accidentally jabbed him instead. "Sorry," she mouthed, all her energy concentrated on her dual enterprise. In a pretense of helping her tie the knot, Stephen brought his other hand to his wrist. Sure he was going to stop her, she was surprised when he used his own fingers to help her tear it.

Just as she secured the knot, the bottom half came apart in her hand. With feigned disappointment, she held it up for the room to see. "Sister, the string is weak. It is a shame you didn't take the time to buy one at the temple for your brother. Then we would have two." Amisha released her pent-up breath while avoiding Deepak's eyes.

"It does not matter," Stephen said, his gaze on Amisha. "I am not meant to be your brother after all."

THIRTY-FOUR

Ravi used a hammer to finish the siding on the house in preparation for the rainy season. Last year, water had leaked into the structure and left the wood weakened. Ravi and Amisha had spent hours mopping it up with towels and old saris as the boys slid through the water, playing.

This year, Ravi purchased the nails from the local carpenter. The carpenter had thrown in some free ones that were used but still in good condition. Ravi had started the project as soon as he arrived in hopes that it would be complete by the end of the day.

Amisha came out at midday, insisting that Ravi come in for a rest and to eat lunch, the heaviest meal of the day. Afterward, Indians would sleep while the sun passed over the horizon.

"Ravi, you will be of no use to the wood or the hammer if your body is burning from the heat. Eat your meal and then work." Amisha stood on the porch, using her hand to shield her eyes from the sun.

"Shrimati." He continued to hammer. "I will be in shortly. The rain will be here soon enough, and then you will wish I had finished."

"Fine." Amisha grabbed an extra hammer and began to randomly pound on the wood.

"What are you doing?" Ravi tried to pull the hammer from her hand without touching her. She pulled it back, and soon enough they were having a tug-of-war.

"Helping. The rain will be here soon enough," she parroted back to him.

He stared at her in exasperation. Mortified that she was outside doing a laborer's work, he put the nails down and left her to enter the house. With a quiet smile, Amisha laid the hammer down next to the other supplies and followed him.

The rain started while they napped, and by dinner it had become a downpour. Ravi said nothing but gave Amisha a look that would have made a lesser woman cringe. She winked back at him and applauded him for having the foresight to start the job early.

"The rain will soften the wood." Amisha peered out the window at the darkened sky. "You will not have to hammer as much."

"Thank you." Sarcasm dripped off his every word. "Maybe I should wait for the end of the rainy season, and then the whole house will be filled with water and we will not need the wood. We can be like fish and wade from room to room." He wrapped plastic around his head to shield it from the rain.

"You are cross?" Amisha asked. She squinted through the door at the downpour. Worry gnawed at her, and she bit her lower lip until it bled.

"At you? Never, Shrimati." Finished tying the plastic, Ravi started toward the door. "The rain is letting up. I should be able to finish in an hour or so."

"Ravi." Amisha tried to stall him, afraid to have him working in the rain with little light. But she knew he would argue. She had overheard him promise Deepak that he would have the job complete before her husband returned. "It is dark, and with the rain it will be hard to see."

"Shrimati, please let me do what I must." He sighed before adding, "It is my duty."

Amisha nodded quietly. Though Deepak would have understood the delay, Ravi would never forgive himself for reneging on his word. She shut the door behind him and allowed the soft patter of the rain to soothe her guilt for having kept him from the job earlier.

Both the volume of the scream and the moans of agony that followed it caused Amisha to rush outside. Ravi had been working for hours. The rain had stopped, leaving wet puddles in its wake. The children had fallen asleep, wrapped in wool blankets to ward off the chill that had permeated the house. The other servants had retired to their own homes.

Earlier, Amisha had lit two oil lamps and taken

them outside to Ravi. She had made some fresh chai to keep him warm and left the thermos at his feet. Neither one said a word to the other, but Amisha knew that he would not stop until the task was complete, and both knew she would not sleep until he was done for the night.

Amisha flew down the steps where Ravi held tight to his leg. Blood oozed from an open gash on his thigh and over his fingers to pool on the ground. "Ravi," Amisha cried, "what happened?"

"The knife." The blade was on the ground next to him, soaked in blood. "I tried to cut a small piece of wood. It slipped." His words were uneven and his breathing was labored.

Amisha quickly cut a piece of cloth from the bottom of her top. She pulled his leg onto her lap and wrapped the cotton around his leg, attempting to stop the flow.

"Do not touch me, Shrimati." Ravi tried to pull his leg away. "My blood, touching you . . ."

"Shut up, Ravi." She secured the knot as she desperately tried to stop the flow of blood, but in seconds the sari was drenched and limp. "I have to get a doctor."

"No doctor will come at this hour," Ravi murmured, his eyes fluttering closed. He was losing too much blood, too fast.

He didn't say what they both knew—no doctor would treat an untouchable. Their guilt would at times force them to dispense medicine but no more.

"I have to try." Amisha refused to let him drown in a pool of his own blood. She rushed into her bedroom and pulled all the money Deepak kept in the bureau.

"Do not bother, Shrimati," Ravi said when Amisha returned and he saw the cash in her hand. "He will watch me die rather than touch my blood."

Amisha knew Ravi was right: no amount of money would convince the village doctor to abandon his prejudices and help an untouchable. Ravi struggled to keep his eyes open. Soon enough, his mind would rescue him from the pain by plunging him into darkness. She tore another piece of her shirt and wrapped it above the wound, tighter than before.

"You are not allowed to die, Ravi," she ordered. The bills fell into the pool of blood, soaking through. She barely kept her tears at bay. "Do you hear me?" she begged, but he stayed silent.

With no options and desperation at her heels, she stood and began to run. She headed toward the only help she could think of. She did not know how he could or even if he would try, but she had no choice. She would beg if needed and fall to his feet pleading.

When Amisha reached his door, she pounded

and raised her voice above the fierce wind. "Stephen!" Amisha screamed.

"Amisha?" Stephen yanked the door open, his face filling with concern at the sight of her. He grabbed her hand and tried to pull her into the house and out of the rain. "What's happened?"

Amisha swiped at her tears. The wind pushed her disheveled hair around her face. Fear permeated her words. "Please help me," she cried. Her hand fell limp in his. "Ravi is hurt, and I don't know . . ."

Her legs buckled, and she collapsed against his door frame. She had been foolish to come here, she realized. What was there to do but face the fact that her friend was dying if not dead? All their money and influence did not matter if she could not force a doctor to treat an untouchable.

"One minute." He rushed back into the house. In seconds he was back, keys in hand. "Let's go." They both ran to his small car. Amisha jumped into the passenger side while he turned the ignition. "Your house?" he asked.

"Yes." They sped silently through the dark alleyways with only the wipers breaking their silence. The car had barely come to a stop before both jumped out and ran toward Ravi on the ground.

"He's still alive." Amisha reached Ravi first. She placed her hand on his chest and felt its rise and fall.

"Let's get him into the car." Stephen hauled Ravi into his arms and settled him in the backseat. He then pulled off his belt and used it as a tourniquet before rushing to the driver's seat.

"Where are we going?" Amisha asked, opening the door to the passenger side.

"I'm taking him to the military hospital." Over the top of the car's hood, he said, "You're not going anywhere."

"I am." Shocked he would assume anything else of her, she said, "I have to be with him."

"I have to drive three villages over. What will Deepak say if someone sees you in the car with me?" The rain, which had stopped momentarily, started to fall again. Before Amisha could respond, Stephen asked, "What would happen to your children?"

Amisha had no answer to his question. She slowly stepped back. If fate deemed it Ravi's time, then she did not want him to die alone. But circumstances refused her the choice. "Take care of him," she said, her head downcast.

Amisha's steps slowed as she neared the temple. The night sky loomed and shadowed her every move. She had asked her neighbor to watch the children so she could come pray. In the past, she was hesitant to believe destiny could be determined by a prayer. Right now, however, she would do anything to alter the course of fate. Her friend was en route to death and she was not sure any human, including Stephen, could save his life.

The empty walls watched Amisha as she entered the sanctuary. She reached for the bell and rang it until the peals filled the night sky. The birds in the trees awoke and cried out in protest, but Amisha had little concern. Her only thought was of Ravi and his survival.

She lit a set of jasmine incense sticks before sinking to her knees in front of the statue. The smoldering fragrance wafted up and surrounded her. Her eyes burned, but she wasn't sure if it was from the smoke or her tears.

"Life should not be gambled," she declared, staring down the force of the all-powerful gods.

She had come to beg but found herself instructing instead. There was no compromise for the life of her friend. She had no interest in fate or cycles of life. She would offer no quarter in this fight. Ravi had to live, because life had to be fair.

"I will not accept his death," she threatened, calm replacing fear. "You have no right to him. Not when life has at last begun to make some sense for him." She thought of his impending marriage. "His happiness is not yours to take." She thought of his wife and parents. The brother and sister he provided for. All who loved him unconditionally.

She wiped furiously at the tears gathered on her face. "I make no concessions for your lack of concern for human life. He is an innocent who has done nothing but live within the shabby means you have provided." She rose from her kneeling position, standing face-to-face with her creator. "This fight is not his own. Assume you have been forewarned. I stand with him, and if you want his soul, then you must take mine first." Saying nothing further, she left the temple, sure God had heard her words.

THIRTY-FIVE

Amisha swung back and forth on the settee, barely aware of her actions. She stared into the dark and counted the minutes until they melded into one another, leaving her with no sense of time. The knock came just as she was sure her worry and fear would render her senseless. She rushed past the children asleep on the floor and yanked open the door to see Stephen.

"Is he alive?" she asked desperately. Her hand clutched the door, digging into the wood until the pain numbed her fingers.

"He's alive." Stephen rubbed a hand over his worn and tired face. "In pain for a few days, I'm sure, but nothing that will not heal."

"Thank you." Amisha tried to swallow past the sob lodged in her throat, but it refused to move. At the sound of his mother's distress, Jay began to stir, murmuring incoherently. She motioned Stephen to follow her into the back room so they wouldn't wake the children.

Inside, Stephen filled the small room. He shut the door, his gaze resting briefly on the bed before he glanced away. Shadows danced off the wall from the dimmed lamp on the desk.

"I don't know how to repay you." In the small space they faced each other. She blinked rapidly, trying to clear the cobwebs in her head. "Without you, I don't know what would have happened."

"You don't have to thank me." He searched her face where streaks of tears covered her cheeks. He cupped her chin and smudged the wetness away with his thumb. "I know how much he means to you."

Amisha closed her eyes at his strokes. Exhausted from the night's events, she couldn't summon the strength to tell him they couldn't do this. Instead, she covered his hand with her own. She pressed his palm deeper into her skin, feeling safe with his touch. "I knew . . ." She paused. He waited for her to finish, his patience a balm to the fear that had consumed her all evening. "I knew you would help him." She could barely speak. "You made Ravi's pain your own and saved my friend."

Stephen moved toward her, closer than he had ever been. She saw the uncertainty on his face, his surety that she would tell him to stop, that they could not do this. She knew it was not proper and would hurt others if they knew. But right now none of it mattered. Instead, she moved forward, matching his steps. When she laid her head on his chest, he wrapped his arms around her waist, pulling her in tight. With her touch, she heard his breathing accelerate. At last she let the sobs that had been threatening all night spill over. Her tears soaked his shirt while her cries shook her body.

"Shh." He ran his hand over her hair and down her back as he tried to soothe her. "He's safe."

Amisha cried until there was nothing left. When she was spent of her tears, she still held on with her arms around his waist. The night had started with her empty and afraid. But because of Stephen, Ravi had survived the hard fight death had fought. High from emotion, she tightened her fingers on his back. Tonight she needed him, and he had come through.

Stephen's hand pressed deep into her bare back, pushing her into him. Amisha raised her hands to his chest and began to draw circles on his heart. Wanting to touch more, she laid her palm flat and dug deep into his skin, hoping to touch his soul. He responded in kind, losing his other hand in her hair. She could feel his heartbeat and knew he could hear her rapid breathing.

He moved his hand slowly down her back and clenched her long shirt. He paused, giving her a chance to protest. Amisha laid her hand over his. She dropped her head onto his shoulder and took a deep breath. She wanted him. The realization slammed into her, unmooring her. It threatened everything that mattered to her. She had no right to be with him. She was married and had three children. She had a responsibility to honor Deepak and their union. Her place was not with Stephen, and it never would be. Yet she ached more at the thought of pushing him away than of being with him.

She moved her hand off his and waited. He slipped his beneath the cotton, moving it lower until it was resting below her hip. The heat from his hands permeated the layers of cloth. He brought her even closer until she was settled intimately against him. He nestled her between his thighs, his reaction to her unmistakable.

Amisha's legs shuddered between his. Her nails raked the back of his neck as his fingers roamed from the sides of her breasts down again to below her backside. Her other hand snaked around, beneath his shirt, and touched bare skin.

"Amisha," Stephen whispered in her ear.

"Stephen?" She felt his body tense beneath her hands. Her mother had never spoken of the feelings churning inside her or the desire pooling between them, leaving her weak and wanting more.

"It's all right." Stephen brought her in tighter. He shut his eyes and moved them slowly against the wall.

Amisha felt her own shudders, which only increased her confusion. During the times she had been with Deepak, she had seen his face tighten and his body tense seconds before he released. Her own body had never reacted that way. She had felt the faint stirrings of pleasure at his touch, but never the sensations she experienced now.

Stephen's arms tightened around her. His body pushed hers against the bare wall. Amisha moved closer into him, her lips meeting his. She opened and let him in. His mouth traveled from hers to over her cheeks and onto her neck. She could hear his breathing accelerate at the same time she couldn't catch her own. She dug her fingers into his forearms. Amisha shut her eyes as everything went black.

When at last her body was sated, Amisha dropped her head onto his shoulder. She felt naked, as if Stephen had undressed her. Not fully understanding what had happened, she tried to make sense of the act. They hadn't made love but had reached a level of intimacy she had yet to experience with Deepak. Ashamed, she loosened her grip on him and dropped her head.

"Don't do that," Stephen warned, his voice strangled. "Don't hide from me."

"What just happened . . ." Amisha stopped, unsure.

"Happened because of how we feel about each other."

"You said it was friendship," she reminded him.

"I said what you needed to hear," he told her. "To give you an excuse for the way we feel."

"I don't know how I feel." She was sure she could convince them both at the same time. The room suddenly felt very small. Amisha stepped out of his arms and to the side.

"That's a lie," he said, but his words were void of harshness. Instead, his face was filled with understanding and his own pain. "We've been avoiding our feelings for a very long time."

"I'm married. I don't have the right to feel anything for you." Shame rendered her unable to make sense of the situation. "What happened between us . . ." Amisha trailed off, words failing her.

"We are . . ."

"No." Amisha couldn't let him finish the sentence. Because then the gods might hear and it would make it real. She wasn't ready to face that. "Please, I can't."

Stephen searched her face. He cupped her cheek and gently kissed her. "All right."

Amisha saw Stephen's frustration, while her own guilt weighed on her. The night's emotional upheaval had left her drained even as she sought some sense or reason.

"Good night." He cradled her head in his hands, murmuring against her lips. He walked out the door, leaving Amisha to stare at it long after he had left.

Ravi arrived to work through the back entrance. It had been only two days since his injury. Amisha and the children had visited him at home. Ravi's family fussed over Amisha as though she were royalty. She had laughed at their desire to please, telling his parents they were elderly and she should tend to them. She gave them a stack of rupees to cover any medicine that Ravi would require.

"I am here to work," Ravi announced when Amisha spotted him in the house.

"You should still be in bed," Amisha scolded, helping him in. He used a long stick as a makeshift cane.

"So I can stare at the ceiling?" he asked, rolling his eyes.

"So you can get better," Amisha lectured, encouraging him toward the settee. He ignored her and instead moved toward the kitchen to start on the dishes. "Go home."

"No. I am fine," he said.

"You were bleeding to death, and now you are fine?" Amisha followed him in. Bina and another servant had taken the wash to the river, leaving Amisha home alone.

"Yes, it is a miracle." Ravi picked up a dirty pan.

"The miracle will be your returning home to sleep." She yanked the pan that he had picked up out of his hands, only to have him grab another to wash.

"If I sleep, who will work?" Ravi asked. He hiked up his pants, squatted on the floor, and began to scrub the pan in earnest.

"There are other servants."

"But none who do as fine a job as I do. Besides, I must earn the money you gave to my family." Once the pan was scrubbed, he began to divide the pots from the dishes. Since Amisha hadn't had a chance to clean, the pile of dirty dishes was high.

"Fine. You want to work—work. But if you have any pain, do not come crying to me," Amisha replied, her face contorted in concern.

"I will suffer in silence," Ravi said, a grin playing at his lips.

"Even if you suffer by wailing, I will ignore you," Amisha returned.

"Perfect."

For the rest of the morning, Ravi worked alongside the other servants, and Amisha helped. She fed the children their meals and washed their clothes for school the next day. Afterward, they ran off to play until it was time for them to sleep. The other servants left in the early evening to make their own families' meal.

"Thank you." Ravi had worked tirelessly all day until all the chores were finished.

"For allowing you to work?" Amisha asked. With his palm, Ravi pressed down on the closed wound. From the grimace on his face, she knew it was aching.

"For saving my life."

"No." Amisha turned away, refusing to listen to him. "None of that."

Unswayed, Ravi limped around to face her. "Without you—I would not be here." He clasped his hands together. "I am deeply grateful."

"Well, right now I don't want you here. And if you continue this nonsense talk, I shall hurt you again to keep you quiet." Amisha still recalled every detail of that night and the terror of not knowing what would happen to him. Now, more than anything, she was thankful he was alive for her to argue with.

"What you did for me . . ." Ravi stopped, overwhelmed.

"You are my friend," Amisha said matter-of-factly, assuming no other explanation was necessary.

"People have many friends," Ravi replied.

"I don't." Amisha shrugged when he stared at her. When he stayed silent, she began to fold clothes. Her own words resonated deep within her, leaving her bereft and unsure.

"Your lieutenant would not allow me to die," Ravi finally said. "He demanded I live."

"He is not mine," Amisha said, an unexpected warmth coursing through her at his words. Memories of what they did swarmed around her no matter how hard she tried to push them away.

"Why him? When you left, I thought you went to find a doctor."

"No doctor would have come." She refused to lie to him. "I couldn't let you die. In the time I have spent with the lieutenant, he has shown that he cares deeply for people."

"He must care about you to do what he did for me."

"He would do it for anyone," Amisha said.

"Shrimati," Ravi confided, "when we arrived at the clinic, I heard the administration argue with him. They insisted it was for members of the Raj only, not for anyone off the streets. The lieutenant threatened to contact a commanding officer of the Raj to order their assistance. The warning was enough for them to move forward and help me."

Amisha kept her face blank, trying in vain to hide her feelings. "I did not realize," she said.

"It is my fortune that you call me a friend. It seems he is your fortune."

THIRTY-SIX

Amisha rested her head against the pillows as she fiddled with the blanket. Anytime she tried to lie down, her stomach grumbled for food. She had tried writing, but words refused to come. Her hunger made even the most mundane chores feel impossible.

"It has been three days since you've eaten." Ravi entered the bedroom without knocking. He was still limping, but his leg was better. "He has not come."

"He will," Amisha said. She and Stephen had not seen each other since the night of Ravi's accident. With the school closed for the holiday, Amisha hadn't missed teaching any classes. "The baby?" she asked, concerned for Paresh.

"Is no longer a baby." Amisha knew that Bina had bathed and dressed him earlier. "Bina took him to the market for supplies." Ravi sat in the chair and rifled through the sheaf of papers Amisha had used in some failed writing attempts. "He refused to hold Bina's hand, insisting he is old like his brothers. Five minutes later, he told her he needed a change of clothes. He had soiled them with milk."

"He is growing up too fast." Amisha smiled at the story. "All of my babies are." She thought about her children and their father. Her smile faltered. "Deepak has not telegrammed?" she asked, anxious for the answer.

"No, Shrimati." Ravi watched her carefully. "I don't believe he remembered the holiday."

Relieved, Amisha nodded. "It is best."

When she lay back, Ravi looked anxious. "Should I go to the school?" he asked.

After Ravi told her about Stephen's behavior at the clinic, she had admitted that they had become closer than she imagined. Without judgment, he listened. When she told him about her plan for today, the day of Karva Chauth, he did what he could to support her.

Celebrated by women across the country, the day was spent fasting without food or water. At the first sight of the moon, a woman would take her first sip of water from the man for whom she had fasted. In return for her sacrifice, the gods were asked to give the man a long and healthy life.

"No." Amisha wouldn't allow Ravi to make it easier. "He must come on his own."

"You have not been to the school since the accident." Ravi was confused. "How could he know to come?"

"If he doesn't know, then I am a fool." Images of their night together played in her head. She had relived it hundreds of times, wondering if she should have done something different. "But

I don't believe myself one." The knock sounded just as Amisha finished her sentence. Ravi stood immediately when they heard Bina open the door. From her murmured greeting, both knew it was Stephen. Relief and happiness flowed through her. For all the confusion surrounding their relationship, she had not read him wrong.

Bina led Stephen to the bedroom, where he stood in the doorway. His concerned gaze fell on Amisha before he turned to Ravi.

"Sir." Ravi bowed, his hands clasped together. "Namaste."

"Namaste." Stephen glanced at Ravi's leg, clearly pleased at seeing Ravi up and about. "How are you?"

"I am walking, and I have you to thank, sir," Ravi said. Next to Stephen, he looked small. "I am indebted to you."

"No debt," Stephen answered easily. "Just stay healthy and please, no more near misses." He glanced at Amisha. "I don't know if Amisha could handle it."

"I will try my best, sir." Ravi motioned him into the room.

"Vikram mentioned that Deepak was in Bombay?" Stephen said, not directing the question specifically to either of them.

"He has been in Bombay since before my accident, sir," Ravi answered before Amisha could. "He will not return for another week."

"I see." He came fully into the room and straight to Amisha's bed. His gaze locked on hers, he asked, "What's wrong?" Both barely heard Ravi leaving. "Do you need a doctor?"

"No, I'm fine." She had hoped he would come—had depended on it. Her voice was gravelly and weak from lack of food and water for three days. "You are here." She fingered the wool blanket, holding her emotions close.

"The school was out for the holiday, but I had hoped you would come for a lesson. When I didn't hear from you, I was worried. After the other night . . ." He trailed off, his eyes searching hers. "I thought about you but wasn't sure you wanted to see me."

Warmed by his concern, she reassured him. "Then we will both live to a hundred, according to a Hindu myth, because I too thought about you."

She hesitated to play this game, but vacillated over whether to tell him the real reason she was in bed and ailing. She had staked everything on his arriving without her summoning him. "I haven't seen you since . . ." She stumbled in her attempt to speak about that night.

For days and nights she had thought of little else. She had convinced herself that their behavior that night was a reaction to the crisis. But as each day passed, and the memory continued to warm her and her yearning for him only increased, she was forced to face the truth she had avoided. This man meant more to her than she meant to herself.

When she was with Stephen, she was happy in a way she had never known. She struggled with her feelings but was past the point of fighting them. In caring for him, she wasn't taking from Deepak. He needed her to be someone who kept house and cared for his children. She did both without question or complaint.

"I have a request for you," Amisha said.

"Your food, Shrimati." Ravi entered with a tray filled with food and a glass of coconut water. "Would you please, sir?" Ravi handed the tray to Stephen while avoiding Amisha's sharp gaze. "She has not eaten in three days. It would be most helpful if you would assist her with the water while I see to the rice." Secure in Stephen's nod, Ravi headed out.

Stephen took the glass from the tray and set the rest of the food on the table. He sat down on the bed next to her. "What's going on, Amisha?"

Shame kept her from explaining immediately. With Stephen, she walked the line between their two ways of life, hoping to find a balance. According to everything she was taught, her actions with him the night of Ravi's accident were reprehensible.

Yet she couldn't convince herself it was wrong. The slightest contact with him felt more right than anything before in her life ever had. She had been given to Deepak without a choice. She made a life with him because she had to. But Stephen was the first choice of the heart she had ever made for herself. The way she felt about him was hers alone. Thus, when Karva Chauth came upon them, she knew without a doubt what she would do.

Amisha had fasted for Deepak every year since her marriage. At the end of her fast, Deepak would offer her water and food, and then hurriedly return to the mill. Amisha had never minded before, assuring herself that her actions were not in vain. She refused to allow Deepak's inattentiveness toward her hunger to affect the basis of the sacrifice.

This year, Deepak had spent the holiday away and didn't bother to ask about her. Ravi had prepared a full meal on the day of the fast, but Amisha fed only the children. When Ravi asked why, she told him she was fasting this year. Just not for Deepak.

"Shrimati?" Ravi had questioned. The moon had already risen on that first day, and women across the village were enjoying their first meal of the day. "What are you going to do?"

"Wait for him to arrive." Amisha was confident in her belief.

"If he doesn't?"

"Then I starve," Amisha had said, though she was sure he would. In time he would seek her out, and then she would guarantee his lifeline. But now, with Stephen sitting next to her, she was embarrassed by her actions and feared he might not understand the ritual that she found so meaningful.

"Amisha?" Stephen repeated, waiting for her response.

"There is a practice among Indian women. Once a year, a woman starves herself for a full day and full night in the hope that, in return, the gods will grant a long and happy life to the man for whom she has fasted—usually her husband. After the rise of the moon, the woman waits for the man to feed her the first bite of food and offer the first sip of water." Amisha recited the purpose of the holiday as efficiently as she could and then waited for his response.

"You have not eaten?" Stephen sat back.

"No." She eyed the food on the table with hunger.

"For three days?"

"I had to wait to be fed."

"Deepak did not feed you?"

"It was not for him that I fasted," Amisha said, revealing her feelings for him in the only way she could.

She waited, unsure, for his response. For all the times she had been hesitant or afraid in her life, nothing compared to the uncertainty facing her now. With her actions, she was telling him that she cared for him. That he mattered to her equally if not more than Deepak did. If she had misread his actions from the other night, then she would feel like a fool for having admitted her feelings.

"What if I had not come?" Concern creased the lines above his forehead.

"But you did," Amisha said slowly, still trying to read his reaction. "And now I'm waiting."

Stephen edged closer to her. He moved strands of hair off her face. His eyes searched hers, and in them she saw her confusion and uncertainty mirrored. When he hesitated, she turned her face away, sure she had made a mistake and revealed too much. He cupped her chin and slowly turned her face back toward him. His thumb stroked her cheek.

He gently tipped the glass into her mouth, watching as she emptied it in seconds. With his palm, he wiped away a trickle of the sweet liquid off her chin. He tore a piece of the naan, dipped it into the lentil soup, and fed it to her. His fingers lingered against her lips.

"Thank you," he whispered, his words choked. "For your sacrifice."

"Now you will live to a hundred years." Amisha breathed a sigh of relief. No matter that they were in limbo—having crossed the boundaries of friendship but knowing they could never be together—she was happy for having guaranteed his lifeline. Without words, she had shown him how much he meant to her.

"So, how do I repay you?" he asked when the silence stretched.

"Don't ever die," she answered before lying back and letting her satiated stomach lull her to sleep.

JAYA

THIRTY-SEVEN

After the first miscarriage, I stayed in bed for two days. Any longer and I started to feel guilty for not doing something, anything to make the situation better. I began by reading every book I could on miscarriages and how to prevent the next one. I spoke to doctor friends and joined a support group. On a mission, I would do whatever it took to make sure the next time I got it right.

Patrick supported my endeavor, seeming to understand my need for control. Assuming he was taking his own steps, I asked him about it one night after finishing yet another book on women and their bodies.

"Nothing," he said. "When it's meant to happen, it will."

I was frustrated with his response for days. Maybe I thought he didn't care enough to work at it, or his inaction was a betrayal of my pain. No matter the reason, I put distance between us. Now, hearing about my grandmother's sacrifice on the night of Karva Chauth, her willingness to show Stephen love with no guarantee of a future, I can't help but think when we have nothing else, when there are no answers, faith is our greatest ally. Maybe for Patrick, it was the only answer he had to hold on to.

I knock on Ravi's door and then wait. In my head, Amisha's story swirls together with mine. For every choice my grandmother didn't have, I think of the ones I do. For all of Amisha's sorrows, I think of the times I told myself I didn't care. For the woman she was, I think of the woman I'm not.

Misha opens the door and offers me a large smile. One part of her hair is pulled into a braid while the other side hangs around her shoulders. She holds a brush in one hand.

"Hi, Beti." Happy to see her, I wrap my arm around her shoulder and bring her in for a hug. I hear Ravi in the kitchen and call out, "You didn't tell me your beautiful great-granddaughter was coming today."

Ravi enters with a washrag in hand. "My beautiful great-granddaughter is coming today." Ravi smiles at Misha's giggles.

Misha returns to the mirror and struggles to brush her hair. I gently remove the hairbrush from her hand. "May I?" On her nod, I brush out the knots, being careful not to pull. I wrap the strands around one another into a braid. "So, what are the plans for the afternoon?" Ravi had mentioned taking the day off to see more of the village and surrounding community. I had readily agreed.

"The Ashram." At my look of confusion, Ravi explains. "An orphanage. It is a place Misha and I go often. Misha wants to show it to you."

"I'm going to be a teacher when I grow up," Misha announces. She and I sit in the back of the rickshaw while Ravi takes the front. When the vehicle drives over some rocks, she grips my hand.

"That's excellent," I say. "What type of teacher?"

"A nice one." She raises an eyebrow in confusion when I burst out laughing. "My teacher hits our palms with a ruler if we get an answer wrong. But he gives us candy if we get the answer right, so I always get it right."

Shocked at the archaic behavior, I glance at Ravi, who says calmly, "The ruler is made of foam pad. It would take the force of God for it to hurt someone."

We spend the rest of the drive with Misha jumping from one random topic to another. From cooking to her friends, she tells us in detail about every part of her life. By the time we arrive, I have heard stories from the time she was three onward.

I follow Ravi and Misha up the steps of a nondescript building simple in design. It is barely one story, and brown pane windows cover the worn white-painted wood. A bulky door opens into a cluttered entrance hall and then a large room. Nothing I have seen on the streets or read about in schoolbooks could prepare me for the scene inside. Bedsheets cover a carpeted floor. Unattended infants and toddlers are scattered about. Crying and the stench of urine and feces fill the room. I cover my mouth, trying to quell my nausea.

"Ravi?" I scan the room, searching for an adult. "This?"

"Yes," he says quietly, seeming to understand my shock. "It is home to many children."

The building is divided into four rooms, each one smaller than the last. The kitchen stores lentils and rice, the children's main source of nutrition. Glass canisters of milk sit atop melting ice. They have only one small refrigerator, the type I had in my dorm room in college.

A back room stores washing provisions and extra clothes donated by the community. They are thrown into a box in disarray. Threadbare blankets cover those children who are sleeping while crying toddlers cling to one another in lieu of stuffed animals. There are no pillows or mattresses, so the carpeted floor and sheets serve as their beds.

"Where are the caregivers?" I ask quietly.

"The temple has funding for only two." Ravi watches as Misha finds a group of children to play with. "Parents who can't afford or don't want their children leave them here. Many are either deformed or handicapped."

The cry of an infant catches my attention. I slip

off my shoes and gently bring the wailing baby into my arms. He has a flat face and short neck—both telltale signs of Down syndrome. As I rock the little boy, I spot two children in the back with missing limbs and countless others with their own special needs.

"The women's days pass in preparing food and cleaning the children as best they can," Ravi says. "If a child survives past age six, he is sent to an orphanage in a neighboring village. Running water is scarce. Because of government restrictions, the flow is turned off for most of the day. There are times where the water is contaminated with bacteria, so the children feel ill with stomachaches and unexplained rashes." He shakes his head. "Those are the most difficult of days."

We spend the next couple of hours helping the caregivers clean and feed the children. Afterward, I play and sing songs to the little ones. I teach them duck, duck, goose, though most of them just turn it into a game of chase. After hours of being there, I'm past the point of exhaustion. Desperate for a break, I search and find Ravi in a back room, resting on a folded chair.

I take a seat on the floor and lean against the wall. "Two adults only. How do they do it?"

"For some, India offers the life of a king," Ravi says simply. "But there are others who live their lives as best they can." When a toddler wanders into the room, Ravi teases him with his cane before the child runs out, laughing. "I imagine it is this way in your country also, yes?"

"Why do you come here?" I ask. He's right—every person, in his own way, has to find his path given his individual circumstances.

Ravi scans the larger room for Misha. He finds her busy playing a game with a group of children. "She tries hard not to let her condition bother her," Ravi says. "But one day she came to me and asked, 'Dada, why did God make me weaker than all the other children?' So we came here. I thought—let her see she is not the weakest. That there are others who are less fortunate."

My gaze locked on her and the children she's playing with, I say, "That's why you told her God gave her braces. Because she was too perfect otherwise."

"Would you disagree with my great-granddaughter's perfection?" Ravi asks. He calls out to Misha to say her goodbyes. "In Indian mythology, when the moon covers the sun, darkness has the power to cover your life." Slowly, he makes his way out of the room and toward the exit. "But it is not always the sun that must shine to have light. In darkness, we must seek out the stars. Their brightness has its own power."

"Why did you bring me here, Ravi?" I ask.

He gives me a sad smile. "You told me you

came to India to escape your pain. I thought about what your grandmother would say to you if she were here." He drops his head. "I could never think to speak for her, but . . ."

"But?" I ask, waiting.

He motions around us. "Maybe today, in helping to ease others' pain, you ease a little of your own?"

I smile, realizing he's right. In the few hours that we've been here, my own heartbreak has eased in the face of these children's.

"Ticket please." The woman at the foot of the bus is dressed in khaki shorts and a white shirt. Her hair is tucked beneath a broad-brimmed hat. She offers me a friendly smile when I hand her my ticket and says in perfect English, "Welcome. Please take any seat inside. We'll be serving drinks in a few minutes."

When I mentioned I was eager to see more of the area, Ravi had recommended a guided trip through the picturesque waterfall towns of Madhya Pradesh. Inside the air-conditioned coach bus, I take a seat near the front. After settling in, I watch as other passengers fill the seats until there are only a few left. I listen with interest to the range of accents and dialects as the travelers talk among themselves.

"Welcome." The woman taking tickets hops up the steps of the bus and stands near the front.

"I'm Mona, and this"—she points to the driver—"is Zane, short for Zev." She smiles at everyone's laughter. "I am your tour guide today. The tour will be approximately three hours." She runs through the choice of drinks and complimentary snacks. "Our first stop will be the Dhuandhar Falls in the Jabalpur district."

I stare out the window as the bus rambles down the freeway. The road twists past modern infrastructure and climbs toward wooded forest. Thirty minutes outside of the city center, the air is saturated with humidity, and a fine mist covers the windows.

Over the speaker, Mona starts to detail the history of the state, first in Hindi and then in English. "Madhya Pradesh has been nicknamed the heart of India due to its geographic location. With more than seventy million people, we are the fifth largest state in population." As the bus continues to climb, she says, "During the British occupation, they incorporated the state into Central Provinces and Berar and the Central India Agency. After India's independence, the state of Madhya Pradesh was created." Mona raises her voice to be heard over a loud roar of water in the distance. "Rich in mineral resources, the state has the largest reserves of diamond and copper in India. More than thirty percent of its area is under forest cover."

As the bus comes to a full stop, Mona

announces, "We have arrived at one of the most magnificent falls you will ever see. The source of the water is the Narmada River, which makes its way through the world-famous Marble Rocks, then narrows before it plunges into a waterfall known as Dhuandhar."

I follow the group of passengers as we exit the bus. Mona adds, "The hundred-foot drop, which creates a bouncing mass of mist, is so powerful that its roar is heard from a far distance."

The glistening water flows over rocks and into a sparkling pool of water. A rainbow shimmers at the edge of an overhanging cliff. Spray from the water falls over us like a light shower. Parents sit on the soft bed of grass while children throw pebbles and try to catch darting fish.

"It's so different from the villages," I murmur aloud.

"India is a vast land containing various topographies," Mona says in response. As requested, she takes some pictures of a couple before returning their camera. "Similar to America." I glance at her, and she smiles. "I did my business degree at the University of Chicago."

Impressed, I ask, "Do you miss the United States?"

"Parts of it." She takes another picture for a family from England. "But India is home. Plus, I'm excited to have started my own company."

"This is yours?" I ask.

"My second bus," she says proudly. "I bought the first one with a bank loan. This one I bought with my earnings."

"That's impressive." Amazed at her business savvy, I say, "You should be very proud."

"My family comes from a village on the outskirts of town." She gets a faraway look. "My father was a farmer and my mother a day laborer. It is good to see them happy."

"What's it like?" I hope I'm not being too personal, but she's piqued my interest about the women of today versus my grandmother's generation. "Starting a business?"

"Hard," she answers, and then laughs self-consciously. "If I had known exactly how hard, I might not have done it. Can I be honest?" She waits for my nod before continuing. "Business school in America was the best and worst thing. The education was second to none, but it gave me a false sense of ability. I was sure I could do anything."

"From where I'm standing, you're not too far off," I say kindly.

"I have women friends who have failed many times in their ventures." She motions around us. "India is a destination many wish to visit. Our state has an abundance of natural beauty." She smiles. "I was fortunate to be in the right place at the right time."

The journalist in me is fascinated and pushes for

more. "Being a woman—would you say it's easier for a woman than a man to start a business here?"

"Not easier." She pauses before trying to explain. "We are a country that's trying to keep up with the rest of the westernized world. Knowing that, there is an eagerness to open all avenues for everyone, regardless of gender. It's a country of opportunity. I'm simply taking advantage."

She smiles before walking away to answer some questions from other guests. I watch her as she mingles with the passengers, a seasoned pro at offering both entertainment and information. I imagine the pride Amisha, if she were here, would take at the strides her country has made in the years since its independence. Smiling, I spend the rest of the afternoon taking pictures and listening to the rush of water as it hits the walls of rock.

I dress in the traditional Punjabi suit—a long silk top over formfitting pants—for dinner with Ravi's family. They invited me and, excited to meet the whole family, I gratefully accepted. The outfit's light-yellow material contrasts with my dark brown hair.

I grab the bag of gifts sitting next to the bed and join Ravi in the living room. He takes the bag from my hands and peers into it. "This is for me?" he asks. "Very kind, but I no longer play with toys."

"I should be having them over for dinner," I say. "Not imposing on your family."

"You forget, I've seen your attempt at cooking," Ravi returns. "Besides, from what my son tells me, Misha will not stop talking about you. You are doing them a favor by joining them for dinner, if only to appease Misha."

The rickshaw drives us to their village. The asphalt turns to an unpaved road. A cluster of huts sits apart from larger shacks. Stacks of garbage are piled in front of each home. The dwellings spill over one another, with little space in between. A long line of women wait their turn at the water pump. They each carry two buckets apiece to fill. While waiting, they talk and laugh with one another. Children run free in the streets, dust kicking into the air with their play.

Ravi leads me to a smaller group of shacks. "It is more affordable housing." A curtain covers the entrance where a door should have been. He pushes it aside before announcing, "We are here."

Immediately, two men come forward. Dressed in traditional clothes, each one clasps his hands together. "Namaste. Welcome," Ravi's son says. He's a younger version of his father, whereas Ravi's grandson looks like Amit.

In stilted English, the grandson says, "Thank you for coming."

"Thank you for having me." I stare at Ravi's son, imagining Ravi when my grandmother was alive. I clasp my hands together and bow slightly to the two women who hang back, watching. "Namaste. You have a beautiful home."

Mud blocks create the walls, and a thatched roof covers the small hut. Torn bedsheets and a worn rug cover the hard floor made of cement. A half wall separates the kitchen and living room. There is only one chair, and several pillows are scattered on the floor. A narrow opening leads to a hall where two small rooms face each other.

"Ravi Dada speaks so highly of you," Misha and Amit's grandmother says. Her daughter-in-law remains quiet. "You have honored us with your presence."

A shriek of joy interrupts us. Misha comes barreling from the room down the hall with Amit close behind. She runs right into my arms. I hold her close, touched by her happiness and grateful to be spending time with her.

"We've been waiting all day," she says. I tighten my arms around her and run my hand down her hair. "I helped Mummy and my grandmother cook."

"I can't wait to eat what you've made." With Misha still in my arms, I glance at Amit, who stands quietly to the side. "Namaste, Beta."

"Welcome," he says in perfect English. "Would you like a tour?"

I slip my hand into Misha's as Amit shows me their humble home. There are three small rooms in addition to the kitchen. We end the tour in the main room, where more than a dozen glazed pottery vases are stacked in the corner. An embroidered rug hangs on one wall with the tale of Krishna depicted in the artwork.

"My daughter-in-law makes them," Ravi says when he notices me admiring the pottery.

"May I?" At her nod, I run my hands over the ceramic. "They're amazing." Each one is painted in dark hues of blue and purple. She watches as I sort through them, admiring the detailed color schemes.

"These are *gharas*," she says, pointing to the waterpots I'm admiring. "*Surahis*—pitchers, and *gamlas*—flowerpots." Each has a different design, with figures of elephants, birds, and serpents adorning them.

"She helps the family pay for the house and food with her work," Ravi says. "She is an exceptional artist, yes?"

"Yes," I say. "Your work is extraordinary."

She picks out the best one and then hands it to me. "You keep," she says.

"No, I couldn't." I hand it back to her. When she pushes it back toward me, I look to Ravi for help.

"It is a gift," Ravi says, pleased with the exchange. "She has never given one away before. You should feel privileged."

"Thank you." I reach out and give her a hug.

She hesitates and seems surprised, but then returns my embrace. "I will treasure it."

I follow the women into the kitchen, where a small kerosene stove burns. In the sitting area, Ravi's son puffs on a vegetable leaf hand-rolled and filled with tobacco. As everyone starts to gather the food for dinner, I ask if I can help.

"You are the guest," Ravi's daughter-in-law says. "Please only enjoy."

"After dinner, I can give you a tour of the neighborhood," Amit says, joining us. "There is much to see."

As they start to take dishes out to the main room, I insist on helping. Misha grabs a plate of appetizers. She walks carefully with it into the main room. She stumbles twice but shakes her head when Amit moves to help her. Nonetheless, he follows her out. Both her mother and grandmother watch her carefully until she makes it into the main room.

"She's beautiful," I say.

"Thank you," her grandmother says out of Misha's hearing range. "She is our God-given angel." She smiles. "Come, let us eat."

In the main room, atop a bedsheet, they've placed the food dishes and plates. The men are seated cross-legged. There's a small chair for Misha. I take a seat next to her and cross my legs like the others. Amit settles next to Ravi.

Amit's mother passes around the food, and

everyone fills their plate. Bowls are filled with mint and ginger water. There's a pan of mixed vegetables sautéed in a cream sauce and a plate of warm naan. I rip off a piece of naan and scoop the vegetables, savoring the spicy concoction. "Homemade buttermilk?" Ravi's daughter-in-law offers me a glass of thick white liquid.

"Thank you." I take a sip of the creamy liquid to help cool the spicy food. "It's delicious— like the rest of the meal. I really appreciate your having me over."

"It was our honor." Ravi's son ruffles Amit's hair. "My grandson tells us you are a reporter."

"Yes." I wink at Misha, who slips her hand into mine. "I know Misha plans on becoming a teacher. But what about you, Amit?" I ask, smiling at him.

"He should be a reporter," Misha answers for her brother. "Like you." The whole group laughs, her admiration never more apparent.

"I haven't decided." Amit falls quiet and is suddenly reserved. Ravi glances at him but says nothing.

"All he's ever wanted to be is a doctor," Amit's mother says, her love for him radiating. "He wants to help other children like his sister."

"Mummy, no," Amit says, shaking his head at her. "It is not possible." The room goes quiet. Amit's father drops his head and focuses on eating.

"Amit, why won't you be able to become a doctor?" I ask.

"He has top grades, but it is not always easy to get admission to university," Amit's mother says for him.

"Mummy, I can do something else." He fidgets with his napkin and then pushes away his half-eaten plate of food. "I will find something else."

I think about the young woman I met on the tour. I describe her experience and then wait, my unspoken question hanging in the air.

"India is a vast country," Ravi explains, "with no man or woman having the same experience. Every day we move forward. That is what gives me hope." But when he glances at Amit, I see the concern of a parent and a palpable yearning for a better future for his loved one.

"What would you choose?" I ask Amit when the room falls silent.

"Maybe reporting?" he says, and everyone laughs, lightening the mood.

I think back to when I announced I wanted to be a journalist. My mother questioned my decision but nonetheless paid for my education and celebrated my every success. Before the miscarriages, my battles were minimal, but whenever I was faced with disappointment, my parents were silent stanchions standing by my side. My mother's admission that she wanted only my happiness gave me a glimpse of what it means to be a parent who wants only the best for his child. Unsure what to say, I quietly finish my meal.

AMISHA

THIRTY-EIGHT

"Papa is home!" Paresh cried out in excitement as they neared the house and saw a light. With a break in the rain, Amisha and Bina had taken the boys out for some *kulfi*. Jay and Samir ran after their brother into the house.

Amisha hadn't seen Deepak since before Ravi's accident. She felt another wave of guilt for what had happened between her and Stephen. But just as it was impossible to stop the rains that came every year, it was impossible to quell her feelings for him. Without the benefit of choice, the only decision she could make was to care for Stephen while continuing in her duty to Deepak.

She smoothed the front of her shirt, seeking courage from the simple movement. She raised her head and followed her children inside.

"And then I played cricket with Samir, and I won." Paresh was in his father's arm, relaying everything Deepak had missed in his absence. Jay and Samir were standing alongside their father, smiling up at him.

"Welcome back."

Amisha stared at her husband, as if seeing him for the first time. In her brief interlude with Stephen, she had felt like a woman. She

403

felt worthy and capable, and for just a moment believed she had a purpose.

Now, with Deepak's return, she wondered how she could return to the reality that demanded she stay in her place. She imagined announcing she couldn't, and that if given a choice, she wanted something else. Just then, Samir shouted at his brother, jolting her from her thoughts. Watching them, she knew, no matter what choice she might have, she would never make that call.

"Can I prepare dinner for you?" she asked, falling seamlessly into her role.

"I ate on the train," Deepak said quietly, staring at her. "Where were you?" There was a bite to his tone that Amisha had never heard before.

Her tongue felt heavy, and sweat pooled in her bra. Had he found out what had happened? But she knew Stephen would never betray her. "I took the boys out for treats."

He picked up a package off the settee and tossed it to her. "For you."

Surprised, Amisha opened it. Inside, neatly folded, was an extravagant sari—a type she had seen only in movies. "It is beautiful." Her voice trembling, she asked, "What is the occasion?"

He made no reply, instead passing out gifts to the boys. Amisha watched him, sensing something was wrong. A quick scan of the house assured her nothing was amiss. Bina shrugged her shoulder when Amisha glanced at her in question.

"Your trip went well?" Amisha asked, unsure. "Are the presents a celebration?"

"Do I need cause to spend my money on my family?" he demanded.

"We are grateful." Amisha had never seen him like this. She wrapped a protective arm around her boys. "Right, boys?"

"Bina, watch the children," Deepak said before the boys could answer. "Amisha, let us speak in the other room."

Amisha gave the boys a reassuring smile before following him in and shutting the door. Off the desk, Deepak held a sheet of paper out to her. "This is what you are doing with your time at school? Teaching children to wish for death?"

Amisha knew without looking that it was Neema's final story about choices. She had been reading it earlier and left it on the desk. She watched in horror as he tore it to pieces and threw them at her feet.

"What did you do?" she cried as she gathered the pieces.

"If the parents learn you're filling the youngsters' minds with this kind of garbage, we will be destroyed in the community." His voice rose with fury. "Do you have any idea what you have done?" Outside the bedroom door, the sounds of the boys playing ceased as Deepak's roar reverberated.

Amisha finished gathering the pieces and laid

them on the desk. "The girl was heartbroken about her marriage. She was playing with words."

"Who was the girl?" Deepak demanded.

Amisha fought her sudden nausea. "Neema."

His face filled with fury. "The girl who set herself on fire." He would have heard about the girl from gossip. He glanced away before returning with his verdict. "You will no longer teach at the school."

"What?" Amisha clutched her stomach, pain searing through her at his words. "The students count on me. Please, I must . . ."

"The decision is made." He scooped the pieces off the desk and threw them into a wastebasket. "You will not jeopardize our family."

Amisha barely slept all night. Her thoughts were of Stephen, the school, and everything lost with just a few words from Deepak. In the morning, she fed the children their breakfast and was seeing them off when Ravi arrived.

"You're up early," Ravi commented. "Normally you are running around, screaming that everyone will be late while the children are laughing at the spectacle you create."

"Normally I would tell you what to do with your thoughts, but since you nearly died, I find myself grateful you are here to speak." Amisha didn't tell him that she had been up all night, thinking about Deepak's decision. Or that her heart ached at the thought of not teaching at the school and seeing Stephen.

Ravi handed Deepak his jacket and tiffin of food. Her husband slipped on his shoes, then left without a goodbye to Amisha. Ravi, noticing the silence, waited until the door was shut behind Deepak before turning to her.

"Why are you not attending school today?"

"He found the story Neema wrote. I'm no longer allowed to teach at the school," Amisha whispered.

"Shrimati." In his voice was all the sorrow that Amisha hadn't allowed herself to feel. "He could not be convinced?"

"No." Amisha scribbled a note to Stephen, detailing the assignments for the children. She slid it into her satchel along with the children's graded stories and held it out to Ravi. "Would you please take this to Stephen?"

"What reason should I give him for your absence?" Ravi asked.

She hadn't seen Stephen since three nights ago when he fed her the meal. Now she wondered when they would meet again. "Tell him . . ." Words failed her. The truth would tell Stephen what they both already knew—that she belonged to another. "That Deepak is back and he needs me at home."

"If he asks about your date of return?" Sympathy shone from Ravi's eyes.

"That I will return if I am able," she said, knowing the decision rested in Deepak's hands.

Amisha stood on the porch and watched Ravi walk toward the school. When he was out of sight, she went back inside the house and shut the door.

Ravi returned with a note from Stephen. With shaking fingers, Amisha opened it.

> Amisha,
> Ravi told me the news, but I fear there is more he did not wish to say. Until I know more, I will trust the delivered message. The children will miss their teacher, and I will miss our tutoring sessions. The garden already seems emptier without your smile and laughter gracing it. When you are able to return, your classroom will be waiting, as will I.
> Stephen

Amisha clutched the letter and read it a dozen more times before writing her own back to him. With a broken heart, she admitted the real reason, telling him in words what she couldn't say in person. In ending, she told him that more than he could imagine, she would miss her students and their tutoring.

Ravi delivered the letter immediately and from

then on, for two weeks, they wrote each other daily with Ravi as the messenger. The letters started to get longer and filled with more honesty. Though not a replacement for their conversations, they served as a balm for Amisha's loneliness.

She missed him every day. The emptiness left in his wake created a deep chasm within her. But if their letters were the only way she could hear his voice and know his thoughts, she would take them with gratitude.

To keep herself busy, she began walking with Paresh daily. Two weeks after Deepak's decision, Amisha was in the village when she heard a commotion. Women were rushing toward the edge of town. Men called out for people to follow.

"What is it?" Amisha demanded of a passerby who rushed to join the throng.

"The British have a man in custody."

Amisha scooped Paresh up and followed the pack to the outskirts of the village. There, in the midst of a large crowd, she spotted Stephen. The sight of him jolted her. The horde had circled him and other members of the British military. In the foreground stood a group of Indian men, all handcuffed to one another.

"Under the laws of the British Empire, you are under arrest." Stephen held tight to a frail Indian man. Infantrymen continued to handcuff others.

"You have no place in this country," the man

returned. In hopes of riling up the crowd, he yelled, "They are arresting me for breaking their rules in our country."

The uproar was swift and loud. The crowd began shouting protests. Some of the teenagers picked up rocks and began to throw them. When one hit Stephen, Amisha cried out in distress.

"What happened?" she asked a woman standing next to her. Her heart raced as the teenagers continued to throw rocks at the officers.

"That man there," she said, pointing to the one who had spoken, "started speaking about Gandhi's words of freedom. An officer ordered him to stop when a crowd gathered. He refused and was arrested."

"He was beaten?" Blood dripped from the man's forehead.

"He fought them," the woman explained. "One of the officers hit him with his stick."

Amisha didn't ask which of the officers hit him. She knew Stephen would have had to act, but she didn't want to know whether he was the one who raised his hand to her countryman.

The officers grabbed the offending teenagers and restrained them. When their parents started to protest and fight, the British began to strike out randomly, hitting both women and men in their effort to control the crowd.

"No." Amisha covered her mouth in horror. She brought Paresh close, trying to shield him from the view. When a full riot broke out, Amisha picked Paresh up to leave. Just then, Stephen's eyes met hers. In them she saw his confusion and questions. Not having an answer, she gazed at him for a few more seconds before walking away.

THIRTY-NINE

"You haven't seen him in weeks," Ravi said. While Amisha darned holes in the boys' clothes, Bina brought in buckets of water to wash dishes. "Is that why the letters are so heavy that my back is sure to break from carrying them?"

"If your back is so weak that it can break from letters, then it is deserved." Amisha missed her mark and pricked her finger with the needle instead. She stuck her finger into her mouth. "If I go to the school, I worry what Deepak will say." She set the darning down. "And every day that I don't speak to Stephen, I feel alone, though surrounded by my family and friends."

"You care for him," Ravi said, not asking.

"More than I should."

Amisha had not seen him since the day of the riot. She heard from other villagers that they had arrested more than a dozen men and teenagers. It was hard for her to see him as the officer she knew he was. She missed the man she knew him to be in the garden. In a letter following the riot, Stephen spoke about his place in the country and his purpose. Though he didn't apologize for his actions, Amisha could detect his regret and confusion.

412

"When I married, I was only told of responsibility and duty." Shrugging, she stared out the window. "Maybe that's all I'm allowed."

"What do you hope for?" Ravi asked. "With him?"

"If I were a child, I would dream of a future," she admitted slowly. "But I am not; nor am I foolish enough to believe I can have anything but what is given to me by fate." She wrung her hands together. "Deepak is the only future I can know."

Before Ravi could respond, Deepak returned from making his social rounds in the village. Amisha waited until the other servants were in the kitchen; then she sought the right words. "It has been weeks since I've been at the school. It is time for me to go back."

"Why?" Deepak asked absently. "Vikram mentioned the lieutenant is leaving. I'm sure the new head of school will find someone else to teach your class."

"What?" Amisha faltered, her hands shaking. She was sure she had misheard him. "When?"

"He is to leave immediately." Deepak picked up the paper and briefly glanced at the news. "It seems he requested a transfer. He is leaving for the front lines of the war."

Amisha's heart slowed between beats. She saw Ravi glance at her and knew he saw the hurt and shock she barely showed.

Deepak, oblivious to her reaction, said, "I have been away from the business for too long. I am scheduled to leave on the train tonight. Maybe you and the children would enjoy a visit with your parents?"

"Go to my parents?" Amisha asked in a daze. "No." She had to see Stephen and ask him what had happened. "I cannot go."

"What?" Deepak asked. "Why?"

"It is—uh . . ." She stumbled over the words, unsure.

"The boys have plans to stay at the house with us tonight," Ravi said, interjecting before Deepak suspected anything. "They have been very excited, looking forward to being spoiled by my wife and parents." Ravi's parents had become surrogate grandparents to the boys over the years.

"Another time, then." Deepak glanced at the clock. "I'll have to hurry to make the next train." Once he had packed, Amisha waited by the door and watched him leave in the rickshaw.

"I will take the children to my house for the night," Ravi said quietly.

"Ravi?" Amisha asked, unsure.

"Go ask him why," Ravi said quietly. "You will not rest easy until you do."

Amisha stood in her empty house after Ravi left with the children. Her stomach turned; thoughts in her head spun past one another, each one more urgent than the last. It seemed only yesterday she was begging for Deepak's permission to teach at the school. That desperation felt trivial now. Then she was fighting for her mind. Now she was trying to hold on to her soul.

The emptiness mocked her. The bedroom reminded her of her short interlude with Stephen. She could still see him in the kitchen, from when he shared a meal with her family. No matter where she turned, he called to her. She tried to ignore thoughts of his fighting in the war. If he lost his life in the war, how would she continue with hers?

She waited until it was dark before leaving her house so no one would see her. She had to beg him not to go. She ran toward his home. Once there, Amisha took a deep breath. The last time she had stood on Stephen's doorstep, she had been frantic to save her friend's life. Now she was here to save her own. Her stomach tensed as she knocked on the door. She started to call his name, when he opened the door.

"Amisha? What are you doing here?" His face tightened with concern when he saw her anguish.

"May I come in?" She moved past him into the small house. Built only months before the school, it had many of the same modern conveniences. She swiped at her tears.

"Amisha, tell me what's wrong," he said softly.

She saw the towel in his hand. "You were getting ready to bathe?"

She was desperate to continue with small talk. Anything to avoid the conversation that would have him speak the truth. Because once he said it, there would be no turning back. No way to undo the damage to her heart.

Amisha had lived in the shadows for most of her life. She had hidden her dream of writing as if it were a curse to be ashamed of. She bore Deepak his sons and sated his needs. But the tales in her would not die. When she wrote, she was transported to a place where she discovered who she was but could never be.

Then Stephen came into her life. He offered her a freedom she hadn't imagined. He valued her words and encouraged her voice. Her life since childhood had been about doing what was expected. He gave her another choice. With that choice, she cared for him. On the night of Ravi's injury, she accepted she needed him. But now she had nothing to give him to make him stay, to show him she loved him.

He threw his towel on a chair and ran his hands through his hair before clasping them behind his neck. She saw his anguish, and hers doubled with it. "I thought I was imagining your voice."

Amisha stepped closer to him. "They said you were leaving."

He shut his eyes and moved away, unwilling to face her. "I have to," he said, his voice catching.

"Why?" Amisha demanded.

"India." He paused and swallowed deeply. "I don't belong here. This is not my fight."

The day of the riot, she had seen his confusion and disgust. His people against hers. She knew she and Stephen couldn't keep going as they were—letters and random sightings. He was young and deserved to live his life. She had nothing to offer him.

"Were you going to tell me?" Amisha whispered.

"You were the one person I didn't know how to tell," he said with a broken laugh. "Not seeing you every day." He shook his head, and Amisha saw his pain. "I have missed you." He paused. "But we both know there are no choices."

"You could die," she said on a sob.

"No." He reached out but stopped before touching her. "I promise you I will not."

Amisha took him at his word and clung to the promise. But life had not always proven fair, and she knew it might be the last time she would ever see him. To turn away from her feelings would be dishonoring him and what they meant to each other. She was tired of living life within the boundaries set for her.

She grasped the front of her sari above her breast and pulled. The silk fluttered to the floor. Soon she was bare but for her blouse and the skirt she wore under her sari.

"Stephen," she said, reaching for him.

He turned, his eyes widening at the sight before him. She stood, exposed and vulnerable, calling to him in the only way she knew how. "No," he said. His fingers curled into fists at his side. "Don't do this."

"Should I beg?" she asked, her hands limp at her sides.

He covered her mouth with his fingers. His hand fell to her neck, taking the freedom she gave him to touch her. She moaned and he crushed her to him, sighing when her body was fully against his. He fit against her perfectly, and she molded to his body.

He kissed her, and she opened her mouth. She matched his thrusts, tangling her hands in his hair to bring his head into alignment. The need to be bare against him overwhelmed her, and she began to undo the buttons of his shirt.

Amisha instinctively knew that Stephen would welcome her need to touch him and to see his body. She explored the skin she exposed, and when at last she had the shirt off, she lost herself in the hair on his chest. It was coarse and soft at the same time, and she bent forward to kiss him.

"Did I hurt you?" Amisha moved away when Stephen sucked in his breath.

"Definitely not." He brought her back.

She touched him in all the ways she wanted to be caressed. She felt his hitch in breathing when her fingers danced across his stomach. She savored the strength of his arms and the gentleness of his hands. When she reached the buckle on his pants, she hesitated, unsure and shy. He took her hands and brought them up to kiss. Then he unbuttoned her blouse and unhooked her bra, freeing her into his palms. She felt the tears pool in her eyes and saw his tears swimming beneath his eyelids.

He undressed her slowly, baring her to him. When she was naked, he kissed her again. "We can do this?" He lifted her into his arms, ready to carry her into the bedroom.

"Yes," she answered, sure she could. Because, right then, she refused to belong to those who had claimed ownership of her. Not to the father and mother who bore her and decided her partner for the rest of her years. Not to the husband to whom she had been passed for the sake of bearing children and keeping house. Not to the expectations steeped within her. For one night she would belong to herself.

When he laid her on the bed, she opened her arms, welcoming him. When he separated her thighs with his knees, she moved them farther apart and encircled his waist, waiting for him to enter. As he crossed her barrier and lost himself within her, she saw the shadows clear and the light finally shine.

Amisha and Stephen spent the rest of the night together. He turned to her twice more in the darkness, and she awakened him early in the morning with kisses on his neck. He pulled her over him and encouraged her to experiment. She was shy in the morning light, anxious about exposing her body to him. He responded by tracing the lines of her stretch marks from her three pregnancies.

She showered in his tub, relishing the indoor facility. While she dressed, he prepared breakfast. She barely touched her food.

"Amisha." Stephen sat down next to her.

"Is this goodbye?" she asked, tears streaming down her face.

Tired and worn, with few choices, he said, "After the war, I will try to come back."

"Then what?" she asked, scared for him and herself. "I will still be married."

"I know," he said gently.

Left with no other answer, she kissed him softly. He deepened the kiss and held her for as long as he could before she left him, sitting there, and returned home to wait for her children.

FORTY

Every new day brought exhaustion. After Stephen's departure, Amisha received word that the school no longer needed her services. The days turned to weeks, and she spent more time in bed. Ravi and Bina were at her bedside regularly, bringing her food and medicine from the local holistic doctor. Six weeks after her joining with Stephen, she began to vomit. She rushed from the bed and heaved near the outhouse until her stomach was empty. Ravi handed her a glass of water and wet towel.

"Shrimati?" Looking uncomfortable, Ravi moved closer to her. "Has the time come to celebrate?"

"Celebrate?" Realizing what he meant, Amisha collapsed against the wall of the house, using the support to keep her steady. "I am with child," she choked, her hand over her stomach. Her symptoms suddenly made sense. Having given birth three times before, she couldn't believe she had missed the signs.

"Sahib will be pleased?" Ravi asked. The question burned between them.

Amisha stared at him. Ravi was the only one who knew her feelings for Stephen. "It is not his." Happiness flowed through her. She had lost

Stephen, but with his child she would have a part of him forever. "When you took the children to your house . . ." It seemed another time when Amisha had lain beneath Stephen. Given him her body long after he had taken her heart. "Before he left."

"Rest," he urged. To his credit, he didn't comment on her revelation, but Amisha knew he would keep her secret. "You must think of the child."

"I have to . . ." She paused. She thought of her boys, and the truth behind her situation hit her.

"Shrimati?" Ravi stood near her, caught off guard by the ashen look on her face.

"Deepak can never find out." She stared at him, wide-eyed and desperate. "My children—what have I done?" She fell to the ground, both hands protecting her unborn.

Amisha planned Deepak's arrival home meticulously. But with every step she was weighed down by the burden of her deception. Her options were limited, however. If Deepak knew what she had done, regardless of the pregnancy, she would be thrown to the streets.

No matter where Stephen was, she still loved him. That was the only explanation she had for her heart-wrenching ache whenever she thought of him. But she was first and always a mother. To fail her boys would be to fail the only responsibility that the heavens had given her. She refused to do that, so instead, she waited for Deepak to return to set her plan in motion. When he arrived two days later, she was ready.

"You are very active tonight," Deepak said when Amisha entered their room. She had put the boys to bed early and sent the servants, including Ravi, home after dinner.

"Am I not allowed to show pleasure at my husband's return?" Amisha brushed her hair in front of the small mirror.

"You are." Deepak watched her with renewed appreciation. As she had hoped, he took her subtle cue and approached her, taking the brush from her hands. "The servants mentioned you had been ill."

"The servants worry too much," she said.

He closed the door and reduced the oil in the lamp. He undressed her, slipped into the bed, and motioned wordlessly for her to join him. Amisha tempered her memories of the last time she had lain with a man. She had forced to the deep recesses of her mind how Stephen had held her. Now she prepared for Deepak's touch. Her unborn child was the gift to her from the night she spent with Stephen.

Amisha loosened her sari and slipped under the covers. She felt the cool length of his body against the warmth of her own. When his hand traveled below her breast, she gently pulled it back up. She could not chance his feeling the slight swell of her belly. If he noticed, he did not comment. In seconds he was ready and brought her underneath him.

"It is time," Amisha murmured when he prepared to enter her.

"For?" he questioned, pausing.

"A child. The boys are eager for a little one to tease." She waited with bated breath for him to comment.

He nodded with a grin, and when he slipped through her dryness, she moaned in pain into the pillow. He began to stir, and she sent a silent call to the heavens above. As his sperm traveled within her, she pled for his essence to penetrate the fluid surrounding the baby. She begged that his sperm join the child in her womb, permeating the protective layer surrounding the fetus. Her hope was that the baby would absorb Deepak's characteristics, thus feeling familiar to him on its arrival into the world. And the child would see Deepak as its true father, leaving no memory or longing for the real father who would never learn of its existence.

FORTY-ONE

Six months into her pregnancy, the fatigue had begun to take a toll. She had vomited twice already that morning. She nibbled on biscuits and ginger water in hopes of keeping the nausea at bay. One foot on the ground, she swung back and forth on the settee.

"The boys left for school early," she said to Ravi. Deepak had left on the train three days prior. He'd rarely been home for the duration of the pregnancy, though Amisha barely noticed. "Was everything all right?"

"They woke up early to the sound of your heaving and dressed faster than ever before," Ravi said, refilling her water. "I fear they haven't mastered the concept of empathy yet."

Amisha mustered a smile for him right before another wave of nausea hit her. Grimacing, she rubbed her hand over her slightly swollen belly. "Maybe I am being punished for my deceit."

"Do you believe that this is punishment?" Ravi placed a bowl near her in case she vomited again.

Amisha thought about Stephen and the child they had created. Their love had been powerful enough to create life, and that life was their bond. "If it is, then I welcome it. Any price is worth having known him."

"Then you are fortunate, Shrimati," Ravi said. "Few know the value of what they are given." He gathered the soiled clothes and tossed them into a basket to wash. "I'll be in the back if you need me."

"Thank you, Ravi." Amisha laid her head against the pillows. Bina and another servant had both stayed home today due to illness, so when the knock at the door came, she was the only one home to open it. "One minute," Amisha said loudly so the visitor could hear. She wiped her hands of crumbs, then opened the door.

The sight of Stephen made her legs buckle, and her eyes welled up with tears. Her hand gripped her chest as pain ripped through her. "You're here." Sure he was an illusion, she reached out and grabbed his hand while they stared at each other. His hair was longer than before, and his face was thinner. But the eyes that held hers were the same.

"I'm here." He came fully into the house and closed the door behind him. "Deepak is traveling?" His eyes held hers.

"Yes." Amisha soaked up the sight of him. She had to convince herself that he was not a hallucination. That her mind, from the deep recesses of the grief that had gripped her since his departure, had not conjured him as a means of survival. "It cannot be you."

"I'm here, Amisha." Stephen gently held her

shoulders, his gaze running over her face. "Is anyone home?"

When Amisha shook her head no, he pulled her in, closing the distance between them. She dropped her head to his chest, her soul anxious to lessen the burden that had sat heavy on it since his departure. He cupped the back of her head and lowered another hand to her waist. The sound of his racing heart echoed in her ear. She willed her own to settle down. The first tears soaked his shirt, but soon she began to cry and shake with sobs that had been stifled ever since he left.

"Shh." He tried to console her, but there was nothing he could say to lessen her pain. She had worried about him throughout the day and at night had dreamed of him in faraway places.

"You left me," she cried, the memories haunting her. "I broke without you."

"Amisha." He started to speak, when he felt the soft swell of her waist beneath her sari. "What?" The question was in his eyes as he began to take her sari off.

"No." She tried to step back, but he held fast. She knew he felt the difference from the night they were together.

"Whose is it?" He stared at her swollen stomach.

Amisha stood at a crossroads, though only one path was hers to take. Stephen was the only man she loved and would ever want. Before she met him, she had accepted her life's course, but he had allowed her to dream. He was her soul, and she was tearing it apart.

"Deepak's."

"No." He turned away.

"I'm sorry." Amisha cried the tears he was unable to. "This child . . ."

"Deserves its father," Stephen answered, defeated.

"I love you," Amisha admitted.

"My love for you is irrelevant."

"Your love is my salvation," she gasped, trying to speak through the sob lodged in her throat. The child she carried was a gift from their union, offering her a part of him and yet forcing her to live without him.

"I have to go." He stepped back, giving her the distance she had asked for only moments before.

"Where?" Amisha needed to know where he would be when not with her.

"I don't know. Back home?" His eyes strayed toward Amisha's stomach. "I only came back to see you." Stephen moved toward the door, his hand blindly reaching out for the knob.

"Wait." She swiped at her tears as she rushed toward the bedroom. From beneath the bed, she pulled the stack of stories. Every written word that came from her was in a neat pile. All the tales from her heart, both in English and Hindi. From the doorway of her bedroom, she stared at him. She knew she would never see him again, so she imprinted to memory his every nuance and feature. With measured steps, trying to hold off the inevitable, she returned to him and held out the papers.

"What is this?" He stared at the bundle through the moisture in his eyes.

"My stories."

"No." He tried to hand them back, but she refused them.

"They are yours, Stephen," she insisted. "I have not written since the day you left. Not one word. The words left me when I knew you were no longer going to be with me." She stopped to take a deep breath.

"Then come," he begged. "Be my family."

"This is my world." She gestured around her. "My children belong here as I do. We have pretended, you and I. In our garden, we raised our roses, but they have thorns and we have been pierced. Spilled blood is all that we have left of our fantasy."

Stephen hung his head, unable to argue.

"And this," Amisha said, seeing his pain match hers, "is a village that you have no use for."

"Amisha," he began, his hurt clear, "we can make a life together."

"Where?" Amisha demanded. "In your country, I am a brown. In mine, you are hated. There is no place for us." He started to say something, but

Amisha interrupted him. "Please, let me speak while I am still able." She laid her hands on his arms, garnering strength from him because she had none left. "I wish I could make a life with you. I will never know happiness again without you."

"You would be safe with me; I give you my word."

"It would be without my children, and I cannot choose you over them. So I will surrender to the rules I must live by, but in doing so, I promise you and the gods that only if we are ever together will I write again. They put me in this world, and now I shall live in it," Amisha vowed, left with nothing but anger.

"That is not a sacrifice you can make."

"You have my heart, Stephen," she sobbed, "and without it, I have no tales to tell." Amisha felt her world shift and her balance disappear. The sense of loss was stronger than the happiness they had shared.

Her stories allowed her to create fantasies and determine endings. But this tale had only one possible conclusion, and she was helpless to reverse it, powerless to alter its predetermined course. Fate had exacted its payment for allowing them to have known such happiness. They were to be left with nothing but memories of a love they would never know again.

Stephen caressed her cheek with his hand and

brought her close. He laid his hand on her belly. "I would give anything for this child to be mine," he whispered. "Even though it is not, the child is a part of you, and because of that, I wish it all the happiness life has to offer." He bent down and brushed her lips with his own. Then, releasing her, he walked out, refusing to turn and see her crumpled on the floor, broken and alone, holding the child that was the only part of him she had left.

JAYA

FORTY-TWO

I swipe at the tears as Ravi finishes. We walk together along the river's edge. "She loved him so much."

"Yes," he says softly. "Their love was true and binding."

"Does my mother know?" Though I assume the answer is no, I still ask. "That Stephen is her real father?"

"She was never told," Ravi says quietly.

"Why not tell her?" She would have been loved completely, and yet she has lived her life never knowing how wanted she was. "Why wait all this time?"

"I couldn't," Ravi says slowly. "Until now."

"Because of my grandfather?" I ask.

"Yes."

"She had a right to know." Angry at the circumstances before my time, I yearn for my mother to have had the love and support of her parents. "She deserved to know her father."

The secrets of my mother's past have lain dormant for two generations. The father she assumed was hers never wanted her, while the father who didn't know of her existence would have loved her unconditionally. I grieve for the choice my grandmother had to make and the secret my mother never learned.

I am empty for never having had a child, as is my mother for never having had her father. In our loss I am linked to my mother—the woman I am just starting to know.

"Stephen would have been a good father," Ravi says, his voice broken. "He was an exceptionally good man."

"Is he still alive?" I ask, hopeful.

"No," he whispers, and disappointment slices through me. "Not anymore. I think neither could live in this world without the other."

I choke back a sob at the profoundness of their connection. "When I came to India, I never expected to hear such a story."

"Maybe it is why you came?" Ravi says. "Your grandmother hoped I would tell her daughter the tale, but maybe you were the one meant to hear it, yes?"

"Maybe," I say. "I'm telling my mother bits and pieces of the story."

"Will you tell her this?" he asks.

"Not yet." She will need my father by her side as she hears of her heritage. "When I go back, I'll tell her everything."

In the distance, women are waist deep in the water as they wash their clothes. Children play nearby, splashing one another as they bathe in the warm water. Men lead their cows to the banks to drink. After spending the morning on the story, Ravi recommended we take a walk.

"Watch your step." He leads us away from the edge of the river and toward the grass. "There can be snakes hidden underneath."

"What?" I stop and search the ground for slithering creatures. "Snakes?"

"Yes." Unconcerned, Ravi continues to casually uproot the rocks as we walk.

"But everyone is in the water." I gesture toward the crowd. "Someone could get hurt."

"If a snake comes upon the women, they will simply push it away." Ravi considers the children, and his mouth turns down. "The children, I fear, may consider the snake a toy and use it for their amusement."

"Shouldn't they kill it?" My voice rises a notch. "It's probably poisonous."

"Ah, but are we not the ones who are a bother to them?" He points his cane at the river. "Who is to say to whom this land belongs? The snake would argue it is its home that we have disturbed. Its poison may be its only defense."

As if on cue, the shriek of a child shatters the silence. A young boy holds up a small snake like a prized possession before flinging it to his friends.

"I hate snakes, and I don't want them near me." I wrap my arms around myself as a shiver courses down my spine.

"So you claim your rights are superior?"

"Yes, I do." I give him an evil eye and dare him to disagree.

"Then I shall recommend we move away from the water and into town. I worry we may come across a snake and you will find your superiority lacking as you run for your life."

Loud Bollywood music and laughter welcome Ravi and me back into the village. There's a large gathering of young men in jeans and shirts and women dressed in colorful knee-length skirts and blouses. A hush falls over the crowd as a young man in an embroidered red wedding top and cream pants rides into the village, seated atop a baby elephant.

"What's going on?" I ask.

The men take the rider and carry him atop their shoulders toward a table near a tent. The women link their arms and form a wall, preventing him from reaching a young woman sitting at the table.

"It's the henna ceremony," Ravi says. "That man"—Ravi points to the man who was just on the elephant—"is the groom. The girl at the table is the bride." The groom makes a mad rush toward the bride, but the women hold their ground, blocking his attempt to reach his betrothed. There's laughter and teasing every time he tries and fails. "It's a sacred part of the wedding. Though the wedding is a physical act, the spiritual aspects of it are most celebrated."

On my wedding day, I wore traditional white, and we were married on the beach. I never thought to have an Indian wedding. "Why is it sacred?"

"They paint her hands with henna. Intricate designs that symbolize the depth of love the husband will feel for her after marriage." Seated next to the bride, her friends paint her hands and feet. The groom makes another playful run to reach her while his friends stand by, laughing. "The artist will subtly blend their names into the design. On the wedding night, the groom can't consummate the wedding until he finds them." Ravi smiles. "There are many tales of a groom searching all night."

The bride's girlfriends begin to sing songs in Hindi, and soon the men join in. They seem oblivious to the heat even as sweat lines the back of their clothes. "What are the women singing about?" Though I can decipher some of the words, I still can't make sense of the entire song.

"They are teasing the bride about her husband and future in-laws. They are saying he will get so fat that one day he will fall asleep on top of her and she will be stuck. They are cautioning her not to cook too well."

A large crowd starts to form. Parents join their children as the festivities continue. "Who are the rest of the people?"

"An Indian wedding can be as small as two hundred people or up to six hundred." In front of the small campfire, the *pujari* cuts a coconut and lays fresh flowers and uncooked rice alongside it. "The coconut represents fertility," Ravi explains. "The flowers are for beauty, and the rice symbolizes sustenance." The priest pours melted butter onto the fire to keep it alive.

As the sun starts to set, the party intensifies. The music gets louder, and everyone begins to dance. The future bride joins her fiancé. He says something to her, and she throws her head back and laughs.

I envy them their happiness. Their life is ahead of them and their opportunities are limitless. On my own wedding day, I was sure nothing could break us. Pain and heartache seemed impossibilities given the amount of joy we shared. My thoughts stray to Amisha and her choices. Watching the couple, I can't help but feel grateful. For as long as Patrick and I were together, I knew true happiness. No matter the despair that followed, I loved him, and I wonder if I always will.

FORTY-THREE

Two days later, I wake up on the anniversary of my first miscarriage. I dress in one of the outfits I bought from the market. I head out, cognizant of each step as I take it, wary of whether I am doing the right thing.

At the temple, I slip off my shoes and climb the steps. "Namaste." The temple is quiet with only a few families in attendance.

"Welcome." The Brahmin accepts my offered plate of fruits and flowers. "Thank you. You will have a long and happy life."

"I appreciate that." I search the faces of the deities. Each one is mesmerizing.

"Is there something you are seeking?" the Brahmin asks.

"I just came to ask . . ." I pause, searching for the right words. "Not ask—maybe get some answers," I try again. "That's the Goddess Parvati?"

"Yes, and Durga." He gestures toward the statue next to her. "Both very powerful forces."

I kneel between the two goddess figures that stand together in graceful harmony. Their eyes are the color of crystal lavender, and their hands are painted gold. I shut my eyes and imagine my babies playing, their laughter a balm to the wounds that refuse to heal. I would have shushed their cries with hugs and joined in their laughter. To them I would have given more of myself than I had ever given before.

"My grandmother came to this temple," I say to the silent sculptures. "I never knew her, but I have no doubt she was stronger than I will ever be." In this moment, I feel younger than my years and even more naive. "But I am here to ask you for a child of my own," I whisper. The tears fall, my sadness refusing me a reprieve. I lower my face onto my knees and hide from the Brahmin and from the eyes of the goddesses. I hide from the world and from myself, still uncertain of my place.

"Jaya?" Amit approaches me with trepidation.

I quickly wipe my tears. Hours have passed, and the sacred statues are now draped in shadows. "Amit? How are you, Beta?"

"I'm fine." He holds a plate full of flowers and fruits. He notices my tear-streaked face. "Are you all right?"

"Your great-grandfather says the temples have an abundance of power." I run my hand over my face one last time, hoping to remove all traces of my tears. "I may have gotten caught up in it." I wrap an arm around his shoulder. "I'm surprised to see you here in the middle of the day. You don't have school?"

"We were let out early today." He glances away. "May I ask you something?"

"Of course. Anything." I lead us toward the far edge of the temple where we can have some privacy.

"Do you believe in miracles?" He's hesitant but seems eager to hear my answer. "You seem to be very smart." His face is full of admiration.

"First of all," I say, smiling at him, "from what your Ravi Dada tells me, I can't hold a candle to you in math. Top of your class, I hear." My compliment earns me a blush across his face. "And what I believe doesn't matter." I hedge, not answering his question directly. "What matters is whether you do. Do you believe in miracles?"

"Misha." He hesitates but then after a minute says, "The polio—there is nothing that can be done." He stares at the marble pillars. "So I come here daily with offerings in hopes that God will heal her." He pauses, his throat convulsing. "Then she can run and play like the rest of us."

I stare at the boy in front of me. He's a man before he's even crossed the boundaries of childhood. It seems impossible to me that one family, one bloodline, can exhibit so much loyalty. "Does your Ravi Dada know?" I ask.

"I would not want him to know of my false hopes." Amit stares into the distance. "In America, have you seen prayers answered with miracles?"

"There are miracles every day," I say, although I have never witnessed one and stopped believing in miracles after my miscarriages. "Is that what you want for your sister?"

"Yes," he answers. He motions toward the statues. "And there is nothing I can do but pray."

That evening, I head to the café and in the phone booth dial the number I know by heart. My breath catches as the distant ring gets louder.

"Hello?"

Patrick's voice carries over the line, sounding the same as the last time we spoke. I realize it's close to midnight his time. Suddenly feeling foolish, I wonder if he has someone there.

"Hi," I say when he says hello again. "It's me."

The sound of his voice has caught me off guard. When we first started dating, we would talk for hours into the night. Soon enough, his voice became the calm in my storm and the cheerleader for my aspirations. It was when I lost myself in grief that I forgot how much I needed him.

"Jaya?" I hear rustling in the background, and I imagine he's putting his pillows up and leaning against them. "I didn't expect you. Is everything all right?"

"Yes," I quickly say. "I know it's late. I didn't calculate the time until I'd already dialed." I'm rambling, but I can't stop myself. "If Stacey is there, I feel bad . . ."

"Stacey's not here," Patrick says softly, interrupting me. "We haven't seen each other again since I told you about it."

"Oh." Stunned, I fall silent. I was so sure she was the final break in a marriage that was shattered from grief. Confused, I want to ask him more, but I hold back. The time when I was his confidante is long past. "I'm sorry."

"How are you?" His voice falls low, and even with the distance between us, I can feel his confusion. "I tried calling you, but the line disconnected."

"I heard your voice, but you couldn't hear mine. I called you back, but . . ." My voice drifts off. It feels like lifetimes ago when he called. Then, I had only started learning the story of my grandmother, never imagining where it would lead.

"You hung up. Because of Stacey," he says in the silence. I don't confirm the answer he already knows.

"I'm calling to say thank you for being there during the miscarriages," I tell him quickly. "Today is the anniversary of the first one." When I hear his indrawn breath, I swallow the sob that lodges in my throat and pray to get through this without crying. "You tried to be there for me. I couldn't see it then, but now I do."

"I miss you," he says, shocking me. It's the last thing I expected him to say. I hear him shift the phone from one ear to the other, and I know that he's turning on the lamp next to the bed. "I missed you then too—so much."

Unbidden hope blooms inside me. I miss him in my life. Amisha's story drives home how precious love is. I took our love for granted, and when it became too hard, I stepped away, sure I was stronger standing alone. But loving him was not a burden; nor was it a blessing. It was two people who desperately loved each other while making a life together. With him I could breathe, and I was happy.

"I was lost," I whisper. I bring my knees to my chest and wrap my free arm around them. "The grief made everything dark."

"I'm so sorry I couldn't get you through it," he admits. The pain that has held a tight grip on my heart loosens. "I wanted to, but I didn't know how." When my sob finally breaks through, I hear him take a deep breath on the other side, and I know he's fighting his own emotions.

"Thank you for trying," I tell him. "I'm sorry I never told you that."

"We're married," he says, not seeming to realize his word usage. "It was my job." When I don't say anything, he says, "I've been reading your blog pieces. They're amazing."

I let out a laugh in between my tears. "Still have your rose-colored glasses on, huh?" I tease. No matter how many drafts I would go through,

Patrick always told me my work was great. "Good to know."

His laugh echoes mine, and then we both fall silent. There's so much I want to tell him, but I don't have the right anymore. He's not my sounding board or my confidant. In walking away from our marriage, I lost my best friend and my love.

"I miss you," I admit. "More than I thought I would."

When friends would announce they were getting a divorce, I always wondered how the bond could break so completely that the love was forgotten. When Patrick and I separated, I was so focused on what had torn us apart, I didn't remember what brought us together. Now a small seed of hope blossoms, but the voice of caution, the one that demands I tread carefully, tells me to take it slow.

"When are you coming back?" he asks into the silence.

"I don't know." My editor recently sent me some assignments I can do remotely. It feels good to be working in addition to writing the blog pieces. "Being here . . ." I think about Amisha's story and her journey. "I believe it's helping me to heal."

"I'm glad." He pauses, and I wonder if, like me, he's still afraid to let me in. "I've been checking in with your parents," he says, surprising me.

"I asked them not to say anything," he explains before I can complain. "I just wanted to make sure you were all right."

"Patrick," I start, and then stop. I want to censor my words, but they spill out. "I wish the miscarriages hadn't happened," I whisper. Caution warns me to keep my thoughts hidden, but I am tired of holding back my feelings. "I wanted a family with you so much. I wanted us to be parents."

"I know, honey." His voice is filled with hurt. "More than anything, I wanted that with you too."

When my tears make it impossible for me to talk, he stays on the phone and listens to me cry. Across the oceans and countries, he offers me comfort, and for the first time since the pain started, I let him in.

FORTY-FOUR

I arrive at the orphanage late at night. I had tried to sleep, but thoughts of my conversation with Patrick kept me awake. We talked for hours about memories from the past and the hurt that felt impossible to overcome. I started to tell him pieces of Ravi's story. Though hesitant at first, I was encouraged by his interest. For those few hours, it felt like we had never been apart.

I climb the steps, feeling foolish for visiting when the children are likely sleeping. I knock once, quietly. If someone doesn't answer immediately, I will return home.

"Yes?" The caregiver I met on my last visit opens the door. Her eyes widen with recognition. "Shrimati, what are you doing here?" She ushers me in. The room is dark, with only a small light flickering in the back room. Though most of the children are asleep, a few are stirring.

"I'm sorry. I know it's late." I keep my voice low. "I wasn't sure what time the children went to sleep, but I thought I could come by . . ." Shrugging, I thrust my hands into the pockets of my capris. "See if I could spend some time with them?"

If the caregiver thinks me odd for the late-night visit, she keeps her thoughts to herself. "There are always one or two children who wake up hungry." In the kitchenette, milk is warming in a pan on the stove. "Would you like to pour it into the bottles?"

"Of course." I find some clean bottles drying on a napkin. "You stay up all night?"

"The woman who usually relieves us at night is ill, so we are taking shifts."

The caregiver works efficiently and quickly. Her clothes are streaked with milk and food. She's pulled her hair back into a tight bun, though escaped tendrils hang down the side of her face.

I finish filling the bottles just as a child's cry reverberates through the room. When she goes for him, I ask, "May I?" When she nods her approval, I lift the crying child into my arms and feed him the bottle.

My back against the wall, I slide down until I'm seated with him in my lap. He draws hungrily from the bottle until it's nearly finished. The child lying next to me scoots closer, seeking warmth in the cool night. My throat thickens with happiness.

"You do it well." The caregiver feeds another child nearby.

"He's hungry. He's overlooking my clumsiness for the sake of food." When the milk is finished, the boy keeps sucking. I gently pull it out of his mouth so he doesn't swallow air. I stroke a finger down his cheek and wipe away beads of milk off his chin. "What made you want to do this? Care for these children?" I lift the child onto my shoulder and pat him gently. It takes a few pats before he burps. When his body relaxes in sleep, I lay him gently down.

"I was raised in an orphanage." She rocks her still-crying child, soothing her when the cries get louder. "It is what I am meant to do." I get her another bottle. "You don't have any of your own?"

"How did you know?" I say after a long moment. I want to change the subject—to keep to myself that I tried and failed to be a mother.

"You hold the children like a new mother. Unsure but excited," she says.

I withdraw into myself as I remember the countless books I read on everything from how to soothe a fussy child to raising a happy one. But no amount of research was the same as caring for an actual baby. Even surrounded by a roomful of children, I am still alone.

I take a deep breath to calm my nerves before asking, "Do you have any?"

"These are my children." She yawns, clearly exhausted. "My own family abandoned me just like these children's families abandoned them." She scans the room, her face filled with love for her wards. "We only have each other."

"They are lucky to have you."

"On nights like these, I must agree with you." The woman laughs even as she tries to stifle another yawn. "So, what brings you to our door in the middle of the night?"

"I was thinking of the children I don't have and found myself here," I say, more honest than I meant to be.

"You're looking to adopt one?"

"What?" Though Patrick had mentioned adoption, we never discussed it further. When I had dreamed of a child, it had been one from my womb, an image of either Patrick or myself. Adoption felt like admitting failure, and I wasn't prepared for that. "No, I never thought about it."

"I'm sorry. I misunderstood."

"Are many of them adopted?"

"If it is an auspicious year, then a few are adopted." The woman calls to an older child who wakes up whimpering. The little girl runs to her and nestles into her lap. "They arrive here lonely and leave as a family. If desperation weren't the only motivation, more people would learn the true joy of bringing home a child."

"What do you mean?"

"Don't all parents dream of having their own child? Raising someone who is a reflection of themselves?" she asks. "The parents who come here accept that their dream has died. They have moved from desperation to resignation. They can't have a child of their own, but their hearts still lie empty. They walk through the door and hold their arms out."

"But the child is neither a reflection nor a continuation of their bloodline."

"True, but in that moment, that child makes them a family. And the parents leave here knowing that being a mother or father is a gift, no matter how it comes about." She carries the sleeping child back to her place. "I wish it weren't just the few forced onto the path that learned the reward of giving your heart to a child not born to them."

I waited for a miracle from my body, but it refused me. These children are waiting for their own miracle—for fate to bring them someone to love. I imagine what it would be like if one of them were mine, and suddenly my heart feels lighter and my mind at peace. I stay there, helping, until the sun rises and brings a new day.

AMISHA

FORTY-FIVE

Nine months and two days after her joining with Stephen, Amisha's labor began under the shadows of the new moon. Though she continued to fulfill her duties to her children and the household, she had lost all sense of purpose. The labor was oddly a relief—the pain that ripped through her abdomen offered her a reprieve from the months of numbness. For the few hours that her child struggled to enter the world, Amisha was able to forget her loss.

The cry of the child yanked her from her thoughts, and she watched with a thrill as the midwife pulled the blood-soaked body from her womb and cut the cord.

"It is a daughter." Scooping water from a bucket, the midwife washed away the blood. "On the night of Amavasya?" In quick steps, she suctioned the mucus from the baby's mouth and then bundled the child in a wool blanket. "You have been cursed." It was a well-known superstition—a daughter born on the new moon brought bad luck.

Amisha dismissed the woman's claim with a shake of her head. Too exhausted to argue with the woman and eager to see her newborn, Amisha held her arms out for her daughter. She caught her breath as a replica of Stephen stared back at her. She brought the baby close and kissed her with all the longing and love she felt for the child's father.

"You are not a curse but a gift," she whispered into the baby's ear. She sent a silent call to Stephen. "Our daughter is here," she whispered. She wished, more than anything, that they were sharing this together. "Thank you for giving her to me," she said through her tears.

Ravi entered after getting the midwife's approval. He stood next to the bed and watched the child cry for her mother's milk. "She is gorgeous."

"She is her father," Amisha said without a second thought. "We will call her Lena."

Deepak entered after paying the midwife. Ravi immediately moved away and began to clean. Deepak stared at his daughter as she suckled on Amisha's breast. He barely hid his shock. "Her skin? It is pale—lighter than the skin of a Brahmin."

"It is a blessing." Amisha searched for a plausible answer. "Your mother once said to me that a child with fair skin is the child of a goddess, given to us for safekeeping." Deepak continued to stare at the baby and then glanced at Amisha's face. She waited, anxious, until he finally nodded his acceptance.

"With her complexion, we will have suitors

lined up at our door for her hand in marriage." Lighter skin in India was considered higher status. Finally smiling, Deepak said, "I am happy for the dowry I have saved."

"She must go to America." Amisha summoned the strength to raise her voice. "Her hand in marriage must be given to a groom in America."

It was the only way she could assuage her guilt for having kept her daughter from a life with her father in England. She had to secure for Lena the opportunities that remained elusive to her. It was Amisha's gift to her, and to the father Lena would never know.

"Amisha." Deepak was stunned by her insistence. "We have many years before it is time to decide. We do not know . . ."

She held her hand up for silence. "Deepak, I respect your place and mine; however, this I cannot stay quiet about. Give me your word, now, in front of the child that heaven's keepers have just given to us. You will not promise her hand to just anyone. She must go to America."

Amisha knew that Deepak could easily negotiate Lena's hand in marriage without consulting her or their daughter. As was often done over a cigarette or at the temple, a discussion could ensue and hands would be shaken. The husband would proceed home and inform his wife and family that the marriage had been decided and that an exchange of brown sugar would soon take place, signifying an engagement.

"Amisha," he started again, staring at the child she was holding.

"Promise me, Deepak." Amisha pulled the sheet around her daughter, shielding her from Deepak's curious gaze. "Please."

Finally he nodded. "You have my word, Amisha."

"Thank you." Amisha closed her eyes in peace and finally succumbed to sleep, her newborn close at her side.

The weeks after Lena's birth were quiet. At night, the baby suckled at Amisha's breast. Lena's eyes soon changed from light brown to a green hue—the same color as Stephen's. Once, when Amisha caught Deepak staring at them, she scooped her daughter up and left the room. They continued with life—Deepak in his role as a provider and Amisha as a mother and the home's caretaker.

"America?" Ravi asked one day, months later when they were alone. "Why there, Shrimati?"

"If nothing changes here, then it is a place where she can have a chance to be who she wants," Amisha said. "Whoever that may be." When he still stared at her, uncomprehending, she tried to explain. "What are you and I in this life? We have no rights, no place to go except where destiny deems worthy."

"Did the lieutenant tell you about it?" Ravi asked.

"Yes," Amisha admitted. She still recalled their conversation in exact detail. "In America," she continued, voicing the words Stephen had spoken to her, "her bloodline will have choices. Lena will have a voice, Ravi. It is her destiny to be free."

"But across the world?" Ravi pushed. "Your only daughter so far away?"

"You watch." Amisha smiled, heady at the thought of her daughter's future. "She will come back, this child." She kissed the baby's forehead.

"What of our lieutenant? What will you do if he returns?" Ravi began to sweep the house. The relentless rain poured day and night, leaving the streets flooded and small puddles in their home.

"He won't," Amisha said, her mood darkening. Their goodbye had been forever and certain. Neither a day nor night passed when she didn't wonder where he was and how he was doing. In her heart, she was sure he relived the memories of their time together. She never stopped wondering what they could have been together, given the chance.

"Do you think he survived the end of the war?" Ravi wondered. The war was over, and with its end came hope for India's freedom from colonialism.

"Yes." Amisha knew Stephen was still alive.

She couldn't imagine living in a world that did not include him. That had been the only thing that saved her—even if they could not be together under the conditions of their birth, they were together on earth. They were waking and sleeping under the same stars and sky. They felt the same heated rays of the sun, and their nights were lit by the same moon. "I would know if he had not."

"Yes," Ravi agreed. "I was witness to your heartbreak from having loved and lost." He glanced at Lena and smiled. "And to the birth that gifted you light back into your life." He headed toward the kitchen to help prepare dinner. "For that reason alone, he has to be."

FORTY-SIX

As promised, Amisha still hadn't written again more than a year after Lena's birth. There were no words left in her to string together or characters that haunted her dreams at night. The only dreams she had when she slept were of Stephen.

The monsoon season had ended, and, as expected, the insects arrived after the torrential rain. The puddles and sewers were their breeding ground, and in a country that could not prevent the homeless from dying on street corners, mosquitoes were merely a nuisance.

Ravi had set mosquito tents over the floor where they slept. But the bites in the early morning and after sunset could not be helped. The children often scratched them until they bled.

"Do you want me to summon the doctor?" Ravi tore an old sari into small pieces to be used as washcloths. Amisha was dragging a bucket of water into the house to give Lena a cool bath because the child had felt feverish to her.

"Let us see how she does through the night. She must have gotten a chill, because she was coughing this morning." Amisha swatted at her bare arm. "Ouch." The water bucket fell out of her hand.

"What?" Ravi asked.

"A stupid mosquito." Amisha stomped on the offender when it hit the floor.

"Your skin is rising." Ravi pointed to the small hive on her arm.

"Excellent. My due punishment for killing the miserable thing." Amisha laughed, water sloshing on her feet as they went in.

The throbbing began three days after the bite. Fever and nausea hit Amisha in the middle of the night. She stumbled toward the back of the house, barely making it outside before she spewed vomit. Her body shook and her teeth chattered. "Samir," she cried out. She crawled back into the house. "Samir."

"Mama?" Half-asleep, he searched for her. He spied her on the ground and ran to help her up. "Mama, what is it?"

"Please get Ravi," she whispered. Samir ran to do her bidding. When the nausea hit again, she barely made it back outside in time, where she vomited bile and then, when nothing was left, dry heaved.

"Shrimati," Ravi cried when he saw her. His hair was disheveled, and he still wore his night clothes. "What happened?"

She began to heave again. Ravi pulled her hair back and ordered Samir to get her water. In seconds, Amisha's oldest was back with a full glass. Ravi held her head carefully upright and tipped the glass into her mouth.

"Small sips," he cautioned. Amisha pushed it away, but Ravi brought it gently back. "You must drink, Shrimati." She drank half while the rest dribbled down her chin. He wiped her forehead and chin with his sleeve.

"Something is wrong." Amisha held on to him. "My body feels . . ." Flashes of pain hit every nerve point in her body. A heavy weight bore down on her head, and her vision danced.

"You will be fine," Ravi said, seeming to try to convince them both. "As a good mother, you absorbed Lena's illness and doubled your own." Together with Samir, they carried her into the house, past the other children on the floor. Once she was settled on the bed, Ravi ordered Samir, "We need a doctor. Now."

After checking Amisha thoroughly, the doctor poured out a dozen small pills from his bag and handed them to Samir. "It's a virus. Give her one every four hours for the fever."

"How long will she be ill?" Ravi asked from his place against the wall. Amisha lay nearly unconscious on the bed.

"It should pass in one to two days," the doctor answered. "She needs to stay hydrated. The virus will not harm her, but the loss of fluids will."

Ravi counted the money from inside the

cupboard and handed it to Samir, who passed it to the doctor. "Call me if it worsens," the doctor said, smiling at the amount. "Anytime."

"Sleep, Beta," Ravi said to Samir after the doctor left. "I am here, and in the morning, we will telegram your father." When Samir started to argue, Ravi said, "I will wake you, Beta, if she needs anything." He laid a hand atop the young man's head in comfort. "Sleep. Shrimati will be disappointed if you miss school tomorrow."

Samir rubbed his worn eyes. "You will wake me?" At Ravi's nod, a smile of relief flitted across his face. He crawled between his two younger brothers, where Amisha normally slept, and pulled them close. To the rhythms of their steady breathing, he finally fell asleep while Ravi kept vigil over Amisha.

Deepak arrived two days later to find Amisha barely able to sit upright in a chair. Ravi had been continuously feeding her a diet of lemon sherbet. Deepak gripped her shoulder. "Amisha?"

"She is weak," Ravi cautioned, keeping his voice subservient.

"Amisha." Deepak shook her shoulder. When her eyes fluttered, he sighed in relief. He took the glass of sherbet and forced it against her mouth. "You need to drink," he said. Liquid dribbled down her chin and onto her lap.

Amisha opened her eyes slowly and stared at the two of them. "You've come," she whispered, seeing Stephen. She took a large swallow of the sherbet and then smiled widely, rejoicing at the intimacy of their actions. There was a heavy pressure in her head, but she pushed against it, trying to hold on to the moment. "I thought I would never see you again."

"I came as soon as I received the telegram," Deepak said.

"Have you seen your daughter?" Anxious to show Stephen the beautiful child they had created together, she searched the room for Lena. "Every day it is the only wish I have— that you could see her." When she failed to find Lena, she begged Ravi, "Please get the baby." She gripped Stephen's hand. "She has your smile."

"Shrimati." Ravi forced a smile and raised his voice to drown out hers. "Sahib knows how beautiful your daughter is. Right now, however, his concern is for you." He stepped in front of Amisha and reached for the glass of sherbet. "I will make sure she drinks the rest, Sahib."

"What did the doctor say?" Deepak asked. Behind them, Amisha fell back into a slumber.

"A virus. He gave medicine for the fever but assured us she will recover." Ravi pointed to the pills. "I have been crushing them into the sherbet."

"Make sure she finishes the sherbet." Calm replaced the anxiety on his face after he heard the diagnosis. "I will be at the mill. If there is any change, send someone for me."

FORTY-SEVEN

Three days passed with little change in Amisha. Ravi and Bina cared for the children and the house while Deepak worked in town. On the third evening, he stood in the doorway as Ravi fed Amisha naan and potatoes.

"She's eating?" Deepak asked from the doorway.

"A little," Ravi said, giving him the good news. "It is more than before, so it is good news."

"Amisha." Deepak took a seat next to her on the bed. Though Amisha sat upright, her eyes barely stayed open. "I have something for you," he said loudly to get her attention. Circles darkened the area beneath his eyes, and his jaw was tight from strain.

Amisha once confided to Ravi that she feared the boys saw Deepak as a favorite uncle rather than a father. Though they had his blood running through their veins and were excited when he was home, he did not know them. Their fears or what calmed them remained a mystery. He was ignorant of their aspirations or of their intentions to follow him in the business as he had followed his father. Since his arrival home, however, the boys were turning to their father for guidance. He offered them as much as he could.

Amisha finally turned toward him. Her lower lip hung low, and her eyes had trouble focusing. She was skin and bones, having lost nearly ten pounds. He opened her hand and laid a set of keys in her palm. She stared at them first and then at Deepak in confusion. "What is this?" She struggled with the words.

"The keys to the school." Deepak met Amisha's shocked gaze. He glanced briefly toward Ravi and then paused, seeming to search for the right words. "I know it was important to you, so I thought you might enjoy it."

"You purchased the school?" Amisha fingered the keys that Stephen had kept with him daily when the school was open. After the British left, it was shuttered. "How?"

"Vikram said the government had no use for it, and I hoped it would help you." Deepak shook his head, seeming confused as to why the building had any worth to his wife. "You seemed happy while you were there."

"You noticed?" Amisha whispered. At Deepak's shrug, she yearned to ask him why he had kept her from it. Those last few weeks, when he had refused to let her continue attending, she was sure she hated her husband. "It mattered to you?"

"I see you now—broken from a virus—and I think I would give anything to have you as you were," Deepak answered honestly. "When you were at the school."

Amisha fought the tears that threatened. It was the first time that Deepak had told her, in so many words, that he loved her. She had forgotten about him over the span of time during which Stephen occupied her every thought. And now, though they were still strangers, he was trying to do right by her.

"Quite an amount of our money went toward the acquisition," Deepak teased in the face of her silence. "It would be wise for us to make no purchases until the children are adults."

"Thank you," Amisha finally whispered. She watched him leave and then fell asleep with the keys next to her.

It took a few days for Amisha to garner the strength to make the trip. Ravi stayed close to her as they approached the school. Eight days had passed since her illness began. Each new day sapped even more of her energy, leaving her weaker. Amisha slowly walked up the steps of the school that had altered her life forever. With shaking hands, she inserted the key into the lock. She had not set foot in the building since Stephen left. She had believed it to be her past, and though it was only blocks from her home, she'd assumed she and the school were destined never to be a part of each other's life again. Now she owned it, free to roam the empty halls and visit its garden without fear of reprisal or questions.

This was hers, a gift from the husband she had betrayed.

Her thoughts were lost in an earlier time as she and Ravi entered. She looked into the barren classrooms as the memories hugged her heels. Their footsteps echoed in the silence as if they were the first to walk the empty halls. For Amisha, however, the spirits of people filled the hollow space. She could hear the laughter of the students and the instructors who taught with sternness meant to mask an earnest desire to teach. Amisha ran her hands over the blackboards and erasers before leading them toward the door to the garden.

"Is this real?" Ravi exclaimed when she opened the door to the schoolyard.

"Paradise, my friend, in our small village." Her sandals dug deep into the soft ground. Buried beneath the bloom of the flowers and alongside the roots of the trees were her memories of Stephen. Here, the ghosts did not haunt her but beckoned, willing her to forget the sorrow of loss and rejoice in the thrill of having loved. She yearned to return to the time when she and Stephen were together even while they stood separate. In their garden, they danced to silent music.

"I am not well, Ravi." Amisha turned to him beneath the shade of her beech tree. The branches of the tree had sprouted over the sterile land. She stood against it and faced what she could not accept before. "I need you to make a promise to me."

"Shrimati," Ravi said, refusing to hear her.

"Listen to me," Amisha ordered. She feared the worst. Her body was enfeebled, and her mind tangled the days from the past with her present. The boys' names swam together, and Amisha could not differentiate their faces. She feared what she could not comprehend. Her body was alive, but her mind was withering. "When I die, you must tell my daughter my story."

"Amisha, hush your words." Ravi used her given name for the first time. He had to convince her that nothing terrible would happen to her. That life was hers to live, and their friendship would always endure. "Do not let the heavens hear you. They may take it upon themselves to believe you."

"The heavens have shown they have a dark hand though the sun shines bright each day," Amisha cried. "How can I believe I have a tomorrow when today I feel so lost?" Tears poured down her face. "You will do more for me than any medicine if you promise me. Please, Ravi," she begged, clasping her hands together.

"You have my promise, Shrimati." Ravi grabbed her hands and held them tight. She knew he would give her anything—all she had to do was ask.

"Thank you," Amisha said, her mind going blank. "Ravi?" Her voice quavered. She leaned against the tree, desperate for the support it provided.

"Do you want me to send for the doctor?" Ravi demanded.

"No." She shook her head. It felt heavy, and no matter how hard she tried, the load would not lessen. She rubbed the skin above her skull and then began to pull at her hair, desperate to relieve the pressure. Her movements became frantic, and she succeeded in tearing a lump out.

"Stop, Shrimati, stop!" Ravi tried to pull her hands away. She struggled against him, craving the pain of her hair loss to distract her from the agony.

"Get out," she cried, not seeing him. She tried to focus, to remember who Ravi was, but now he was a stranger. She struck his head and his stomach. She heard a cry, not realizing it was her own. She pounded harder and harder.

She began to laugh, because something told her it was a game. "I am writing a story," she said. "My children are playing." Her three boys tossed a ball to her, and she smiled with joy because it was a glorious day and the sun was shining and everything was right.

"Stephen." Amisha reached out, and her arms embraced the air. "You have our daughter." Amisha clapped her hands in joy. Her face moved from side to side as she searched for her boys and found them. "Samir, Jay, come, Beta. Bring your brother." Happiness shone on her face. "Stephen is here, and he will help me as he helped you, Ravi," Amisha said, her eyes unfocused. To Stephen she whispered, "I am so sorry for sending you away."

Then the throbbing began again, and her voice escaped her. She searched for her tongue with her hand, but the pressure was excruciating. Her eyes went blind even as they remained open. Amisha tried to reach out, but her arms refused to move. She tried screaming, to tell them something was wrong.

"Don't go!" she screamed.

But Stephen stepped back and took Lena with him. Her boys returned to playing, and soon they were out of sight. She tried to hold on to Ravi but couldn't reach him. It was starting to get dark, and she was all alone. She fumbled for a branch, but the world continued to spin, and moments later she fell beneath the shelter of her beech tree.

RAVI

FORTY-EIGHT

"The Brahmins say it is dark energy." Deepak had just returned from a visit to the temple, where he spoke to the *pujaris*. "Demons have entered her body and are playing with her mind." The doctor had washed his hands of the case, telling Deepak that only God could help her now. Deepak's eyes darted to Amisha, who lay in a deep slumber. Her wrists and ankles were tied to the bed to keep her from hurting herself. "They are coming to perform a ceremony. The children should not be here."

"Bina will take them immediately to your sister's," Ravi said, his nerves taut.

Ravi and Bina shepherded the children out of the house and searched for a rickshaw. "I'm not going," Samir said as the other children watched. Since Amisha had fallen ill, Samir had been the one who repeatedly checked on his mother. "I will stay here." His chin quivered.

"The Brahmins will help to heal her." Ravi tried to calm the boy who had already seen so much. He had to fight to protect him from seeing any more. Refusing to tell him about the demons, he said, "They will pray for her."

"Then I will pray with them." Samir crossed his arms over his small chest.

Ravi knew the child wanted the same thing he did—to help however he could. He grasped the young man's hand in his. "God will listen to the prayers of Shrimati's child more than anyone's. But your father has asked for the home to be empty so that the Brahmins can do their work. Please?"

As a child, Ravi was taught that death was a matter of time, neither to be feared nor fought. Life was a punishment, and the time spent on earth an ordeal. For an untouchable, death provided relief from life's misery and a welcome return to oblivion.

Ravi was unsure whether death meant a reunion with God. The question that begged for an answer was if God existed, then why were there untouchables? When he was a child, Ravi watched his aunts and uncles wither lifelessly on the street corner. He was told that they were going into a deep sleep. Just as when he slept and the world became softer in the darkness, they would sleep.

Death was a gift given to them because, once dead, they no longer had to fear life. In death, they were free of the terror of children pelting them with stones for entertainment. They no longer had to battle stray animals for food, only to be beaten by humans if they won the fight. Death was freedom. Never should the hand of death be fought; rather, it should be welcomed as a savior into the home.

Yet he rejected these teachings in the face of Amisha's failing health. Her illness was to be neither celebrated nor welcomed. He would not accept her passing as a gift from above. And he would do whatever it took to save her.

Finally Samir nodded his agreement. Bina herded the children into the rickshaw. Ravi stood back and watched until Amisha's children were safely on their way. Only then did he return to her home.

From his place against the wall, Ravi watched the priests fill thirty bowls with ghee and light the cotton wicks. Burning incense sticks placed in small brass holders filled the room with smoke.

The younger priests rang their handheld bells while the elders started chanting. They called on the deities as the fires danced in their bowls, creating a haze. Ravi watched, agonizing as two priests stood over Amisha's head and rang the bells. They chanted louder and louder until they were screaming around her in hopes of driving the demons out.

The smoke filled Amisha's weakened lungs, and she began to cough. "Water," she moaned. "Please."

Ravi moved toward her to do her bidding, when Deepak raised his hand, silently ordering him to stay back. Unable to defy him, Ravi stayed in place. Every time an incense stick burned out, they lit three more, depleting the room of all its oxygen. Amisha screamed in agony. They continued, ignoring her cries. On instinct, Ravi stepped forward, desperate to push them away from her. Somehow he had to protect her—to keep her safe.

"Step back," Deepak ordered.

"There are no demons," Ravi cried, his heart breaking at the sound of her cries. "Please tell them to stop."

"Can you heal her?" Deepak demanded. When Ravi stayed silent, Deepak said, "That's what I thought."

Ravi turned away, unable to watch. When her screams grew louder, he fled the house. As he tripped over himself in his haste to get away, he remembered the first time she invited him into her home. His head lowered, he gasped, trying to catch his breath. She had made him part of her life and her children's lives when he had no reason to live. By doing so, she gave him a sense of self-worth for the first time.

He picked himself up off the ground and continued his flight, faster than before. The tears blinded him, but he kept running, desperate to be as far away as he could go. Amisha had given him everything, and now all he could do was run as he saw her stripped and left with nothing.

FORTY-NINE

Deepak held the leather whip with the wooden handle. "The temple leaders believe it is our last option. The dark energy has surrounded her, so we must beat it out of her," he said quickly.

Ravi stared at a man he no longer recognized. "You choose to beat her?" He made no attempt to hide his anger. "She is weak and helpless."

"Do not question me!" Deepak shouted. "This is the only way; otherwise she will die. Is that what you want?"

"It is not what she deserves," Ravi argued, surprised he would find the nerve to do so. But he did not care anymore. If Deepak beat him or released him from his job, he did not care. He would not allow this to be done to her.

"This—her in this state—is not what I deserve," Deepak said. His words echoed in the still air, mocking them both. "The children deserve their mother. What are we to do without her? You have answers. You think this is not right, then you tell me. What are my options?"

"She will get better," Ravi insisted, though in his heart he didn't believe it.

"Like I thought—you do not have a solution." Deepak threw the whip at Ravi. It skimmed his torso before falling to the ground near his feet.

"The clerics will tie her to the beech tree in the garden and perform a ceremony. Then you will use the whip. They said once at night and once in the morning. They have promised it will only be a matter of days."

Ravi stared at him in horror. "You expect me to do this?"

Deepak stared out at the water before answering. "Who do you think she would prefer do it?" He blinked, and Ravi saw him fight his emotions. "She told me once she would trust you with her life."

"I cannot." Ravi's body shook.

"Fine, I will hire other men to do it. From the mill." Deepak turned away in disgust.

"No." He could not allow them to do that to her. To beat her as if she were an animal. "I will do it." He held his hand out for the whip.

Deepak picked it up off the ground and handed it to him. "She will be ready soon."

Ravi watched Deepak stare at the woman who bore him four children and stood by him before he became a man. In the school garden, the Brahmins used rope to wrap her arms and legs tight against the beech tree, leaving her shoulders and stomach bare. Her head hung forward. Her eyes were closed, and her body appeared lifeless.

"Will you stay?" Ravi asked Deepak, his hands shaking as he sweated in the heat. When Deepak shook his head, Ravi bit out with uncharacteristic defiance, "Then leave. Let me perform in peace the task you have assigned me."

Deepak jerked at his words. They both stared at the woman they loved. The woman who had bettered their lives and was now fighting for hers. With nothing further to say, Deepak walked out of the garden and away from the school.

Ravi kneeled before Amisha and laid his hands on her feet in the manner she had forbidden years earlier. "Please forgive me," he whispered. His tears fell on her feet, and he wiped them off, ashamed he had allowed them to touch her.

Slowly he removed his tunic, baring his back and chest. He picked up the whip, one hand on the handle and the other on the leather. He yanked and snapped the rawhide, ripping into his own hand and drawing blood. With precision, Ravi lifted his other hand and flipped the whip backward, lashing his back. He then pulled it forward, purposely weakening his momentum, and allowed the lash to slice across Amisha's stomach. She cried out, her mind unable to comprehend the source of piercing pain.

He repeated the maneuver, slicing his back until blood dripped from the wounds on his skin. With every lash to his own body, he lessened the sting of flaying her. His skin inflamed and then shriveled in response. With every stroke, she unleashed a bloodcurdling scream.

Amisha begged her unknown assailant to stop. She pleaded with him to have mercy upon her. She was sorry, she howled. She implored his forgiveness. To excuse the behavior that had sentenced her to this punishment. With every plea, Ravi beat himself harder, his face blinded by his tears. Only when there was a pool of his own blood and his hands were numb did he stop.

Amisha's face fell, her mind at last plunging her into unconsciousness. Ravi collapsed at her feet, his face pressed against the ground. His body shook in convulsions from anguish.

"I'm sorry," he sobbed. "Shrimati, I am so sorry."

He begged for forgiveness for having used the hands she had held in friendship to harm her. For being the one—the companion she had trusted and cared for and made her own—to draw her blood. As that blood mingled with his own in a puddle on the ground, he looked to the heavens to a god with whom he had never spoken, and wished his closest friend the gift of death.

Amisha remained tied to the tree for two days after Ravi's beating. The clerics had insisted in hopes that the demons would become impatient and move on to afflict someone else. When Deepak ordered him to repeat the performance, Ravi told him, "I will cut off my hands before doing such a thing again."

"It is the only way," Deepak insisted. "If not you, then I will bring someone else."

"Then bring two, because I will stand in front of her and your person will have to kill me to get to her," Ravi said, refusing to stay quiet. If nothing else, he owed Amisha a voice when she was unable to speak for herself. "She has little time left on this earth. Let her pass on in peace. She is worthy of that."

Deepak escaped to the mill. When Ravi sent for him a day later, Deepak called the doctor. He checked for a pulse as Amisha hung limply from the tree. She was dead.

They prepared the cremation site for her funeral. Ravi helped to untie the ropes that bound Amisha's corpse. They laid her gently on the wooden stretcher to transfer her body to the pyre. The mound of wood sat high, and Amisha's body, now dressed in a white sari, was placed upon it. Deepak and Samir, as the eldest son, took a burning branch and set her on fire. Those gathered watched as the dancing flames engulfed her body.

When there was nothing left of her but ash, Deepak opened the urn and allowed her ashes to fly unencumbered into the air, scattering throughout the land. Some, lighter than others, flew farther and freer, rising above the clouds and beyond the horizon, at last taking Amisha to places of which she had only dreamed.

JAYA

FIFTY

We sit on the porch as the village comes to life under the rays of the early-morning sun. Tears course down my face as Ravi finishes telling me of Amisha's death.

"What was it?" I whisper.

"Encephalitis from the mosquito that bit her." Ravi swallows repeatedly as he struggles with his emotions. I fight to keep my own in check. "The hallucinations are caused by the swelling of the brain."

"A mosquito?" I ask in disbelief.

"If it is any consolation, because your grand-mother smashed it to death, no one else was harmed by its poison." Ravi grips his cane and brings it close.

"How did you know about the encephalitis?"

"The disease became an epidemic years later. As more people succumbed, the government took notice." His voice low, Ravi says, "The government warned us to stay indoors or stay covered after monsoon season." He shakes his head, angry. "The symptoms were the same."

"Mom has no idea about this." I grieve for how much was kept from her. She had a right to know the story of the past that cemented her future.

"No," Ravi affirms. "Your grandfather rarely

spoke of your grandmother afterward." He clasps his hands together in his lap. "It was our secret— the way we had treated your grandmother in her final days."

"Why beat her? And the smoke?" I try but fail to keep the anguish out of my voice.

"We lived in a different time, Jaya," Ravi says, but regret and heartbreak are in his voice. "Choices were limited for us. Our country has come a long way in the short time we have been free."

"I wish I had known her." I yearn for the grandmother I never knew. I mourn her death and lament how she died.

"Your grandmother would be proud of you," Ravi says. When I meet his gaze, he says, "But I think she must rest in peace, knowing her sacrifice was not in vain. You live a life filled with possibilities, yes?"

"But my mother's wasn't, right?" I ask. "My mother's heartbreak began with her mother's death."

"Yes," he says, slowly. "She almost lost everything after your grandmother died."

"Ravi," I start to ask, desperate to know more, but he holds up his hand.

"Today I would ask you for time." With weathered hands he wipes the tears off his face. "I didn't believe I could grieve any more from her loss." Broken, he sighs. "I fear I was wrong."

He pats my shoulder before leaving me on the porch and heading for home.

Wound up and restless, I roam the streets of the village. With every step, I wonder if my grandmother and mother walked the same path. I wander toward the outskirts of town. With time, I lose count of where I walk and how many miles.

My mother has meditated for as long as I can remember. She always seemed happiest lost in the musings behind her closed eyes. She said she started as a child. Given her love for the discipline, I tried it multiple times over the years. Each time I failed to quiet the thoughts that pervaded my mind. From work to pregnancies and everything in between, my senses were overwhelmed with daily happenings. When I asked her the secret, she said to find peace in that moment, you have to cede control of life. I didn't understand what she meant, but now I wonder if it was the only way she could survive having lost so much so young.

The revelations of the last few weeks have been overwhelming. I had come to India to escape the twists my life had taken and to find a way to cope with my loss. Now I find myself unable to comprehend the losses that my grandmother and my mother faced. With Amisha's story, I was transported to a foreign world, and yet it was as much a part of my mother's history and mine as the lineage we shared with Amisha. No matter how separate and apart I was from Amisha's time, without this village and its haunted history, I would never have come to be.

I find myself at the door of the school. I take the key from where Ravi hides it and unlock the chain bolt. Though Ravi and I have strolled through the uninhabited halls numerous times, now, alone, I see it through different eyes. I enter the garden where I imagine Amisha searching for herself and finding Stephen instead.

My grandmother never believed love was her right or that she would be valued for her writing. Yet I had attained success in both, never having had to make a sacrifice for either. When forced to decide, she refused to walk away from the sons who needed her. But at the same time she made the sacrifice to remain in India, she secured the promise of America for my mother. I grieve for having never known my grandmother. I yearn for the woman with whom I share blood. But the strength that coursed through Amisha's veins has, until now, eluded me.

The caregiver's words echo in my head. The story Ravi told me in detail replays until it's all I can hear. I stare at the garden, struggling with how to honor Amisha's memory and uphold the standards she set.

I arrive home that evening to see a rickshaw idling in front of the house. Curious, I come closer just as a man steps out after handing the driver payment. When he turns, my breath catches.

"Patrick?" I whisper. His face has day-old scruff on it. Wrinkles line his shirt and his jeans. He has a large duffel bag thrown over one shoulder and his computer bag over the other. "What are you doing here?" I take the few steps to bring myself in front of him. I reach out to hug him but then, unsure, step back. After our conversation, I felt closer to him than before the miscarriages, but given all that has happened between us, I'm still hesitant.

"I came to see you." He grabs my hand and pulls me forward until I'm in his arms. They wrap around my waist and hold me tight. In flats, I push up on my toes so my head can rest on his shoulder. Want and love envelop me, reminding me of who we used to be. "I hope it's all right," he says into my hair.

"Yes." I step back and stare at him, still in disbelief. "More than."

Hope swirls around me, but I remind myself that our one conversation can't undo years of hurt. I curl my fingers into the palm of my hand, fighting the urge to run them over the bristles on his cheek and down the front of his shirt.

"Can we talk someplace private?" The edge in his voice betrays his exhaustion and nervousness.

"Yes, of course." I motion him toward the house. "Let's go in."

He follows me up the stairs and waits while I unlock the door. Inside, he leaves his bags in the foyer and then looks around. "This is your mother's childhood home?"

"Yes." I feel a fierce pride at the humble surroundings. "It is where my grandmother wrote her stories." I try to see it through his eyes, remembering my own reaction when I first arrived. What seemed small and inconsequential then I now know is the cradle of the events that shaped my family's destiny. "Where I'm learning who I am," I say quietly.

"And who is that?" Patrick asks. He comes to stand next to me. His eyes search mine as he waits for my answer.

"Someone who had to put all the pieces of myself together again," I say softly. "I had to learn . . ." I pause. "I had to learn who I am. Who my mother is. No matter what role I play in my life, I needed to be sure of me." He nods his understanding, and I ask, "Why are you here, Patrick?" I need him to tell me the truth—to tell me what's in his heart, if only to help me understand what's in mine.

He glances away before meeting my eyes again. "You weren't the only one who lost yourself during the miscarriages. I couldn't breathe," he admits. He runs his hand over his neck before slipping it into the pocket of his jeans. "I wanted to save you, to save us, but it just felt easier to walk away."

"Stacey," I say, and he nods.

"I thought she would help me forget. I was a fool." He reaches out to touch my cheek but then, seeming to realize what he's doing, pauses. "You're all I have. All I need." He swallows deeply, and moisture pools in his eyes. "I'm so sorry I left."

"What happened?" I ask, still afraid to believe.

"It wasn't easier without you," he says slowly. "It felt like all we had at the end was pain, but when I moved out, I missed everything about you. Your smile, your laughter, your obsession with making sure every word you wrote was perfect." He takes a deep breath. "I missed my best friend. I missed my wife."

The final bits of darkness fade away with his words. I think about my grandmother and the choice she made in this house between love and her life. It was a choice that no person should ever have to make, but she did it with grace and a heart that always thought of others first.

Patrick is the man I have always loved. Even when my heart was broken, it belonged to him. I was sure I had lost him when I lost myself. Now he's standing in front of me, his arms open and his heart willing. Unbidden, tears pool in my eyes, and happiness settles into my heart.

"Are those happy tears?" With the pad of his thumb, he wipes them away.

"Yes." After having been adrift for so long,

I can't believe I have found him again. "I love you," I whisper, feeling lighter than I have in a long time. "I always have. Even when I couldn't remember I did."

"Sweetheart." His lips find mine, and I open to him, to all the memories, to the laughter, the pain and the love. "I love you." His tears mingle with mine. Desperate to touch him, I lift his top up. He steps back to let me pull his shirt off. I run my hands over his chest. He tries to unhook the button at the base of the back of my neck. I laugh as he struggles to get the unfamiliar clasp undone.

"You look beautiful," he says when I reach back to undo it. He runs his hands down over the long simple cotton shirt like the ones the women in the village wear. "I've never seen you in anything like it."

Once the clasp is undone, I lift my arms up, and he tugs the shirt over my head. We slowly undress, savoring each other. He runs his palm slowly over my abdomen where I carried our children for a short time. I cover his hand and rest my forehead against his, mourning with him. His lips meet mine again.

We were thrown into a storm, and for a while it proved more powerful than both of us. Our sails weren't stronger than the wind's rage, and we nearly drowned in the currents. Just when I was sure the lighthouse couldn't guide me home,

I heard my grandmother's story. Her struggles and her determination taught me that each day is precious and love is something to be protected as a priceless treasure that only the fortunate find and keep.

He picks me up and carries me to the settee, where in quiet whispers we offer a balm for our wounds and remind each other of our love. When we finally come together, I close my eyes and hold him tight, grateful to have found my husband again.

RAVI

FIFTY-ONE

For two months and two days, Deepak searched for a wife. He sent word to the surrounding community that the dowry requirement would be waived. Janna helped him filter through all the offers from fathers, but Deepak said no to every one. Frustrated, Janna threatened to stop helping him. "Amisha is dead," Janna bit out. "The sooner you accept that, the faster the children will have a new mother."

Ravi, who was playing with Lena while Bina cooked, stayed silent. They had taken over raising the children while Deepak searched. "Choose someone," Deepak finally said. "It doesn't matter who she is. Just make sure . . ." He paused, staring at Lena as she hit a spoon against a pot. "Make sure she is willing to love the children."

Janna chose a woman whose family had wealth but whose heart was cold. Deepak's new bride, Omi, cared little for the children who came with the marriage. She often complained that everywhere she turned, the villagers spoke only of Amisha's thoughtfulness and love for her children.

"I am living in the shadow of a martyr!" Omi screamed months after her marriage. "This family is lucky to have me." Lena, frightened by the screaming, began to cry. "Be quiet," Omi yelled. To Omi, Lena was a reflection of the woman who preceded her. When Lena didn't immediately quiet down, Omi slapped her across the face. Lena fell to the ground, wailing in pain. Ravi rushed to her side to comfort the girl.

"Do not touch her," Omi yelled, freezing Ravi in his steps. "If you do, I will beat her more."

"Please," Ravi begged for the child who couldn't beg for herself.

"You plead for the child who killed your shrimati?"

"What?" Ravi couldn't have heard right. "Killed Shrimati?"

"She was born the night of Amavasya."

A daughter's birth on the night of the new moon, when it was fully covered by shadows, brought darkness upon the family. But not Lena. Not the baby girl Amisha had adored. "It is not possible."

"The child was born under a veil of darkness, and demons killed the mother," Omi said. "It is fitting someone like you would try to protect her." Omi knocked Lena into the wall, leaving her crying in fear.

That was the beginning of the woman's torment of Lena. Omi beat her for even the smallest infractions, leaving Lena whimpering and shaking in her presence. The boys were older, so they escaped their stepmother through school and outings with other children. But Lena had no escape.

Ravi tried repeatedly to stand between the woman and Amisha's child. Twice she beat him instead, but it did not matter. It was two fewer times that Lena was harmed. Desperate, Ravi sought out Deepak at the mill on a rare night he was in town.

"She is hurting Lena," Ravi said to Deepak the first opportunity he had. Since his remarriage, Deepak had begun to spend even more time away from home, sometimes not returning for months. "I beg you to make her stop," Ravi said when Deepak barely showed any emotion. "She is Shrimati's child."

"And the lieutenant's," Deepak said, shocking Ravi into silence. He held Ravi's gaze and shook his head. "You knew." Deepak bit out a broken laugh. "Of course. You kept all of her secrets. Omi found the letters between Amisha and the lieutenant. Love letters." He ran his hand over his worn eyes. In a broken whisper, he said, "My wife was a cheater. A liar."

"No, she . . ." Ravi struggled for an explanation. He had forgotten about the letters. Even as Amisha was dying, she had never mentioned them, and Ravi had assumed they were gone. "She was a good person. The letters meant nothing."

"Don't lie to me!" Deepak roared. "Amisha

betrayed me." His eyes bulged, and his mouth turned down in disgust. "Omi is raising a bastard child. I owe her my gratitude and more."

"Lena is just a child. She deserves better," Ravi begged, trying to make him understand. "You don't know what it's like to watch her cry."

"Then don't watch her." Anger laced his every word. Deep in thought, he considered Ravi before seeming to make a decision. "Omi has complained often to me about your familiarity in the house. That may have been acceptable to someone like Amisha, but Omi deserves better," he said, throwing Ravi's words back at him.

"What are you saying?" Ravi whispered.

"It is no longer acceptable for you to work in my home." Deepak began shuffling through the papers on his desk. "Today is your last day. Lena is no longer your problem."

Shocked, Ravi stared at him. "Please, Sahib," Ravi begged, "I meant no offense. I will do anything. The children—"

"Are not your concern," Deepak said, interrupting him. "You are dismissed." Ravi started to beg him, to plead to allow him one more chance, when Deepak said, "And one more thing—if you ever mention Lena's true parentage to her or anyone else, I will leave her at an orphanage in the city and never look back. I have a reputation to maintain." He stood up and threw open the door. "Since you are a master at keeping secrets, this one will be easy for you also."

Ravi tried one more time. "The lieutenant. He would take the child. Please call him."

Deepak shook his head. "The lieutenant died in an accident. Vikram received the news a few weeks back."

Ravi bit back his cry of distress. He remembered Amisha's words that her only solace was that they lived under the same sky. Amisha was sure she would have known of his death. Ravi wondered if somehow the lieutenant knew of hers. But now both of Lena's parents were gone, and she was truly alone. Heartbroken, Ravi could only nod before taking his leave.

He found employment as a city worker who picked up the feces left by the wandering animals. As the years passed, he sought Amisha's boys out weekly to get updates on their lives and Lena. With broken voices, they told Ravi that Omi had stopped hitting Lena but called her the *apasakuna*—a bad omen. Lena did her best to stay out of the way and made sure not to invite her stepmother's wrath. Deepak was still traveling, but when he was home, he barely spoke to Lena.

Distraught, Ravi listened to the news each week. He encouraged the boys to do well in their studies and brought them sweets to celebrate their birthdays and accomplishments. It was easy for Ravi to stay in touch with the boys, but since

Lena was given limited freedom, any contact between them was made impossible.

Years passed, and Samir and Jay left for England to study on scholarships, against Deepak's wishes. Paresh was getting ready to leave for Australia, also against his father's wishes, when he sought out Ravi. "There are two offers of marriage for Lena," Paresh said. His features were similar to Deepak's, and his voice sounded like his father's. "One is a boy in another state who comes from a family of seamstresses. Omi wishes her to be sent far away."

When he paused, Ravi asked, "And the other?"

"A boy who's going to America to be a doctor." Paresh rubbed the back of his neck with his hand. "There haven't been any others."

Omi had spread the word when Lena was young that she was a bad omen. She cautioned the villagers that it was in their best interest to keep their distance from her. She blamed the girl for her mother's death and held regular *pujas* to help clear the house of her negative energy. She told tales of Lena's odd behavior, though Lena had never been anything but a sweet young girl. Soon enough, the townsfolk believed Omi and, for the safety of their children and family, kept their distance from the girl. It seemed to give Omi odd pleasure to see her suffering.

"She told me that she wanted to marry the boy

who is to be a doctor, but . . . ," Paresh started, and then paused.

"But?"

"Omi has said no. The dowry is too high," Paresh said. "He is highly sought after, since he is to be a doctor in America." Ravi saw Paresh's struggle to do right by his sister. "Lena has been crying. She and the boy have seen each other in passing and like each other. She begged Papa, but he refused to listen. I also tried, but without success."

Deepak's increased absence after Amisha's death had created a rift between the boys and their father. His tolerance of Omi's treatment toward Lena had only exacerbated it. Ravi was grateful that the boys still trusted him after all the time that had passed. Samir and Jay had the most memories of Ravi in the household and often talked about how much Amisha valued Ravi's friendship. Paresh, trusting his older brothers, had formed a strong bond with him also.

"Papa is to announce the engagement in a few days." Paresh stared at the village, his thoughts lost amid the crowd. "If Lena is forced to live the rest of her life with the garment boy . . ." He stopped and swallowed deeply. "She deserves to be happy."

Ravi showered in the public outhouse that he and his family shared with ten other families. He used the same soap to clean both his body and hair of the filth from work. He dressed quickly in a fresh tunic and pants. Using a broken comb, he pulled the knots from his hair.

After slipping his feet into a pair of sandals, he walked toward the mill. As he neared the factory, the memory of his first meeting with Amisha assuaged him. "If you can hear me, Shrimati," he whispered, "then help me to do right by your daughter."

The bell over the door jingled as he entered. The manager was different from the one years ago. "Is Sahib here?" Ravi asked.

Ravi swiped his sweaty palms on his pants while he waited. When Deepak followed the manager out five minutes later, Ravi didn't hide his shock. Deepak's hair had gone gray, and stress lines covered his face. He had lost substantial weight, and his clothes hung off his frail body.

"Ravi," Deepak said. His face held none of the anger it had fifteen years before. Instead, it was filled with fatigue. "It has been many years." He motioned for Ravi to follow him into his office and take a seat in the visitor's chair. "How are you and Bina?"

"We are well." Ravi didn't tell him that a day didn't go by where Bina didn't speak of the children she had loved as her own. He took a deep breath for courage before saying, "I heard the wonderful news that Lena's marriage was to be decided." He had rehearsed each word a hundred times in his head. "Paresh told me that his sister wants to marry the boy who is to be a doctor."

"You speak to my son?" Deepak demanded, but there was no fire in him, just exhaustion. "You told him the story?"

"No," Ravi rushed to assure him. "I promise Sahib I haven't said a word." He tried to regroup, afraid he had made it worse. "He told me in passing. Out of concern for his sister."

"The marriage to the doctor is not possible," Deepak said, seeming to accept his explanation. "Omi thinks the seamster is better."

"Amisha wanted her in America," Ravi said, his voice harsher than he meant. "The night of Lena's birth, you made a promise to Amisha. Do you remember?" From the light of recognition in Deepak's eyes, Ravi knew he did.

"Unbeknownst to me, I promised my wife to send another man's child to America," Deepak said. Anger lit his face and brought the corners of his mouth down. "I was foolish. A child with brown hair, white skin, and green eyes. I believed Amisha when she told me Lena was mine. Why would I think anything else?" Disgusted, he shook his head. "I have no reason to keep the promise. Lena will marry the garment boy." He stood up, indicating the discussion was over.

"He came for her," Ravi said, desperate.

Deepak stopped moving toward the door and stared in confusion at Ravi. "The lieutenant loved her. He wanted her to go to England with him. Promised to raise the boys as his."

"A Hindu woman?" Deepak sagged against the desk. "A member of the Raj?"

"Yes." Ravi silently prayed for guidance. "Amisha said no. Knowing the child she carried was his," Ravi said slowly, letting the words sink in, "she still said no."

"Why?" Deepak begged, his voice torn. "If she knew the child was not mine, why deceive me?"

"Because she loved you," Ravi lied, frantic to help Lena. "And she wanted her life to be with you." Ravi finished with the only words he thought would help. "Shrimati could have given birth to her daughter in England, but she trusted you to raise her. To do right by Lena. She stayed in India to be with you. And she paid for her loyalty with her life."

Ravi stood on the outskirts of the small gathering. Omi had refused to spend any more money than necessary on the wedding. She had planned the ceremony in less than three days and invited only immediate family. Paresh had invited Ravi to the wedding but cautioned him that Omi didn't know. Ravi promised to keep his distance. He only wanted to see Amisha's daughter be married.

The *pujari* spoke the words in Hindi that

512

bound Lena to her new husband for lifetimes. He showered them with rose petals and blessed water. The *pujari* tied the edge of Lena's sari to the groom's garment, then asked the couple to repeat seven oaths to each other before circling the fire.

There was a small round of applause as the ceremony concluded. Ravi closed his eyes, silently wishing his friend were here to witness her daughter's marriage. Lena went first to Paresh, who pulled her in for a tight hug. Paresh kissed the top of his sister's head and wished her well. Because the wedding was so sudden, neither Samir nor Jay was able to make it back in time. Lena then bent down and touched Omi's feet in a sign of respect. Omi only nodded and stepped back, refusing to embrace the stepdaughter she despised. Next, Lena approached Deepak and touched his feet in the same show of respect.

"Be happy," he said to the daughter who was not his own. "For your birth mother."

Lena's gaze flew to his, and Ravi saw tears pooling in her eyes. She nodded, her movement jerky. "I will, Papa." She glanced at her husband, who stood silently next to her, before facing her father again. "Thank you," she breathed. "For the wedding." She stared at the man who had raised her. Her chin quivering, she whispered, "For allowing me to marry the man I wanted."

Ravi saw Lena's new husband reach out and

briefly clasp her hand in his before releasing it. He smiled at the act that only a generation ago would have been frowned upon. The show of affection and support would have made Amisha's heart soar.

Deepak nodded. Ravi saw him struggling with his own emotions. Turning to his new son-in-law, he said, "In America, take care of her. She is yours now."

"I will, Papa." Lena's husband called him father out of respect. "I promise."

With a hand on her back, Lena's husband led her toward the waiting car his family had hired. He opened the door and motioned for Lena to precede him. As she bent her head to get into the car, her eyes met Ravi's across the hood. She paused when she saw the tears coursing down his cheeks, and her face clouded with confusion. Raising one hand, Ravi offered Amisha's daughter both congratulations and a goodbye at the same time.

Likely having no memory of him, Lena nonetheless raised her hand in return. Her husband said something Ravi couldn't hear. Nodding, Lena broke eye contact with Ravi and moved to get into the car. Her husband followed her in, and seconds later the car drove away. Ravi watched it until it was no longer in sight. When he started to leave, he caught Deepak watching him. Ravi brought his hands slowly together and with a bow of his head thanked him. Not waiting for a response, he turned away and went home, assured that Amisha's wish for her daughter had come to fruition.

JAYA

FIFTY-TWO

The temperature cools, and the shade from the tree chills the air even further. The garden is quiet, as if the animals know something is amiss. The flowers turn inward, and the leaves on the tree hang limp as if in mourning.

"My mother was a bad omen," I whisper as Ravi concludes the story. "Her stepmother faulted Mom for Amisha's death?" I choke back a sob. Everything makes sense now—her insistence about following all the rules, making sure never to take the wrong step. Her torment when I lost the babies. Her refusal to get close to anyone for fear that her energy would hurt them. She was made to believe that anything that went wrong in her life, her mother's, and then mine was her fault. "She thinks she's a curse."

"Yes." He's drawn and tired. His eyes are vacant as he stares past me. "Your stepmother warned any man who wanted to marry her that their lives and their children's would be cursed. Your mother was told from the time she was a child until she was married that she was a curse. Deepak never told her differently, so in time she came to believe it." His shoulders sag. "And I could not tell her the truth."

As a journalist, I saw and heard the cruelties

humans were willing to commit toward one another. We were trained to keep an emotional distance and recite the facts for the readers. I struggled early in my career but quickly found a rhythm. Soon I was recognized for my ability to tell a story with an objectivity others envied.

Now hearing about my mother's treatment, I cannot stay neutral. Rage rushes over me. If the choice were mine, I would demand her path be changed. But I am helpless to alter her past. Her fortune was to live the life that she refused to reveal to me. Maybe keeping her secret was the only way she learned to accept it.

"Why did Deepak ask her never to come home?"

"I do not know," he admits, looking confused by the request. "It could have been a number of reasons—Omi's insistence, Deepak's fear their reputation would be ruined if the story ever came out." His voice cracks. "He never told me about the promise."

"But before his death he asked for her?" I ask, trying to make sense of my grandfather's actions.

"Maybe, before his death, he hoped to right his wrong." He pauses. "He loved Amisha. I don't know if he ever fully recovered from her betrayal or her death." He takes a deep breath. "Lena became an easy person to blame."

"She has a good life," I say quietly. "With my father." I have seen my mother's demons over my lifetime, but given what her life could have been, I know how fortunate she is. "You gave her that." I'm about to say more, to tell Ravi how grateful I am that he stepped in and changed the course of my mother's life, when he shakes his head.

"The story is not over." Ravi holds up a hand. "I have not told you everything." He clutches his cane tightly. "I waited a lifetime to unburden my soul, but now that the time has come, I find I fear the truth." His eyes meet mine, and I recoil from his fear. I start to ask, when he says slowly, "I lied to her."

"To whom?" I ask, confused.

"He came back." His words are barely audible as a light wind rustles the trees and causes the flowers to sway in protest. Tears flow unencumbered down his cheeks. "After Amisha sent him away, the lieutenant came back for her."

"Stephen?" Shocked and confused, I try to make sense of what he's saying. "She told him no."

"She never knew." His body starts to shake. "Three days before she was bitten by the mosquito, he came to the house for her. She was at the river, and I was home alone. I told him . . ." Ravi tries to catch his breath. "I begged him to leave. I told him she was happy. He believed me and promised never to return."

"I don't understand," I whisper, my heart hurting. "Why would you do that?"

"If he had seen the baby, he would have known," Ravi says slowly. "He would have wanted his daughter with him. Amisha would have had to choose between her boys and the baby." His sobs mask his words. "I thought I was saving her from heartache. Instead, I sentenced her to death." He raises his face, and his eyes meet mine. "Because of me, your family faced nothing but heartbreak." His body shakes with grief. "I am so sorry," he cries. "She could still be alive."

Stunned, I stare at the man who has carried the guilt and burden of a lifetime. In broken words, I say slowly, "You didn't know what would happen." My tears fall freely as I lay my hand over his. My grandmother faced a choice no person ever should—her children or the man she loved. "Her choice was an impossible one." I refuse to criticize the man who lived his life with integrity and always supported his friend without judgment. "Her death was a tragedy, not a fault."

I bow my head, fighting my own heartbreak. But I cannot blame a man whose only crime was trying to do the right thing. My own miscarriages, coming to India, reuniting with Patrick—all of it has taught me that there is never a guarantee of life's path.

For the first time since the story began, I sense a whisper from my grandmother. I stop and listen, sure I can hear her voice, encouraging me. From the sway of the beech tree's branches to the bloom of the flowers, I believe Amisha is standing with us. With soft words, she guides me to help him.

"You were her friend." I grip his hand in mine. "Amisha loved you and trusted you. It would break her heart to know you blamed yourself. It wasn't your fault. It wasn't my mother's fault."

"Amisha's children and Stephen needed her. They loved her and had to live without." He cups my cheek. "You had to live without a woman who would have loved you unconditionally." Refusing my forgiveness, he says, "For that I will do penance for lifetimes."

Ravi stands slowly and leans on his cane as he starts the walk home. I watch him until he's no longer in sight.

I spend the rest of the afternoon staring silently at Amisha's garden, replaying every detail of the story in my head. Patrick is spending the day sightseeing to give Ravi and me time to finish the story. When the sun finally sets, I leave my grandmother's haven of flowers. I flag the first rickshaw I see and ask the driver to take me into town. Once there, I enter the café's familiar surroundings. After dialing the number, I wait as it rings across continents.

"Hello." My mom's voice is gravelly from

sleep. It's still the middle of the night there.

"Mom," I say, and then pause. In time, I'll share with her the story of her parentage and the circumstances surrounding it. But for now, I need to tell her how I feel. "I love you," I whisper.

"Jaya?" she says, suddenly alert. I can hear her sitting up in bed and my father next to her asking if everything is OK. "Beti?"

"I'm so grateful for you. For everything you've given me," I say, tears clogging my throat.

Fate passed its judgment and sentenced my mother at birth. She was destined to live a life without the presence or guidance of a mother. Though sadness always accompanied her, she carried the weight of her hurt silently. She believed herself a curse and kept her distance. She loved me the only way she knew how while living her own life in shame.

I mourn my mother's need to keep the events of her childhood hidden. But because of it, I traveled across the world to a home I never knew. And with my journey to India—in the laughter of the people, in the wounded souls of the beggars on the street, in the greatness and the sadness—I discovered the true story of my mother and grandmother. The women who created me. Though there is no playbook on how to navigate the path of life, if I do it with the grace and heart of the women before me, then I will have lived my life with honor.

● ● ●

"God gives you only what you can handle." It's a common belief across cultures and languages. As a young reporter, I covered the funeral of a beloved small-town mayor. He had served for twenty years and left behind a legion of devoted constituents and a young son. After hearing the phrase repeated by those who came to pay their respects, the widow finally turned to her friend and asked, "What if I can't handle it?" It was a fair question but one without an answer.

My grandmother loved another man and bore a child without his knowing the child was his. This parentage and the story behind it, unbeknownst to me, shaped my future. The combination both gave me definition and created limits and opportunities.

When my grandmother was still young, fate intervened, and she passed on before having fully lived life. Her secret remained untold until now. The man whom she considered her closest friend kept her confidence even in her death. But with the story, he carried a burden of fault—he was sure he was to blame for her untimely death. One decision made in hopes of protecting her he was sure led to her demise. His guilt is something that can never be assuaged no matter what we say. So it begs the question—was it his decision that put her on that path, or was the decision part of her destiny that couldn't be rerouted?

I had three miscarriages. Each one was an outcome I never would have invited. As time passed, I did everything in my power to change my circumstances, but fate proved more powerful. Yet the heartbreak of not bearing my own child weighs heavy, as does the question, is there any decision I can make to change my destiny?

Life is a puzzle with pieces that seem to constantly be reshaping themselves to alter the picture. So often I have been sure of my path, only to choose a different one. A soul mate at sixteen became a stalker at seventeen (I joke—a bit). The college I knew would be lucky to have me decided I didn't measure up, and I had to embrace another. Some turns were my choice whereas others were a forced detour. Each one led me to where I am standing today.

This is my final entry from India. I'm ready to go home. This means facing the despair I ran from. I'm returning with a new sense of purpose and understanding. Maybe life is a series of decisions with destiny thrown in. Maybe it is accepting that the impossible means opening another door. And maybe it means that you have to stand the strongest during the hardest of life's times. My darkness has not disappeared, but it is fading. With gratitude for all that I have and a glimmer of hope for what I can be, I release my past and look to the future.

"What are you writing about?" Patrick asks over my shoulder.

I turn to see him carrying bags of mementos from the village shops. "You've been shopping."

"Yes," he says sheepishly. He holds up his bags. "The kids in the town are pretty persuasive."

"You were fleeced," I tease, my voice drawn. Hearing the shift, he immediately sets down his bags.

"Is everything all right?" He cups a hand around my cheek. "You finished the story?"

I lay my hand over his and nod. "About my mom and what happened to her."

I had introduced Patrick to Ravi and his great-grandchildren the night before. As I suspected, he loved them as much as they did him. When he started a game of kickball in the street with Amit, Misha, and a group of neighborhood children, I watched with a happiness I hadn't felt in too long. Ravi, seeing my reaction, leaned over and whispered, "He is a good man, yes?" At my nod, he said, "He is very lucky to have your love."

"As I am to have his," I whispered.

"Her upbringing—what she went through . . . ," I say, continuing my response to Patrick, then pause to catch my breath. "It explains so much." She feared getting too close because she was sure that anything that went wrong in my life was somehow her fault. She tried to protect me by keeping her distance. "Ravi told me about a choice he made. He's been living with it ever since." I hand him the computer. "Choices. Destiny versus decision."

"Would you have done it any differently?" he asks after scanning the words.

"I don't know. I would never have made the decision to lose them, but if given the chance to do it again, would I have gone through the pregnancies?" I pause as I think about all the years of hope that turned to despair. "If I hadn't tried, I always would have wondered." It is the first time I've been able to admit that to myself and acknowledge that I did have a semblance of control. "How about you?"

He takes longer to answer but finally says, "Maybe. Losing us on top of them was hard." He caresses my cheek. I cover his hand with mine, welcoming his touch. "What happened to you at the apartment?"

He's asking about the spells of darkness and loss of time. I had seen his concern then, but if he had asked, I wouldn't have had the answer. "I think it was the grief. I didn't know how to handle it, so it was just easier to black out." At any other time, the symptoms would have been frightening, but then I barely realized what was happening. "It got better once I got here, and soon enough they stopped." I point to the computer. "This will probably be my final entry from here."

He holds my gaze. "You're ready to leave?"

"I'm ready to go home." I take his hand. "There's something I've been thinking about that I wanted to discuss with you." When he nods, I spend the next hour detailing my ideas about Amit and Misha. I conclude with telling him about the orphanage. "I want to adopt a child," I say, hesitant. "I know the process will take a while, but . . ." I trail off, waiting for his reaction. When he smiles, I can feel the burden on my heart lighten.

He pulls me into his arms. "Yes," he says softly. "Let's bring home our child."

FIFTY-THREE

Ravi arrives in the early morning. Patrick is spending the day with Misha and Amit, who wanted to introduce him to their parents. When I open the door, Ravi seems older and worn. He smiles and holds out a stack of papers. "As promised, this is what your grandfather wanted to give your mother. The reason I asked you to stay for the story."

I shuffle through the papers and glance up in shock. "The letters from Stephen to Amisha?"

"Your grandfather wanted your mother to know she was loved and wanted." His voice cracks. "He knew she didn't believe that."

I bite back a sob and clutch the letters close. "Why did he keep them?"

"I think in the beginning they were a form of self-punishment. A reminder of Amisha's betrayal." Ravi pauses, his gaze clouding over as he stares at the floor. "Then he kept them for your mother. He told me before he died that he couldn't undo his past mistakes, but he hoped the letters would be a first step toward making things right."

I scan the letters—reading Stephen's unconditional support and deep yearning. His words detail their love for each other in a time where they should have been nothing more than friends. Their love was never more apparent than when they were forced to be apart.

"I will give them to Mom." I swipe at the tears as they flow unbidden. "Thank you."

Though it seems like only yesterday when Ravi welcomed me into the home, so much has happened since. With his story, he gave me the gift of my heritage and a source of salvation for my mother. For that I will be in debt to him for lifetimes.

"What is wrong, Beti?" Ravi asks as he sees me struggle to compose myself.

"I am leaving." Sadness mixed with resignation crosses over his face at my announcement. "It is long past time."

"With your husband," he says before I can. He smiles in understanding. "You have been happy since his arrival."

"I am," I admit. "I know how fortunate I am to have the love I do and, because of your story—my grandmother's—the importance of holding on to it."

"Then the story served its purpose," he says gently. "When?"

"In a few days," I say. "But there is something you must do for me. This home . . ." I pause and glance around the small abode, searching for the right words. Though the people who lived here were only human, their story and spirits were larger than life. They have changed me, and because of them and their history, I will be forever grateful. "I want you and your family to move into it."

"Jaya, no." Ravi holds up his hand in refusal at the same time he shakes his head.

"Listen to me," I say, unwilling to back down. "I've transferred this home plus the school property and the mill into your name." With all the letters from other family members renouncing their claim, it took only a few hundred dollars to transfer the titles. "You did what you promised, Ravi. Now please, take what my grandmother would have given you."

"After what I told you?" Ravi stares at the documents. "How can you offer me this?"

"You told me once that my grandmother was not perfect, but her heart always tried to do right by others. I think she would say the same of you." I search for suitable words. "You were only trying to protect her. She would have known that."

"When she was alive, it was filled with happiness and joy." Ravi glances around, his words filled with grief. "Afterward, it became a mausoleum."

"You have treated it with so much care and love since. It is rightfully your home," I say. When he starts to argue again, I say, "Blood does not define family. Love does." I take his hand

532

in mine. "If you asked my grandmother today who Ravi is, she would say you are family." He swallows deeply. "You could lease the school for commercial use and even put the mill back in business. Please, Ravi," I ask, "for her, for your family, say yes. She would want you to have it."

"You have given us a great gift," Ravi whispers. He clasps his hands together and bows. "Thank you."

"There's something else," I say quietly. "What I'm about to offer is not . . ." I pause, desperate not to insult him or his way of life.

"Tell me, Beti," he says, confused.

I consider my words. "I have a spacious apartment in New York. Patrick is a wonderful person." I think about the past and all the steps it took to bring me here. For the first time in so long, I look forward to the future. "I don't know if anything can be done, but I would like to try to help." Thoughts of my mother and my childhood give me the strength to continue. "My mother showed me that the most important thing you can give a child is support and love. And I promise you I will give that completely."

"Give to whom?" Ravi asks, confused.

"Your great-grandchildren," I say quickly. "Allow Misha and Amit to come to America for Misha's medical care and both of their educations. It would give me great happiness to provide this."

"Jaya?" Ravi says, watching me.

"My grandmother's writing was her gift. It gave her an entrance into a world where she was happy. There she found Stephen and true love." Never again would I take the gifts of my life for granted. "Your story showed me that life isn't always about what I want to be but instead what I can be. Amit and Misha have a family who loves them and this is their home, but I would be honored to be the person who shares another world with them, if only for a short while."

"You will be their entrance?" Ravi asks.

"No," I say slowly. "I think they will be mine."

EPILOGUE

RAVI

Ravi closes the brochure, his heart swelling with pride. His eyes blur with tears as he watches his great-grandchildren dance with Rokie, who is barking in camaraderie. They are set to go to America. Jaya sent tickets for both Amit and Misha, along with information about a children's hospital near her home in America that specializes in orthopedics and polio management.

Ravi holds the glossy pages to his chest and slowly wobbles toward the back room. As he opens the door, the memories fill him. The same room where Amisha composed her stories for so many years now beckons him. He takes the steps slowly, in no rush to be anywhere. He closes the door behind him, leaving his family to celebrate as they will.

"Thank you," Amisha says to him, standing at the foot of the bed.

Ravi stares at her, having seen her so many times before. Yet never was she as real and alive as she is right then. "It was your story to tell," Ravi says softly, wishing, as always, that she could have been the one to tell it.

"You did a finer job than I ever could," Amisha assures him, her smile still in place. The laughter reaches her eyes as she teases him. "Made a hero of yourself, did you?"

"You have always been my hero," Ravi admits, his heart light and his mind unburdened by the weight of all the years. "How are you?"

"Happy," she promises, seeing the tears gather in his eyes.

"Stephen?" His hope blooms when he sees her smile.

"Yes." Her simple answer tells him she has been reunited with her true love. "I have some stories I have written." She reaches out, her hand open and inviting. "Will you read them?"

"Always." Ravi slips his hand into hers. Amisha's hand encircles his, and with his friend of lifetimes, he knows he can finally be free.

JAYA

Two weeks before the children's arrival, I receive a letter in the mail informing me that all the plans are set and the children are packed and ready for their trip. At the end of the letter, Ravi's grandson speaks of Ravi's passing. He died shortly after they received the photographs Patrick and I sent of our home and the school my parents helped to find for the children. Ravi's son said he smiled as they perused the catalog of the school and hospital facility. He then left for bed, where they found his still body the next morning.

I don't shed any tears at the news of Ravi's passing. The man I met lived to fulfill the promise he had made to his friend years before. He related the story of Amisha to me and assured himself that her legacy would be revered. Because of him, my mother and I found our way toward each other. As I repeated the story to her, together we celebrated and grieved the lost love that brought her to life. When I told her about our plans to adopt a child from the orphanage, she hugged me with tear-filled eyes and told me she couldn't wait to meet her grandchild.

Once Ravi accomplished his mission, he finally allowed himself to sleep. I believe Amisha was waiting for him so she could welcome home the truest friend she ever knew.

Acknowledgments

Mark Gottlieb—I will be forever grateful for the day we began our partnership. You are invaluable, and I feel so fortunate to be working with you. I look forward to a lifetime of friendship and many books together.

Danielle Marshall—You make the publishing experience so enjoyable every single time. Because of you, I trusted in this story. Thank you for your words of wisdom and encouragement.

Gabe and Author Team—Thank you for everything you do, including all the behind-the-scenes work that brings everything together so seamlessly. I am deeply appreciative.

Dennelle Catlett—Thank you so much for all the work you do to bring the books to the readers. I am deeply grateful.

Tanya Farrell—I am so excited to be working with you. Thank you in advance for everything you do.

Sarahlou C.—Thank you, my friend, for your keen sense of understanding and for always being there no matter what. You are the voice of calm and reason when I need it the most. I love you like a sister—but still a no on the insane vacations. ☺

Tiffany Y. Martin—Your insight and ideas for

the book are instrumental. Every time you make the story better. Thank you for always being such a true pleasure to work with.

Nicole Pomeroy, Sara Addicott, Jane Steele, and Nicole Brugger-Dethmers—Thank you so much for all of your efforts, ideas, and corrections to make the book shine. It is so much better because of all of you.

To the readers—Thank you for reading the stories. There are no words to express my deepest gratitude.

About the Author

A former attorney, Sejal Badani is the author of the bestselling novel and Goodreads Fiction Award finalist *Trail of Broken Wings*. When not writing, Sejal enjoys reading and traveling.

Books are produced in the United States using U.S.-based materials

Books are printed using a revolutionary new process called THINKtech™ that lowers energy usage by 70% and increases overall quality

Books are durable and flexible because of Smyth-sewing

Paper is sourced using environmentally responsible foresting methods and the paper is acid-free

Center Point Large Print
600 Brooks Road / PO Box 1
Thorndike, ME 04986-0001 USA

(207) 568-3717

US & Canada:
1 800 929-9108
www.centerpointlargeprint.com